PARAGON'S FALL

The Hero's Code
Book 1

A.R. KNIGHT

The Champion

From the snow-slicked street, Aegis saw the lights, heard the sounds of his targets. Voices didn't carry the sixty-some floors down the sole lit span in the tall, wide building dominating the abandoned business park, but the shots did; rattle-cracks from old model guns, tattled on their owners with their rat-a-tats. The noise proved Aegis had a reason to be out here at a time of night known for villains, and perfect for those hunting them.

The pod behind him gave a warm beep as it began rolling towards its next request. The sound triggered a quick inventory check: gloves, a plated vest over a thick dark wool sweater to keep Aegis warm, a pair of Paragon-uniform pants belted over with accessories, including everything Aegis would need to disable, kill, or call for help. Nestled over his nose and cupping his eyes sat black-and-blue goggles that kept incoming light optimal for anything.

No helmet. Aegis wouldn't go that far. News crews would chase his pod signature, and they would be here. The Paragons ran the world. Their mascot couldn't hide.

His boots, with soft pads built into the heels to keep old feet comfortable, did a fine job conquering the concrete walk towards the building's entry. Snow piled up on the sides, plowed with precision by automated labor so cheap the cities could keep it running for ghosted buildings like this one. Two tall, shock-white columns flanked the entrance, bearing an etched logo not quite strong enough to overcome decades of irrelevance to find a trigger in Aegis's memories.

Between rounds of cracking fire from above, Aegis crunched snow to the thrum of New York. Trains pulsed beneath him, the rushing keeping pace with his steps, while a vague decay seeped through the breeze into every breath. Broken business parks surrounded the compacting city now and they all smelled like this. Felt like this while they waited for someone to save them.

Double-doors provoked a majesty marred by shattered glass, by the bent handle showing reckless force applied to the opening. Aegis used his predecessor's handiwork and stepped over the shards. He'd send a rep offer out tomorrow, get someone to clean it up. Image mattered, even out here.

"You're there?" Celice came through his earpiece. She chewed something, teeth gnashing thick.

Eggplant. One reason Aegis had taken this call personally. He looked forward to dinners with his daughter, but now she kept insisting on recipes meant for old men and goats. Aegis would eat the leftovers when he came back, though. After he'd had a bit of aggression to work up his appetite, when he could justify some protein to go with the veg-tastic dish.

"I'm here," Aegis said. "They broke in. Not subtle about it."

"Do you need back-up? I can send the call," Celice paused, except for her chewing. "A couple drones aren't too far. Ten minutes."

"I'll be fine."

"Dad."

The lobby held up better than the door, possibly owing to its barren blandness. A long desk blocked an empty wall the same white as the columns outside. Space for chairs, receptionists, and, where Aegis stood now, customers and employees. Working so hard for dollars, euros, at the cost of family and friends. While the

Paragons had much left to do, they had at least ended the mad scramble for cash.

"Call the drones then," Aegis said. "But I'm not waiting."

The elevators posed a problem. If the criminals up top had any sense, they would have someone watching the only reasonable entry to their floor, and elevators like these displayed their location in white numbers on black bars atop their slate-gray doors. The moment Aegis punched a number, his imminent arrival would be clear to anyone paying attention. Stairs lingered as a possibility, but for sixty flights, not a sane one.

The drones would beat Aegis to the targets if he took that route.

"Going in," Aegis said, both for his daughter and the recording.

Every mission, every word the Paragons spoke in action sat in their vaults. Ready and waiting to counter the dual threats of hyper-inflated media and the myth-making enterprises involved in making the Paragons seem like arbitrary gods. Recruit anomalies, keep the normals from getting scared. Two birds, one stone, etc. The more the public saw the Paragons as not only the world's guardians, but its friends, the less trouble would be thrown their way. For that matter, it'd been too long since Aegis sent out his own release, proof that the Champion himself still performed, still chased down evil.

Inspiration came from the top, and if providing it required a few hits, then Aegis could take them.

The elevators matched the front entrance, one suffering violence extreme enough to leave its door hanging while the other waited for passengers, though its sharp squeals signified good looks wouldn't keep the elevator long from forced retirement. Aegis ought to survive if the thing fell apart with him in it, but those people already up top likely would not. Which means they were both brave and stupid, or they'd made the safe, slow call and climbed the stairs. Knowing the sorts of people who would take potshots with weapons in an abandoned tower at night, Aegis bet the former.

The elevator's speed preached new definitions of the word *slow*, which gave Aegis another chance to stretch out. Feel his shoulders crack and stretch his lungs with a few deep breaths. His stun gun had a loaded dart, and he kept the weapon ready in his right hand as the numbers on the panel climbed. He shifted to the left side of the elevator, minimizing his profile. Years ago, Aegis would have stood stock center, hands on hips and ready to win through cocky intimidation alone.

That time ended when the bruises started following him home, haunting him the day after. When the concern in Celice's eyes stole away his macho grin.

The elevator announced its arrival with the sound of a dying balloon instead of a cheery ding, but the lift made it to the sixtieth floor. The doors began their same, slow crawl and the *blam blam blam* of heavy weapons fire poured through. Not at Aegis, though. The morons continued their party. They'd had every opportunity to prepare, to set an ambush, and instead they'd opted for more champagne.

The opened door cleared the way to a smaller, nicer lobby, as though its height preserved the glass-lined white furniture from the seeping decay down below. A circular desk sat off to the right side, required chair and anything on it gone, ransacked for what could be carried. The lobby's sole occupant leaned against the desk now: a man holding an old-model handgun down at his hip and staring at his Tama and the image it projected above the man's forearm.

Aegis lowered his own gun and left the elevator, making it halfway across the lobby before the man bothered to look up. Seeing the armed and armored Paragon leader, the world's most famous Champion, the man's head cocked to a side, eyebrow raised. Questioning the impossible.

Aegis decided to prove it.

A long stride, Aegis's right quad leading into a solid right hook, took the man's just-opened mouth before he could make a sound. With his left arm, Aegis caught the fallen guard and set the suited figure onto the pearl-white tile.

"Trig blink neutral," Aegis said, following a hunch.

His goggles took the command and shut off their processing for a solid second, giving Aegis a true look at where he operated. Line lights, with their bright trails, filled the gaps between the ceiling tiles and sprayed such a harsh glow that the lobby seemed like a snow-covered mountain at noon. No wonder the guard had trouble reacting to Aegis—keeping the floor this washed out would make identification impossible without goggles like his.

The lobby played security for a single path, one locked by a walnut-wood door whose key card seal stood out on the wall with a small red speck showing power. A look behind the reception desk revealed any bypass that might have existed had gone the way of the chair and the monitor.

"Trig P-Lock," Aegis said to the room, then held his left, Tama-bearing wrist against the card reader.

Paragon technology worked again and the reader beeped its submission to Aegis's rank, jutting open the lock and allowing Aegis to open the heavy door via the chrome-metal bar on its front.

Another ambush opportunity came and went as Aegis, with the door opened just enough to see around, looked into an empty hall-way. At the far end, past secondary split-offs, the hallway opened into a broad, overlooking space so favored by the high floors in these buildings. A chance to look down upon all those you'd managed to rise above.

The weapons-fire stopped and, from the door, Aegis could see why. The morons had shattered several windows, and the intact pair Aegis could see sported bullet's tell-tale starburst. Bullets that likely came from the big, turreted gun in the room's center, facing outside.

"Are you seeing that?" Aegis said.

"Looks like we've found our target," Celice replied.

"They could take out the drones with a weapon that size. Tell them to keep off."

"I'll tell them to watch out. Mynx can always make more."

Aegis wanted to say that Mynx made enough of the things already, but stopped. These jerks might not have an ambush ready now, but they could change their mind any second. Better to use surprise while you have it, than lose it arguing about things that didn't matter. Besides, Aegis knew the real reason he didn't want the drones around: they'd take away the glow. That oh-so-sweet vindica-tion Aegis would get when he stood in the courtyard below, speaking to the media about another successful Paragon operation. Sharing the spotlight with a pair of Mynx's mechanical monsters would mean . . . sharing.

Aegis slipped through the door into the hallway, hugging the right wall and watching the far glass for any sign of motion. Every step came with a rolling heel, his hands holding his stun gun forward and ready. He crept closer to the first cross-section, quick-stepped up to the bisecting hallway and leaned to give himself a view without exposing his back.

Empty. Aegis reversed to the other side of the hallway, stun gun aimed along the opposite direction. Nothing there either. Closed office doors. Clear white walls with brighter, square blotches exposing art's former home.

Aegis took a breath. Slow, shallow. Listened.

Laughter. Towards the windowed room. Liquid splashing into glasses. Not laying a trap, then, but celebrating.

He'd spent too much time going after hardened criminals. Enemies who knew full well what Aegis and the Paragons could do and prepped to fight them. These, these were the bottom-barrel criminals you fought when all the others were gone. Who filled the void left when you'd eliminated the truly terrifying.

Aegis shook his head at nothing. He'd be surprised to get a single interview after this one. Who cared if low-level bums shot up some abandoned buildings? He slipped the stun gun back into its holster. The least he could get from this would be some fun.

Aegis wheeled left, into the side hallway whose end revealed another cross-section. He moved quicker now, padding his feet to the sounds of chatter, talk of weapons moved and weapons made. New deals struck. Despite all efforts, the Paragons could never get rid of every under-the-table transaction, couldn't quite cleanse the world of its muck, but Aegis felt they'd at least made sure to punish the main offenders. You could swim in the swamp, but you would pay a price.

At the new hallway's end, Aegis peeked right and saw the party. A quartet of chuckling nobodies, wearing drifter-style gear confirming their neophyte status in the criminal game. Two cylinders occupied the center space on a pop-up plastic table otherwise covered in a garbage dinner; synth food Aegis wouldn't touch. One cylinder bore whiskey or bourbon's telltale brown, the other looked like water. No surprise which held less.

The real shock, for one of the four, a capped man whose eyes floated past his friends in mid-drink, was Aegis making his way in long strides down the final stretch of hallway. The man paused his swig, his bloodshot stare struggling to understand what came towards him, before his hand lost grip on the glass and the man stumbled back, shouting a warning.

Aegis connected his first swing, the capped man's glass hitting the tiled floor and shattering. Not that his target, whose puffy, pale cheeks took Aegis's blow with a satisfying squelch, appreciated the timing. Nor, Aegis figured, did the man enjoy having his face collide with the dinner and the pop-up table, but a criminal's life was often disappointment, especially when Paragons were around.

The next one in line, a gibbering, shorter man whose coats and sweaters belied a tropical ancestry, didn't get enough distance on his scrambling back-step to escape Aegis's reach. With both hands gripping the short man's coat, Aegis whipped him to the right, into and through the thin, decaying wall into what was once a high-profile office. Now, in a far cry from the monetary mountains once moved in its confines, the short criminal laid unconscious and covered in drywall on the office's floor. One more injustice leveled in the building, and not the last to come.

Two left. The capped man, who'd made it as far as the glass windows on the level, who's hands were reaching for a gun somewhere on his person, and a lanky, suit-sporting specialist. Aegis had seen enough fighters in his time to know the leader, to know who posed the greatest threat, and he could dissemble a thousand clues to find that one person in a group of enemies. This time, it didn't take much: the specialist's eyes were narrow, his hands weren't twitching, and he didn't appear to be praying to some deity for salvation. In other words, the specialist was everything the capped man wasn't.

Aegis broke for the specialist with a barreling charge, using his sheer spectacle for intimidation. This tended to result in cowering collapse, with the true cowards fleeing at first look. The specialist, though, reached into his jacket, pulled out a handgun style the Paragons had banned decades ago, like the one the elevator guard had held, and fired.

For most of his life, Aegis had a cordial relationship with bullets. They would greet him with their usual ferocity, and Aegis would disarm their damage with the very thing that made him the Paragon's icon: an invulnerable skin. The shots would sink against Aegis, and then fall away to the ground, leaving nothing so much as a mark for their trouble. Missions had gone by where hundreds or thousands of rounds had poured into the Paragon and found themselves rendered useless, whether they struck his arms, legs, eyes, teeth or anywhere else. As though a divine cloak covered Aegis and kept him safe from harm.

That cloak did its job again now, catching the bullet as it struck Aegis's left shoulder, outside the reaches of the vest where the shot tore through Aegis's clothes and rendered its ineffectual verdict against the Paragon's body. The specialist managed to snap off a second round that went directly into the vacuum hole of Aegis's vest, causing nothing so much as a microsecond's pause in the Paragon's momentum.

There was no third shot.

The capped man, having seen his partners laid to waste, took the safer road and awaited his arrest with the simpering pleas of the over-matched and guilty. Any thoughts of further escape vanished when Mynx's drones arrived, shattering the remaining glass and hovering inside the room, stun guns at the ready, lethal options awaiting an algorithm's calculation.

"Late, as always," Aegis said to the machines, standing near the capped man with the specialist's unconscious body hanging from his right arm.

Aegis took the specialist down himself, leaving the drones to watch over the other three. At the building's base, a few pods arrived and disgorged news crews looking to feed popular content's ravenous beast. And the media found nothing more popular than a

Champion conducting a raid. Aegis strode out to meet the flashes, the cameras, the pouring of questions from reporters and fans alike.

Before answering a single one, though, Aegis directed the other late arrivals, the lower Paragons whose job covered this district, who had asked Aegis to cover for them. Who would have taken the bullets he bore instead. The motley anomalies, wearing their Paragon blues, swept by Aegis towards the tower. They'd take the other three, plus this one, and divine the proper punishment. The cost in reps owed, and the best methods of repayment.

"Are you all right?" Celice's voice, coming through the ear piece, cut through the calls from the press.

"I'll live," Aegis gave his classic comeback, then dumped the specialist on the ground in front of the cameras as snow fell between the lights.

He had a speech for this, a modified version of the stock Paragon set of warnings, lessons, and calls for a better tomorrow. The difference this time, what made Aegis's words come slower, and forced him to focus to keep standing tall, was the spreading pain in his left shoulder.

An aching, deep, bone-crunching pain that he'd never felt before.

2

A Hunt

Nightfall brought five-minute frostbite weather, perfect for the hunt. Kat gave herself one breath of the outside air when she left the vehicle, and that was enough to nearly freeze her lungs solid, so she snapped shut her face-mask and completed the custom tracker suit's closed system. The seal caught her, even those long auburn strands that escaped everywhere else, keeping her safe from the elements.

And what she found among them.

A beep behind her turned Kat around—she'd forgotten to close the vehicle's door and shut off its engine. All things you didn't need to do with a pod, but here, well off the grid, Kat had to use one of these big-wheeled rovers. Kat leaned into the spartan interior—all seats, restraints, and nothing else, and looked for a button or a switch before she remembered.

"Trig rover, off," Kat said, her words muffled by her mask.

The rover, vocal recognition parsing Kat's blurred, somewhat dehydrated, deadpan voice, followed the instructions and its batteries wound down to silence. When Kat shut the door, a tiny meter appeared in her upper-right view, showing a bright green bar estimating the time until the rover became an expensive icicle. The hunt wouldn't, shouldn't take that long.

"Seeker?" Kat said as she stood up from the rover and took in the snow-cloaked pines.

The turn off to this little enclave in the woods hours north of Chicago looked like it hadn't been cleared all winter, and amid the deep snow drifts, which the rover handled with brave competence, Kat's best friend plumbed the joy only available to those creatures of the husky persuasion. Seeker burst out behind the rover, spraying fluff all over Kat's crystal-white suit, which rejected the offered flakes with the best in all-weather technology. Few things made a hunt as miserable as getting wet, cold, or covered in husky slobber, and Kat's suit provided the antidote to all of the above and plenty more besides.

For the reps it'd cost her, the suit ought to.

"What'd you find?" Kat said to her dog, who replied by shaking the rest of the snow off himself and staring back at her with his big baby-blue eyes.

Kat laughed. Seeker had a secret path to her heart, and the big fur ball never failed to spring a smile. Kat's, though, faded when Seeker gave a low huff, turned, and loped back into the snow, towards the forest's dark edge. The moon glowed bright tonight, giving clear sight above the carved road, but underneath the thick woods . . .

Well, she'd planned for that.

A rapid check confirmed Kat had what she needed, and, with the suit's equalized temperature keeping her comfortable, Kat set off after Seeker. The frigid air, at least, meant the snow kept itself light. Her boots stamped down, pushed away the drifts one motion at a time.

"Trig range to target?"

Her goggles flashed the estimated distance. Almost a kilometer from the nearest road. It'd feel like twenty in these conditions, but Kat wouldn't mind the effort. She'd had enough rest sitting in that rover for the last few hours. She lived in the city for many reasons, one being she could use her own legs to get where she needed to go. All the same, the tromp through the woods proved meditative. A nice break from the constant urban onslaught. Lights and sounds and people pestering her every moment. Here, Seeker's boundless energy as the dog rolled and ran his way all around her made the biggest distraction, and Kat could watch that all day.

By the time she hit the clearing, her legs burned and Kat devoured one of the protein pills she'd packed for the hunt. Slotted inside slim pockets in her face-mask cheeks, the pills held packed energy. That they tasted like chalk and stuck in her throat half the time were minor inconveniences—letting an anomaly escape because Kat didn't have enough strength to make one more sprint made a major one. And reports suggested her prey could run.

"Trig dossier," Kat spoke to her suit, then winked her left eye.

A picture flashed over her left lens, displaying a scrawny man, bags underneath the eyes and defined facial bones suggesting an austere existence. One fleeing from Mynx and the trackers. Text splashed across next, at first blurred and then focusing into clarity as the lens read Kat's eye and determined the optimal projection.

The mask's next update should fix that; cut down the time-to-clarity. Would be nice if that ever shipped.

Vedder, the target, belonged to an offshoot anomaly group. The names all ran together for Kat, so she blew past the text's diversion into Vedder's exploits. Suffice it to say that Vedder had earned the rep bonus for his tracing. Mynx still preferred the anomaly taken alive, surprising given Vedder's record. The Paragons tended to take an extreme view of threatening anomalies—a dead one wouldn't cause any more problems—which meant Mynx thought Vedder still had a shot at redemption.

She wondered how many trackers Vedder would have to take out for that shot to go away.

Kat winked her left eye again and the picture-text disappeared, giving back her full view just beyond the forest.

A cabin waited. Ramshackle, dark wood and so far behind the times that Kat shuddered. A slight chimney, more a lucky brick stack than a deliberate effort, spat polite smoke into the sky, haloed by the moonlight. The front door, facing Kat, stuck in at an angle, adding to the sole window's orange glow. Somebody was home.

Seeker, reading Kat's mood the way a pet could, stepped up

next to her and stood, head up above Kat's waist, his eyes matching her look at the cabin.

"Cover," Kat said to the dog, and Seeker huffed an agreement, loping away towards the cabin's back side.

While the dog made his round, Kat walked towards the door, keeping her right hand on the stun gun clasped to the belt on her waist. The first time she went on an official hunt, the lack of lethality bothered her: rogue anomalies could go hostile, and getting in a fight with a powerful being without a means to cancel it didn't seem fair. Then she'd caught her first anomaly. Found fear in that face far greater than her own, even though that anomaly could have killed Kat with a finger snap—oxidizing a human body is a scary thing—and Kat knew, if she'd had a deadly weapon, she'd have used it.

Lacking a killing punch didn't mean Kat went in hoping for the best. Instead, when she made it within a couple meters of the cabin's front door, Kat lifted her left arm, made a fist and pointed it towards the wooden entry.

"Trig cable."

From the white-metal gauntlet on her wrist, a small panel raised up and launched a black-steel cord with a tri-hook on the end. The cable whistled the distance to the door and embedded into the wood with a crack that sounded at clear odds with the serene night noises. The surprise had started, and now Kat had to move quick.

"Trig door buster," Kat said the words and, with her right hand, she drew the stun gun.

At the same time, the gauntlet jerked the cable back towards Kat. With its hooks embedded, the cable tore the door off, ripping it down into the snow and giving Kat a clear view inside. The interior matched the cabin's spartan surroundings; a small, circle table and a single rotting chair. The fire flickered behind the furniture, a hunched figure, wearing a blanket, fronting the flames. Kat had a clear shot, but dragging Vedder the kilometer back to the rover sounded like a terrible idea. Kat could stun and trace Vedder, leave him out here, but without the cabin's front door and in cold like this

. . . Kat wouldn't get much reward for a frozen anomaly. Which meant the diplomatic option.

"Vedder?" Kat called, not moving from her spot in front of the cabin. "It's over. Time to come in."

The hunched figure didn't move. Didn't reply. Kat tried the name again, in case Vedder's ears were frozen already. When that didn't get a response, Kat shifted her stance. Loosened her legs, snapped her left wrist to change the gauntlet's prepped gadget, and took a deep breath.

This was why they called them hunts.

Kat clenched her left hand and the gauntlet launched three small, silver orbs. All connected by a tiny fiber strand too small to see unless you were on top of it. The three spheres spread as they flew until they landed about a meter apart inside the shack. Each one flared a blinding white in turn, Kat shading her eyes with her right hand, and then settled into a dull green glow.

The green meant nobody hiding. Yet, Vedder still hunched over right there in front of the fire.

If the obvious seemed incorrect, then Kat had to move fast.

She kicked up snow with a sudden sprint, again snapping her left wrist to send the gauntlet back to the steel hook. Kat kept the stun gun as level as she could while plowing through the deep drifts. Stepping onto the wood floors came with blessed stability, and quick glances to the left and right as Kat advanced into the shack confirmed her sphere's assessments; the place was empty.

As for Vedder, when Kat reached the hunched form and put her left hand out to grab the fabric, with the stun gun aimed where the neck should be—better there for complete paralysis—her hand went right through. Vedder vanished, and not a slow fade like in old movies, but a one-second-there-next-second-gone flash. Which, of course, fit Vedder's profile.

An illusion anomaly. Truly, the worst.

Kat picked up the orbs and slid them into the gauntlet's slot, and as they clicked into place a new sound joined in with the wind and driving snow: Seeker.

The dog had a thousand different barks, from happy chirps to intruder-defying snarls, but this was long, loud, and targeted. The sound told Kat to come and fast, because Seeker had found what she hadn't. Vedder was out there, and depending on how the anomaly felt about dogs, Seeker could be in trouble.

Seeker's calls came from behind the cabin, so it took Kat more time than she'd like to admit running out and around to the back through the deep snow. Her legs made it known that all the hiking would make for an unpleasant tomorrow, and Kat told the suit to relax its temp setting so she wouldn't drown herself in her own sweat. Not that the sudden rush of frigid air made things much better. Two seconds of death-wish cold and Kat turned things back to the warmth.

Behind the cabin the woods scattered over a looming hillside, giving the moon ample opportunity to glow through the snow-dropping clouds. It would've been picturesque if Kat had been looking up. Instead, her eyes focused on Seeker's tracks and how they paralleled the depressions made by a man fleeing in the same direction. Her mask took the hint from Kat's focus and outlined the prints, keeping her clued in even as the shadows and swirling flakes made naked vision a laughable idea.

Then again, hunting an anomaly at night, in a deep forest, during a blizzard was also a laughable idea.

What Kat did for reps.

Seeker's barks kept coming, but not moving, which meant the dog had pinned his quarry and that Vedder either lacked a weapon or the dark heart required to attack the animal. Still, when Seeker's form finally revealed itself near a solitary pine at the hill's top, Kat couldn't fight off a relieved grin. The dog, which she'd originally adopted on the advice from another tracker, had been a tool with a purpose. Now . . . well, now wasn't the time to get emotional.

The pine had branches extending out and down like a cloak, covering anything lurking up in it with plenty of black-green needles. Despite the snowstorm's growing intensity—Vedder's powers weren't supposed to include weather manipulation, but Kat didn't rule anything out—the tree's base was a shed blanket. Something had been climbing this thing, knocking the needles off as they went.

"Good boy," Kat told Seeker as she caught up to the dog, who spared her a single glance then went back to barking up the tree. "Let's see who you've found."

Even up close, she couldn't see Vedder, which made the probability of a surprise attack too high for comfort. But it was so cold, and Kat was so tired from marching all the way up here, that Vedder taking her out with a dropped log or something didn't seem so bad. Either way, without a target to shoot at, Kat only had one weapon.

"Vedder!" Kat yelled up through the storm. "You're cornered. It's cold as hell. Get down here and let's go before we both freeze!"

No response. Seeker kept barking.

"Vedder!" Kat tried again. "If I have to cut this innocent tree down, it's not going to be good for either of us."

"Behind you!" Vedder's voice came from up the tree, and as he cried in the shrill, dry tones of someone for whom hydration was a luxury, Kat's mask beeped a warning.

Kat whirled, stun gun raised, as Vedder charged through the snow at her. She fired. And watched as the numbing bolt flashed right through Vedder's illusion and off into the night.

A weight landed on her back and drove Kat into the snow, her face pushing into the flakes. Something tried to get through her suit, pressing against her lower back, but the suit turned the strike and gave Kat the time she needed to drive an elbow into her attacker's chest. Vedder—because who else could it be?—grunted, then yelled as Seeker dove into him, the dog more than heavy enough to drive the thin man off of Kat's back.

"Dammit, Vedder," Kat said as she pushed herself up from the snow, turned towards the man struggling with her dog. Vedder lunged at Seeker with a crude knife, but Seeker kept his distance, barking and hopping away from every swing. "Did you have to be such an ass?"

Kat raised the stun gun again, and Vedder turned to her, then split into three versions of himself, all turning to run in different directions. Seeker, though, wasn't fooled, and the husky took the one fleeing right, grappling Vedder's leg and driving the man to the ground, where an easy shot from Kat put the anomaly down.

She stood over Vedder's body, put away the stun gun, and caught Seeker's panting tongue and happy grin. Shook her head.

"You going to help me drag this guy back to the rover?" Kat asked the husky, who gave a single bark in response, then scampered away into the snow. "Thought so."

3

The First Sign

Used to be, when the sun rose over Lake Michigan, Zhan-Yo would get a look at the beautiful orange start to the day. Now, with the sight line from his balcony to the water leading through a spider's web of looping, interconnected architecture, Zhan-Yo saw refracted light's rainbow burst instead. Like a child's toy grown large.

The older skyline still stood, steel towers reaching back to a time when Zhan-Yo's parents mattered, when he mattered, when the people milling through the street below counted. Unlike the new buildings, coated in translucent solar-sucking material that gave them their prismatic glow, the elders were dark in the fresh dawn. Obelisks that some, including the columnist whose weekly rant Zhan-Yo had just finished reading, considered out-dated. Not worth saving.

Zhan-Yo waved away the article and it shrank back into the table's round surface where the rest of the city's, the world's, breaking news sat plastered beneath the breakfast remnants. One daily ritual ready to give way to another. Zhan-Yo stood from the metal chair, designed to last through all the weather Chicago could throw at it, and let the chill run through his light jacket, the flannel pajamas that fell over his slippers and dusted the frosted balcony floor. He fumbled in his pocket for a lighter and a musty cigarette pack, lit one with a flick and went to the chest-high railing. A habit passed on from father to son, taken in moderation and with murderous delight; Zhan-Yo ruled his body and could do what he liked with it.

All the people out this early were getting ready for a market, selling fruits and vegetables that didn't belong in this climate this time of year, but that were now grown in hothouses on roofs, or inside micro-gardens that ran on drip-feed technology. No soil required, minimal space. Miracles upon miracles leading to a northern city with a verdant bounty. Yet for all these wonders, stands arose in the streets and voices hawked wares to one another. Passing people chose to spend reps and collect these local delights by hand, even as they used their Tamas to order up countless plenty from bigger warehouses with drone deliveries on Chicago's outskirts. As if a little bit of community compensated for all the stale distance of modern life.

Ziran, his father's company now his son's, had worked to create this world, and Zhan-Yo collected the benefits. In between puffs, a smile made a halting advance on his face, stretching past the few wrinkles that had managed to take hold on his tight skin over the decades. Yes, he'd done well. They'd done well. Everything Ziran set its corporate eye towards, it completed. Everyone wore their Tamas, everyone stayed connected through Ziran's massive network, and when the Paragons decided to throw their invincible weight behind the company, the takeover had been complete.

The smile ended when shade interrupted the sun's rainbow display. Zhan-Yo tracked the disappearance, knowing what he'd find and wanting to see it all the same: a galaxy-blue oval, twice the balcony's size, drifted overhead. Get close enough and Zhan-Yo would see the sectioned pieces for every one of the drone's functions, the escalating options as encounters went from passive to deadly. The only open spot gave view to the drone's camera, a glass eye staring and scanning.

A reminder that some takeovers are more complete than others, and their costs more dire. For all Ziran's accomplishments, for all

Zhan-Yo's efforts, one decree from Aegis or the local Paragon leader, Innis, and everything his family had worked for would be cast aside. No vote, no say. While the people believed Ziran had tremendous power, Zhan-Yo knew they had no power at all.

The table dinged and Zhan-Yo turned away from the drone, hoping for something to salvage the morning's mood. Though messages swamped Zhan-Yo's accounts, many handled by assistants and automated algorithms, a select few found his person no matter where Zhan-Yo happened to be. Sylvie's name, spread across the table's surface and wrapping around his boiled eggs and steamed carrots, was one. Flipping his right hand, the burning cigarette in his left, Zhan-Yo brought the message up, projected it over the table's surface.

Watch this. Then call me.

Beneath the message sat a video, what looked like a media broadcast from the previous night based on the amount of labels hovering over the video's edges—square boxes hailing Zhan-Yo to earn reps or spend them on various things he neither needed nor wanted. What mattered, though, stood in the center: Aegis.

Zhan-Yo tapped the projection and the video began to play, sound piping from speakers embedded into the table. The combination device and surface had been an expensive purchase, yet necessary if one wanted to maximize their moment-to-moment productivity.

The video began and reporters asked Aegis inane questions about who the Paragon had apprehended this time, whether anyone had died, and so on. These weren't interesting, and Zhan-Yo wondered if Sylvie had decided to waste his time today. But no, that wasn't her style. Sylvie did not joke, she plotted. If she had sent this video, there must be a reason.

So Zhan-Yo sat back in his chair, smoked, and watched. Studied the Paragon and his uniform, front and center in the camera. Until he found it.

"So it's true," Zhan-Yo spoke the words softly, like one does when they're speaking nonsense and want no others to hear.

Because this video showed nonsense. He couldn't believe it, but the smudge showed plain on the screen. Aegis kept his left shoulder still, favored it, and where the bullet had torn the fabric, beneath there seemed to be the slightest wet. Blood, maybe. With that clue, Zhan-Yo found more evidence: Aegis pressed his eyes every so often, his mouth closed tight when he wasn't talking. Sweat hovered on his forehead.

The invincible man felt pain. Aegis had been hurt.

Sylvie never joked, never wasted his time, and this might be her greatest find.

Zhan-Yo wiped away the video, sent the wounded Paragon back into the void. Stood up and took one more look at the drone, which had settled in to watch the market below. For now, Zhan-Yo could do nothing to the machine.

On his way inside, Zhan-Yo stubbed out the cigarette on the wall, adding another black ash mark on the red brick, next to so many more. The blotches rose above his height to the limit of his reach and were now nearing his feet. Soon he would have to wash it and begin again.

But perhaps only one more time.

4

Inside The System

Mynx woke with the sunrise glowing in her western windows. Beyond Mynx's overlay and down a steep, sandy cliff, the Pacific ocean lapped a rocky beach spotted with runners. A playful sea, frothing amid dark and deep water. A contrast to the smooth surfaces around Mynx's bedroom, coated and ready to transition to whatever her mood required. Right now, a soothing light blue that mirrored the sunrise did the trick.

"I'm awake, but keep it going a little longer," Mynx said, brushing black curls from her eyes.

Her hair considered sleep a chance to march about her head like explorers, branching out in all directions and getting into trouble. The tangles and knots could wait a moment, though, because this sunrise looked good. Deep oranges bleeding into purples, with a few clouds fighting for wispy relevance. All this coming through a mounted camera catching the eastern sky from atop her home, her lab, her everything.

She savored the seconds, all ten, before the drum of tasks to be done grew too loud to be ignored and Mynx slid herself out of the covers. Things went well until she swung her long legs off of the mattress and her hip popped. Her breath caught.

"No damage, all signs are normal," Reeves said, his voice a pleasant British monotone. "At your age, your muscles take a little longer to find their places."

"Good morning to you too, Reeves," Mynx replied, closing her eyes to summon the extra energy to shove off the bed.

Her feet settled on the hard floor, a rippled false wood Mynx herself had made in a bid to design a more natural armor for her drones. That bid had failed, but as with most failures, she managed to extract something useful; in this case, a beautiful chocolate surface that kept firm without wearing down. Hardly a revolution, but before the Paragons changed the world to value better things, selling that flooring and the recipe for its production had brought in much-needed cash.

"I'm ready," Mynx said, standing straight. "Show me the day."

The sunrise faded, and the ocean-facing glass wall shifted to show three columns, one holding the day's calendar, another the day's tasks, and one more highlighting the weather, news, and so on. While Mynx read, activity burst around her: the closet door behind Mynx opened and a four-propeller drone glided into the room carrying a sky-blue Paragon uniform while two other, humanoid, drones came in through her main bedroom door, a beach-white piece that blended with the teal walls to give the room an ocean vibe.

"Jones. Who is she?" Mynx asked, raising her arms as the drones combined to remove her nightgown and begin the Paragon spectacle. "I'm assuming that's the reason for the uniform?"

"You approved the visit last month. Doctor Denise Jones is a geneticist, who is looking into—"

"The aging. It's coming back now." Mynx sighed. Things always came back, they just took a while. "Think I still have time to do a run through?"

"How are you feeling about breakfast?"

"Keep it light, and I'll eat it while she's here." Mynx made it past the tasks, to the headlines and caught one about Aegis performing heroics again. How many times did she have to tell him to leave little things like this to the drones? "The next model has to be ready *soon*."

"Of course."

With the uniform on, the drones returned to where they came from, and Mynx tore herself away from the view . . . and nearly trampled a new delivery. Wheeled, with only a single large tray on top, this drone held a set of pills and two water glasses. One, Mynx knew, in case she spilled the other.

"Feels like these are multiplying," Mynx said, reaching for them.

"Each one as recommended by the database," Reeves replied. "You can ignore them if you like."

"What would you do?" Mynx asked, then began swallowing the pills with rote habit.

"As an inanimate construct, I have no opinion. However, I do run a number of extra operations to keep my own capabilities at optimum efficiency."

"Point taken."

The long walk through her living area, to the thick, stainless steel doors marking the Factory's start covered three stories in height, a hundred meters of reinforced corridor bored through thick rock and coated in security measures designed to stop anyone save Mynx herself lasted long enough to get the dry chalk taste of the pills out of her mouth. The entry doors had no opening mechanism. They stood tall and silent, perfect smooth slates with not a notch on them. As if they had emerged, seemingly, from the false-natural rock design that made up the walls and that proved convenient for hiding cameras, weapons, and worse.

"Going to let me in?" Mynx asked Reeves.

"Your own protocols forbid me."

"Good answer."

Always worth testing an AI. When they started to develop their own ideas, that's when things got dangerous. In lieu of a switch, a command, or the massive knob that would have been required to open these doors, Mynx set her hand on their smooth exterior instead.

And *fell in*.

She'd designed these to be simple: a daily task couldn't take too much time. So when Mynx placed her hand on the doors and slipped her mental self inside of them, the space she occupied looked as plain as an empty, new apartment. Tiled floor, clean white walls, a big yellow light in the ceiling, and a single silver dais in the middle with a big red button on it. A little homage to the cartoons she'd watched as a kid. Mynx pressed the button, closed her eyes, and slipped back out.

The doors opened with the silent sliding of exact dimensions and precise cuts, swinging inward and revealing a gigantic, open space. The Factory. Her lab, her playground. The place where Mynx made the world for so many in Pacifica, Atlantis, and, slowly, the rest of the world. Beyond the doors, the corridor ended in a single, two-meter wide disk whose coated, silver floor ended with yellow-rimmed edges.

Safety first.

"D block." Mynx stood on the disk and spoke, which sent the platform moving. A sole strut beneath the disk slid along a groove several stories beneath Mynx, dipping down into that groove to bring the lab's owner and Pacifica's Champion down to D block's level. A constant chill breeze slithered through her midnight hair, and Mynx tasted the coppery texture of hot electronics. "Get the gladiator ready, Reeves. We don't have a lot of time this morning."

"Of course."

Now Reeve's voice came from the disk, and with it sounded a thousand purring, whirring, and stirring parts as Mynx's lab awoke. Multi-colored lights lit up the various blocks as experiments in progress commenced. Gunfire, spoken commands and crunching metal played out as projects whittled down to-dos to production. Automated, yes, but guided. Following Mynx's grand design.

D block held the gladiator drone's newest model, her trickiest creation. While most drones spent their time patrolling the skies or skimming the globe's vast information networks in search of threats or crimes, the gladiator drone should replace . . . her. Aegis. The other Paragons risking their lives getting face-first into fights with anomalies or normals.

Mynx would stop those funerals. And, if this Denise Jones knew her stuff, maybe Mynx could stop the other, more natural ones too.

The Paragons' salvation sat in D block's center, a squat container not much larger than Mynx's bedroom and bereft of anything interesting other than the jumbled parts in the middle. Mynx walked off the disk, across a granite-tile floor made of the smooth mountain rock she'd hollowed out to craft this place. The moment she stepped onto the ground, the parts began to snap themselves together. What had been junk formed itself into a four meter tall, menacing, modular, metal machine.

"I like the new disguise," Mynx said. "The production model will need to look worse, though. I could tell it wasn't junk."

"I have three new coatings in development. Rust, of course, but also forest floor and dust-covered."

"Good." Like with the doors, Mynx went right up to the massive construct and placed her hands on its legs, which stood as tall as she did, and went *inside*.

The steel doors had nothing on the gladiator drone's space. Here was a mansion. Towering, vast, and with rooms for each and every function. Mynx started in the lobby, looking around at the various wings, each one labeled with its primary feature. The core components lived here. The wing she wanted sat towards the back —out the back, actually.

She'd used a tribal motif with this design, seeing as the gladiator drones were meant to join in with the Paragons. African highlights decorated the walls: masks, ornaments, and the mansion's own material seeming to come from the jungle's heart. When Mynx built with her mind, adding flair came easier, more pleasant and focused at the same time.

As she went by algorithms fashioned as standing totems, clinging to the walls outside the section dealing with evidence collection and prosecution, Mynx glimpsed herself in a floor-to-ceiling mirror spacing the wide central hallway. A concession to vanity, a marker of her inventions, Mynx always threw these in, because they showed her what she was.

What she used to be.

The Mynx staring at her had lost decades from the Mynx that woke up in her bed on the cliff-side that morning. The Mynx looking back in the same Paragon blue uniform had lived in a different, scarier world. She hadn't proven herself yet, didn't have the lab or a whole region of the world under her thumb.

"You would probably think I'm evil," Mynx whispered to her younger self. The mirror image matched the movement of her lips, but said nothing. "But you were naive. Beautiful, but naive."

Past the mirror and out the mansion's back sat rolling sand dunes. As if the mansion had emerged from some desert. Above, a cold sun glared down from an even-blue sky. On the nearest dune stood the gladiator drone, standing over a small boy. Arms, legs coated in plated armor to protect the wires and weapons beneath. Unlike the actual drone, this one stood no taller than Mynx's knee. The boy not even reaching her ankle. Easier to judge these sorts of things when she could see every angle.

Mynx couldn't feel the sand when she stepped on it. She breathed no hot air—no air at all, really—and when she spoke the words to start the test, they didn't come from her lungs, her voice, or anywhere except the electrons that burst around the gladiator drone's circuits. In here, inside the drone's very core, Mynx was God, and God wanted to see how her drone performed.

The test began without a sign, a switch, or a saying. Two drifting, faceless thugs rose up from the dune as if they'd been lurking in the sands all along. They reached into their identical brown trench coat pockets and drew knives, then advanced on the small boy. The drone picked up the newcomers, shifting its relative bulk to put the boy behind it.

Protect first. Good.

But the drone decided to take the protection command too seriously. It waited for the thugs to close, for the two enemies to split apart, like a widening V, which neutralized the drone's crowd-control options. Mynx would have to dial up the initiative—the idea of waiting for an attack before reacting had died away a long time ago, now strategy was all about the threshold: at what point was an attack a certainty?

The drone reached that point when the thug pacing to its right came within arms length and still had its knife out. The drone issued a verbal warning, which the thug ignored. The drone, then, committed to a lightning-fast, incapacitating assault on that thug. A trio of stunning darts flashed out from openings in the drone's left hand and struck the thug, digging deep while, with its right hand, the drone grabbed the thug and slammed the adversary to the floor.

And failed.

Mynx shook her head and wiped away the simulation, with the second thug holding its knife to the child's throat. The drones kept over-committing, but if Mynx lowered the aggression, then they sat and waited until they were trapped, it was—

A tug on her mind. Attention. Mynx slid, the dunes, the mansion, everything disappearing until she opened her eyes back in her lab. Behind her, one of Reeve's floating micro-drones retracted its steel claw from her shoulder.

"She's here," Reeves said. "Dr. Jones."

"I'm coming," Mynx replied. "And Reeves? I'll have that tea now."

5

It's About That Time

Smooth, creamy, and loaded with sugar. Aegis sipped the latte from the top floor of his—no, the Paragon's—tower. Beyond the penthouses' blast-proof glass walls, beneath him, Manhattan's chaos spread into late-morning life. Industry churned down in those streets, in those buildings blending old and new architecture, and beyond sat the water, bustling with ships.

Anomalies, normals, living and working together. No longer at each other's throats, no longer scared of what might come. The Paragons had built this, a new world standing tall on its forebear's ashes.

"Would you sit down?" Celice said, walking barefoot on the wood floor and carrying bandages and ointments in her arms like she was going to perform an amputation.

Aegis followed his daughter's orders anyway, relaxing back into the wide chair that sat near the window. His command station kept a perfect view, with monitors available to rise from floor slots at his request. Right now, right now he just wanted to drink his coffee, but he shrugged the thick robe off of his left shoulder, ignoring the ache when he did so.

"Is this really necessary?" Aegis said as Celice set about unraveling the bandages from the night before.

Blood spotted the gauze, faded and far from the drenched wounds Aegis had seen on other gunshot victims. Yes, he might not be as invincible as he'd been decades ago, but Aegis could still take a hit better than anyone else.

"If you can get hurt, you can get infected," Celice said, tending to his shoulder with caring exactness. "What would the world think if their greatest Champion fell to disease?"

Aegis slugged the latte. The ointment chilled his shoulder. Aegis counted two deployment drones making a slow crossing route through the sky, their deep blue bodies looking so much like floating pills.

"I expect you to lie if that ever happens," Aegis said. "Claim it was a hidden attack by Outbreak, or Patient Zero."

"Can't do that, Dad." Celice put the new wrap on, tight and soft. "Both died years ago."

"Did they? How?" Aegis should know this, but there had been so many anomalies, so many normals the Paragons had sent away.

Celice stood back, cocked her head. "The same way all your villains die, dad. Rotting in the ocean."

Ah, yes. That place. Mynx handled that grim business, so Aegis tended to ignore it. Once the fight finished, he was happy to turn over the aftermath to those more interested in it.

"I noticed my calendar is empty today." Aegis swapped topics.

"I cleared it." Celice pointed at the wound. "You need to rest."

"I do not."

"You do, and you will." Celice looked so defiant, all set up in the Paragon's professional uniform, though she'd left the blue blazer behind for her dad's medical dirty work. "I'm telling you, dad, you have to stop this. You're worth too much to the Paragons to risk yourself."

"Just to the Paragons?" Aegis cracked a smile.

Celice rolled her eyes. "To me, too. But I'm serious. Have you thought about what would happen if you didn't come back from one of these? What happens when you retire?" His daughter ended the question with a flourish to the city below. "All this rests on what you made."

She wasn't wrong. The world had been run by fear; anomalies and normals facing off with their abilities and their guns. How easy it would be to go back to that without the mantel of the original Champions and their Paragons covering the world. Time after time, Aegis, Mynx, and the other six had saved civilization from itself, and then they'd taken the reins to run it. What would happen when they let go?

"You're right." Aegis delivered the admission with the straight-eyed slate speech he'd been doing almost since birth, a determined look that guaranteed honesty and follow-through. "I'll call a summit. We'll talk transitions. Get a plan together."

Celice stood up, stepped back and leaned against the glass, putting her body one structural failure away from a short, fatal trip into the city. With the sun giving back-light, and her dark, shoulder-cropped hair staying in perfect balance through some magic Aegis couldn't fathom, his daughter looked the image of a business executive headlining an article on corporate power. The sort of thing Aegis had grown up reading about, had matured into working for, and then disposed of when it stopped being useful.

"Not good enough," Celice said. "You want to transition, you have to live to see it."

"What?"

"Stay on the sidelines, dad." Celice didn't plead, she ordered. "You've done enough. Find someone to take over, and, for once, enjoy yourself."

"Talking with my daughter, overlooking the greatest city in the world with a delicious breakfast isn't enjoying myself?"

Celice shook her head, stared at the ground like she did whenever she wanted to hide an emotion. Aegis guessed laughter, this time, based on her hand coming up to shade her eyes. When Celice looked up, though, gravity had retaken its hold on her face.

"Promise, dad. You're not going out again. Not for these little things."

Another sip. Truth was, the small runs were tiring, even if he enjoyed them. Stopping crooks was a hobby, a way to keep his skills sharp, but small fry weren't worth dying for.

"I promise, Celice. I won't go saving the world anymore, just for you."

"Good." Celice glanced at her wrist, where a wrap-around bracelet turned from stylized silver-black to blue at her look and displayed a calendar too small for Aegis to read. Celice always had the fashionable Tamas. "Have to get going, dad. Northeast wants to discuss their new headquarters project."

"Hold on," Aegis said as his daughter started going past him. "We spent all this time talking about me. What're you doing? I haven't had to chase away any new boyfriends lately."

Celice stopped, quipped a laugh. "Boyfriend? After taking care of you and all your Paragons, none of whom know what they're doing outside of a fight, by the way, I don't have much time for dating. Besides, once someone hears who I am, who my dad is, they stop acting normal."

"Ah, I'm not so bad."

"Sure." Celice tapped the glass-metal side table where Aegis's remaining breakfast sat, bordered by a circular, plastic case smaller than Aegis's hand. Inside it, split into sections, were little colored ovals. "Remember to take them all. The new ones are for the pain."

Before Aegis finished his latte, Celice vanished into the elevator. He looked at the pills. The water in a new glass waiting. Conditions to treat, and Aegis rattled them off in his head. Each one its own surprise when it came, another marker of Time, that invincible foe the Paragons hadn't been able to defeat.

Yet.

But they'd been able to win against everyone else. No military, no police. All the governments dissolved into parts beneath the Paragon's protection. Peace covered the planet, and anyone who disturbed it was dealt with in swift, final fashion. At first, complaints. Then, the people learned. The normals accepted and the anomalies understood their role, the part their gifts needed to play in helping the world.

Aegis took the pills. One in, one sip, one down. Stood as he started, took the long step right up to the glass and watched the mass beneath him churn.

All of this depended on him, and Celice was right. When—if—Aegis couldn't protect them all anymore, when he couldn't deliver on the promises the Paragons made to the world, someone else must. Better for him to choose that someone than rely on the Paragons themselves to sort it out. Better for all of the Champions to choose.

"Polly," Aegis spoke loud so the system's receivers could catch it. "Send a message to the Champions."

"Ready."

Polly's voice was always so cheerful. Aegis had found it annoying, but then the AI's relentless optimism had grown on him, peppy light on a gloomy day. There were enough difficulties in life, having a computer that spoke with bubbly joy wasn't one of them.

"We need to meet. It's time to decide what happens next."

6

Homecoming

Passcode. Key. Insert. Turn.

Kat operated in monosyllables. She didn't have energy for more, not after hauling Vedder back to the rover, tracing him, and then dropping the anomaly at a hospital on her way back. Barring some bad luck, Kat would never need to see Vedder again. With some good luck, the anomaly would earn Kat plenty of reps through his new, forced career as a Paragon.

Her apartment's stench, a potent mixture of old laundry and dog hair that grew into a toxic cloud whenever the windows were shut, wrapped Kat in its strangling embrace and the tracker stumbled into a space best described as stricken. It wasn't clear what had happened, or was happening, in the apartment but something terrible had occurred. Clothes, food and things that may have once been food but were now entire ecosystems, jumbled boxes from prior moves never opened, and treasures Kat once knew yet now regarded as stuff lumped throughout the one-bedroom space. Without the lights on, with the curtains drawn, the junk shadows loomed.

Seeker burst by Kat and tackled the horrors with tongue-wagging delight, barking up a storm that would annoy the neighbors excepting it was noon and nobody was left in this working stiff complex. With the apartments too small for comfortable at-home offices, Kat watched the every-morning escapade as the building emptied out into the streets of Chicago, people struggling to find their way to support the Paragons, earn their reps, and come home to a place no doubt cleaner than hers.

"But you like it this way, don't you?" Kat said to Seeker, who bounded up to her covered in random laundry, a pink-and-yellow, bone-shaped chew toy in his mouth. She began taking off her suit, dodging around the dog at the same time. "You know, you could help."

Seeker took the suggestion and ran with it, dropping the bone and gnawing a hold on Kat's boot, causing her to trip and fall onto a faded blue couch that'd seen more years than she had. Age left the cushions jelly-like, so Kat sank into them with the soft pleasure pain from sore muscles given a chance to relax. While Seeker took over stripping Kat of her shoes, gloves, and gauntlets—the dog was precise with his teeth, able to hit the pressure points that snapped off the techno-armbands—Kat laid there, breathed. Settled into the headache approaching as her body succumbed to sleep deprivation.

"Tap, open the windows," Kat muttered, but the hyper-sensitive mics dotting the apartment's corners picked it up anyway, and moments later fresh air began its war with the stultified apartment. "And get me some breakfast. The usual, from *Brickhouse*."

"You got it, Kat," the AI replied in its cheerful, surfer-boy voice. "Anything else? You sound tired. Want coffee?"

"Nope." Kat had managed to remove the suit's mask, and Seeker had picked it up and dumped it in the marked bin. Her eyes were closed and she wanted to keep them that way, for a little while. "I want sleep."

"Does that mean you don't want your daily report?"

Kat groaned with the despair of one who knows the right call and hated to make it anyway. "Fine. But make it fast."

"I'll read it at one-point-two-five speed."

Tap followed his warning with numbers, a statistics barrage Kat filed away with force of habit. First came anomalies she'd traced that hadn't amounted to time-wasters and had earned her royalties over the last day. A percent of contracts completed. Reps to pay her rent, and the best reason to be a tracker at all.

Not her reason, but the best reason.

Today's results were pretty good; one anomaly with a penchant for detoxifying sewage had found a lucrative set of contracts with Chicago, and those kept paying. She'd found him after reports came in from western Illinois of a series of crystal clear lakes that'd been algae-covered for the longest time. His earnings beat out all the other anomalies, including the deadly ones, Kat had ever traced. And she hadn't had to drag him through deep snow, either.

"I have one priority message too, if you're still awake?" Tap asked when the readout finished.

"I am. Who's it from?"

"Gordon Holyoak." Tap was an AI, but even the computer knew to say Gordon's name with trepidation.

The fan on the ceiling didn't move. She hadn't turned it on. At Gordon's name, Kat stared hard at the blades, daring them to break her from the memories, emotions, and other garbage ruining the nap she wanted to have. After a moment's glare, the fan failed in its mission and Kat rolled off the couch, landing on and continuing to roll off of Seeker, who'd adopted his usual sleeping spot near her side. With her chin planted on one of the few clean spots on the carpet, Kat now looked through a slim door at blankets, pillows, and renegade stuffed animal forces that occupied her bed. That, too, did not help in her quest to avoid reflection.

"Uhh." Kat said into the floor, then pushed herself up to an unsteady stand. "Fine. Read it."

"Hey Kat! I know it's been awhile, and I know you won't believe me, but I'm in town, and contacting you, for business reasons! Can you meet tomorrow? I know that's fast, but we don't have much time on this. Hope you're doing well!" Tap concluded. "There's a geo-marker attached for The Spit Roast, in six hours."

"I don't wanna," Kat said, rubbing her eyes and looking at Seeker, who provided no valuable insight whatsoever.

"It's not priority, but you may want to know Gordon just put out a general call to Chicago's trackers," Tap said. "Same time, same place."

So Gordon did have a reason to be here, aside from messing with Kat. If he put out an open call, that meant a big target, because Gordon would be divvying up reps for the trace to everyone who helped.

"How long ago was Gordon's message?"

"Last night. While you were gone."

A solid half-day's lead time to an old partner. That's what Kat was worth. She looked at the couch, considered the possibility of getting that nap, and discarded it when a series of sirens broke out somewhere in the distance. A drone responding to a call, and a sign that she'd missed her window.

Shower time.

In the meditative steam and hot water, Kat's exhaustion pulled her to Gordon's arrival on her scene. He entered stage left, walking in on a ruin as Kat scrambled to sell what she had to survive. Gordon wasn't wealthy, wasn't someone looking to take advantage, but he wanted Kat's company and that'd been enough. When Gordon made her laugh, something that hadn't happened for a long time, Kat gave him a chance at dinner. Gordon wound up paying for that, and Kat for everything else.

But she was a tracker now, and Gordon had put her on that path. Which made up for, what, ten percent of the grief the man had given her?

By the time she was clean, the *Brickhouse* breakfast had arrived without a coffee Kat now regretted missing, and she wolfed down the eggs, the vitamin-infused potato hash. Threw the remnants into the slot near the door that'd carry the trash to some magical place Kat never worried about. That the containers weren't in her apartment was enough.

After all that, and putting on an outfit that countered the Chicago's winter chill, which was winning its war against her apartment's heater in the continual bout between breathable air and livable climate, Kat looked at Seeker, who'd grabbed his leash while Kat had finished eating, and sighed.

"Guess there's enough time. C'mon."

Tap locked the place down after Kat left. Sealed the window too, and Kat made the questionable call to ask Tap to find someone, something that could clean her apartment. She had enough reps now that living on the brink of plague wasn't necessary.

The afternoon sidewalks weren't too crowded—it was cold, people were working, and Kat's neighborhood wasn't great walking material. For every older building reaching back for simpler times with brick and mortar, a dozen others boasted modern efficiency's shiny, pre-fab gloss. Chemicals forged together and greased with anomaly powers turned what would have been cold metal into watercolor creations that withstood everything nature could summon up. Which, given most major cities had anomalies tasked with weather manipulation, wasn't much at all.

"Can't seem to keep it comfortable, though," Kat said, watching her breath poof into a gray cloud.

There were reasons, of course, to maintain the usual climate. Reasons Kat neither had the time, nor the desire, to contemplate. That's what the Paragons, that's what Mynx, were for. Keep the planet alive so Kat could walk her dog to the park and throw a disc.

The park hit all the right notes for a city oasis: surrounded by imposing structures, nonetheless fenced, and a formerly fountain-dominated center bulldozed to flatness in order to give the dogs more freedom. Seeker took advantage, bursting away as soon as Kat let him off the leash to go inspect a roaming canine horde barreling around the park like a force of barking nature. Seeker's excited yips had the happiness Kat wasn't sure she'd ever experienced, but the vicarious joy she drew from the husky's leaps and bounds dulled her exhaustion's edge.

At least until she saw a familiar face meandering through the park in her general direction, hugging the fence's inside as though to take one more step into the dog's territory would be a crime punished with overwhelming slobber.

"Stan." Kat threw the anomaly, walking stiff in a jean jacket and faded, black baseball cap a greeting.

"Kat," Stan said, his teeth making a chattering clack Kat

would've attributed to the cold if she didn't know Stan so well. "You look tired."

"Thanks, Stan. Needed that today."

"Sorry." Stan sought to salve with an awkward smile. Kat let him go, returned it. "Rough night?"

"Let's just say not every anomaly is as nice as you."

Kat spoke with a sigh, but she meant it. Stan had been hiding low from Mynx's searching drones and the Internet sleuths that hunted anomalies by working locally with small time carpentry. When he'd finally made a mistake and completed a job a little too fast—the neighbors were surprised to find a house that'd been white yesterday all baby blue the next without a swarm of scaffolding and sweat—Kat had cornered him in a bar not three blocks from here. Stan had ordered stiff, cheap bourbon for the both of them and held out his arm for the trace.

"Never thought running away would be good for me." Stan tried to look to some horizon, but wound up staring at a corner grocer's sign instead. "Always thought Chicago was my town."

Kat nodded as a brisk breeze shot through. The dogs didn't notice, barking up a storm at some poor bird in a tree.

"Things aren't bad, either," Stan kept going. "Paragons give me plenty of work, the reps are good."

"I know." Kat saw the receipts, took her cut from every gig Stan did. Reliable, but not as rich as the sewage guy.

"Suppose you would." No malice, only acceptance there. Stan hesitated, and Kat felt him searching the side of her face for permission. "Can I ask you a question?"

"Go for it."

"What happens if you don't make it back from one of these things?"

"You mean if an anomaly burns me to a crisp? Shoots me a dozen different ways with her super speed?"

"Uh. I guess?"

Kat launched her blue-eyed, tracker stare at Stan, let him know the question was both impolite and annoying, but she'd answer it anyway. "You'll get another tracker. Someone close by. Nothing changes on your end."

Stan struggled to get a response going, so Kat unhooked him with a *nice seeing you* and let the anomaly whistle for his chocolate lab and head out.

His question, though, lingered. If Kat didn't come back from one of her hunts, the only one who'd notice would be Seeker. The headache, sensing Kat's lowered defenses, surged back and the tracker leaned back against the fence, pressed her fingers to her temples, and tried to lose herself in the endless barks of happier creatures.

7

Inviting All The Players

Zhan-Yo wanted to take a wheel that wasn't there. The pod rolled along the street, both following and being followed by other pods in an unceasing, efficient line pulling up to the mall. Every time he sat in these things, their cushions stale from too many riders and too few cleanings, Zhan-Yo wanted to trade the efficiency and safety for the hard leather circle that steered his father's car. The one Zhan-Yo himself had driven for a few years before manual drives were eliminated in the name of protection.

Zhan-Yo found the logic a poor substitute for emotion.

Yet when the pod paused at the mall's main entrance, its door flashing green LEDs around the edges, the seats vibrating to let Zhan-Yo know his destination had been reached, Zhan-Yo didn't mind not having to park. On a cold afternoon like this, a short walk inside was a welcome benefit.

If the pods were an evolution for an older, obsolete machine, the mall had evolved too. Glitz backed by substance: lights called out various vendors, with projected squares shouting sales, false fireworks drawing eyes to new stock, and a few old drones standing on the entry walk offering limited opportunities on their bodies, where armor had been replaced by screens. People abounded, the mall serving as a rescue from the cramped confines of massive population, the ones coming in and the ones going out carrying the same amount of product:

None.

Zhan-Yo smiled at a young girl and her mother, both carrying the satisfied shopping glow. He held the pod's door open, accepting the little girl's encouraged thank-you, and then went through the gaping entrance. No doors here, but Zhan-Yo felt the slight shift in the air, his thin gray hair catching the subtle breeze as the mall's pressure gate served to keep out the chill. His skin broke out in momentary goosebumps as Zhan-Yo went through the gateway, blue-neon-lined tile that served as the mall's sole spot without advertising.

The main floor beyond stretched for blocks in both directions, every dozen meters or so broken up by another storefront. The three-story complex filled every space with stuff, floor and ceiling tiles doubling as screens playing one silent ad after another. A lazy saxophone floated above it all, contrasting with the wealth immersion on display. What should have been overwhelming to everyone had become commonplace, a media menagerie made irrelevant by its own success.

Across from him, a clothing store occupied the prime position; the first target for all the eyes coming in. Designer outfits and accompanying ads hung large. One in particular called out to him, a red leather jacket with gold trim, hanging on the mannequin in a front window. His parents would have found it garish, but it spoke of rebellion, of spirit. Zhan-Yo wasn't here to shop, but he strode across the showstopper avenue and took a closer look.

Smooth, well-made. He touched the sleeves, frowned. Synthetic leather. The real thing was so hard to find, but a few brands still catered to it, still cared about authenticity. He slid his eyes to the price hovering in a small display beneath the jacket. Alongside the number of reps, Zhan-Yo noted the small, slanted Z. He knew it would be there, because nobody would dare not. Ziran benefited everyone, except those who didn't play by its rules.

The Paragons required a new currency, and reps required a means to be spent, earned, and distributed.

"You want to image it? There's nobody in the dressing room right now?" a man said, and Zhan-Yo saw a teen wearing metal accessories and half-matched clothes Zhan-Yo himself could never get away with, the teen no doubt wondering what a man Zhan-Yo's age was doing looking at such a stylish outfit.

"No, thank you," Zhan-Yo said, giving the teen a nod in thanks for his time. "Just admiring."

"It's a cool one," the teen agreed. "Let me know if you need anything."

As soon as the boy turned away, Zhan-Yo tapped his right wrist, where his Tama wrapped around in nice gold links. As soon as the Tama made contact with the price tag, it beeped three times, letting Zhan-Yo know that the product was available in his size, at the same price as listed, and could be delivered within a day to his apartment. With his left hand, Zhan-Yo tapped the Tama's face and accepted the order, never taking his eyes off the jacket.

Something to wear when he met Aegis, perhaps.

Ziran parlayed in actual provisions too—Zhan-Yo entered one of their tech outlets not far from where he bought the red jacket, nestled between sportswear brands and looking neither as stylish nor as interesting. But then, when Ziran's target market was the corporate buyer or the desperate, disgruntled civilian hunting for some way to make their life simpler, it paid to have a store look, well, simple. Zhan-Yo gave the overhanging sign with the blue-tinged Z on a soft white background a nod as he passed beneath.

A man ought to pay respects to the things that made him.

His Tama vibrated, letting Zhan-Yo know he was late, so he didn't spend any time checking the shelves, but he managed to give the sales associate a quick look that said the inspection would be happening later. Time for the young woman to get the store in perfect order, a warning most, including Zhan-Yo, didn't get.

There were two doors at the store's back, both bearing big placards declaring them for authorized personnel only. That the same personnel were not authorized for each door went unsaid, and

Zhan-Yo used the left one brushing his Tama against the black square on the pearl-painted wall. A soft chirp, a lock's click, and Zhan-Yo opened the portal. Unlike its partner, this door swung into a steep concrete stair. Zhan-Yo followed the steps—the door shutting by itself behind him—beneath the mall's back hallways and into a section carved out years ago for a very specific purpose. The landing did nothing to reveal that purpose, keeping the gray concrete look and adding stiff chairs, a small table, and nothing else. You might wait here, the setup seemed to say, but not for long.

Zhan-Yo's goal sat beyond the next door in the line. This, too, required a swipe from the Tama on a black scanner embedded into the wall, but unlike the one upstairs, the scan alone did not unlock the door.

"Zhan-Yo." He always felt strange saying his own name, but, according to the program now analyzing his pronunciation, a person's way of saying their own name was unique.

The program accepted his style without argument, letting Zhan-Yo into the second, and last room. Unlike its predecessor, this space embraced pre-rep luxury, opulence for its own sake. A mahogany table, with wood the color of barrel-aged whiskey, played out like an ocean, filling the room and making the five others already sitting around it seem tiny, even though this group combined as much power as existed in the world beyond the Paragons.

To Zhan-Yo's left, basic needs were over-met by distilled taps for both plain and sparkling water. A fruit tray, with yellow pineapple dominating the center per Zhan-Yo's request, filled in the black-granite counter. Above the tray, retracted when not in use, hung the delivery pipe, allowing workers or drones to send refreshments without accessing the room itself.

"We're all ready," a thin, blond man sporting a black suit too formal for Zhan-Yo's taste, said, making the effort to push his chair away and stand while he spoke. "Should I open the call?"

"Yes," Zhan-Yo replied, moving towards his own chair at the head of the table. The seats were rescues, tanned leather from a century ago that Zhan-Yo took care to maintain. He and Wexley would remove the chairs from the room themselves when repairs were needed. "A glass of plain water, if you would."

Wexley took the ask like a son, moving to fill a glass taken from a tray covered with them, and, at the same time, stating a set of commands for the room's AI, baked into the center of that table, to follow. Zhan-Yo took the moment to look at who'd bothered to come in person today and found himself satisfied at the cautious, curious faces meeting his own. What had been zero for so long was now four. The impossible moving to the possible.

Nobody spoke. There would be time for questions later.

After Wexley completed the command to launch the call, the room's wall across from Zhan-Yo brightened as a projector in the ceiling spooled up. At first, only white with a single name on the right side, *Ziran-Alpha*, displayed. This room's title. Over the next thirty seconds, however, another dozen names appeared, almost all meaningless letters and numbers.

This is why Zhan-Yo respected those who came in person— nothing to hide behind. They were the true committed ones, and it was Zhan-Yo's job to turn every faceless number on the call into faces at the table.

"Welcome," Zhan-Yo began as the white screen shifted from nothing to a polite close-up. A few wrinkles, that wispy white hair, black stubble . . . the inexorable march of time hadn't taken all of Zhan-Yo's youth yet. "To those who have been here since the beginning, thank you. To those only now coming to see our cause, I hope you find what you're looking for here. Today, to illustrate why our efforts are so important, we will begin with a story."

Wexley took his cue well, raising a single finger on his right hand and not flinching when his own face replaced Zhan-Yo's on the projection. "Many of you know me as Ziran's Chief Operating Officer. Many of you don't know that I am a product of the very thing we're working to end."

The story Wexley told was a familiar one. Zhan-Yo had heard it from Wexley before, of course, but most everyone here knew someone like him. Knew lives ruined by anomalies, lives that trusted the Paragons to save them and, when the Paragons failed, had no recourse. No voice.

"I didn't get to go home, because my home didn't exist." Wexley stayed cool, composed. Heartless, except for the tremor in his voice. "The Paragons called it an accident. An undiscovered anomaly who lost control, like so many others. My only option was to move on, deal with it. I'm here because I think we can do better."

"How?" The question came from the call, an unknown speaker distorting their voice so it sounded like a broken drone talking. "How do you think we can do better than the Paragons?"

"By giving people a say." Zhan-Yo took over the lead from Wexley with a look. "The Paragons have had their time, and it's clear their hearts lie with the anomalies. We are nothing more than a burden, a collection to keep happy while the Paragons cement their power."

"So you would replace the Paragons with yourself?"

"I would add our voices to theirs. Return us to a democracy, where everyone is heard, not just those with the strongest abilities. Don't you want to have a say in your own future? You control your companies, but you do not control your own society."

Silence. A good pause. Let the thought mature, and like wine, everyone here, whether they'd heard Zhan-Yo's arguments before or not, would come closer to embracing his ideals. Power intoxicated, and the chance for more, the chance for *any*, was impossible to resist for a group like this. Ziran had taken its position as much through manipulation as innovation, and Zhan-Yo would not abandon subversion for principal here. Not when they were so close.

The eyes at the table told Zhan-Yo when it was time to speak again, by the way they turned to him, by the way those men and women waited to hear him guide them on the path to this future.

"Our exact plans," Zhan-Yo started, "are, and will remain, secret. The Paragons have spies everywhere, and they will not look on our democratic dreams with our same hope. But we are making progress, and we are closer than ever to announcing, publicly, our stand against the Paragons. To prepare for that moment, I ask you to look to yourselves, find those reps you can sacrifice to a noble cause, and do so."

There were more questions, and Wexley answered them, leaving Zhan-Yo to watch the callers and the faces in the room. Progress was what they wanted, and Zhan-Yo would have to give them something tangible soon. Proof of their commitment, proof that the Paragons were vulnerable, that challenging the established power would not bring about their ruin.

Sylvie's plan would solve this. If Aegis fell, then Ziran would rise.

8

Impressions And Suspicions

As entrances went, Mynx wanted hers to be grand. The Factory, as she called it and as it now appeared on every map, in every database, and on every tongue, existed as a monument to technological prowess as defined by Mynx. That meant no offices, no vast parking lots, nothing except the core components run by Reeves and controlled by the Champion that powered the Paragons.

The Factory's front door encapsulated Mynx's mechanical grandeur, opening its copper-and-silver Paragon logo with arching gears. Five meters high and three wide, the open entry framed Mynx from a distance, and, in the afternoons, served to pitch sunlight on a golden lip where Mynx stood to greet whomever decided to visit. As it was morning, and as there were no journalists or prying eyes—Reeves confirmed this—Mynx didn't go for the full glory and walked out to greet Dr. Denise Jones instead of the other way around.

Glasses, rugged jacket and frayed jeans. Denise looked like a scientist that belonged to the outdoors, not a laboratory, though the sheer size of the bag slung over her shoulder gave a hint as to Denise's true passion. In there, Mynx would bet, sat notebooks waiting to be filled, recorders to be used, and a computer capable of running a simulation just in case it was necessary.

If Denise could deliver on her promise, then Mynx wouldn't care how big her bag was.

"Dr. Jones, welcome," Mynx said. "I trust the pod gave you a nice ride?"

"It did," Denise said, accepting Mynx's wave to walk by the host and into the Factory. "Thank you for sending one."

Mynx watched as Denise went through the same steps every new Factory visitor experienced. First there was awe at being inside a place mentioned in countless videos, books, and stories. Then came the searching, the placing of the Factory into the person's own perspective, deciding whether to exclaim aloud about its size and brilliance, or to hold the emotions inside and suppress them in a futile attempt at control.

Denise chose the latter, turning from her first view to Mynx with a straight smile. "It's a beautiful place."

"It's a functional place that happens to be beautiful," Mynx replied. "Come in, I imagine we both have other places we need to be."

The Factory's entrance hall led to a circular foyer serving up potential destinations. Mynx caught Denise staring at the gated entrance to the Factory's Lab, where Mynx had been playing with the gladiator drone. For a scientist, that wasn't surprising; always hunting for knowledge, for secrets.

"Maybe later," Mynx said, guiding Denise towards the first section, her home. "The Lab's not as exciting as you might think."

"I doubt that."

Denise didn't fight Mynx on the change in course and together the two went into Mynx's cliff-side abode and found space at a glass table on a white-wood deck that launched out like a spear's head from the mountain. Drones proffered coffee, tea, and Mynx's delayed breakfast.

"Would you like any?" Mynx asked, nodding at the plate and its spinach-stuffed omelet. Two strips of vitamin-loaded, synthetic bacon and melon chunks completed the ensemble. "It's all made here."

Denise eyed the food, then declined, "Just coffee. Black."

"You don't like synthetics?"

"I'm not hungry." Denise pulled her bag up and set it on the table while Mynx set about to eating.

Denise watched Mynx take the first bites, which Mynx might have found annoying except she'd spent so much of her life under the sharpest lenses. People always wanted to know what the Champion was up to, always dug for her life's smallest details. She'd built the Factory inside a mountain to hide it from those same eyes.

The food, as promised, was delicious. Mynx wasn't going to let a little staring ruin her breakfast.

"I asked you here for a reason," Mynx said between bites. "I think you know why."

Denise took the first sip of the hot coffee, shook her head. "I do, but you won't like my answer." When Mynx only responded with another omelet bite, Denise went on. "The research isn't progressing. We're stuck."

"But you've come so far?"

"The changes don't stick," Denise reached into her bag, pulled out, as Mynx suspected, a notebook. "We can't wipe out all of the translation errors, and then the cells collapse back to where they were. We get a few days. A week. Then you're reverted to your old self again."

Mynx hid her disappointment with the practiced ease of someone who'd stumbled through so many roadblocks that their presence no longer fazed her. That Dr. Denise Jones, premiere aging expert, had hit a dead end was expected. It answered one of Mynx's own questions.

"That's why you agreed to come," Mynx said. "You think I can help."

"I know you can."

"How?"

Denise leaned towards Mynx, one hand around her coffee and the other flipping open the notebook to a blank page, fingers twisting around a pen that'd been slotted into the notebook's spiral binding.

"Your database. The one the trackers use." Denise spoke like she was searching for confirmation. "I know what you store there."

"I have the links to their locations. Who traced each anomaly." Mynx took a bacon strip, popped it into her mouth and then wiped her hands on a white cloth napkin. "I don't see how that will help you."

"That's not all you have."

Mynx stared into Denise's fire. It'd been a long time since she'd seen, heard the kind of energy Denise put into her frame, her words. Sharp, determined, and Mynx would bet, willing to go beyond what was proper to get what she wanted.

"Who told you?" There would be a limited list, and Mynx would hunt down every last one to find out who'd broken her trust.

"That you keep DNA samples?" Denise said, allowing a cocky smile on her face and sitting back, now that she'd achieved her goal. "You just did."

Ah. Denise thought she was being clever, protecting someone, but that's not how this worked. Someone must have clued the scientist in, but that was a mystery to resolve later. The thread in front of Mynx needed pulling first.

"You believe anomaly DNA will help you somehow?"

"Anomaly samples are rare," Denise said. "They're also the only thing that I know of that drives controlled, permanent changes to a person's DNA of the kind we need. If you want to end aging, Mynx, give me access to your records. Let me learn how anomalies function and apply my techniques to their cells, and we'll find a solution. I swear."

The samples, taken by Paragons and sent to Mynx for storage, existed to identify anomalies, and to try and find common threads between abilities. To understand how they worked. Reeves did, was doing, the analysis while Mynx worked on the science she preferred —the drones. Handing all of it over to Denise would be . . . dangerous. The Paragons had already dealt with would-be villains whose schemes revolved around twisting anomaly cells. Mynx had no desire to create another one.

"How about we continue this conversation at your own lab," Mynx said. "Let me see your methods, what you're doing, and if I'm convinced having access to my records would help, we'll see."

"Mynx." Denise used her name for the first time, and she said it flat, like an order. "You're the one that asked for this meeting. You want my research, my solutions, to keep going, then help me. Don't waste my time."

So much for the humble researcher.

"I won't." Mynx pushed herself back from the table, and Denise matched her rise. Together, they walked back to the Factory's front door, with Denise again halting for a long moment by the Lab's entry. "Send me a time, and I'll be there. Prove that this is legitimate, and I'll help you."

"I will," Denise said. "We can change everything, Mynx. Everything."

When the scientist had left, Mynx went back to the table. The drones had cleared away breakfast, but fresh black tea sat steaming for her. Mynx sipped it while watching the waves.

"What do you think?" she asked.

"Her readings were all over the place," Reeves replied, his voice coming from speakers embedded beneath the table. "I believe she is sincere, though."

"She's ambitious," Mynx said.

"She's passionate. Like you."

"She could be dangerous."

"Also like you."

Mynx wanted somewhere to throw her side-eye, but with Reeves being a computer, all she could do was sigh. "You work for me, remember? Stick a drone on her, quietly. I want to know more about who I'm dealing with."

"Of course," Reeves said. "I should also mention we received a call while you were with Dr. Jones. From Celice."

"Reeves, we need to work on your priorities. If Aegis or Celice calls here, you interrupt me. Whatever I'm doing."

"Sorry. I've adjusted my algorithms."

"Good. Play the message."

Celice's voice, tight and tired, came through the speakers.

Mynx, I'm sorry to call you like this, but it's about my father. He got hurt last night, playing hero again. It's worse than the other times. I think he believes he can still do this, that he can still take a bullet and keep on going. But he can't. Not anymore. I need you to help me get him to stop, or I'm afraid one of these times, he won't come home.

Mynx finished the tea. Had Reeves play the message one more time. Celice did sound worried, and it'd been a while since Mynx had seen Aegis. With the gladiator drone stuck, and with Reeves handling the Denise Jones investigation, maybe a short trip away wouldn't be a bad thing.

"Reeves, get the jet ready. I'm going to pay our Champion friend a visit."

9

Troubles At Home

Atlantis called in. The Paragons stationed in the Gulf, New England, the Midwest and Appalachia appeared on the screens while the afternoon sun drenched New York's skyline in cold fire. A weekly touch base, not his retirement call, though Aegis had been planning to drop the announcement towards the end.

As usual, though, his plans were sidetracked.

"There's one issue, man, that we keep having," Cornelius, Appalachia's lead, broke in after a discussion over new uniforms petered out the same way it always did—nobody could agree on color, logo, anything. "And it's getting worse."

"If this is about the cockroaches, I don't wanna hear it." Pixie, New England, said. "I have enough nightmares without your giant bugs."

"I'm not talking about the bugs. I'm talking about the Elementals."

Aegis winced at the name. Every few years, the Elementals came back—

"Wait, you're seeing them too?" Innis spoke up, the burly Midwest captain hailing from Chicago. "Just last week they were helping an anomaly get outta my city when he wrecked a whole block after drinkin' too many rounds."

"You caught him?" Aegis said.

"No, we didn't catch him. Elementals stole him to the border. He's Mynx's problem now."

Aegis shook his head. "No, he's all of our problems. Make sure a bounty gets posted on the tracker board. We may have regions, but we're all Paragons. A threat to one is—"

"A threat to all," Cornelius finished. "We know, Aegis, we know. I happen to think the Elementals *are* a threat. They might not be trying to kill us, but they're helping anomalies hide. They're getting in the way. I've even had a Paragon drop out and join'em."

"Messages of hope play to everyone," Aegis said, keeping his face straight. Eyes calm. See the commander, feel the command. "Cornelius makes a good point. Talk to your Paragons. Hold calls like this one and make sure everyone understands our goals. They ought to know we support them, we value them."

"That's fine, but what about the Elementals?" Innis said, and Aegis wondered whether he'd given them too much freedom to talk. All this venting only fueled frustration, it didn't lead to solutions. "You wanted us to stay clear of them, and now they're taking advantage. I think one good thrashing would teach'em that they're not welcome."

"Yes. Anomalies fighting in the streets. That's what will give people confidence in our leadership." Aegis waved his hands towards the screens. "I'll think on it. Let you know what I decide. We're done for now."

The Paragons began to drop off, but when the tones of cut calls stopped beeping, two faces were left staring back at him. Innis, with his stubbled, red-faced mug and Pixie, who'd picked up one of her sons and rocked the infant on the screen.

"What?" Aegis asked, when neither one jumped on the chance to speak first.

Innis looked at Pixie, who looked at Innis, and then the woman sighed. "Fine, I'll go. Aegis, like Innis said, the Elementals are growing, and they're causing problems in Boston. I arranged a meeting with their local leader, but she told me they wouldn't talk to anyone but you."

"Why?"

"No idea. But since we're not that far, think you could make the trip?"

Go to Boston? It was close, and getting out of this tower and away from Celice's constant watch might do Aegis some good. His shoulder hurt, but the medications and ointments kept the pain away. Besides, this came with leading the Paragons—he couldn't very well tell his team to lead their own if he didn't do the same.

"Send me the details. I'll make it happen."

"Thanks, Aegis. I mean it." Pixie smiled, then the baby started to cry and, with a roll of her eyes, she cut the feed.

Which left Innis, who looked a little stunned at the sight of a child. Aegis wasn't certain, but Innis had to be nearing forty years old. Not that the Paragon ever struck Aegis as a family man.

"Never had a kid before?" Aegis asked him.

"Never wanted one," Innis replied, shaking off the wide eyes and turning a grim face back to Aegis. "No place for them with what we're doing. Pixie's a brave woman."

"She is." Aegis nodded at the man. "What do you need, Paragon?"

The formal title was deliberate: Aegis had things to do, and the call had gone on for hours already. Idle chit chat could wait.

"Trouble," Innis replied. "The Elementals, I'm handling best I can. But there's something else going on. I think there's a move happening."

"That's it? A feeling?"

Innis turned red. "No, no. I mean, I don't know the details, and I've got my people on it. Just letting you know that if you could head my way when you're done with Pixie, it might be good. If this gets as big as I'm thinkin' it might, having you around . . . it might keep things from getting out of control."

"You're being cryptic, Innis. What's going on?"

"Eh, you know, maybe I'm too early with this. Let me dig further." Innis stammered his way through his words, unusual for a fighter who broadcast bravado with every sentence. "I'll let you know what I find out."

The call blinked out and Aegis stared at the monitor. Weird. Not like Innis to be that way.

Aegis might have thought more on it, but his shoulder started aching again. Time for the next medication round. As he reached for the pills, Aegis realized he hadn't mentioned retirement. Or the wider Paragon summit he was planning with the other Champions, the eight companions that formed the overall heads of the entire Paragon organization.

"Guess I'll keep working for a little bit longer, then," Aegis muttered to himself, not all that sad about it.

10

Offers From A Past Life

Kat took the train to Gordon's meeting. Faster, quieter, and cheaper than a pod car, the train came with one other advantage: the chance to find and trace an unsuspecting anomaly. Just because Mynx's drones hadn't found them and pegged the anomaly onto the tracker board meant nothing. Some anomalies didn't even know they had any abilities until a tracker with a careful glance caught something strange, like a teenager showing off a 'trick' to their friends.

All of 'em were dangerous, all the anomalies needed to be traced, and Kat wouldn't say no to a few more reps in her account.

Going out casually meant leaving her suit behind. Kat ventured into the chill city wind and its constant smell of refined *anything* in a thick jacket, some lined jeans that took her movement's kinetic energy and turned it into extra heat, and a full set of gloves-and-baseball cap.

The cap made her sigh every time she put it on—its bright red blaze with a swooping C logo did nothing to preserve the low profile Kat craved. The trackers, though, had a contract with the company that made the tracer equipment, and that contract paid out bonus reps if someone took, and posted somewhere, a picture of a tracker in their hats. CytoGenX was a burden, but those little kickbacks let her upgrade from boxed to bottled Chardonnay, so Kat didn't complain too much. Did it hurt her subtle search for anomalies on the go? Yes, but a sure rep in the account was worth two in her dreams.

In her blizzard-ready apparel, with some stray strands catching hold of the wind and snapping around her face, Kat marched with those other souls who found themselves required downtown, or at least somewhere in that direction. If, during the day, Kat could ignore the Tamas and their constant presence, at dusk such obliviousness wasn't possible. Most walking along had their eyes basking in the halo of the projected person they were talking to, the game they were playing, or the video they were watching. The Tamas knew where their owners were going and helped, with subtle lighting cues, to direct the walkers in the right direction.

What annoyed Kat most was that if she'd had someone to call, she'd be doing the same thing. Instead, Kat wished she'd stayed in bed, or put on a movie from her couch instead of marching her sore, tired self out to Gordon's meet-up. Reveling in self-pity passed the time as she walked to the train. The pod's chirping warnings on the street beside her, the occasional sewage belching up from a nearby grate, and the inane chatter around her seemed to sympathize with the walk's dismal drudgery.

The L train stood on the steel foundation laid down almost two centuries ago, but the trains didn't touch the tracks anymore. Kat still had to climb stairs, both an indication of Paragon priorities and, in her frustration with the cold metal steps, an embarrassing amount of entitlement. She could have gone in the elevator for those who couldn't walk, after all, and not one around her would have cared. But no, she pulled herself up, grumbling in her mind the whole way.

Gordon. That miserable bastard.

Kat brushed her Tama through the fast stalls—if you didn't have one of the ubiquitous things, a squat box would take your reps and, without those, listen to your pleas with zero cares—and strode out onto a platform drenched in the deep fryer smells finishing the evening's rush at full, boiling speed.

If Gordon was getting Kat to go this far, the place better have food, and he'd be buying.

The train came whisper-quiet, magnets pushing and stopping the cars with what seemed like the force of God himself. The platform edges lit up in harsh, neon red whenever the trains came close while a soothing voice played, in several languages, a warning to step back. The crowd around Kat had filtered out onto the platform, so she wasn't so much crushed anymore as enclosed. Didn't matter: live in the city long enough and you get used to people everywhere.

Two stops later and Kat hopped off into a neighborhood redesigned for a younger, hipper, richer caste. Not that Kat was old, but there's a particular type of youth that comes with an unlimited supply of reps and the time to spend them. Here, too, among the normals, Kat noticed the first anomalies. Some paraded themselves around in various Paragon uniforms, their blues drawing them space as they walked in clusters, laughing and chatting through the slight snow that had started during the ride here.

Other anomalies, ones Kat's contacts touched and ID'ed at a glance with names and abilities floating over her eyes, kept to themselves or tried fitting in with the normals. Only trackers had gear that could tag an anomaly on sight, so it wasn't as if all the random families and larks getting off the platform with her knew what they were walking near. A good thing, because trackers and anomalies tended to make normals nervous.

And nervous people made Kat nervous.

THE SPIT ROAST LOOKED, from the outside, like a sweaty, squat dive at hard odds with the upper-tier apartments on top, the boutiques next to it, and the huddling high-repped people getting into pods in front. A neon pig, complete with its own spit, occupied a swath of steely silver wall on the front, ending with its apple eyes staring right at the double-length door.

Kat made it up to the building before she stepped aside, leaned against that hard wall and took a deep breath. Cast away the lingering remnants of her exhaustion. No matter what happened in there, she was in a different place now than when she'd first met Gordon. Kat wasn't a new tracker, for one. She'd climbed the boards, had plenty of reps, and didn't need his help.

Maybe she should have worn the suit. That alone would work, would show him she wasn't a pushover.

"You're here now. Do it," Kat muttered the words.

Something her dad had taught her—say what she meant to do, and she'd manage it. Nobody caught Kat talking over the sounds of a city in motion—not that Kat checked—and she pulled open *The Spit Roast*'s heavy glass door and went inside.

A large, lit-up barbecue sauce bottle greeted her, its eternally dripping orange sliding down and out to fall and illuminate a steep stair. The red haze coming from that direction, coupled with the strong wave of smoked everything gave the impression that Kat was about to walk into Satan's own cook pit. Apparently laws against animal meat hadn't put a damper on this place, and Kat saw why as she descended.

The Spit Roast had decided to extend the art of barbecue and smokehouse tradition to the lab, and small windows, bracketed by the falling sauce lights, gave clues as Kat took the steps. Through the portals, vats of growing proteins formed in vast clusters, shaping formless globs that would make enough muscle, fat, and their tender combination for a steak, chop, and, with some help from molded plastics, rib infinity.

The changes had become mainstream by the time Kat was old enough to know what she ate, but her parents had talked plenty of the older, barbaric days. They'd sounded almost wistful about it, though Kat couldn't imagine either of them wanting a return to all that slaughter. Like most things with her parents, though, that desire went unrealized, unexplained.

Cavernous, dark, and honey-glazed. Kat hit a wall of people waiting for tables, looking for those who'd found tables, or deciding, via a muscle-bound approach to the bar, to make do standing. Without her suit, and with shoes more suitable for walking than a cocktail party, Kat decided not to wait behind coat-bound shoulders and resorted to a time-honed tactic to get herself through: free-flying elbows coupled with light feet brought Kat further through the crush, confused grunts in her wake.

There he was. Gordon Holyoak. Pint already in one hand and mouth wide open, holding forth to what looked like three other trackers at a big brick table. Gordon's black hair, like him, spiked out in all directions, coupling with the marker stubble and ringed eyes of a sleepless haunt. As if to emphasize his place outside reality, Gordon wore a heavy tactical jacket inside this sweltering place, the pockets coating its sleek gray surface acting like cups to gather the sweat dropping from Gordon's face.

"A cleanse," he told Kat ten minutes later, when she finally sat down at the table with a double whiskey in hand. "Sure, it's miserable while I'm sitting here draining all of myself out of my pores, but tomorrow I'll be ready for anything."

The other three trackers appraised Kat as the friendly rival she was. Kat had seen them before: Chicago regulars. Trackers didn't mark out territory, exactly, but they had a pecking order for hunts and Kat stood atop the local one. If she slapped her name on a request, these three knew enough to stay away from it. If they didn't, any transgressions were handled between the two trackers, however they chose.

Kat preferred up front, clear, and with no compromises.

"You know Kat?" Gordon said over the silence. "You ought to. She's got a hold on this town of yours."

"We know her." Desi, a transplant from the west coast who wanted to reach for the stars before she deserved them, said. Desi leaned on her elbows, her arms clothed not in fabric but a nest of beads, weaves, and charms. "She made sure of that."

Kat dished a sweet smile Desi's way, then turned to Gordon. "Spill it. I'm tired and I'm hungry."

"Sounds like your problem," Desi said.

"Was I talking to you?"

"Hey," Gordon, leaning back in his chair, walked his chill eyes between Kat and Desi, as if the supreme coolness of his being was enough to halt any argument. "We're all on the same side."

"We're not," Kat said. "I know you like to say that, but we're out here working for our lives. If Desi takes an anomaly, those are reps I don't get. She's my competition."

Desi, for once, agreed, and the other two trackers nodded along with her. "Unless you're offering this up as a team job?"

"All right." Gordon took a long quench from his amber brew. The drink did nothing to erase the thick sweat sheen coating his face. "I'll be up front: this isn't a team issue. The target's only a single anomaly, and we don't think he's dangerous enough for a coordinated effort."

"You mean you're too cheap to pay for one." Kat tasted her own liquid fire, enjoyed the caramel burn.

She caught it. The trademark Gordon crack. The man was flash, flimflam and pizazz, but beneath it all roiled a gooey soft interior looking for approval. Looking to be told it was doing good. Exposing the flaws in the constructs Gordon made of his life was delicious fun. Kat would hate herself for it later—she always did— but right now, Gordon's twitch to a frown and a cut sigh had her cover up her own satisfaction with another drink.

"We have to keep things fair." Gordon swapped strategies, appealed now to a higher purpose, reaching for that charisma. "Think. If Mynx handed out reps to every tracker for everything, nobody would do anything else. Being a tracker is supposed to be hard. You have to be good, you have to *earn* it." Gordon paused, took a long breath and let the sentiment lie. "When we heard the anomaly might be heading here, I chose to come personally because I knew, I knew Chicago had the trackers to handle this one. Otherwise we could have waited, let the anomaly glide on to another town. Instead, with one of you, I want to stop it here."

Gordon spoke like this anomaly was walking devastation, but if things were that apocalyptic, then the Paragons would have taken control themselves. The trackers only existed because the Paragons didn't have enough bodies or desire to hunt down all the minor anomalies that didn't want to obey their laws. So Kat threw on her skeptical face and waited. Gordon had the attention back on him now, and he wouldn't let it go yet.

"Now," Gordon started back in, "this anomaly hasn't killed anyone, at least that we know of. But there's been some incidents. A restaurant in Denver where the dishwasher noticed their fastest chef was cheating physics and churning out cooked meals in less time than it took me to tell this story. Two weeks later, our guy pops up again in Kansas, this time working miracles in a dry cleaner's. Things go in ruined, come back perfect in record time."

"Seems like this anomaly's a real monster," Desi cracked.

"It's not what he's done. And we should be thankful he's stuck to the small stuff. It's what he's capable of, Desi. We don't know the extent, and Mynx doesn't want us scaring him into doing something drastic."

"But you're going to antagonize him anyway."

"We can't let a power like that one go un-traced," Gordon replied, and here again his composure slipped, not into embarrassment, but fervor. Belief. "It's our job to make sure anomalies like him have support, have training, and, if things go wrong, can be found quick."

The slick smiles, the friendly words, drew people to Gordon's orbit, and once they came close enough to see it, his passion drew them the rest of the way in. The man believed in the Paragons, in the good he thought they were doing to the world. Kat's acid cynicism had been too much for that before. Today, now, she drenched it in a long gulp of water some blessed waiter had dropped off. With its low ceilings, crowded mash of tables and drinkers, *The Spit Roast* had no room for serving drones.

"So it's a seek-and-find," Kat said. "We track the anomaly, give you a call, and then snag him together?"

"Yes." Gordon raised his wrist, showing the black Tama around it. "I've already sent what we have. The contract starts now."

Like a starting gun, Gordon's words had the other three trackers jumping up from their seats and making breaks for the exit. Kat stayed, took a long, curious stare from Desi as the latter made her way through the restaurant towards those steep stairs. No doubt wondering why Kat wasn't sprinting off like the rest of them.

Gordon didn't share that question. He looked at Kat's almost-empty glass, finished his beer, and asked, "Another round?"

"I didn't come all the way out here for one drink."

Gordon laughed. Flagged the waiter down and ordered. Looked at his soaked self. "This is the stupidest thing."

"I know. Would've told you if you'd asked me."

"I'm a sucker for fads, Kat."

"Because you want to believe in everything." Kat finished her first round. "You don't get that things don't work out."

Gordon stared at the table, then at her. "No, I get that. I just choose to hope that they will." He paused. "You doin' all right?"

"Tired."

The new round came.

"Long night?"

Kat laughed, a happy-sad mingle. Looked straight down at her drink, which caused her hair to fall in front of her face, haloing the glass and its amber contents like it was a portal to some alternative, boozy dimension. One way for the evening to go: drink until decisions made themselves.

"You know I put it behind me, right?" Kat said, lifting her eyes to Gordon's. "I get it, now. You. This whole thing. I thought it was an act, but really, it's who you are. I can't hate that."

Gordon had the humility to look elsewhere for a moment, turned back with a shrug. "Never promised I'd become someone else. Didn't mean to hurt you, either."

"You did. I got better. Don't want to talk about it." Kat buried the conversation with a slanted head and a slanted smile. "So tell me, Gordon, just who are we hunting?"

Sharpen The Knife

Cold, austere and beautiful. City lights scattered against the ice floes bobbing on the water, turning each one into its own lit platform, as though inviting Zhan-Yo to take a run and jump from one to the next. Wind whisked around him, the thick wool cap, scarf, and jacket he'd picked up on his way out here doing their best to keep Zhan-Yo from freezing. Nobody else was on the path this late, despite the full moon midway up in the clear night making a silver counterpoint to Chicago's rainbow skyline.

So many people resided here and so few bothered to brave its elements, to know what it really meant to live in this part of the world. Then again, Zhan-Yo wouldn't be here either if he didn't have a reason.

"Doesn't this make you feel alive?" the reason called, appearing as if from nowhere. Zhan-Yo looked around for the pod car, for a trace of where Sylvie had come from, and saw nothing. "Oh, stop it."

"I have to check," Zhan-Yo said as Sylvie headed up the wide walk towards him. "Assumed success makes a person lax."

If Zhan-Yo fought the winter with deep-woods warmth, Sylvie employed all technology could give her. Black and sleek, her outfit looked like a wet seal, almost plastic, but beneath its skin, heaters pulsed. Her coat's collar rose up, fanning beneath her chin so that it appeared as if the clothes were a part of her, necessary to keep Sylvie's temperature ideal. A purple-black headband worked over-time to do the same for her hair, her ears. Her deep tan hid any rosi-ness on those cheeks.

The first time he'd seen the get up, Zhan-Yo had laughed. Decried the garment's inefficiency when so many other, more prac-tical clothes existed. When Sylvie, though, had taken out his old bodyguards, using the outfit's flexibility to dance around their fumbling swings, Zhan-Yo had stopped laughing. When Sylvie continued eliminating his enemies, continued to keep Ziran moving forward through back alleys, Zhan-Yo had stopped questioning her.

Now he listened.

"The meeting went well," Zhan-Yo said, the two falling into a slow walk along the lake shore. "More and more call in every time. We are turning their minds."

"But will they commit? When you actually ask, will they act?"

"I don't know." The admission, as with any hard look at a dream, came with a wince. "They risk little with these meetings. They risk everything by rising up."

"Which is why you cannot give them a choice."

"They depend on structure for survival, and our plan would tear it away." To their left, pod cars streamed by as some event at Soldier Field let out, thousands jumping in the waiting vehicles and heading home. "Ziran, though, needs that same structure. We need to change the world, not destroy it."

"Then drive the change," Sylvie said. "You saw the video?"

"He is vulnerable."

Even saying the words felt wrong. Like denying gravity. Aegis had been the leading Champion since the Paragons existed, and his immortality, at least from physical harm, had been a constant in the world for almost as long as Zhan-Yo had been a player in it.

"He's your change. Your opportunity."

"You want to kill him."

"It would help."

So many reasons why Zhan-Yo kept Sylvie hidden. Paid her salary, her budget, and kept her off Ziran's rolls. Brutally effective, and often just brutal, Sylvie approached situations with the cutting black guidance of ends justifying means. She always had, and she'd always been good at it, even if the messes left behind had Zhan-Yo questioning his conscience more than he wanted.

"Murder doesn't inspire," Zhan-Yo said. "We're not cleaning up a mess here."

Sylvie's hands had stayed stuffed in pockets this entire time, but Zhan-Yo caught the shift in the coat as Sylvie crunched them into fists. "Stop it. You're not this weak. All those people joining your meetings? They're sharks, Z. They'll smell the blood when we spill it, and they'll follow your lead into the frenzy."

Zhan-Yo didn't say he never wanted to be a bloody leader, that restoring normals to some say in world affairs wasn't meant to be a violent uprising. The idea had been the slow amassing of power in the back-channels. Fill all the cracks with normals, until the Paragons had to admit their society would crumble without the normals' contribution, without Ziran and the others. Then, a peaceful change. The incorporation of the offices like the ones his father, his mother held. A government representing all its people, not only the ones with power.

He'd been naive. Ziran had grown massive in Zhan-Yo's decades, and every step had tainted the mission more and more as Zhan-Yo found those paths to real power closed to him. Playing by the rules let his company grow while Zhan-Yo shrank, more and more a Paragon tool than a leader. The break came years ago, when the Paragons dictated Ziran's priorities to him. He'd found Sylvie not long after, in a desperate search for a lever to lift the Paragon's crushing weight.

With Sylvie's help, Ziran cemented its hold across markets in secret, erasing any who dared opposed Zhan-Yo's secret buy-outs, arms acquisitions, and more. With Wexley's savvy, minor Paragons were bribed and manipulated, and Zhan-Yo nursed his vision and used it to inspire employees, the other companies falling in line through pressure both philosophical and actual. None of it had been clean, all of it had been necessary to build the revolution.

Would he back down now, over one more body?

"If Aegis is taken out of the picture, we can fill the vacuum." Zhan-Yo said, nodding Sylvie's way. "With our leverage, we can ensure the Paragon that takes his place is sympathetic to us."

"More than sympathetic. We can own them. Ensure their compliance."

"Then we get our changes. First here, the east coast, all across Atlantis. Then Pacifica." Ziran and the other companies were global. The pressure they could push here, could be pushed anywhere. "It wouldn't take long."

"All it takes is a start, Z. We've been looking for an opening, and now we have it."

"It will take planning. Time."

Sylvie's hand shot out, grabbed Zhan-Yo's arm and turned him towards her. "Not too long. Aegis is old. If he retires, selects one of his Paragons, then we've lost our chance. We have to move while he's still out there, while he's still the face of their oppression."

They were nearly at Millennium Park's north end now, and to their left the gaudy spectacles adorning the mammoth space buzzed with later evening crowds making frosty stabs at ice skating. In addition to the big rink, the Paragons installed dynamic motion-glass statues, each one representing a founding Champion, moving, ever so slowly, in creeping orbits around the park. The theme had something to do with motion, continual improvement . . . Zhan-Yo didn't remember and it didn't matter. The statues were ugly, and at night their own lights washed out their features so it seemed as though faceless luminous giants stalked downtown.

"You wouldn't be saying this if you didn't have a plan already." Zhan-Yo nodded past Sylvie, towards the moving statues. "Absolute eyesores."

"I think they're neat," Sylvie said. "How many pieces of art do you know that can actively hurt someone?"

"Stop. I'm too tired for your bloodthirsty routine tonight."

"Then be serious with me." Sylvie pointed at Aegis's moving statue. "We have to bring him down, and soon, or we'll lose momentum. I do have a plan." Sylvie paused, and the way her eyebrows darted up for a second, along with the corners of her mouth, told Zhan-Yo to stay silent. "If I'm being honest, and I am, for once, I've already started it."

"That's not the way this is supposed to work."

"You gave me latitude. Told me to get the job done. This is me doing that." They started walking again. "I have a team coming into town."

"You want to do it here?"

"Right in Ziran's headquarters. Nobody will doubt us then."

The bitter chill seemed to bite deeper and Zhan-Yo pulled his jacket tight. Sylvie didn't seem to notice at all as she kept going, talking through one detail after the next and weaving such a beautiful net that Zhan-Yo found himself believing, in spite of himself, that Sylvie might be right. The time to strike *was* now. Aegis would fall, and the Paragons would be vulnerable.

"I'll start the revolution," Sylvie finished. "You and Wexley can end it."

12

A Not-So-Friendly Visit

Even amid Manhattan's spires, Mynx had no trouble finding Bastion. The steel forest grew every time she visited, but finding Aegis's physical fortress never took more than a second's stare across the skyline: it wasn't the tallest building, not anymore, but Bastion glowed a deep crimson along its edges. Towards the top, those red lights coalesced into a solid luminous core, as if Bastion was a super weapon charging up for some skyward blast. Knowing Aegis, it could even *be* a weapon now.

Mynx's jet adjusted the approach, sliding its engines up and getting ready to angle them for a straight landing. Mynx monitored air traffic from the splash screen on her cockpit glass, an overlay on the view highlighting any concerns in hues ranging from a safe leaf green to a warning yellow. No reds to worry about this late, with the clock getting close to midnight. Her own drones drifted over the city and kept watch on a grateful populace.

She grimaced at the time: later than Mynx wanted to get here, but Reeves had pestered her with updated statistics on her changes to the gladiator drone, and she'd fallen down a deep algorithmic well until Reeves, again, insisted that she leave.

Celice had asked Mynx here to keep Aegis from doing something stupid, and here she was, far later than she'd promised. She'd have to make it up to Celice somehow, maybe set stealth drones on Aegis's trail to keep him safe.

"There she is," Aegis's voice burst into the cockpit over the Paragon channel Mynx left open for emergencies. "Celice said you'd be hopping out this way. I'd begun to think she was joking. Trying to keep me in for a night."

"I'm coming." Mynx covered up the relief at Aegis's voice with the logic-honed edge she'd employed all her adult life. "It takes a while to fly from coast to coast."

"Nice try. Reeves already told us why you'd be late," Aegis said. "You ought to teach your AI to lie."

"Hard to think of anything more dangerous than that." Manhattan's towers were beneath her now, and soon enough Bastion's red arrow showed on the small screen under the windshield, one Mynx had set to show the plane's bottom camera. "You mind letting me land?"

"I guess it's the least an old friend can do."

AEGIS'S WOUND looked worse than Mynx had imagined. She traced a circle around the black and blue bruised edges, shaking her head while Aegis sighed. Celice, standing behind Mynx in Bastion's top-level command center and observation deck, pointed out, for the third time already, that Aegis could have died.

"She's not wrong." Mynx offered Celice token support, though, really, any Paragon could die at any time. It was part of the job. "You said it's been a day since this happened?"

"About that," Aegis said.

"You're getting slower." Mynx stood, put a finger to her lips, still staring at Aegis's wound.

"Slower?" Celice asked. "What does that mean?"

Does that mean Aegis hadn't told her? Mynx sent Aegis the question in a look, and Aegis's sudden stare towards the ground while he put his shirt on gave all the answer Mynx needed.

"Your father hasn't been invincible for decades now," Mynx

said, moving out from between father and daughter to lean on the railings pressed against the glass. "But he repairs—heal isn't the right word, more like the damage disappears—so quickly that it's more or less the same."

"Still is," Aegis grumbled. "I'm fine."

"You're not fine!" Celice said. "You've been favoring that arm all day! You were bleeding when you came back last night!"

Aegis looked like he wanted to be annoyed at Celice but couldn't bring himself to yell at his own daughter. The man always was a softy when it came to his own family. Mynx would never say it, but if pressed she'd admit that lax attitude was the very reason Mynx stood here instead of Celice's mother. But since Tessa wasn't here, Mynx had to play peacemaker.

"Aegis," Mynx said, raising her arm, and her Tama, up. "Let's see if you're really fine. Trig shield."

From the ceiling, what had looked like metal support beams folded in on each other and dropped to the floor, arranging and standing up into a lithe, murderous drone. Pinwheeling arms and legs, all ending in vicious edges, stood two meters high and ready to slice apart any intruder attacking Aegis or Celice.

"Dummy protocol," Mynx continued, and the shield drone froze in place. "All right Aegis, take a swing at it. Show us."

Aegis threw Mynx a look that said she'd hear plenty about this later, but Mynx wasn't Aegis's daughter and didn't care. Keeping the Champion's pride in check, so he wouldn't die doing something stupid, mattered more.

Celice moved and let Aegis walk up to the drone. The tall Paragon, aside from the silver stubble and gray in his hair, the wrinkles glazing his face, had all the muscle of his youth. Formidable, even if such fist work was outdated. No matter how many benches Aegis pressed, Mynx's drones would be stronger. Aegis tried to push back on that here, but when he raised his left arm to go for a swing, he winced, dropped it. Cursed.

"Exactly!" Celice cried. "That's what I'm saying! You can't do this anymore!"

"She's right, Aegis. You're too important to go fighting thugs at night."

Aegis looked at the two of them, and for the first time since they were young, since they were exploring the limits of their abilities on the New York streets in the early morning hours, Mynx saw the frantic worry of someone who no longer knew where he fit into his own world.

13

Rebel With A Cause

Aegis left Mynx to take a nap in Bastion as the sun blitzed the city with its winter light and took a Paragon pod car to a Paragon jet that, with the high-powered whine of concentrated battery power, shot Aegis up to Boston in thirty minutes. As such, the Champion, sporting a demure gray Paragon fleece and jeans, sipped hard black coffee and looked at brave winter runners jogging through Boston Common before nine.

Pods paraded by in the street between Aegis and the park, which, coated in snow, appeared an oasis from the activity going on around him. The coffee shop, resolutely refusing to be automated, had morning arrivals delivering demands for drinks in harried and hopeful tones. A new day starting with stress, with a shot at success. Aegis didn't see a single Paragon blue among those waiting in line.

Which meant everyone here had a hard upper limit to how far they could go before they hit the Paragon's rep cap. A necessity to curtail greed, civilization's wanton destroyer.

A person took a bench across the street, the cue for Aegis to finish his coffee, slip the ceramic mug into a plastic bin some drone would take back and rinse—the coffee shop wasn't so rebellious as to keep its most menial tasks in human hands—and head out into the chill. If the caffeine he'd consumed took one half of keeping Aegis awake after the long night, the brisk wind accomplished the other. By the time Aegis took his spot alongside the person, he couldn't keep a grin from his face—this was life.

"A smile? Not what I would have expected." The woman's own amusement leaked into her voice, along with her southern roots. "This isn't going to be a happy conversation."

"It never is," Aegis replied. The unbroken and hyper-efficient pods streamed back and forth, their only variance coming in which ads displayed along their roofs and the paints: shades and translucent shapes like diamonds and circles so everyone knew what districts a given pod car would cover. They sped along with their tires crunching and nothing more. "But it's your fault we need to talk at all."

"For both of us, I'll ignore that," Rosamund said.

Aegis wasn't sure what to call her—the Elementals had a hierarchy in the same way a tree ordered its leaves: some were better than others, and they were all related, but it was difficult to trace a path from one to another. Rosamund, though, seemed to be the one Aegis met with whenever the Elementals caused enough trouble to warrant Paragon attention. And according to Pixie, who waited, and possibly watched, from somewhere nearby, the Elementals had crossed that line.

"You're helping anomalies hide," Aegis said. "We've let you get away with that for a long time, but we can't let your campaign carry over to the criminals."

Pixie sent along details after the call yesterday. There'd been attempts to free dangerous anomalies the Atlantis Paragons kept in a remote northern prison nicknamed "The Icebox". Ranging from slipped-in devices to prisoners intercepted during transfers to open protests, the action gradient involved was too large to be isolated efforts. The Elementals were the only substantial anomaly group that would dare try something like this, and Aegis hadn't been shocked when he received the Elemental's quick reply confirming this morning's meeting.

They wanted something, and now they had his attention.

"Not all are criminals," Rosamund said. "Just because they don't want to join your empire doesn't mean they deserve to be imprisoned."

"I don't need them to join the Paragons. Not really. But they need to be tracked. These people could be dangerous. You know that."

"They're innocent."

"And you're naive. Either you—"

"Look." Rosamund pointed up, at a car-sized drone doing a slow flyover. "Every moment we're being watched. This isn't freedom. Even if you mean well, if we don't remind you that what you're doing is wrong, you'll put every anomaly in your box."

Aegis rubbed his hands, shook his head. "Ah, right. All the anomalies get to run around. No checks. Then, when one gets angry and blows up a city block, or another one has a bad day and poison's the water supply just by looking at it, what do you think is going to happen? The normals won't take it. They want protection, and if we don't give it to them, they'll kill all of us."

"You have such little faith in your own people."

"I know them."

"Do you?" Rosamund turned to him, and Aegis saw the wrinkles in her face as she saw the grays in his hair. "What's going to happen when you go? Will all the Paragons see the world the way you do, as a spectrum of power and who has the most?"

"There will be a transition. The Paragons will continue."

"I'm sure." Rosamund glanced at her Tama, back to Aegis. "I came here with an offer for you. We'll cease our activities here, and keep quiet everywhere else, if you invite us to your summit."

The Elementals knew about that? The message had only gone out to the Champions and a few higher Paragons yesterday after his touch base. Then again, how surprising was it to learn the rogue anomaly organization had ears inside the Paragon's command? For all Aegis knew, they could have someone with the ability to read Aegis's mind and transcribe his musings.

That was the problem with anomalies: literally anything was a possibility.

"I won't have you disrupting it," Aegis said.

"You claim that the Paragons represent all anomalies. If that's really true, then you'll let us, who speak for the so many invisible you refuse to recognize, attend. You'll let us have a voice for the future."

"Or what, Rose? We could crush you in a moment if I gave the order."

In response, Rosamund stood up. Held her sleeves together as she clasped her hands in front of her. "There are always consequences, Aegis."

"I don't like threats, Rose." Aegis raised his voice, calling after her as Rosamund walked away, crossed a street and stepped into a waiting pod.

Aegis sat back against the bench. Invite the Elementals to the summit? So many Paragons that would attend had spent their careers fighting the organization, turning back their attempts to undermine what the Elementals believed was an unfair, authoritarian government. What the Elementals refused to realize was how necessary the Paragons were, how dangerous the world had been and would become again if normals and anomalies could live with absolute freedom. It would be chaos. Everyone would live in constant fear.

Joggers rushed by and Aegis wanted to wave his arm towards them, continue making the argument. But Rosamund was long gone, and she'd made clear the terms. What she hadn't demonstrated was the cost for ignoring them.

Which is why exhaustion crept back when Aegis's Tama buzzed. Pixie's face appeared on the black band's small screen. No children this time, only a strict Paragon uniform, one meant for a mission, not for the office.

"I'm guessing the conversation didn't go well?" Pixie said.

"What's wrong?"

"We were doing a cell transfer, and someone hit Thane with adrenaline a minute ago. He's breaking out, Aegis. We're scrambling, but we could use some help."

Celice would beg him not to go. Mynx would say it wasn't necessary—she could summon a drone army to streak on over. Both would take time. Both would cost him leadership and reputation ahead of the summit. Both were unacceptable.

"On my way."

There were always consequences.

14

Don't Want Any Part Of It

Seeker's lick woke her up. The light sliding in through her east-facing windows said mid-morning, and by the third blink Kat realized she was alone. She stretched out, branching legs and arms through canyons in the sheets, feeling muscles no longer sore luxuriate in the exercise. Seeker watched it all, sitting near the bed and staring with his tongue hanging out the side of his mouth.

"What? I'm allowed to enjoy my morning."

Kat looked from the dog to the window; a clear winter's day. Then at her still ceiling fan. An old model with blades. It held no answers. So with a sudden energy brought about by a restless bladder and the knowledge that Seeker, if left to founder much longer, would take to dive-bombing the bed, Kat lurched from her cushy prison and took care of things, not bothering to read the short note Gordon had left using the only available writing option: Her computer. There it was, in static type there on the screen, blown up so she couldn't possibly miss it. That was the problem with proximity passwords—just because her Tama was in the room and Kat hadn't locked it down, Gordon had been able to get right into her most valued possession. Which Kat wouldn't have cared about, but then she read the note.

"Asshole," Kat swore, then glanced at Seeker, whose head had tilted and whose eyes were wide. "Not you. Gordon."

The tracker had left a couple lines. One saying sorry that he had to leave so early, and the other telling why: another tracker sent a tip on the anomaly, and wanted to chase it down. That Gordon hadn't woken Kat meant he didn't want her showing up, making things awkward when the other tracker tried to claim the anomaly for his or herself. Or maybe Gordon just didn't want to talk in the morning.

Fine. Whatever.

Kat deleted the note, flipped up her reports and read the rep counter. A few more had flowed in overnight. Paragons getting things done at all hours. Then over to the tracker board, to see if any other tips had been posted for the area. Two. Both for small anomalies, minor powers that'd been spotted by a drone. Kat could go after them, hope they turned into quality earners. Neither would pose as much trouble as Vedder had.

But.

"You know it's stupid, right?" Kat said to Seeker. "I should just take the safe options."

Seeker huffed.

"What, that's not being a coward."

A slight growl, then Seeker came up next to Kat, put his nose on her lap and looked up at her. His cream coat glistened in the sunlight, that tail swishing back and forth, demanding activity soon or restless destruction would follow.

"Fine. Fine. We'll go for a wander. See if we can't spot something."

Trolling for anomalies wasn't a great use of time—compared to the infinite eyes of Mynx's drone network, Kat digging herself didn't even register, but the machines looked for a certain anomaly type: one using their powers in the open, or causing problems. With Seeker sniffing everything, Kat could walk slow, keep an eye out, and see if she got lucky with a garden-variety, non-threatening anomaly.

This time, Kat went west. Took a short trip on the train, with

Seeker sprawling on the car's floor for the uncrowded, midday ride. Parks were more plentiful over here, less crowded. Few drones bothered to patrol these skies too, which meant more opportunities.

One percent. That was the estimate for the anomaly population. One percent and they had changed everything when they first appeared, and now ran the very world that made them. Kat couldn't recall the specifics of how the anomalies came to be—far too much chemistry and people hoping for one thing and getting another—but the overriding belief was that if you drank the water when you were young, you had a shot at being something much greater than your parent's genes alone would get you.

Sometimes, the parents won that lottery. Sometimes, the kids got nothing.

Seeker saw the park from the moment they left the train. Unlike the one they'd gone to the day before, this one had trees, and even a small frozen river. All things that demanded Seeker's immediate and undivided attention. He pulled at the leash till they made it down the steps from the station, and then Kat let him go. Even though Seeker had to cross a street to get there, the pods saw him coming and paused their routes for the exact seconds it took the husky to sprint by.

"Brave woman, letting your dog go like that," said a man selling hot coffee and chocolate at the station. "Wouldn't trust those things not to hit it."

"When was the last time you heard of a pod car hitting someone?" Kat asked, eying the coffee and debating whether the cup of it she'd had back in the apartment was enough.

"Know why you don't?" the man replied. "Because they pay the people they do hit. Give'em reps to keep'em quiet, keep the system going."

So the man was crazy, but the coffee smelled good, so Kat tapped her Tama and took a mug. Sixteen ounces of metal-forged, indestructible drinking glory complete with a tracker so that if Kat removed it from circulation, some drone could find it, clean it, and restore the mug to its designed purpose. It might be heavy, but it sure beat having the constant plastic and paper litter everywhere.

With Seeker invested in some snow-buried bushes, Kat kept going past the park to the next block, where older houses betrayed their owner's neglect through long ice spears hanging from every edge. In front of the third one down, a light blue two-story that looked newer than the others, a boy piled fluff in an attempt to make a snowman. At first Kat wondered why the kid wasn't in school, then counted all the possible reasons she wouldn't be privy to and stopped.

"You live here?" Kat asked the boy, who only noticed she was there when she spoke.

He studied her with the practiced evaluation of someone who'd had encounters with less-than kind strangers, a coldness that made Kat frown, before the boy concluded Kat, in her jacket, gloves, and CytoGenX cap, didn't register as a threat. He dropped the snow, turned to her, then pointed at the house.

"You mean my house?"

"I do," Kat said, then squatted to even out their heights. "When did you move in?"

"We built it!"

Kat hung for a second. Built it. Supposed they would have had to. The porch was different, now that she looked at it. Longer, with straight, functional rails instead of the looping, carved ones that'd been there before. And the second story was larger too, maybe an extra bathroom. Upgrades all around.

"Hey, you want something?" a man opened the front door, in a sweater and jeans that said this was his day off and he wasn't thrilled about the interruption.

"Sorry, no," Kat said, standing up. "Just used to live around here."

The man didn't say anything. Stood and watched her while the boy went back to his snowman until Kat, feeling more and more awkward, left. Went back to the park to collect Seeker, now bounding around with another dog he'd befriended. She scooped up some snow, threw it and watched as the two dogs chased after and were then mystified by the snowball's disappearance into a sea of itself.

As if she'd come here searching for anomalies. Kat liked to deceive herself. Get herself going into situations that weren't going to end well, like pursuing Vedder once it'd become clear he'd left the city for the more-work-than-it's-worth haunts of rural, snowy Wisconsin with sly promises that, she knew, were fake. When the lies played themselves out, as this one did while she threw another snowball for Seeker, Kat had to confront the real reasons, and those were never as fun as the ones she made up.

Hard to believe that it'd been rebuilt already. Last time Kat had taken a ride over here, the house had been nothing more than a shell. Burnt-out, ash still scattered along the yard. A condemned sign warning passers-by to stay away while telling them nothing about what had happened inside the walls. It would have been a strange thing to see for anyone unfamiliar—as if a fire had been lit and carefully controlled to burn only certain parts. Pocket explosions, maybe, like fireworks set off in designated spots to blow out all the windows but keep the structure intact. Nobody would ever guess—

Seeker woofed at her feet. His friend had vanished. Kat sighed, reached down to scratch his ears.

"You feeling hungry?" Kat said, shuddering as a cold breeze brought with it the smell of the hot dog maker. "I know I am."

There were restaurants here, sandwich shops, or even that cart vendor, but Kat could feel her memories stirring. If she stayed here much longer, she'd fall into a funk that'd knock her out the rest of the day. Time to head home, see if Gordon's tip on that anomaly had paid off. See if he'd be going away again.

See if she'd even care.

15

The Right Hand Man

The mid-day market, even in the cold, flexed with the workers on their lunch breaks. Zhan-Yo sensed Wexley's discomfort as they walked through the lines for every sandwich, kabob, or taco they could imagine. Ziran's corporate cafeteria served food with professional efficiency and at a subsidized rep cost that made it affordable to the technicians, salespeople, and support staff dominating its Michigan Avenue tower. What it lacked, and what this market, squeezed into an intentionally vacant space between high rises, had, was character.

"We're wasting time," Wexley said. "Don't we have meetings this afternoon?"

"I'm sure we do," Zhan-Yo replied, then, catching sight of a stand selling what he was looking for, made a sharp cut into the end of a line. Wexley joined him, looking between his Tama and the people around them as if the crowd was, somehow, responsible for him being there. "Yet, as we are the number one and two of this company, I'm sure they will wait."

Wexley muttered something non-committal. Zhan-Yo, his sunglasses killing the reflected light, took a quick look up towards the sky and the drone hovering there, then back along the line in front. An economic medley brought together by their Tamas, many connected to the networks his company built, maintained, and perfected. All so they could take orders for their friends, so they could share pictures of the food they were about to get, so they could keep their lives in order.

And soon, soon, for them to participate in the order that defined their lives.

"You seem different, Z." Wexley said. "Today, I mean. Don't take this the wrong way, but you seem happier?"

"Today, I have clarity." Zhan-Yo kept his hands in the pocket of his fine, gray slacks. The thick blazer kept him warm enough, kept the wind from touching him, even as his breath misted and joined that of everyone else's. "We all look for purpose, and while you and I have known ours for some time, how to achieve it has been a mystery."

"Because of the call yesterday? I thought it was progress, but not the leap you're making."

Decisions needed to be made. Zhan-Yo trusted Wexley with Ziran's operations, of that there was no question, and Wexley had earned that trust. The man worked with a fanatical zeal, spending too much time making sure Ziran met each and every deadline, that its employees carried out each and every task in professional fashion. Zhan-Yo might be the company's spiritual leader, but Wexley kept Ziran running.

And yet.

Zhan-Yo already had one dangerous ally in Sylvie, who took a carefree approach to crossing moral and legal lines. With Wexley's tortured past, how would he react to the darker ideas? There would be chaos with the revolution, opportunities for the unscrupulous to take advantage. Zhan-Yo would trust in Wexley's honor, but he would watch his friend nonetheless.

"What would ya like?" the stall's clerk asked Zhan-Yo as they reached the front of the line.

. . .

A WARM PITA stuffed with all manner of meats, onions, cucumbers, and sauces in his hand, Zhan-Yo and Wexley found the stone edge of a raised garden to sit on. If the air felt cold, their seat was ice, but Zhan-Yo didn't want to leave the sun behind. Besides, another place had offered hot cider, and while the apple drink didn't exactly complement the Mediterranean meal, its sugared heat made up for the clashing flavor. Such things were meant to be had outdoors, shoes crunching snow too low for shovels and noses red in the wind.

"You've worked with us for a long time," Zhan-Yo said as they finished their sandwiches.

"My whole career," Wexley said.

"And you still believe in our mission?"

"The one on the sign in the lobby, or the one we talk about in the basement of a shopping mall?"

Zhan-Yo nodded. "The former has brought us all the wealth we could want. The latter will give us the freedom to use it."

"What aren't you telling me? I've known you a long time, Z, and you don't talk in riddles like this."

True. A blunt approach tended to accomplish more than building a maze out of words. Still, before he went further, Zhan-Yo needed to confirm Wexley's loyalty, that no matter what, Wexley would side with Ziran, with Zhan-Yo and Sylvie.

"We are reaching an inflection point," Zhan-Yo started. "The Paragon Champions are getting older. Vulnerable. Our opportunity will come soon, before new anomalies can take their place."

"You think the Champions will be more open to our ideas now?"

"No. I think we need to force them to listen." Zhan-Yo paused, watched Wexley's narrow face. He kept it still, looked right back at Zhan-Yo. No terror in those green eyes. "They will not respect us unless they see us as a threat."

There it was. If Wexley wanted to, the man could wave down the drone above and report Zhan-Yo's statement. He'd be taken away to a Paragon cell, where they'd pull some anomaly with mind-bending abilities to break Zhan-Yo's brain and make him spill every secret he'd ever had.

"You have a plan, or you wouldn't be telling me this." Wexley looked at his gloved hands. "You know what the anomalies cost me. I want justice, and I can't get it because I'm normal. I'd do anything for that chance."

"Even if it meant violence? Even if it meant total disruption to all of this?" Zhan-Yo nodded at the market.

"I would fight them tomorrow if I thought we could win," Wexley said. "If I thought all the normals would rise up with me and our numbers could destroy the Paragons, I would do it. But you and I both know that would only get us killed."

"Not that way. Not with the Paragons united. Not with the Champions still standing."

"You want to murder them? How?"

"I don't need them to die," Zhan-Yo said. "They just need to open their eyes."

"Stop. Nobody has time for your cryptic sayings." Wexley pulled his wrist out from his coat sleeve, looked at the Tama. "You've kept me outside. It's cold, we're late for the meeting, and you've got me interested, so tell me. Straight."

So Zhan-Yo did. Kept Sylvie's name out, kept it high level and broad. He didn't say Aegis but Wexley did, picking up the likeliest target that would be here in Atlantis, in Chicago. Going after the Paragon's greatest Champion didn't make Wexley blink, didn't cause him to call down the drone or declare Zhan-Yo insane. Instead, hunger burned in Wexley's eyes.

IN ZIRAN'S LOBBY, centered behind four double-sliding doors providing a barrier between the cold air outside and the cold office atmosphere, just after metal detectors and security drones, sat a bronze fountain scrubbed to a gleaming gold orange. A statue stood in the fountain's square base—a small pool's size—and, with short jets spraying around it, served as the idol to Ziran's mission.

The statue began on the left with a young boy, no more than three and still finding his footing, looking up to and holding the hand of an older sister. She, too, turned to her left, repeating the same combination of stare and hold with a man who must be her father. He, too, connected with the grandmother, the last holding herself strong with a cane in her left hand. Only she looked back to the right. Beneath their feet, with land a brighter copper than the oceans, sat a world map. Along a plaque at the front base, facing the street, inscribed the following: *Connecting all the World.*

Zhan-Yo, as he did every time he came into the office, flipped a coin into the fountain's water. A penny, still bearing Lincoln's face. Plenty of those to be had, and had for cheap. At first cash had been hoarded, people traded reps for it in expectation that the Paragons would realize the insanity of their endeavor and turn back. When years had stretched to decades, though, and having invulnerable protectors became the preferred state, markers of a not-so-golden past became cheap.

Wexley had gone ahead, volunteered for the sacrificial embarrassment of opening the meeting first and apologizing for their delay. Zhan-Yo wanted his fountain moment. His father had put the thing here, after all, and without a grave to visit, this seemed the most appropriate place to pay his respects.

And commit to the future.

16

Lab Work

Mynx let the autopilot fly her back to California. The three hours of supersonic flight she spent napping went a long way towards her showing up at Denise's lab in some semblance of humanity. Aegis's tea, her sole remedy for a night spent talking strategy and telling stories, had the lackluster strength you'd expect from a Champion whose body strove to keep itself in perfect condition and needed no help in the matter—she'd almost fallen asleep drinking it.

"Tell me something good," Mynx said to Reeves as soon as she stepped from the jet and back into the Factory's comforting confines. "How's our gladiator doing?"

"Your changes are having, I believe, the desired effect. Eighty percent of the tests result in neutralized threats and a saved child. Far fewer grisly outcomes."

In the Factory, where rooms and corridors were too large to handle embedded speakers everywhere, Reeves often had to resort to a small bobbing drone, whose quad fans kept the little box aloft and hovering nearby. Beyond the jet's landing bay sat two options; to the left and she'd be back to the Factory's main floor, able to jump into that other twenty percent. To the right, ground transit and responsibilities.

"Keep refining it. I want that twenty cut in half before we release the updated model."

Logically, the choice wasn't difficult. Physically, it was excruciating. Mynx wanted to collapse and sink into oblivion. Instead, Mynx went right, towards the doors leading to the pod approach.

"Leaving so soon?" Reeves asked.

"Aegis was exhausting, but he proved a point, though I don't think he meant to." Mynx tapped her Tama, summoned a pod. She could've asked Reeves to do it and the AI would have been faster, but she liked to prove she could still accomplish tasks on her own. "We're breaking down, Reeves. I hoped Denise would have the solution."

"I didn't think she did."

"Not yet. I think it's time to help her along and see if she can find one."

DR. DENISE JONES commanded an impressive silver-looking lab that grew off of a much larger medical campus near UCLA on the city's west side. With a sharp slant to its roof, the lab building looked like it'd been sliced at an angle, a great metal doorstop connected to its bigger brethren with a highway-spanning skywalk. Mynx listened to various articles about the lab on the drive over, all coalescing around Denise receiving both the building and rep funding for her ideas, yet the supposed miracles had proven hard to realize. Now, with funding drying up, the vultures were circling to snag the building, the staff, the equipment.

The drive took the pod thirty minutes, a route that, at the time and under the old rules where everyone drove themselves, would have taken an hour to get from the canyon where Mynx had built the Factory. That the pods still displayed this advantage almost a decade after universal adoption seemed like rubbing it in, but they weren't wrong. For the loss of control, everyone had gained time. Guess which of the two people wanted more.

For all its splashiness, the lab didn't invite visitors. Beyond a five-spot parking lot for those few who might keep pods on site, the entrance had a small overhang looming above its single glass door. Written on that door, an old-style one with a handle to pull it open, was a sharp-edged text reading *Double Helix, Inc.* That'd come up in the articles too—desperate to save her lab and her work, Denise had split from academia and formed her own company, making enemies in the process. Still, nobody else in the field had come anywhere close to solving biology's inexorable march.

"A subtle name," Mynx said as she read the words on the glass, then looked at herself in the reflection. She wore a loose-fitting outfit she'd classified under 'relax' a long time ago, finding it saved time every day if she set her wardrobe into specific collections for specific moods. Mynx only had to say the word and Reeves would bring out the perfect selection. "Reeves, get me the records for a *Double Helix* incorporated."

Reeves didn't speak, but Mynx's Tama vibrated the requisite times to confirm the AI had received the command. Mynx didn't quite trust Denise, and the articles hadn't helped much, even if they'd all praised Denise's daring in the face of general skepticism. Mynx reached out to tug on the lab door's handle and found it locked. She noticed a small black button labeled *Call* on the door's right side and pressed it, giving Denise points for security.

"Hello?" said a man who sounded surprised he had to speak. "Uh, can I help you?"

"Is Dr. Jones around?" Mynx put on a safe smile. Older lady, tired-looking, hands clasped at her waist. As non-threatening as they come. "She'll want to talk to me."

"Who's asking?"

Ah, the name drop. Whatever pleasure had once come from delivering her title and watching the surprise, doubt, and final accepting stammers from various people had long since dissipated into exhausting seconds Mynx tried to avoid whenever possible. Here, though, she didn't see any other option than to say, with dripping, edged sweetness, her name.

First came silence. Then the uhs, the muttered question to someone standing nearby whether Mynx was really Mynx.

And then . . . "Got it. I'll buzz you in now and you can wait inside, Miss, uh, Mynx."

"Thank you."

The lock popped, and Mynx pulled the door open, took a step towards it and her Tama vibrated. She glanced at it, the screen across the band displaying a message from Reeves:

They've reinforced the walls of the building. It will block my signals.

Interesting. So Denise either didn't want her employees tossing off messages on their Tamas during the day, or the telecommunication waves from outside could disrupt her experiments. Mynx logged the information and kept going.

On the other side, a sparse lobby held some bare chairs picked up from some closeout sale set against a cream-color wall painted by, going by the slapdash striping, the same people working deeper inside. The lights, at least, looked professional grade and blanketed the area in sterile brightness.

Framed posters proclaiming *Double Helix*'s forthcoming products dotted the space. All promised miracles, and all ended with 'coming soon'. On the whole, the lab offered strange initial impressions, culminating in the feeling that Denise didn't care much for appearance.

Mynx could respect that. The results were the important thing.

"Not all of us have a Factory," Denise's warm tones came from a new opening, another keypad-locked double-door, this one solid and lacking the first's see-through candor. "Welcome to our humble lab, Mynx. I'm glad you could make it, even if it was so sudden."

"Circumstances can change suddenly." Mynx shook Denise's hand. Cold, moist. As if she'd just slathered her palms in sanitizer. "I'd like to continue our conversation."

Denise gave her a nod, then waved back through the heavy door in a manner that said the man at the desk didn't need to know anything about the conversation. Good—nothing reeked of amateurism more than evoking some open-minded principle where everyone at the lab needed to know everything. You never knew what a person would do with information, no matter how inconsequential. Best to keep its flow restricted, particularly from people.

Reeves, she could trust. Humans? Not so much.

The office, unlike the lobby, had earned some extra budget. Denise's desk held multiple fixed monitors, an inefficient use of space compared to the projected screens so popular these days, but the superior fidelity was likely a boost when examining molecular strands. Mynx killed a grin threatening to surface; normals and their need for equipment like this.

"May I?" Mynx asked as soon as Denise started describing the experiment whose data scrolled across the monitors.

"May you what?"

"Just watch." Mynx went by the scientist, eased into Denise's chair, then reached out towards the screens.

The gesture wasn't necessary, but it seemed to help with people seeing this for the first time. Then again, Mynx wouldn't know what Denise thought, what expression popped up on her face, because Mynx wasn't there anymore.

Beneath a starless black sky, Mynx stood center in a cabin ring. A far cry from the mansion she'd constructed in the drones with her structured, tuned code. The software trying to analyze Denise's samples showed itself as a networked collection of patched-together shacks. Holes in the roofs, sagging chimneys, doors hanging askew, all showed sloppy quality.

At Mynx's feet, moss-covered stones marked the fragmented functions tying the cabins together, and the set in front led to the part of the program currently churning along, the only cabin whose fire seemed lit, and whose smoke filtered up in a slow curl. She went towards it, careful to keep her feet on those stones—she had to follow the code, and one wrong step into the black void around the rocks could crash the program and send Mynx outside.

Or worse, trap her in a hard freeze that she'd have to escape.

Mynx, though, excelled at walking in a world of her own making. No wind blew, no tilt or slide of the stones conspired to throw her off; in here, Mynx moved with a spirit's silent confidence.

The cabin's door didn't budge when Mynx pressed her hand against it. Physical force didn't exist here, which meant the data Denise's program gathered had a seal blocking access. Mynx tapped the door with the tip of her index finger and the wood flashed ocean-blue before disintegrating into code. Letters, numbers, symbols all swarmed, and Mynx picked through the maze.

"There you are," Mynx mouthed the words, heard the sound in her mind, though no actual noise echoed in this place.

She'd found the link leading from the door back towards the program's center, a bright-blue burning strand tying the cabin's door, and likely all the others, to names beneath the stone where Mynx first appeared. The database. Mynx could go all the way back there, dig through its records and find a name and password that would unlock the cabin, but now that she could see the strand . . .

Mynx reached down, grabbed the glowing rope where it flowed away from the door with her left hand. Like a metal clip bridging a circuit, Mynx connected with the database and pulled out, as if thinking up a memory, a suitable name and password combination the cabin would accept. The data shot from Mynx's right hand, still touching the door, and inserted itself into the messy security code barring her way. With an emerald flash, the door melted to nothing and Mynx went inside, and searched.

"You're close," Mynx said as she snapped back to Denise's office. "Very close."

Denise had the presence to close her mouth, to set the pen down from the notepad where, Mynx suspected, would sit scribbled observations. Denise did not, however, have the grace to blush at being surprised.

"Like I said, I need more samples to confirm," Denise replied. "Right now, I can restore functions, I can repair the DNA, but it doesn't stick, and I don't have any anomalies to try testing with. That could be the key."

"Then take some of mine."

Protect those who could not protect themselves. An obvious ideal for the Champions. Giving Denise the entire anomaly genetic database could expose them. Giving her own cells, with Mynx's armada of drones and the vast Factory resources at her disposal, wouldn't be much of a risk. And the benefits?

Well, those would be worth anything.

"I, I would love to," Denise said, and she stood. "We have a collection area set up. Not that we take many samples, but for when we do . . . Still, that database of yours? We could fashion new cells and try all kinds of techniques."

"Earn it, then. Show me progress, and you'll get your database."

A needle stick, a vial drawn, and Mynx let Denise get to work with her new anomaly DNA. Walking back to the pod, Mynx waited until she was well away before taking up her Tama.

"Reeves, you haven't seen any abnormal behavior out of Denise?"

Nothing obvious. Typical routines for her background, occupation.

"Then pull the records on that lab. Double Helix."

You don't trust her?

What Mynx had seen in that cellular analysis confirmed two things: that Dr. Denise Jones had great possibilities, and that she could be very, very dangerous. What Denise did with Mynx's DNA would prove whether Denise was both, but past often predicted present, and if Denise had left any clues behind, Reeves would find them.

"You know me better than that."

17

Mixing It Up

The Paragon transport jet swooped low over the trees, its engines switching from high-speed thrust to a slower, stable hover.

"I'm dropping," Aegis said, and at the words the side panel door he stood behind slid open and let in chill afternoon air. "Reset to pick-up on my call."

The jet's drone system acknowledged the order with flashes from lights ringing the door, and then Aegis jumped out. A couple seconds in the air, a reach behind his back, and the chute popped out in a clear, synthetic catch that slowed Aegis's descent and let him coast to the ground in a clearing of snow-covered trees. By the time he landed the jet had vanished, leaving Aegis alone with the after-echoes of its roaring engines. The target sat ten meters away, on the ground with his back against a tree. A red pool marked the position in the snow, though Aegis didn't see it getting any larger.

"You still with us, Paragon?" Aegis asked the man, who sported the Paragon's armored uniform. Designed to block bullets and absorb most anomaly-powered energy, the suit sacrificed mobility for bulk, not that it mattered here.

"Been better." The Paragon's wispy rasp told a story of cracked lips, dehydration, and a collapsed lung.

"Medical's on the way," Aegis said. "Where'd he go?"

Only one target for that question, and the Paragon managed to tilt his head westward. Now that Aegis bothered to look that way, Thane's march marked its path with broken branches, bent trees, and so many pine needles that their deep green spikes hid the snow.

"Not too far," the Paragon said. "Tried to stop him, but that didn't work out so well."

"You tried. That's admirable."

Aegis didn't wait with the downed Paragon—nothing he could do for the anomaly, and stopping Thane made for a higher priority. The anomaly's reappearance burned like a cancer as Aegis picked up his run through the trees. Doubts, questions about his own fitness —that shoulder was still sore—and the odds that Aegis could still take on Thane . . . well, those weren't worth asking because he was here, now, and that's all that mattered.

"Dad?" Celice's voice buzzed in his ear on the channel Aegis kept open during missions. "What's going on?"

Aegis summed up the drop, the downed Paragon, with a short growl, "He's out, I'm on him."

"Alone?"

A low branch forced a duck, and Aegis kept his legs pumping, kicking up snow and pine needles. His arms moved too, always drifting on their downswing towards the pair of stun guns belted at his hips. Never knew when Thane might pop out from behind these massive trees.

"At the moment. No time." Aegis ran through puffs of his own breath.

"Then I'm scrambling some of Mynx's drones. They'll track your position." Celice sounded annoyed. "You shouldn't be doing this."

"I'm not letting Thane go. Celice, keep this tight. No press. No broadcast."

"Already done. Who is this guy?"

"Later."

The forest ended with sudden civilization; a black highway and, across, a power station for pods to recharge. What used to be ground-planted plates with a neighboring, squat building with food, snacks, and toilets for those on a long pod trip now looked like a stomped-on child's play set. Wrecked pods littered the area, smoke flew up from the burning, busted store, and someone in that mess still lived.

"Found a damaged power station. Send your drones here." Aegis muted the Tama with a tap from his right hand.

The trees around the power station stood pristine. Thane had come here, had destroyed, but he hadn't left. At least not through the forest. Which meant Aegis had to hear everything. Mostly, he heard screams. He dashed across the road, following the woman's noises as Aegis dodged around, ran over, or jumped across tires, shattered glass, and sparking wires. Burning rubber mingled with melting, cheap food to create a blend at stark odds with the pine around him. Then again, Aegis tended to find himself in broken places.

Ruin felt like home.

Thane didn't present himself, but the shouts drew Aegis to the collapsed station where, mangled with a double door, writhed a woman who looked like she'd found the building's broken glass. Her eyes were closed, and her screams were wordless, sobbing things that would have pulled at the Champion's heart if he hadn't heard the same thing so, so many times before.

"Hold on," Aegis said, crouching near her. "Can you move at all?"

The words of a Paragon, no, a Champion stopped the woman cold, and her eyes opened, sliding a tiny blood rivulet from some cut hidden by her forehead hair from her face to the ground. Her mouth worked, going between the next shout and saying his name. Aegis brushed glass from her shoulder—it looked like she'd fallen on her side when the roof collapsed, and the door frame had splintered down onto her legs. Aegis had strength, but he wasn't one that could lift a ton with a single finger.

"I'm stuck," the woman finally managed.

"See that." Aegis brought the Tama to his mouth. "Celice, send medical to my current location. One civilian down."

Celice affirmed the order with a click.

"Did a big, old man do this to you?" Aegis looked down at the woman.

"Are you going to get me out of here?"

"Can't." Aegis scanned the station in front of him, didn't see anything. Turned around, glanced at the wrecked pods and saw nothing there either. "Answer, please. Who did this?"

"I don't know! Maybe, what you said. I was inside. First the pods—"

"Quiet." Aegis held his palm towards her.

A new noise rose over the small snap crackles of the tiny fires and the occasional bit of metal still making its slow collapse to the ground. A scuffing sound; shoes too large for their feet brushing along the asphalt. Coming from the right side of the station.

Aegis drew a stun gun, gripped it with both hands and brought the weapon up. The woman didn't obey orders, started crying again, but Aegis didn't have time for that. The scuffs stopped, seemed like they were right around the station's corner. Aegis took one step, then another, rolling his heels to his toes. Winced at the glass snapping further under his boots. Nothing could be done about that, though.

How many times had he been in a situation just like this? Creeping closer, again and again, to some villain, thug, or anomaly gone wrong. It would end with a fight, a surrender, and possibly a death, not necessarily in that order. Aegis had lost Paragons on days like this one, beautiful and cold. One of these times it might be him. Honestly, it ought to have been him many times before now.

Aegis rounded the corner in a smooth motion, saw the old man, and pulled the trigger. Thane, proving the malleability of his age, pressed himself against the station's wall and the stunning dart flew by. Aegis swiveled, locked Thane in his sights, and hesitated. The monster's wrinkles dangled white whiskers, while Thane's skin-and-bones frame held a comically over-sized shirt that sank from his shoulders to his feet, all one-and-a-half meters of Thane's height. His hands, translucent, shriveled, raised their palms towards Aegis.

A surrender. A fight. A death.

"Thane." Aegis started. "Why?"

"One of the many curses intelligence burdens its bearers with is that of wanderlust, my friend," Thane spoke with a creaky whistle. "I could not stay in your cell."

"So your plan was to, what, get out, destroy some things, and make us catch you all over again? I thought you were smarter than that."

"Depends on the time." Thane nodded towards the Champion's left shoulder. "Is that where you're hurt? The invincible becoming vincible?"

A churning sound, the air roiling, mingled with the stillness around the destroyed station. Drones on approach. Reinforcements.

"You're done, Thane," Aegis said, ignoring the crack about the shoulder. Giving Thane any satisfaction at all was not in the Paragon playbook. "Lay down on the ground and I won't stun you."

A lie. Thane was far too dangerous to leave capable in any way. Aegis pressed the trigger, ready to fire.

"You know what always disappoints me?" Thane said. "You lack subtlety."

Aegis fired. The dart hit Thane square in the chest, but didn't pierce the skin. It bounced off, falling to the ground as Thane began to change. To grow.

"You're direct, but you never revel in it!" Thane said, his voice hardening, growing deeper and less distinct as he grew, as his bones expanded and his skin tightened. "You are a hammer, Aegis, but you fail to—"

Thane's words descended into a howl as the monster's mind vanished into the giant's anger. Where a frail old man had once stood, now a single lower leg occupied the same space. A four-meter tall, musclebound man loomed over Aegis, drool dripping down from his cocked grin, wild yellow eyes leering at his enemy. The mindless beast. A disaster loosed on the world decades ago, captured again and again by the Paragons. Aegis had tried to kill Thane outright plenty of times, but there didn't seem to be a way to do it. Not through direct physical means, anyway. The only option, the only chance they had, was sedation. Peace.

"Thane, stop!" Aegis ordered, backing away.

Thane responded to the suggestion in the same way he'd now respond to anything—his right fist, the size of a suitcase, swung its block-like self into Aegis and sent the Champion flying back, landing inside the wrecked shell of a pod. The impact should have knocked Aegis out. It only made him mad.

Aegis climbed free, made it to his feet as Thane, walking with the wide, swinging steps of someone getting used to a new pair of pants, approached. Thane roared, snarled, and bit at the air as he moved, like a rabid dog.

"I really, really hate you," Aegis said, putting up his fists like he was going to box with the creature.

Thane leaned into a big roundhouse, a move that telegraphed itself in the pull back and swing forward so clearly Aegis had time to line up his sidestep without the slightest worry. The Champion dodged left as Thane's fist screamed by, then quick-stepped past Thane's right leg and delivered a snap-kick to Thane's knee. The lug collapsed with a grunt, but managed a backhand swing that sent Aegis flying, bouncing along the asphalt.

"Are you winning?" the woman said, still on the ground and now right next to Aegis. "It doesn't look like you're winning."

"Appearances can be deceiving."

Aegis pulled himself up, brushed the dust from his shoulders and tried to suppress a sudden headache, the result of smashing into the station's side. Thane, with a slight limp, came towards him. Over the back of the monster's head, though, Aegis saw Mynx's heavy drones coming in fast. Before, it'd taken a Paragon squad to bring Thane down. Now, it would only take a few machines. Aegis wasn't sure how he'd feel about it later, but right now those two drones gave him plenty of relief. Getting ground to dust by an angry Thane was nobody's idea of a good time.

"C'mon, ugly," Aegis called out. "Keep it up and maybe I'll feel something."

Thane took the insult in stride, and with the woman screaming again behind him, Aegis dodged right to bring Thane's swinging fists away from the civilian. Biding for time, Aegis focused on evasion, slipping under and around those ridged, bony knuckles as Thane whacked the ground, the air, and tossed one pod after another aside trying to catch his smaller quarry.

Until the drones arrived. The first one, a saucer-like craft meant for suppression, launched a cable that caught Thane's fist mid-swing. The drone hovered, sending enough electric current down the cable to make any normal human collapse in a spasm of over-loaded nerves.

Thane wasn't a normal human. Thane did not collapse. Not even when Aegis took advantage of the distraction to make a running, jumping uppercut to Thane's enormous, pointed and whisker-covered jaw. Instead, howling, Thane pulled his right arm, threw the cable and the drone attached to it right at Aegis as the Paragon landed from his own attack.

Aegis saw it coming, saw that black-metal saucer fill his vision as he settled onto the asphalt, fresh from delivering what would have been a knockout blow to anyone but that, to Thane, caused no visible harm.

Aegis, Champion of Atlantis and leader of the Paragons, swore as Thane crashed the drone into him, and saw no more.

18

A Tracker's Regrets

The furry blanket covering her feet ate the noodle that escaped from her fork. Seeker waited for more, and, against her better judgment, Kat scooped out another couple pale yellow ramen strands. If she had a real table, no doubt Seeker would patrol its chairs hunting for scraps. As it was, the husky had to be content with the droppings from Kat's desk.

A lesson she could learn.

Gordon hadn't sent any messages, and the bounty for the anomaly remained open as the day ticked towards night. So either the tip hadn't resulted in anything, or it was a slow-moving stalk. Kat should have been able to ignore it, to focus on something else, something that didn't drag her personal life into business.

She tapped away from a pointless video on her screen to the tracker board, where her anomaly earnings showed themselves in a dizzying array of graphs and tables. Any filter or organization Kat could want lay there: by city, ability level, lifetime earnings, and so on. She had more than two dozen anomalies dumping rep shares into her accounts, but her default view sorted the earners in reverse. The least important up top, so she could learn which anomalies to avoid.

The tracker board had another filter on by default, one which she disabled depending on her mood, and right now the gloomy winter day, the sleepy dog, and the monitor's blue glow had her turning it off. Three gray names appeared at the top—no reps earned within the last year, within the last several for the top two. Dead anomalies didn't make much. But they cost her plenty.

She'd caught Sameer on the Mississippi, gambling on a party boat and using his minor mirror-images to copy face-up cards long enough to collect his winnings and disappear. He'd completed all two jobs before getting staffed to a Paragon task force and, soon after, going gray on her board. They never told her why, and the few thousand reps the Paragons had sent her in compensation were cold comfort.

They'd shared drinks on the boat after Kat had traced him. Sameer had been one of the good ones.

Unlike Crystal Raines, who'd put up a helluva fight in the back alleys of Chicago's New South Side. Her ridiculous penchant for turning, well, anything into temporary sinkholes made chasing her down into a dashing dance. If Kat hadn't hit her with a long range stun dart on a wild, diving shot, Crystal would probably be out there still. Or not, since she'd fallen back on her old thieving habits soon after getting traced. The drones had zero trouble finding her once they'd determined the source of a jewelry store's warped doors and display cases, and Crystal had decided to go out fighting. Kat couldn't decide if Crystal had done the job intentionally—the drones made a convenient, quick way to get killed.

Zach had been different. He'd found her, right after she'd traced someone else. Just walked up to her in the middle of a rest area where tired pod travelers could take a break alongside the highway. She'd been in her white suit and everything, standing over an unconscious anomaly who—she scrolled down to remember—could turn screws with his eyes. Literally screws, and just screws.

"Man, was he annoying," Kat said to Seeker, still asleep at her feet. "You remember him? Took our pod apart while we were in it."

Yet that guy earned a ton of reps. Zach, though. He'd said he was tired of being on the run, looking over his shoulder. So she'd traced him right then, taken him out to dinner. Turned out Zach's whole thing was smells; he could take any scent in the air around him and amplify it. Made the Italian place they were sitting in suffuse with marinara sauce and garlic. At first it'd been reps for that sort of thing, then Zach had caught more dangerous jobs, gas leaks and the like. Hadn't come back from one.

But that was the game. This miracle world held dangers aplenty, despite what the Paragons said. Sure, giant disasters were managed, criminals tended to vanish in supernatural fire, but good, old-fashioned accidents and fights still took their toll.

Kat clicked away from the tracker board, browsed through the local Chicago sites, looking for anything interesting and finding nothing. A pop-up in bottom right corner of her screen indicated some menace in the northeast, too far away for her to care about. Other than that, nada. As if the whole world was as bored as her, waiting for some news worth getting up for.

Slurping her last noodle left Kat with a void, one filled in short order by the same motions that'd been ruling the dead zones in her day for a decade; without thinking about it, she brushed her Tama, started a call to a number that should have been canceled by now. A recording, eventually, answered:

Hi! You've reached Melody Collins, drop your name and number and, if I like you, I'll get back to you as soon as I feel like it!

Kat tapped away the call. Shook her head. Blinked away tears that hadn't formed yet, that wouldn't form anymore. She'd ground away that reflex, but oh, did it feel good to hear that voice again. Her mother's cutting humor, something no doubt annoying to anyone actually trying to reach her. Something so precious now.

Her Tama beeped, cutting through the cloud with a promise of action, adventure, anything. What it was: a question, from a friend. A loose friend. Kat turned the idea over in her head—what even was a *friend* really? Seeker huffed at her as she stood. Oh, yeah.

Given the night's possible activities, from waiting to hear from Gordon to wandering to the corner bar and letting liquors dictate the hours, what her friend offered could be more rewarding, and would definitely be more fun.

"Trig send, I'll show." Kat climbed her way to her closet, brushing her hands along the clothes when she made it there. "Whaddya think, Seek? Red or black?"

Seeker's woof made the obvious choice: both.

Shake Off The Rust

Punch. Kick. Spin and set the stance. The fire felt good in his muscles, taut and sweaty beneath the light white robe cloaking him and the other dozen members working their way through the set on the dojo's matted floor. Cream walls pasted over with posters alternating between move diagrams and inane, inspirational showings played picture to the music's upbeat encouragement, a twist to the usual, more quiet classes.

"Feel the beat and work to it!" the instructor shouted, clapping her hands, as if the thwacking sound her calloused palms made could push her students to new heights.

But then, that's what all the classes were these days. Zhan-Yo had been coming here for years, and the dojo had been, like a parent trying to keep up with their children, reforming itself more and more to momentary fads. Pure martial arts had given ground to exercise routines with less emphasis on techniques that might get you in trouble.

Who needed to know how to fight, to defend oneself, with the Paragons to do it for them?

Still, Zhan-Yo worked through the exercises with dutiful obedience. If nothing else, he could flavor the routines with legitimate strikes, reversals, and lunges. The whole thing kept him limber, strong, and if Ziran was about to up end the world order, strength and flexibility would be useful. Not least because, if Sylvie had her way, Zhan-Yo might find himself in a room with Aegis. The thought terrified, excited him.

The music cut as the class hit its end, the instructor taking up the sudden slack to start cool down motions. Zhan-Yo went through the routine several times, even as most of the class stopped at one. Every extra year required a little more stretching to work out the kinks, and there was something pure about being the only one on the mats, the only one still working.

"Always the last," the instructor—what was her name, Chloe?— came over to him, reached out and adjusted Zhan-Yo's stance ever-so-slightly to even his balance.

Shutting his eyes to whisk away the irritation at being interrupted, Zhan-Yo turned to face the woman, robed in yellow to signify her role. Hair tied back, easily half Zhan-Yo's own age, but without fear or trepidation at approaching him. Then again, Chloe wouldn't know who Zhan-Yo was. Wouldn't know that she had every reason to tread lightly.

"I take my time," Zhan-Yo replied. "Thank you for the class. It was good."

A standard-issue compliment. Now that Chloe had broken his concentration, Zhan-Yo's mind turned to his Tama, safely sealed away in a locker, and the work awaiting him. Polite conversation was a luxury, and now, especially now, he didn't have time for it.

"This class isn't what you want, though, is it?" Chloe didn't adopt a smile, didn't look anything other than curious. "I see the way you add on to the routines."

"Perceptive." Zhan-Yo looked over Chloe's shoulders, towards the locker room. A hint. "Old habits that I would like to remember."

Chloe nodded. "You're not the only one. If you have a minute, and the energy, would you like to spar?"

Zhan-Yo said yes before he realized what Chloe had asked. To spar. To fight with his own hands. Sure, he'd practice every now and then against Ziran's more adept security officers, but they always fought with a hedge, not wanting to strike their own boss. Wexley, too, used to meet Zhan-Yo for pre-dawn bouts, but as Ziran grew more demanding, their sessions grew sparse until they stopped. But beneath all that, what pushed Zhan-Yo to accept Chloe's offer was a nervous doubt, the thought that he'd lost his verve, that by trying so hard to win wars in board rooms and through press releases he'd forgotten how to do it with his fists.

Chloe aligned across from Zhan-Yo, and the two bowed to each other. Straightened. Zhan-Yo settled into a loose crouch as Chloe set one leg in front of her. Enough of the class remained that they had an audience assembled, sucking at their water bottles, towels around their necks, tapping away at their Tamas or, in one case, holding his Tama up to record the fight.

Zhan-Yo struck first—Chloe had spent the workout doling out instructions, meaning she would have more energy, endurance. The longer the session went on, the more Zhan-Yo's already tired muscles would slow down, lack the strength to knock his smaller opponent aside. Chloe didn't seem shocked by Zhan-Yo's sudden run-up into a flying kick. She dropped, fell to the side and let Zhan-Yo rocket past her. As soon as he hit the mat, Zhan-Yo dove forward, dodging Chloe's own snap kick that would have struck his side had he tried to turn around.

They faced off again. Eyes locked.

This time their hands fought the war. Zhan-Yo closed in a quick two-step and from there jabs, cuts, elbows and fists ruled. Hits and counters, blocks and hooks, each one striving for position, each of them running through their repertoire while ditching those moves that belonged to a fight with fatal consequences. Chloe kept up with Zhan-Yo for a while, letting the older man land some minor body blows, then took over, unlocking speed Zhan-Yo hadn't expected. She turned aside his arms, batting them wide and then planted a dual-palmed push into Zhan-Yo's chest that sent him stumbling back.

Before he could recover, Chloe hit him again, going straight at him before spinning to the side and tripping Zhan-Yo with a low kick. Flat on his back, with Chloe's elbow planted in his chest, Zhan-Yo did the only thing he could; surrendered.

After they'd showered, Zhan-Yo waited for Chloe outside the dojo, taking the time to dash off some messages to underlings in need of direction. While Ziran needed him back at headquarters, Zhan-Yo wanted to thank the young woman for the excuse to exercise, despite the outcome.

"There's a group of us," Chloe said after Zhan-Yo's thanks, while they waited for respective pods. "We train once a week, the old style. If you want to join in, I think we'd be glad to have you."

"My old bones would be welcome?"

"You wouldn't be the oldest one there," Chloe replied. "We take turns teaching, too. There's a lot of tradition we don't want to lose." A pod pulled up and Zhan-Yo waved for Chloe to take it. "I'll send you the details. Think about it?"

"I will. Thanks," Zhan-Yo replied.

Normals, taking care of tradition, helping each other. Though he would have to make the time, Zhan-Yo would consider Chloe's offer. He needed more hobbies anyway — the revolution had begun to take over every second, and Zhan-Yo worried he'd make a mistake without the chance to clear his mind. And he could not afford mistakes. Not any longer.

20

Getting The Outside Perspective

As afternoons went, this one matched the bar for southern California: warm, breezy, and full of winter sunlight. Mynx alternated between reading reports on drone model performance and watching the waves from her wide deck. Without anyone else, one would have expected the large, glass, white-framed table to be empty, but Mynx had projections coating every surface. Reeves highlighted each one in turn as the square image flipped vertical, filling in so Mynx could read and watch even with the sun hitting it.

Hot tea helped to stave off the encroaching exhaustion, as did taking a nap after her visit to Denise's lab, and the jasmine mixed well with the speckled yellow flowers framing the deck's edge, which broadcast a strong enough scent to cover the constant burning, cooking metals from the Factory. Yet, despite the ideal, a sound kept tossing Mynx's concentration, until she waved away Reeves' latest dive into battery efficiency comparisons and took a clean look to the waterfront.

"There's someone there," Mynx said, tapping her Tama, which switched her contacts from a near to far focus—age once again laid low by technology. "Multiple someones."

"It's a family," Reeves said. "A mother, two children that look to be under ten years old. Their risk profile is low, so they did not trigger any intervention."

"No, that's fine," Mynx said. "Can you get me a closer look?"

Seconds passed before, from the table, a new square image popped up. This one courtesy of a drone now hovering near enough to the family to get a clear picture. A mother and two kids, the latter seeming to delight rushing into and out of the waves, screaming laughter, while the parent watched with a patient smile, towels and other necessities in a large bag looped over her shoulder. To make it this far from the pod drop off, they must have been determined to get away from the crowds no doubt braving the chilly water. As if to confirm the thought, both kids splashed from the sea and showed off their skin-tight thermal swimsuits.

Seasons were no longer a barrier to enjoying the beach.

Mynx watched the family talk, play, splash for a minute before telling Reeves to pull the drone back. Those were memories she would never make for herself. Never had that chance, or rather, when the chance was there, she chose another road. And she didn't regret that choice either, only that there wasn't time to make *all* the choices, exhaust *all* the options and have a complete life.

"Reeves, why do we age?" Mynx said, knowing exactly what she was going to get and smiling even as the AI started its response.

"It is a function of biology, Mynx," Reeves began, then seemed to notice Mynx's expression. "I believe you are mocking me, but I shall go into more depth if you require?"

"No, you've answered the question." Mynx's tea had hit that cool stage where further drinks were unpleasant, and its loss pushed Mynx to a different frame of mind. "Two more questions, Reeves. First, can you warm this up for me? And second, what time is it in Bangkok?"

"To the first, of course. To the second, it is quite early. I would not expect a normal business to be open."

"Apinya is about as abnormal as it gets. Call him, Reeves."

Reeves placed the call and, again appearing in a square projection over the table, a dark image arose. Too dark to see.

"Mynx," a tenor, melodic voice that was, despite the hour, not at all tired, said. "I trust you are not in danger?"

"Apinya, if I was in danger, would I really call you?"

A joke, if a bad one. Apinya would likely lose a bar fight to a common drunk, but in doing so, he would learn everything about that drunk, including just the thing to say or do that would cause those sloppy fists to stop swinging, for tears to start flowing or laughter to break away the violence. If you needed force, you didn't call Apinya. If you needed to know whether that force was necessary, well, that's when Apinya proved his worth.

The Champion flickered a flame, and with the lighter managed to start up a small lamp that cast an orange glow across his face, the sparse bed, and the screened-off ferns behind him. Mynx didn't know where Apinya was, but he had a penchant for leaving his vast city behind to find quiet. Hard to blame him—Mynx had done the same with her Factory. Only, instead of nature, she'd chosen machines.

Apinya himself looked far better than Mynx felt; while they were all getting along in years, Apinya seemed to wear his in slight wrinkles, in gray tips on his short hair and stubble, and his ash eyes escaped the tiredness plaguing Mynx's own. He curled away from his Tama, whose camera sent the Champion's image across the ocean to Mynx, stood into the dark to pull a robe around himself. No other lights were visible, no glow from a nearby city. Through the connection, Mynx picked out a bird's long hooting calls. How exotic. Mynx eased back into her chair, reached out and took the fresh hot tea from the drone.

"So if you're not in a crisis, then why are you calling?" Apinya asked, taking up his Tama and moving away from the bed, out to a bamboo porch. "Or do you often have friendly chats before dawn?"

"Is this always how you greet your friends?"

Apinya smiled. "It has been a long time. Too long, I think, since we've all seen each other."

Had it though? Mynx didn't ask the question. The Champions had split themselves across the Earth for more reasons than simple proximity. In a world where cross-continent travel took fewer hours than a night's sleep, and a video could beam from one city to the next in no time, they could have all stayed together. Could have all kept their homes in New York, or at their staging base in what had been Singapore.

"Aegis is trying to fix that." Mynx sweetened her face. "But we can talk about that later. I'm calling for another reason." Here she faltered. Strange how easy it was for a question so clear in her mind to smear into nonsense as she spoke it. "Age. We're old, Apinya. And I'm worried about what's going to happen when we're gone."

Apinya sat back in a chair that looked to be made of strung bamboo. He leaned his head against the soft, reddish wood wall and shut his eyes for a long second. The smile never left his face. Mynx knew what he was doing, knew Apinya was, right now, climbing inside of her and digging around for her thoughts, for what had led her to this moment. So she drank her tea and let him rummage.

"You're not only worried about your legacy, you're afraid," Apinya said two long sips later. "You don't want to die at all."

"Is that so hard to imagine?"

"No," Apinya looked off from his Tama, into some distance Mynx couldn't see. "You were always the worrier, while Aegis wanted to charge right in. Always a fist away from victory. He does not fear death."

"I don't know what will happen to it all, Api." Mynx used the nickname, fell back into old habits. "The Factory, the world we've built."

"It's not for us to decide," Apinya replied. "Either the world will keep what we've made, or destroy it and fashion something new."

"So you don't care at all?"

"I do. I'm training those who will replace me right now. I want what we made to survive, Mynx. I think the Paragons are on the right side of things, but I will not let fear of what may come haunt me now." Apinya returned his relaxed gaze to the Tama. "You should be enjoying yourself, Mynx. Let the next generation of Paragons take up the fight. Rest."

Mynx nodded at her Tama, wished she could have the same

sage-like view on things as Apinya. He always seemed to be operating in a different world than the rest of them.

"Thanks, Apinya. Good luck with your training."

"You're very welcome. I hope you find your peace, my friend."

Ten minutes later, all spent staring at the ocean, drinking tea, and puzzling over how Apinya managed to be so aloof all the damn time, Mynx asked Reeves to resume the status reports.

"Did you get what you wanted from the Champion?" Reeves asked as the AI cued up the projections across the table.

"He reminded me who he was, and who I am," Mynx said, leaning forward, taking in the latest test results of an upcoming stealth surveillance drone. "But he did have one good idea."

"Which is?"

"Let's send out a question to all the Paragon regions in Pacifica. I need to find the next me."

21

Villain Problems

Silver faces stared at him in the dark. Like ghosts, and for a moment Aegis considered the possibility that Thane had overcome the Champion's abilities and sent him on to the next life. If that was the case, though, then the next life was cold, blustery, and filled with Paragons. He could make out their uniforms now that his eyes were adjusting. The light turned their powder blue into a menacing gray, and Aegis made a quick note to review the color when he had a chance.

As if he would ever get one.

A Paragon reached out, took the Champion's left forearm and pulled. Aegis caught on, after a second of being very dead weight, to the goal and flexed his legs beneath him, rising up to a stand.

"That could have hurt him," said another Paragon, and Aegis recognized Pixie. "Broken back or something."

"He's Aegis," the lifter replied. "What's going to hurt him?"

"He was unconscious, wasn't he?"

"I'm right here," Aegis said, "and I'm fine."

Not totally, but enough. His head ached, but what should have been thunderous pain was only a mild drumbeat, a reminder that he ought to avoid such blows in the future. Not that Aegis ever listened to his body—the thing was there to do what he wanted, wasn't it?

Pixie dispensed information while Aegis took a long look around. Robotic crews swarmed the site around him, removing rubble and repairing what could be fixed. Pods didn't care about appearances, so long as they could get their power from the big batteries beneath the asphalt, they would be fine. As for the passengers, Aegis bet this place would be up and running again in less than a week. When you had non-stop work and many part-printers to go around, a little destruction didn't cause a big problem.

"Thane's gone west," Pixie began. "He wasn't hard to track. I guess you made him pretty angry."

"He and I do that to each other."

"Right. I suppose that makes sense," Pixie looked like she didn't know whether to laugh or not. Aegis's straight face probably didn't help her. "By the time we made it up this far, he'd already hunkered down in an old plant. Built into a hill."

"You haven't gone in after him?"

A new Paragon might have been embarrassed, might have stammered at the words, but Pixie had been around long enough to know any decision was valid so long as she could back it up. So with Aegis exhausted, beaten, and waiting for reasons, Pixie squared her shoulders and gave them.

"Look, Aegis. We were on our way here when you engaged. When you dropped off communications, we had to make a choice: follow Thane and try to stop him, or find you." Pixie took a deep breath, locked in. "And we chose to follow Thane, but when the drones tracking him showed that he stopped before he'd gone far, we came for you instead."

"You followed the guidelines."

"Your guidelines, yes."

The sheer enemy variety, from armed troops to world-destroying anomalies, necessitated priorities. The latter, those creatures, like Thane, that could level cities or do untold damage, had to be dealt with immediately, before any clean-up or wounded rescue. That

Pixie had followed the rules, even with Aegis himself down in the field, ought to be commended.

"Nice work," Aegis offered. "Any sign of the woman?"

"The woman?"

"There was another here, a civilian. Wounded when the building fell?"

"We didn't find her."

"Thane must have taken her then." Aegis shook his head. "Don't know why he didn't take me for a hostage instead."

"We have no idea."

Thane did tend to lose track of things like plans when he bulked himself up. Invincibility in exchange for imbecility. The key to keeping Thane under control lay in choosing the version least apt to the situation. Aegis, stupidly, hadn't kept Thane from getting enraged. Sloppy.

It wouldn't happen again.

The Paragons had come in a similar jet copter to the one Aegis took to his ill-fated fight with Thane. They'd parked the thing on the destruction's fringe, on untouched asphalt where the copter served as a silent irritant to the repair bots sliding around on their treads. At the Champion's order, Pixie and her Paragons climbed into the vehicle, with Aegis the last one in—and thus the first one out when they reached Thane. Stiff seats, restraining belts snapped on, and with a final check on his squad of five, Aegis told the chopper to lift off.

Nothing happened. Then Pixie did the same, and the engines whirred to life. Sometimes Aegis hated technology.

Pixie had her Tama synced with the craft, so it only listened to her. Pixie set the course by projecting a map of the area in between the sitting squad, which gave Pixie the opportunity to simply point where she wanted to go. As soon as she'd picked a spot near the rise where Thane had settled down, not so close as to bring the Paragons headlong into an ambush, the copter's jets pushed them up above the treetops, rotated, and sent them rocketing through the night.

The ride wasn't a long one, and the Paragons spent it listening to the wind's roar as it blew through the open side doors. Frigid, but these uniforms were designed to handle all weather conditions. They'd live. Being a Paragon wasn't about luxury anyway.

Pixie banked the copter once they came close to Thane's location, swiveling the craft to give Aegis a good look at the hillside structure Thane had taken for his own. For an old mine, this was some fortification. Tall walls, wide ramps for cargo-hauling freight, and, in front of what Aegis assumed was the mine's entrance, a large dormitory. Lights peppered the windows, too many for a single villain and his sole hostage.

"Bring us down here. No closer," Aegis said. That Thane knew a place like this suggested something more than a random escape, and Aegis wouldn't bring his Paragons into a trap. "We're going to try something different."

Pixie landed the copter in the lone road's center, its pitted and potholed pavement showing long neglect. After they came out, Aegis looked up the path towards Thane's hideout and told the Paragons no.

"We're not going in. Not tonight," Aegis said.

"Why?" said the one who'd helped Aegis up. "We're here, we're ready."

"He's ready too." Aegis patted his vest. Still had one stun gun, which he took off and handed to Pixie. "I'm going to go talk to him. See if I can figure out what he wants."

"Why does that matter?"

"Because if we have to fight him, people are going to die." Aegis started up the path. "One of 'em will probably be you."

Every step up the road brought Aegis further away from the Paragons and closer to his enemy, and every step made him feel a little better, a little lighter. Not that he preferred being alone, but Aegis wasn't a babysitter. Had never been one. Mynx and the other Champions had declared the world couldn't be handled with the eight of them alone, and, Aegis had to admit, they were right. The low-level nonsense the Paragons handled made his life immeasurably easier.

But that didn't mean he had to take them along on every

mission. Didn't mean he couldn't get his mitts dirt without worrying about someone else.

Up close, Thane's reclaimed building looked even more imposing. Not in an evil fortress way, but it was large, built solid to support heavy traffic, and any force advancing up the hill towards it would find themselves very vulnerable. And were those sentries? Already?

Three, armed with what looked like long rifles and lit in the soft yellow lights hanging from straight poles. Arrayed on the concrete overlook behind the dormitory and staring out over the slope towards Aegis and the copter. All of those rifles aimed his way, so Aegis kept his arms wide, hands open. No threat here. Not from range, anyway.

Instead of a gunshot, though, what came, stumbling and shivering down the ramp, was the woman from before. Thane's supposed hostage. She went towards Aegis, and when he waved her behind him, towards the Paragons, she understood the message and kept going. No clear injuries, minus the dirt and cuts she'd had before.

"See, Aegis? I've been reformed by your prison's excellent care!" Thane called from above, standing next to one of the guards. He must have appeared while Aegis watched the woman. "I didn't touch her, and I left you alive. I'm practically a saint now!"

"Sure you are," Aegis shouted back. "Since it's been working so well, why don't you come back with me? We can have you set up in time for breakfast."

"Ah, see, that's the problem." Thane raised his skinny arms wide —*sorry*. "The food you're serving truly is terrible. Even this place, where my men have lived for just a week, has better to offer. I'm sorry, my friend, but there is no going back for me."

"Thane, quit the bullshitting. I'm tired, it's late, and we all know how this ends. You huddle in there until we get enough people here to make it impossible for even you to get out. Let's save ourselves some time, some pain. Surrender."

Thane, wearing a thick, long jacket that rippled in the wind above what looked like a robe, nodded. "As you have so often told your Paragons, if you do not fight for your values, then you do not deserve to have them. I value freedom, Aegis, even if I cannot be trusted with it." Thane put a hand on the man next to him. "When you try to take our freedom from us, we will be ready, and you will pay the price."

Aegis sighed. Time was, he would've gone charging up that hill, taking and bouncing bullets like they were nothing. Punch, kick, and shoot his way through Thane's gang and take the monster himself down with well-timed stunning darts to Thane's mouth, head, and other parts that lacked his angry super-armor.

Time was.

"Thane, you're telling me you have no hostages up there? No innocents?"

Aegis could take Thane's blustering, but if there were civilians at risk . . . the Paragons, whether they liked to admit it or not, depended on public acceptance for their power. Aegis held no illusions that if the normal billions rose up they could wrest back control, could murder or imprison every anomaly. But that would be hard, would be deadly, and would be so much more work than letting the Paragons keep the streets safe, keep the world from going to war.

If normals ever doubted that safety would be kept, then the Paragons were doomed.

"What use is another mouth to feed, another person that needs babysitting?" Thane replied. "No, no Aegis. If you come after me here, you risk your own people and yourself for nothing more than your own desires. So follow them if you wish, Aegis. Attack me. Prove you are as reckless, careless as you've always been."

Instead, Aegis turned around and walked back towards the Paragons, Thane's laughter following him all the way.

22

A Night Out

Carver's looked like garbage and not even the night's steadily increasing snowfall could save it. The club's exterior exuded a trashy hostility, like being accosted by a drunk over the beer you'd just ordered. Even its pink neon sign, perpetually in a flickering war to survive, had black patches forever darkened by thrown bottles. Hooded, huddled people stood off to the side, smoking throwbacks to the era *Carver's* belonged to. Kat had asked—nobody knew who the bar's namesake was, only that it'd been around for a couple of centuries, sponging from one generation to the next like a disease.

Through the single door, clotted over with postings for local acts, events, and the like, the bouncer hit her with a half-second bored stare that transitioned to a solemn nod once he realized who was coming in.

"Packed tonight," the bouncer, a bulk-loaded dude named Tracy, said.

"Good hunting?" Kat replied, happy to give Tracy a few seconds of conversation while she scoped out the club behind him.

"Ought to be."

Which was as good as Tracy gave when it came to anomalies. *Carver's* didn't allow Kat to actually trace on the premises, but she had no problems picking up a lead and following them home. Especially on a night like this, when Kat wanted a distraction from Gordon, from that anomaly of his, and from a life that had thus far failed to fill her with joy.

So she ordered a double. Vodka. Neat. It'd go down smooth, she'd sip it, and she'd put in her number.

Carver's, once a week, set up a central ring where its dance floor normally lay. There, amateur fighters could beat the living tar out of each other for five minutes at a time. Buy a drink and you could get a ticket, then drop it in a big, old, fishbowl at the end of the flaking, cherry-painted, metal bar. When the bell rang to finish a fight, another pair came out and the fun continued.

Kat could have come up with theories for why *Carver*'s fight nights attracted so many people, including tonight's packed crowd that swarmed the ring. Cheers, side bets, and the occasional scream when a fighter landed a vicious hit made up the main attraction to the constant pulse-pounding electronica bouncing off the walls. Why, though, come up with theories when the facts presented themselves so plainly:

People were bored. People wanted to feel something. Ergo, punches, kicks, tackles and clumsy headbutts.

"So why'd you tell me to come tonight?" Kat asked when Sandra, the bartender whose long, curled hair hit every color of the spectrum, along with the jewelry dangling from every visible part, set the double down.

"Missed your pretty face," Sandra's voice had that hoarse quality you get when you spend most nights yelling over noise, as if her vocal cords had been roasted to a crisp. "Where've you been?"

"Up north."

"Vacation?"

Kat answered that question with a long drink. The vodka went down easy: chilled, a little burn to remind her that she wasn't drinking water.

"Guess not." Sandra flicked her eyes down the bar, the line of customers legion. "I'll be back. You want to put in a ticket?"

Kat waged a guessing game with Sandra's body. Leaning away

from Kat, eyebrow making the slightest of climbs up Sandra's fore-head, hands gripping the edge of the bar. No obvious sign except those eyes, those bright eyes that said she shouldn't miss this.

"I'm in for one."

With Sandra gone, Kat took another long visual trip across *Carver's*. Anomalies wouldn't stick out, necessarily, in a heavy-drinking, alternative crowd like the one here. But Kat could weed out the regulars, the ones that looked too at home to be targets. Once she did that, the numbers thinned out enough to spot a possibility.

The guy sat on a chair against a side wall, sipping on a pint and throwing his eyes around the room like he was afraid he'd get jumped. He wore a cloth cap pressed tight on a shaved head, its Christmas green contrasting with his chocolate skin. A ragged sweatshirt with a tear where the hood should be went down over stained jeans that had stories to tell. He checked Kat's boxes.

"Don't tell me you found one already?" Sandra asked, choosing to mix someone's order next to Kat.

"Might be. You know that guy? The one with the hat?"

Sandra peeled an orange. Stole a second to peer through the crowd where Kat looked. "New one. Came in a couple nights ago."

"He put in a ticket?"

"Have to order another round to know that." Sandra poured so much sugar into those words that Kat laughed.

That was the deal with *Carver's*: you wanted something, you paid for it, but the return here was too good to pass up. Something about the place's dingy, off-the-road vibe attracted the sorts who wanted to lay low. Who wanted to be part of a crowd without, really, joining it. Kat bet most people here, including herself, were running away from things. When Sandra came back next, Kat ordered another, this time a single, and asked her to get the cap guy's tickets and hers next to each other. Then Kat stood, went away from the bar and to the ring. Get a closer look at the action. That, and the buzz had her feeling warm, restless. Ready to see something.

Beating each other around the ring right now were two middle-aged women, and they'd come to play. These weren't the t-shirt sporting, half-drunk punks that bumbled around the circle throwing haymakers and hitting the wind until one tripped and knocked themselves out. These two, these two were *good*. The ring's small size meant moves had to be tight, and the women had made things even tighter for themselves by closing to a range where short jabs, elbows, and knees were in vogue. Their limbs flashed, batting each other's strikes aside and sneaking into the vulnerable moments to crack a jaw or deliver a kidney shot. At first, Kat thought the two were going to keep at it till one of them died right there.

Then . . . Kat grinned. She saw it now. Invisible to the untrained eye, especially with the reactions. These two were pulling, at the last instant, their punches. Less a fight and more a dance. And the reason why came through in the growing shouts around her: side bets, some no doubt put in by people who knew what the finish to this would be. Profits shared.

A routine that ought to get these two banned from *Carver's* for life, but when the fight ended, the timer at four minutes and thirty five seconds, with a duck-under-and-upper-cut motion that sent one to the floor, motionless, the crowd cheered, groaned, and exchanged cash without pause. Kat found herself clapping along with the rest as the winner held her hands up high, showed that even pulled, she'd earned some bruises for her trouble. Enough entertainment, and even a set fight could be worth paying for.

Kat hit the bathroom, ditched her coat with Tracy back at the bar's entrance, and gathered some space for herself to stretch. Only a couple more minutes, if Sandra had done her job. Kat's outfit tonight had that loose-fitting style suggesting a carefree attitude but that, really, gave Kat room to breathe in tight quarters and flexibility in wide ones. A red, short-sleeved top coupled with warm, dark leggings that'd stretch as she needed them to.

"Next pair to the ring, and it's a good one! We got ourselves a newcomer, Calvin, facing off against the legendary Kat Collins!"

That DJ. She'd have to have words with him later, tell him not to play her up like that. Raise expectations. Sure, she didn't lose much here, but *legendary*? Kat wasn't sure one could become a legend beating random jokers in a dive like *Carver's*. But the stage had been set, and when Kat walked towards the ring—her vodka long finished—the crowd parted to give her room. More than a few hands sprung up for high fives, which Kat gave, and she tossed smiles and nods at the people who knew her.

Knew her. More like they'd made enough money off her wins to keep her popular.

Up close, the ring's scuffed red tape boundary did nothing to hold back the crowd's press, well within a missed punch's range, a slipped kick's hit. They closed in, ready to see the next show, drinks in hand and spilling on each other, the floor. Biker bros—an ironic fashion set since motorcycles had long since been banished to designated tracks—made way for Kat to get into the ring.

Calvin hadn't made it through the press yet, so Kat crossed to the far side. Now the smile vanished. The slight haze from the booze blurred away the crowd's noise as she fought through to her focus, to the moment. Try hard enough and any situation could be just like those woods at night, snow blowing and silence the only sound. A little bit of lingering soreness in her legs, her throat a little dry from the vodka, but otherwise she could destroy the world.

Kat's quarry made it through with the help of pushing hands. He stumbled a bit, the kind of move that made Kat wonder if Calvin was a rookie, a boy way in over his head, who'd thrown in a ticket because a pretty bartender had asked and he didn't know how to say no. Then he looked up at her, and she'd never seen a harder face. None of the usual smirks, the eye rolls she'd get from men lining up against her, but instead an ice-cold pierce from eyes shadowed by the lights above and around them. Kat re-evaluated; Calvin had scars, looked very much not afraid of stepping into it, and maybe wanted to, maybe used things like this to take the edge off.

Calvin dropped his bulky jacket off his shoulders, handing it to someone who'd likely steal it behind him, revealing an addict's wiry shape, or a person for whom food came in fits and starts. A gray t-shirt hung loose, and a few red stains found splotchy homes on its chest. From across the ring, Kat couldn't tell if those came from blood or barbecue.

"Kat and Calvin! Last chance to get your bets, your drinks!" the

DJ announced, before switching *Carver's* screens from sports to a thirty-second countdown.

"You ready for this?" Kat called to Calvin. The music blared loud enough that she had to shout, but the miracle of human hearing meant Calvin caught the sound anyway, and nodded. "Don't hold back! I won't!"

All part of the game. All part of getting Calvin's head in the right place. If the man was an anomaly, if he had a spark hiding in there, Kat wanted to bring it out. And most anomalies, pushed to the brink, would give in and let fly with the last trick they had.

It was a miracle Kat still lived.

Thirty seconds hit zero and mind-obliterating air-horns split through the beat to start the fight. Kat went in fast, running right across the arena in three steps to bring as many jabs to bear on Calvin's face. The man proved his wiry bona fides by dodging to her right, ducking under the punches in the process. But he didn't take advantage of the opening, didn't throw a blow.

Disappointing. Kat had left that split vulnerable just to see what Calvin could do, and if he wasn't going to bite, she'd have to force the issue.

Whirling left and letting her fist swing wide, Kat felt Calvin grab her arm with his own, putting her back to his chest. More importantly, it put Kat's right foot in position to kick back, knock Calvin's matching shin off-balance, and before the man could counter, Kat used her shoulder, planted her left leg, and wrapped her right around Calvin's head, culminating in throwing the man over her body and slamming him down on the floor.

The bar cheered. The bar groaned. Kat didn't give Calvin a chance to catch his breath.

She went for a kick at Calvin's collarbone, that part right where the neck connected. Should have been an easy strike, painful, but Calvin apparently took his throw-down well, because he managed to grab Kat's foot as it hit. He pulled, and then it was Kat falling flat to the floor, butt first.

Sticky, hard, unpleasant. She'd probably burn the leggings.

Calvin turned, pressed Kat's stolen leg to the floor and started to stand when Kat used that press for her own leverage and snapped a kick at Calvin's chest, right there in the solar plexus. If she'd been wearing pointed heels instead of rounded boots, the fight might've ended right there. Comfort over fashion came with costs.

As it was, Calvin let go, stumbled back a few steps with his hands pressed to Kat's strike point. The space let Kat push herself up, bouncing into a sprint that, over the spit-flinging cries of the crowd, let her slam into Calvin before he was ready. Fists, elbows, knees and more than one stomp on his toes had Calvin hiding his face in his arms, trying to weather the storm.

"C'mon," Kat hissed without stopping the hits. "Show me who you really are. Do it, or I'll kill you."

The words were cliche, and she had no plans to kill Calvin—*Carver's* amateur fighting ring conferred no immunity to murder charges—but making a tense moment sound like it belonged in a movie often worked. Kat needed Calvin to believe this was his time, his climax where he'd burst forth, all heroic, and end up with a trace in his arm and a new career as a forced Paragon.

"What are you talking about?" Calvin said, his voice tight and shot-through with the tremors of someone trying and failing to get enough air.

"You know."

Kat backed off for a hot second, long enough for Calvin to think she'd let up, and then she danced back in, this time going low. Beneath the man's long arms and bony elbows. Calvin jumped away, bouncing off the pushing spectators, and wound up only taking a single shot to the quad for his troubles.

"Nah, I don't," Calvin said as Kat followed his dodge.

Now Calvin played host to the party, setting the tone with long, reaching swings meant to keep Kat back, occasionally tweaked with a snap-kick too slow to be something he practiced. We were super-heroes in our minds, and Calvin fought like he was dreaming. So Kat let the man tire himself out as the clock ticked below a minute. Time was running out to get Calvin's ability, if he had one, into the open. As she ducked another wild right hook, Kat closed again with a hugging grab around Calvin's middle. She hooked her left leg around his, pushed and toppled the bigger man to the ground. Kat pulled back her right hand, made the fist as Calvin hit the floor.

"Now or never," Kat said.

"Never." Calvin stuck his hands above his head, wide and palms out. A surrender. "I'm done."

Before Kat could move, could react, the DJ played the air horns again and the crowd who'd made some sweet reps off her swarmed the ring. Carried her off Calvin, who she lost in the mess of hands, faces, bodies. A crush that only stopped when the DJ announced the next two fighters. By the time Kat made it to the bar, to Sandra, Calvin had disappeared.

"Sorry, Kat," Sandra said when Kat asked after her missing combatant. "He took off after the match. Think he didn't want to get hassled."

"Don't blame him." Kat looked towards the exit, as if some glowing trail to Calvin might materialize. None did. "Did he give you any hints about who he is? Where he's from?"

"You still think he's an anomaly?"

"Yeah. He's scarred, which makes him dangerous."

If Kat could draw a line connecting the anomalies she'd traced who'd proven themselves to be terrors, the one common factor was that they *knew* they were hunted. They'd fought, scrabbled, and burned away relationships to survive outside of the Paragon's barred bounty, and the result had turned them hard. Suspicious.

Calvin was walking that same path. Whether he'd blow up a city or create nothing more than a puff of smoke depended on random genetic chance.

And on whether Kat found him first.

Knife Meets Management

Finishing a cigarette always felt like waking up. The final ash knock, slipping the filter into the small pouch Zhan-Yo carried—if a drone saw you litter, it'd cost obscene reps—all signaled a break away from the meditative puffing. Back to the Tama, to the evening's demands. You could get the same effect without the drug and its harmful effects, but habits were habits and Zhan-Yo owned his.

Ice bobbed in Lake Michigan and he watched it as he leaned on the cold metal rail. Not quite as chill as last night, but enough to warrant the heavy coat, a scratchy wool hat and a scarf that Zhan-Yo pulled up to cover his face.

"Those things'll kill you." Wexley approached. Zhan-Yo had seen him minutes ago, walking away from the buildings and into Millennium Park's comparative serenity. Wexley had taken his time to arrive at the meeting spot, and Zhan-Yo didn't hold the reverie against the man. "Don't even know where you find them anymore."

"If I die from these, I'll be a happy man."

Wexley gave a single, dead laugh and joined his boss, looking out over the black water. In the winter, this view always had a special feel to it: without all the shipping and boaters haunting the summer, the shore felt like a dividing line between dark and light.

"Thank you for coming," Zhan-Yo said. "She'll be here soon."

"She?"

"There are things you need to know. In case this doesn't go the way I want it to, and more so if it does."

Wexley, wearing glasses and the boot-to-neck trench coat popular with today's fashionable businessman, took the news without much emotion. Perhaps Zhan-Yo had given his lieutenant so many surprises over the years that Wexley now treated them as standard events, little bumps in the otherwise straightforward climb to success as Ziran's shining star.

"You're being evasive. Which explains where we are." Wexley waved an arm over towards the park, his eyes flicking up. "No people. No drones. But I'm not going to get jerked around, Z."

Wexley didn't need to worry. Zhan-Yo caught the pod's light coming from behind Wexley and looked towards it, his lieutenant following the gaze. The pod slowed and pulled off to the curb across Lake Shore Drive's wide expanse. Sylvie slipped out, coated in formal wear that, on her, could hold any number of weapons.

"Fine," Zhan-Yo said as the pod shuffled off, giving Sylvie a free path across the street. "I won't. That's Sylvie. She's going to ruin us, or help us change the world."

Wexley had the decency to wait for Sylvie to cross before asking questions. After the barrage started—full name, background, why he should trust her—Sylvie glanced to Zhan-Yo with an expression begging permission to kill this annoying fly, but Zhan-Yo's refusing shake turned her irritation into a resigned sigh.

"What? Is this boring to you?" Wexley said. "Here you are, telling me that you've been working under Z for years and—"

"Stop, Wexley," Zhan-Yo cut in. "Stop. I brought you here to listen, to learn. Not to speak, and certainly not to demand."

For however much power Wexley believed he wielded, Zhan-Yo was still the boss, and Wexley's sudden quiet, his back-step away from Sylvie and stare towards the ground indicated he knew it. Which, good. Aggressiveness, ambition, even arrogance could be tolerated. Insubordination, however, was a rot that could not stand.

Zhan-Yo would hate to replace Wexley, but he would.

"Seems we're sorted now?" Sylvie asked, and at a wave of Zhan-Yo's hand, she continued. "Good. If you've been reading my updates, you know things are going well. Don't tell me you've called me here to cancel."

"I want the details," Zhan-Yo said. "That's why I called you here. Cryptic messages are fine, and I'm glad things are proceeding. But what things, and where. That's what I want you to tell me when nobody is listening."

"Someone is listening." Sylvie indicated Wexley.

"If we cannot trust him, then this whole enterprise is pointless."

Zhan-Yo hoped Wexley would stay quiet, and the man did. This was not his conversation.

Sylvie took a breath. Gave Wexley one more evaluating look, then spoke, "We're moving weapons into the city now. Not enough to trigger alarms, but enough to be noticed. Word's already spread up the Paragon chain, and I think, with one high profile leak, we'll be able to get Aegis here. He's still taking things on personally. I've heard he's in the northeast right now, responding to some prison escape. If we can cause enough of a problem, he'll come."

The Champions's vanity knew no bounds. Zhan-Yo had grown up with their photo-ops, their exploits spread across the screens and the lingering remnants of the paper publications. Every opportunity to make a save meant a chance to boost their names, their profile. Give them a big arms bust in the middle of a major city, yes. He could see it. Aegis would want the credit. Would want to be the hero.

"Hold on." Wexley couldn't keep himself quiet any longer. "Z, what is this? Weapons? You *want* the Paragons to take everything?"

"Listen to her, Wexley."

Wexley started to make another noise, and Sylvie, with the slightest, exasperated hiss, whipped a finger-length knife from her coat pocket—or maybe her sleeve, Zhan-Yo wasn't sure—and stuck its point against Wexley's throat. The man's eyes went wider than his glasses and he froze into the perfect stillness only achievable one breath away from death.

"We're listening to her because she knows what she is doing."

Zhan-Yo put his hand on Sylvie's knife arm and the pressure proved enough for Sylvie to abandon the threat. "And because she's very good with that knife."

As much as points could be received, Wexley understood Sylvie's threat and Zhan-Yo's subsequent order. He shoved his hands in his coat pockets and shuddered. Zhan-Yo allowed him that much; it was cold, and Wexley, the administrator and polished business executive, was being pulled into a mad world that, no doubt, had previously existed to him only in stories.

"Please, continue," Zhan-Yo said to Sylvie, who hadn't taken her eyes off Wexley.

"I'm scouting locations around the city," Sylvie said, as if she were reciting her grocery list. "I'll settle on one soon. What I need from you is the communication strategy. Once we take care of Aegis, the world will need to know. They'll have to understand what it means."

"It will be done," Zhan-Yo replied. "Once you have your location, we will have it prepared."

"You're just going to kill him?" Wexley broke in again, but this time he directed the complaint at Zhan-Yo, not Sylvie. "That's it? If you're drawing him into a trap, why not get some more out of him first? We could make him say the Paragons are a mistake, that—"

"Wexley." Zhan-Yo frowned as he cut his lieutenant off. The man continued to say and do things that were shaking Zhan-Yo's confidence in him. Perhaps he had erred in bringing Wexley here, in exposing him to this at all. Perhaps Wexley's steel spine, composed and strong, was really brittle iron rusted and ready to break. "We are not torturers. We will take no pleasure in this. It is a means to a very necessary end, and that is all. The Champion's death will be enough."

Sylvie tapped on her Tama. Calling a pod, signaling the meeting's end.

"I'll let you know when I've found the place," Sylvie said once she'd summoned her ride. "Try to keep this one under control."

"Don't worry about me," Wexley said. "Now that I know what's going on, just tell me what you need. Anything. I'm there."

"Which is precisely where I don't want you to be." Sylvie searched the street for her pod, sighted it, and began walking towards the vehicle even though it was blocks away. "Look, don't touch."

Wexley stared after Sylvie until Zhan-Yo began walking the other direction, steering him away and back north, towards the glittering towers. The cold had penetrated his coat and snarled itself into Zhan-Yo's skin, and the hair beneath his hat itched, and when he scratched it felt like brittle glass. All the same, in his heart, Zhan-Yo held destiny's warm glow.

24

An Unwelcome Surprise

The morning process kept getting longer. Today, after the medical line items, Mynx added a new one; stretching before she embarked on the walk out to the Factory. Her quads, it seemed, were no longer willing to make such a journey without a warm-up. Her quads. Referring to parts of her body as if they were not her, but separate. A result of them feeling less and less like they used to. Less and less like she believed she should be.

"Schedule?" Mynx asked as the drones slipped on the day's casual outfit.

The soft blue Paragon sweater and cream lounge pants were a good sign on their own—Reeves wouldn't choose them if Mynx had somewhere exciting to be. Somewhere public. So even as she asked Reeves to detail the day's demands, Mynx expected a long, blank slate.

She was the leader, Pacifica's Champion. A land and water realm covering everything west of the Mississippi, all across Hawaii and Alaska to Singapore and Japan. Countries and states relegated to administrative domains managed by Paragon-appointed delegates. While some Champions, like Aegis, preferred a hands-on role, Mynx hit all her Paragons with tests and used the results to turf away her duties. Except, of course, the final say. If needed, Mynx could leave the Factory and take it all back. As if she ever would.

"Nothing official, but you should know that Dr. Jones is in a pod heading this way. She should be here in approximately five minutes."

"Reeves, why didn't you tell me? Wake me up sooner?"

"Unscheduled, ma'am. The pod records indicate she made the call this morning."

Mynx glanced out the window. Another sunny day she had planned to bury inside her mechanical mountain, perfecting the gladiator, and getting the final deployment arranged for an aquatic drone squad a long time in the making. Now the pleasures of her simulations, data, and drone development would have to wait.

"Delay her. Long enough, at least, for me to get my tea."

"Of course. I already started brewing some in anticipation. Dr. Jones will have her arrival delayed by ten minutes."

Reeves would go in, tell the pod some street or series of them were under construction and have the thing wind through back roads. A handy trick when Mynx needed some time, or when she wanted a particularly annoying visitor to get so lost as to give up on the interruption. Not that they wouldn't figure it out eventually, but Mynx had stopped caring about the niceties. Time was too important.

When Mynx gestured open the grand doors to her house for Denise, she did so while holding a steaming mug that smelled of wildflowers, though she hadn't changed her clothes. Nor had she bothered to put on anything more than a straight expression. Her stance screamed that Denise was interrupting, and that such an interruption had consequences.

Denise failed, with her pleasant smile and earnest good morning, to pick up on this.

"Can I come in?" Denise asked after her greeting went unreturned, and Mynx offered no invitation.

"Denise," Mynx said. "I know you may believe that we have a special relationship. That because I am interested, very interested, in your work, that you have some special license to arrive here unannounced on a whim. You do not. I'm a Champion, and a busy one. Schedule your visits and I will be happy to receive you. Don't, and—"

"I'm getting somewhere," Denise interrupted. "Your sample. It, it's getting me, us, closer. We made the cells regress, removed the age-damaged ones and replaced them with working cells."

"And?"

"That's the thing. Your anomaly strands seemed to be the key. Not every cell in an anomaly is abnormal. I mean, special."

"I know what you mean."

"Right. So we, uh," Denise looked at her hands, as if she wished they held a screen with data, or maybe a marker she could use to draw her description. "It turns out the percentage of anomaly cells that had age-related damage was very low. Compared to the normal cells, anyway."

Mynx basked in a long tea drink. Played out the logic to a few different conclusions and decided to see which Denise would settle on.

"So what do you think?" Mynx said.

"I think, I think that if you had more of your anomaly cells, you'd be younger. At least in a physical sense." Denise took a breath, pressed her lips together for a second and looked up. Dead at Mynx. "This is why I'm here. We need to confirm that it's not just you. That every anomaly has this opportunity." Another pause. Another breath. "And whether it's something we can transfer to others."

"You want the database."

"Well, you offered before. If there was promise? I think this could be it. Really."

When an anomaly first realized that's what they were, it's almost always a traumatic experience. Even if the ability was something minor, like making their tongue change colors or always knowing the precise humidity in the air, they'd joined an exclusive group.

A consequential ability brought with it responsibilities. Mynx and the other Champions spent years learning that lesson and fighting other anomalies that never did.

The database Mynx built wasn't a product of her ability, but its contents could do as much, maybe more damage if handled without care. The drones were the same; each one had a fail-safe Mynx could activate, one that would shut down the machine if it failed to connect on its own every 24 hours. A code that would descend down a designated Paragon line if Mynx herself died.

The point being, Mynx took her position seriously, and that meant not giving power to people who didn't deserve it.

"If there's promise, then show me," Mynx replied. "Send me the evidence, send me where you plan to go, and if it's good, I'll give you your access."

Denise wilted, then found some spine and straightened. Tried one last shot, "You're the one who wanted this fast. I'm trying, and you're making it harder."

"When you wish for the impossible and someone says they've done it, I think it's reasonable to ask for evidence."

Denise didn't stay after that. Told Mynx she'd send along the details and vanished back into the pod, which Reeves had held for Denise on Mynx's order. This was never going to be a long conversation, no matter what Denise had to say. Words were nothing without proof, and no legitimate proof would come hand-delivered, not in the detail Mynx would need to be convinced.

"You weren't very nice," Reeves said as Mynx finished her tea back on her deck, sun crawling higher in the sky. "I've found humans to respond better to kindness than anger."

"She lied."

"Lied? About which part?"

"Everything," Mynx said. "And she did it poorly, because she's a researcher, not a con artist. Anomaly cells are immune to aging? Then why aren't anomalies all younger than the normals?"

Reeves agreed that theory did seem rather easy to disprove. Then, dropping the subject, Reeves started in on the day's assessments, the drones that needed to be reviewed, the provisions for new parts and raw materials for the Factory that needed to be signed off on. Mynx let it all roll over her while, beneath it all, she stayed on Denise Jones.

Questions abounded. Why did Denise come today, and why

make up such an obvious lie? Why, when Mynx refused, did Denise simply back down and leave? If she wanted the database so badly, Denise should have thrown offer after offer. Tried any technique. Instead, she faded. Took the no and left.

"Reeves," Mynx said, interrupting a long exploration of the forthcoming deep sea defense drones. "Denise has a long track record in this field, right?"

"Indeed." One of the many benefits of AIs over a normal human was that they took being interrupted with no offense at all. "She is one of the premiere geneticists in Pacifica."

"So she knows how to get a conclusion respected. She understands how to present results."

"It would seem plausible."

"Then let's double-check. Reeves, I want you to use the database. Thaw out some samples, run a check on the cells and let me know if Denise's conclusions are accurate. If the anomaly cells are younger."

"And if they are?"

"Then I apologize."

Reeves didn't need to ask what would happen if Denise's conclusions were off. At that point, Mynx would have to make a decision. Either treat Denise as a fluke and disregard her, or treat her as a threat, and remove her.

"There is another matter you should know of," Reeves said after several seconds, drawing out the *there* at the start. A programming quirk Mynx had built in to signify something, well, significant. "A Paragon alert in Atlantis has been issued. It seems Thane broke out of his cage."

If she'd been punched, it would have hurt less. Thane was like a childhood secret, buried so deep that Mynx could forget about him. Forget about what they'd done, what had been necessary. She leaned on the table, pressing down on it with her palms. Atlantis was a long way away, Thane's prison far beyond the border, and yet that still didn't feel far enough.

"How?"

"Details are scarce at the moment. Aegis is calling in a large number of Paragons to assist."

"He'll need every one of them." Mynx stood. "Odds of me reaching the conflict in time to affect the outcome?"

"Difficult to calculate. My . . . information on Thane's abilities is minimal. It is hard to quantify the effect your presence would have on the situation."

Minimal for a reason, and not one Mynx cared to state out loud. However much she depended on Reeves, she refused to forget he was a program. Functions and calculations devised by human hands, and ones that could be stolen by the same. Or forced to reveal their secrets.

"Fair. Keep me apprised. If Aegis has trouble, I want to know about it. And I'll want to get there as fast as possible."

"I will hold a flight plan for you."

Mynx didn't hear that last bit. She'd returned to the man, the villain.

The stain she'd failed to remove.

25

Father Daughter Dilemmas

Compared to Thane's fortified mining manse, Aegis quite enjoyed the view from the beach, munching on a lobster roll under a heat lamp, soaking in a sun that had managed to fight its way through winter clouds. He'd left Thane there, with Paragons keeping watch and more pouring in every hour. Eventually he'd get the call when they were ready to try an assault, or maybe Thane would just starve in his new home.

That'd be too good for the bastard.

Aegis wiped a bit of rogue mayo from his cheek, looked around. Scattered wanderers filled the restaurant, most like him, either alone or with one other person. Empty tables sported happy tourists posing in photos, covered in plastic. The joy when you're suppressing life's hopes and terrors for a second or two. All taken in the summer, a blatant warning that Aegis had chosen the wrong time to make his trek to Maine's eastern seaboard.

But he couldn't have spent another minute in that outpost, listening to logistics, dealing with hero greetings from Paragons whose names he'd never remember. Aegis, they all said, can I get your autograph, a picture with you. Like the subjects on the table beneath his hands, a table getting more smeared by the second as his roll dripped its sauce everywhere, Aegis had faked all the smiles he could to send the Paragons away happy. They were going to be risking their lives. It was the least he could do.

"You're actually here," Celice sounded truly surprised. "I didn't think you'd leave, even after you told me."

Celice could read him. Aegis wouldn't have left, except it'd been clear that charging Thane with anything less than an army would result in unnecessary death. Not a single Paragon in Atlantis had the power to bomb a site from orbit, and the actual capability to do something like that had been disbanded by the Champions a decade ago. Normals were dangerous enough without giving them nukes to play with.

"It's going to be a long one," Aegis said. "Thane's got himself holed up good. You hungry?"

"They're making it." Celice eyed her father's mess with amusement and disgust. "Looks like you're enjoying yourself."

"Too much sauce." Aegis wasn't one for food's finer workings— his big hands made clean dining a disaster. "Glad you came up."

"Not like there was much to do back in New York. You have every Paragon north of Virginia coming to this thing. I set the drones on high alert and left."

Celice took her seat with the casual elegance Aegis had always admired in his daughter. While he bumbled through the world, Celice floated. Her sharp eyes caught details he missed, and while Aegis never quite understood what caused her gleeful innocence— her running around with his own action figure in their first, much smaller Bastion played through his mind on loop all the time—to disappear, Celice had earned his pride, and his dependence.

"Thane beat me," Aegis said, evading the words with a studied look to the horizon.

Celice didn't hesitate, "He should, right? Didn't it take all of you to bring him down before?"

Not wrong. One of the last times the Champions operated as a unit. Before differing strategies became differing ideals became irreconcilable. Before they'd scattered around the world to keep from killing each other and ruining all they'd built.

"Too easy," Aegis said. "I shouldn't have lost like that. Hit me in the head with a drone. I should have been able to shrug it off, keep him there till Pixie and the others arrived."

He didn't say he felt tired. A younger him would have been all fire, ready to take the lessons learned from the fight—namely, don't let a drone smash you into the ground—and go back at it again. Now he had a headache, now he was tired, now he wanted to . . . go home?

By the time he realized his daughter hadn't said anything, it'd been a full minute or more and Aegis turned, wondering where Celice had put her peppy pick-me-ups, or even realistic expectations. Anything to distract him from where, what he was now. Aegis found an incredulous look, the exasperation on her narrowed eyes and in her long, slow breath.

"Don't tell me that you dragged me way up here because you're all depressed," Celice said. "You lost. It happens. The Paragons have lost countless times. What keeps us going, what keeps you going, is that you don't stop trying."

There we go. Aegis laughed, a rumbling low thing, and he leaned back on the bench enough that he nearly fell off.

"I know, I know. And I didn't ask you up here for a pep talk. At least, not just for that." Aegis bent forward, and set aside the self doubt to dive into that distracting topic: logistics. "What I need you to do is get as many drones as you can spare up here. Not the physical, beat-em-up ones, but the artillery. Thane's turtling up, and I want to soften his shell."

"Strategy? Is that the Paragon way?"

"Our way worked well enough for a long time. But I'm done throwing away lives needlessly." Aegis glanced at his Tama. "We've cut his power, network access, all of it. Thane's got nothing, but he's too damn smart. I want to blow him out before he comes up with something terrible."

Celice nodded, then looked at her own Tama, ran her finger

across its surface towards Aegis. A projection, fuzzy and hard to see in the sunlight, played across the table. After a second, the program figured out the most important elements of Celice's show and dimmed everything else, giving Aegis numbers in a deep green color.

"That's all we have across Atlantis. You've been so reluctant to get more from Mynx that we're short as it is."

This argument again. Ever since Mynx had brought the drones to the point where they could capture most criminals without a Paragon right there with them, Celice had been pushing for the robots to be everywhere. Thing was, Aegis had fought against plenty of monster bots in his time. Too many normals, too many anomalies thought all the answers lay in bigger, stronger machines. Any program could be corrupted, any computer controlled by the wrong hands.

But times had changed. The Paragons weren't as popular as they once were, thanks to their own success. Anomalies no longer cared to join an organization that, with no vast evils to fight, would likely set them on a lucrative, dull career. Normals saw the drones as their police now, with the Paragons an almost archaic group of weirdos coming out to scare everyone now and then. All that meant the Paragons had difficulties hitting their recruiting quotas, and there weren't enough trackers running around to make up the difference. Drones might be the only option.

"I'll talk with Mynx after this. Place a large order. You win."

"Yay." Celice withered with the word, then caught herself, forced up a questioning smile. "You're being too reasonable today, Dad. Is this all because of Thane?"

If only it were that easy. Sourcing what was a slow change in his outlook to one pivotal event. That kind of simplicity might seem plausible to Celice, whose life-roster of notable moments could be grasped, analyzed and its conclusions outputted into causes-and-effects. Aegis would have a harder time delineating whether this introspection stemmed from the first time he truly felt pain—well into his thirties—or if it was last night, where the honest thought that he might die panicked his mind. Or a hundred other instances where it seemed all he'd worked for, fought for, was about to vanish.

"We wanted to kill him back then, but couldn't take the risk," Aegis said finally. "Apinya made the call. Said there might not be a limit to Thane's power, and if we tried too hard, he might lose himself in an indestructible rage. That's how it is with Thane—in the end, the only thing that stops him is himself."

"Then why keep him here? Why not shoot him into space or something?"

"Because we wanted to use him," Aegis laughed, a sad and dire sound. "Thane's a spectrum. One end, you have all the power in the world, none of the brains. On the other, you have the smartest man that ever lived. The key was keeping him numb, ready with answers and so far away from anger. We set him up like a patient in the world's calmest hospital."

"Wait, you kept him prisoner and forced him to answer your questions?"

"More than that, Thane gave us inventions. Ideas. Not every-thing, of course. He's not a god. But if we were stuck, we'd go to him for help puzzling out a solution."

Aegis wondered how Celice would handle this. The process of becoming an adult meant the gradual death of all your childhood fairy tales. Celice was well past the expiration date for those, but that last gasp of innocent belief, that the Paragons, and the Champions, were forces for good, Aegis believed she still bought that. Hoped she did.

Because Celice was the future, and if she gave up on them . . .

"I get it," Celice took Aegis's tack of looking towards the ocean. "You're not perfect. I know that. Neither is anyone else."

"You are."

"You get to say that because you're my dad, but I'm not. You did what needed to be done."

She'd hardened. More than Aegis thought. Celice's acceptance made him proud, a sick pride, sadness at the edges. Her mother would've been so disappointed to see this, to see Celice jaded enough to buy into the reality Aegis had made for her. Yet, if her mother had done the same, maybe she'd still be alive.

"We're done with that now," Aegis said. "We've made enough progress. Thane's too dangerous to be worth the risk."

"So you want to kill him now."

"He murdered your mother, Celice. It's long past time he paid for it."

26

An Interesting Offer

Gordon finally tossed Kat a line that morning, though she technically didn't see it till the afternoon. Sleeping way too late happened when, flush with a victory and annoyed at an anomaly's escape, Kat accepted way too many drinks from people who'd just made their reps on her performance. Sandra kept Kat from getting too far gone, though, and a pod took her the rest of the way home.

Seeker's restless licks were a poor hangover remedy, so Kat, after reading Gordon's message three or four times and figuring it didn't have any hidden meanings, forced herself out of bed, popped After-Effects pills to dull the headache, and tromped along a snow-coated sidewalk after her manic dog.

Found him. Not caught, yet. You still have a chance Kat! - Gordon

Sure she did. No name. No leads. No interest. Gradually, as happened when she went on these walks past rows and rows of row houses in her neighborhood, a newer design for density over autonomy, Kat turned over last night and stewed in it.

She'd failed, and that was it. Been sloppy. She'd traced three other anomalies from *Carver's* before, two involving fights like last night's. Those anomalies had given up their gifts in the struggle, and when Tracy or the other bouncers kicked the anomaly out, Kat had been ready to follow. Calvin had split without wasting a second. Which meant he knew all about trackers.

Seeker, ahead, spied another dog at the opposite corner and tugged hard on the leash. Advancing technology still hadn't changed the core features and drawbacks of a strong cord attached to a collar, and Seeker took advantage, dragging Kat after him. The sudden speed corresponded to a slick patch beneath the snow to send Kat stumbling forward, with just enough control to throw herself to the side, into a snowbank.

In a way, the ice-cold white stuff killed her headache more effectively than the pills. In another way, the snow went down her coat, stuck to her leggings and, Kat learned when Seeker started licking, to her face.

"Are you all right?" the dog walker, a woman who looked like she'd seen twice as many years as Kat and didn't bother trying to hide it, said.

Vaguely, Kat thought the woman might be her mom's age, if her mom was still around. The wispy blond hair sneaking out from beneath the woman's cotton cap wouldn't have matched her family's brunette, but the rest would be close.

"I'll live." Kat rotated, pushed herself up rather than take the offered hand. Last thing she'd want is to pull the woman down as she stood up, especially with Seeker still making frenzied attempts to slobber off her face. "Thanks."

"Brave to own a husky around here," the woman nodded at her own, much smaller puppy, who looked at Seeker with fear and awe. "Don't they have a lot of energy?"

"See for yourself."

Seeker obliged, giving the woman a standing greeting as soon as she looked his way. She laughed, which was more than what Kat would've expected. After a lick, the woman ran her hand through Seeker's fur and the husky snapped his mouth shut, settling back to the ground and dropping to a placid sit. He looked at the woman like he expected, and would obey, a command.

Kat drew the stun gun she kept loaded and ready at all times, pointed it at the woman. Arms iron, aim steady. "Want to tell me what you're doing to my dog?"

The woman still smiled, but her face grew a cool edge, matching the weather. "Just settling him down. He looked like he could use it. As could you."

If Kat thought she could get away with it, she would twist her wrist and let the Tama capture the woman's face, match her to the tracker database. But right now, without her tracker contacts, her suit and other gear, she didn't want an open fight in the streets with an unknown anomaly.

"You're going to step away from him right now," Kat said, and the woman obliged, giving Seeker a solid meter of space. "This isn't a chance encounter, is it?"

Threatening her elders. One more childhood lesson dying in the harsh environs of her adult life.

"As perceptive as your rank would indicate. The best tracker in the area, I gather." The woman nodded at Kat's gun. "You can put that away now. I'm not here to hurt you."

"I'll decide that."

"If we wanted it, you'd already be dead." The woman ran her eyes around Kat, as if to point out there were hidden allies waiting for an ambush. "This is an invitation, not an assassination."

"Who even are you?" Kat said.

"We're interested in the anomaly you're tracking. He is dangerous, but in the right hands, potentially everything," the woman said. Kat noticed, now, that the woman's small dog was as placid as Seeker, sitting there without making a sound. Creepy. "We have tried to bring him in, but haven't managed to succeed. We would like your help."

"Didn't answer my question."

Kat continued running through possible organizations that would hire untraced anomalies to make threats on trackers. That behavior could get you on the Paragons's bad side, which would be any company's literal end. Unless you were already blacklisted and didn't care, and the orgs still in operation that could claim both that and tangle with anomalies . . .

"You're answering it yourself," the woman replied. "That doesn't matter. What does is our shared target. Left at large, he could lose focus. Cause a major disaster without realizing it. He needs guidance."

"Then he needs tracing. The Paragons will help him."

"The Paragons will use him. You know this. You get the rep statements every day. They will task him to one job after another until his potential is wasted."

"Sounds like your problem, maybe his. Definitely not mine." Kat clicked her tongue, a sound Seeker should respond to, and, much to Kat's relief, the dog snapped out of his funk, sensed the situation, and rose, standing next to Kat and giving a low growl. "Try again."

At last the woman's composure broke. Maybe it was Seeker's renewed animation, maybe Kat's stun gun had worn down her reserve, but either way she turned and sat on the thick snow bank. Looked at her hands holding the dogs leash.

"My name is Beth. I'm part of the Elementals. I'm sure you know who we are."

Who didn't? If anything, the admission made Kat grip her gun tighter. She risked a quick glance behind her, just empty sidewalk. No pods. In a way, the empty street made the surest evidence Beth told the truth—no part of Chicago stayed this deserted for long.

The Elementals were bad news. A group trackers were warned to stay away from, even though they consisted of un-traced anomalies. The whole reason the Champions, and by extension, the Paragons ran things now lay in the sheer power of anomalies working together. The Elementals had that same power, if not the resources. With all her gear, Kat didn't fear going up against one, maybe two anomalies. But five? A dozen?

"Name's Kat, but I guess you know that already. And I'm familiar," Kat said, still holding that gun. "If you're after this guy, why don't you take him?"

"You could say that we're more into organic recruitment," Beth answered. "You're the ones who like to take people against their will."

"Only ones like you."

"Of course that's what you believe," Beth pulled back the right sleeve on her sky blue jacket, looked at her Tama. "As much as I'd like to debate our philosophies, I'll get right to the point."

"I'm listening."

"We're prepared to give you intelligence you don't have. Information that should let you find the anomaly. In exchange, we want you to capture him. Subdue him."

"But no trace, right?"

"No trace. You'll hand him over to us." Beth went back to that pitying, haughty smile she played so well. "You'll get your reps, of course."

The offer hung in the air, its only companion the wind and the two-streets distant whistle of the mag-lev train flowing to a stop. The terms were, to put it mildly, crap. An anomaly with the talents to get this interest from the Elementals would, no doubt, be worth far more over a lifetime working for the Paragons. Then again, did Kat want to get on the bad side of a secretive anomaly organization?

Eh. She didn't have to make that decision now.

"All right. I'll play. When will you deliver?" Kat said.

"Right now." Beth tapped on her Tama, and Kat's own issued a bright chirp a second later.

Kat didn't look at it. Not that stupid. Instead, she kept the stun gun leveled at Beth and waited. Either Beth would get up and walk away, the deal concluded, or things would get messy. Instead, Beth stood, "Come on, Fluff. Time to get you inside where it's warm."

The Elemental turned her back on Kat and walked off down the street, keeping her eyes forward. Kat let her get half a block away before she did a slow turn around, watching the windows, the roofs. Hunting for eyes. She found none. Seeker seemed on edge, but the husky made no moves in any direction. No immediate threats, then.

"Time to go, buddy," Kat said, and the two hot-stepped it back to the apartment.

As soon as she made it inside, Kat dropped Seeker's leash and let him loose to find any potential intruders while she made a mad run for her closet. In record time, she slipped on her suit, her gadgets, her contacts. Armored, armed, and breathing hard, Kat sat on her bed and stared out the window.

Gray sky. Empty, except for a drone passing by. Her contacts identified zero threats, and when she looked over her apartment, they detected no unusual footprints, aside from Gordon's leftover impressions. No strange molecules in the air from deodorants, perfumes, or a deadly, silent gas. Maybe the Elementals were making the offer in sincerity. They might not be planning to kill her.

Gordon. His tip had been wrong, so maybe he wasn't anywhere close. Gordon matched her tracker rank, but they'd come to her instead. Because Kat lived here? Because she didn't seem quite as immersed in Paragon orthodoxy as Gordon? She dashed off a quick message to him anyway, asking if he was all right.

Then, finally, Kat took a look at the intelligence. Saw what the Elementals had decided to give her.

Kat blew up the message on her big monitors, which allowed her to tap through the numerous links to photos, videos. From the first one, she knew. Calvin. The confirmation didn't surprise her—Kat had a hunch about the man fighting alone in *Carver's* bar, and thus far, her hunches had been solid. Suddenly she was glad Calvin hadn't decided to go nuclear last night and use his ability —if the Elementals thought he was so dangerous, Kat might not have enjoyed being on the wrong end of it.

The first real surprise: Calvin was his real name. The man had chosen it when it came time to register for the standard anomaly test. Paragons dragged every kid past puberty to various proving centers where physical extremes were delivered in an attempt to force out powers. Unsuspecting anomalies tended to get themselves traced then and there. Others, ones who hid their growth from parents or school officials, or who just developed abilities later, had a really bad day.

"Nope. Not going back there," Kat said to herself, and Seeker, catching some snoozes on the bed, huffed in agreement.

Rough memories for her. Same for Calvin, it looked like.

The Elementals had put together a pretty complete package, and Kat filled in the blanks with her own tracker access to Paragon data. Calvin had bounced from one family to the next as a kid, primarily by running away. Starting by age eight, it seemed Calvin had attracted a serious case of wanderlust and learned how to lie well enough to feed it. He'd show up somewhere, give a false last name, always calling himself Calvin, and then make whatever use he could of a place, of a people, before leaving again.

Calvin had aced his anomaly exam too—no powers determined. Either he'd arrived at his valuable abilities later, or he'd been skilled enough to keep them under wraps. Given the fight last night, Kat knew which way she'd bet.

So then, what was the thread? The Elementals didn't spell it out, which meant Kat spent the afternoon and evening piecing together Calvin's life. By the end, she could've given a dissertation on his interests: popular entertainment, obscure wildlife reserves, and dives like *Carver's*. He had no blood family that anyone knew, and he'd trekked from Pacifica's west coast all the way here on a shoestring rep account kept afloat by strange, random payments from individuals that Calvin seemed to associate with for brief instants and then never again.

Of all the things she read, the last bit felt familiar. Anomalies had to earn reps somehow, and because most who refused to join in with the Paragons found themselves outside the traditional means-earning methods, they prostituted their powers. And once you sold your ability, the buyer could blackmail you, threaten to turn you in to the Paragons, and thus you made your way on to the next place. A life of desperation, sure, but a free one.

Calvin, though, had dreams. The one thing in common with his travels were their end goal: Calvin found his way to the conventions. The comics, the movies, the spectacles. Kat didn't know what he hoped to find there, but he kept going. And it just so happened one opened in Chicago tomorrow. One of the biggest in Atlantis.

Guess she'd have to get a pass.

The Price Of Progress

Several years into his fifth decade and Zhan-Yo still considered the glass-walled, window-lit top floor of Ziran's headquarters his father's office rather than his own. The ghost lingered in the possessions, like the black desk, the digital portraits shifting between images of his father's family—Zhan-Yo never bothered with a family to replace them—and the telekinetic carpet that took its navy fabric and overlaid it with a circuit board's branching silver pathways. Anywhere else, the office's odes to technology would feel heavy, forced. Ridiculous.

But his father believed in paying homage to what brought you success, and Zhan-Yo couldn't argue that Ziran had done just that.

"Z," the secretary said. "Mrs. Vanne is on her way up now for your nine o'clock."

Levers needed pulling. Zhan-Yo had spent most of his corporate life tying together the plans and pieces needed so Ziran, in the moment, could make its push to restore power to those who rightly deserved it. That moment, with a strong push from Sylvie, had arrived. Which meant secrets that had been hidden, plans that had made little sense to outsiders at the time Ziran embarked on them, would show their true purpose. Yet, to achieve all this, Zhan-Yo had to wear a full suit. Had to sit in a large chair with the city at his back and look everything like the stereotypical leader he didn't want to be. A revolutionary, sure. A guide to a better future, absolutely. But the wool made him itch, and he found the tight shoes, the tie and collar restrictive. A culture that had belonged to his father and not to him.

He stood when Anna Vanne came into his office several minutes later, the tall woman brushing away her Tama's projected schedule as she walked through the glass door his secretary opened for her. Zhan-Yo gave her a short bow, shoulders only, and she reciprocated with a nod.

"It's good to see you," Anna began, settling into one of the pair of plush gray chairs, which had neon blue running along the sides as the arbitrary concession to sci-fi trappings, and giving Zhan-Yo the sort of smile that asked *what the hell are you doing here?*

Zhan-Yo couldn't fault her for it. He had an earned reputation of being a phantom, floating in for a meeting and disappearing again, reachable more by Tama than by staking out his office. Running a giant company mattered less where he was physically, and he showed as much to Anna with a look towards the window behind him, as if that's where his soul truly belonged.

"I'm not here often because I have you to manage this place, and you do it very well." Zhan-Yo firmly believed in the power of compliments to inoculate against forthcoming difficulties. "Yet, circumstances are changing." A breath as Zhan-Yo pieced together the next sentence. "Our true project is about to begin."

Vague, and to anyone without some very specific knowledge, useless. You didn't get to lead technology company without picking up some suspicions on the way, especially if you were plotting to overthrow society's current order. Anna caught the reference— Zhan-Yo could tell by the momentary freeze, her searching look as she unpacked what he just said. Then, with a tilt of her head and a slight sigh, like a parent coming to terms with their child's choice, Anna let him know to continue.

"I know this is coming as a surprise, but events like this one do not have the luxury of time. We planned, and now it's time to follow those designs." Zhan-Yo tapped the surface of the desk, which had been overlaid with a projection screen a few years back. The slight cerulean haze shifted to mirror his Tama, and the taps brought up a three-pronged series of steps. "Take this. It's the same as the one we gave you a long time ago, but the specifics have been added."

Anna held her own Tama—on her right wrist, unusual—over the projection. It beeped a second later, confirming the data transfer, and she withdrew her arm, looking at it as if it had become a rotten thing.

"Once we start this, it will be hard to reverse," Anna said. "A lot of people won't make it."

"Only if we fail."

"If we succeed, Z." Anna dropped the employee facade and spoke like an equal, like a person worried for what they knew and valued. "If this works, then who knows what will be left? What kind of work, what kind of anything?"

"Are you doubting us now?"

"I'm concerned." Anna took a look behind her, but the only other on this level was his secretary, a luxury Zhan-Yo demanded. "Wexley isn't pushing you to this?"

"He has taken some convincing." Zhan-Yo sat forward, clasped his hands level against the desk so that they bled into the projection. Trust, confidence, strength. Appearance wasn't everything, but it didn't hurt either. "We are not making this choice lightly, Anna. But neither do we want to be so cautious as to miss our chance."

"You're not going to tell me everything."

Zhan-Yo said nothing. The more Anna knew, the more she risked. She laughed, then, rubbed her nose and shook her head.

"You know, Damian and I, we have two children. Four, six. Little girls."

"I know."

He'd sent them birthday cards every year, with a piece of matcha candy from Japan, a flavor they probably hated but that he'd loved growing up. Signed each one personally.

"I didn't think this would ever happen. I thought, when I took this job, when you told me what was possible, that it was a dream.

That I'd be gone, that they'd be older." Anna's hands kneaded the edges of her skirt while she spoke. "I don't want to raise them in chaos, Z."

"I understand. Unfortunately, the rest of the world will not wait for you to be ready."

"All due respect, but you don't have a family. You don't understand at all."

Anger. Fear. Frustration. He'd expected all of those things, felt each himself as Sylvie sent him every update on her progress. Recruiting morally flexible soldiers, importing weapons long-since banned by Paragons. Steps on a one-way stair that, at its end, would likely mean the destruction of Ziran, would likely mean the disruption and dissolution of so many structures depended on by Anna and her family.

But it would mean her children would have a say in their future world.

"Do you know, Anna, how I grew up?" Zhan-Yo said. A digression would cost him time, but if it maintained Anna's loyalty, then time was a small price. "What my parents did to protect me from change?"

Anna didn't speak, but ice came through when she shook her head. He'd broken so many other's resistance, industry titans with stakes as high or higher than Anna, than his own. Zhan-Yo could persuade her too.

"I began in one world and became an adult in another. From the earliest available age, because of my parent's efforts, I had every advantage. Teachers told me I would be able to decide for myself how to live my life. That I would have a voice in the direction of the world, or at least my country, my city. Instead, when I finally achieved the degrees, the station to effect that change, the Paragons took it all from me. My parents told me to give in, like them. We had too much to lose. It took me decades to realize that I'd already lost the most valuable thing."

"Your idealism blinds you, Z." Anna countered. "Who cares what the Paragons do so long as we're able to be happy? Safe and healthy?"

"For now, maybe. But what happens if the Paragons decide normals aren't welcome? They would take everything you have and there would be nothing you could do to stop it."

"Why would they? Have you asked yourself that, with this grand plan of yours? You talk like this great injustice has been perpetrated, but I don't see it. Anywhere."

"Because we're blind. My parents were, I was. You have to see that we're pawns, Anna. Little pieces on a board, easily sacrificed." Zhan-Yo looked at his hands. His normal hands. "No ability, and with no ability, our place in this world is set."

Anna looked like she wanted to make another smart comment, but she held back. Waited.

"Your children may be normal, may be anomalies." Zhan-Yo had to be careful here. Make his point without saying anything that would trip a listener. "That is not your choice. Their future is. You can give them a world to enjoy, or you can let them be prisoners like us."

A little ridiculous. Prone to falling apart if Anna chose to pick at the phrase. But an emotional appeal trumped a logical one, and Anna, if she didn't buy it, at least accepted it with a look towards the floor, a slow stand from the chair.

"I understand. I don't agree, but I understand."

"Then we can trust you?"

"I will execute the plan. Ziran will survive as long as it can."

"That is all I ask. Thank you, Anna."

Another set of exchanged, slight bows, and Anna walked out of his office. To the elevators and down. Zhan-Yo remained standing until she disappeared, then asked the secretary to fetch him a glass of water.

"Will she do it?" Wexley asked over the Tamas a few minutes later, after Zhan-Yo sent a message that the meeting had ended.

"I think so," Zhan-Yo replied. "Keep her watched. We are in her home, yes?"

"Have been since we promoted her."

"Then keep the ears up. We'll need as much warning as possible if she turns. It's the children, Wexley."

"Doesn't she have two?"

He didn't know that about Anna? Zhan-Yo frowned. Wexley ought to understand his officers, what made them come to work every day and what they hoped would be their's tomorrow. He'd have to learn that before Zhan-Yo would ever let him lead Ziran. If there was a Ziran to lead.

"Watch them too. If they have struggles, if there are vulnerable opportunities."

"I understand."

That, Wexley did know. If Anna proved unreliable, if her loyalty wavered, what made her come to work every day could be used to keep her here. An unfortunate turn, but not a dire one. The children would not need to be harmed. Hopefully.

"Are you going to be in the office much longer?" Wexley was asking. "There are a couple of meetings this afternoon I could use you in."

"Send them, but I will be remote," Zhan-Yo said. "There is a class I am taking."

"A class?"

"For my health. Keep me informed, Wexley."

"Of course."

The Tamas clicked off as the secretary came back with the water. Zhan-Yo gulped it down, looked at it, marveled at how the clear liquid could hold everything the anomalies needed to grow. How the chances of billions came through what they drank every day. A simple additive, a possible mutation, and human history changed forever.

If a little bit of water could do it, then why couldn't he?

28

All Anomaly

Millions of marbles splashed with every possible color coiled up through the void. Mynx watched them climb until they cycled back to the bottom, well beneath the blue-gray expanse at her feet, and began the journey again. The endless travel of an organized database being analyzed. Reeves had set it in motion, and, dodging reality's stress, Mynx had gone to see it.

She went closer to the helix, enjoying how, in this place, her aching bones never followed. Mynx didn't have to breathe through the small cold she was getting over, or the dried skin itching on her left knee. And when Mynx reached towards those marbles, her arm grew the extra meter it needed to enter.

Mynx didn't feel the orb she grabbed, not through touch, anyway. More like its contents filtered through her fingers to her mind, allowing Mynx to understand data held within. The secrets contained an anomaly, this one named Sarah, who had passed some years ago. She'd made it to an old age, the record said, a grandmother with the trivial ability to change the flavor of anything she happened to drink. Water could become cherry. Wine, the most perfect blend every time.

"Imagine how much her spit would have been worth." Mynx

said, though there weren't really words in here. More like she chose to display her thoughts in a text that her companion, the ever-present Reeves, could read. "A trick to market, I guess."

"There's not much information on attempts to sell saliva to consumers." Reeves' reply floated by in big block letters, bracketed to ensure its clear status as a comment.

"Almost hard to believe."

Mynx put Sarah's marble back in the helix. As soon as she let go, the invisible current pulled it up as if it had never left. Mynx watched it move. Nobody else in humanity's history had seen this before, been here before. It was likely no one else ever would. Then again, with the anomalies, unique experiences were becoming less, well, unique.

"Are you ready?" Reeves sent another word batch floating by. "I have additional tests ready to perform, but they will alter the database."

"You'll get your copies."

Even in here, work never truly went away.

Mynx grew, stretched taller and taller until the cycling anomaly DNA, their lives and families, fit in her hand. Security necessitated precautions, like keeping Reeves from copying this database. Otherwise the AI could have done this without a moment's effort, sparing Mynx the time.

And costing her the fun.

"Pause your programs," Mynx said. "We wouldn't want to corrupt this one."

"There is always the back-up."

"Remind me to wipe that from your memory," Mynx said. "It's disconnected for a reason."

Disconnected, stored on isolated flash memory deep inside the Factory. Every so often, on dates Mynx tracked on an old-style, analog calendar, she would download the database to a tiny card, take it down there, and copy it over. Three separate passcodes were necessary to get in, and a single wrong entry deleted the stored data-base. Not a big deal when you had a new copy right there in your hand, but a thief would find it annoying.

Mynx picked up the helix—from this size it looked almost like a shimmering silver gemstone—and put her hands together, covering it completely. She passed the command through her fingers—her own bio-markers serving as the keys to the locks here—and felt the functions pouring back as the database built a new version. Millions of stories copied over in about a minute, and when Mynx turned her left hand over, both held identical helix copies.

"How many?" Mynx asked.

"For optimal run times, a half dozen should suffice."

"Then a half dozen you shall have."

Reeves stayed quiet till Mynx completed the copies, till she set each of them down and Reeves' programs began their work. While the original settled back into its churning swirl, the others turned to different colors, and some lost marbles entirely as Reeves' calculations, hunting for commonalities between the anomalies, searching for genetic markers that might be used to halt, or even reverse the biological process that destroyed all living things, nixed failing samples.

Mynx shrunk, watched the spins. She could reach into any one of them and catch the output, try to process it, but this much raw data would be meaningless. A cloud of numbers, text, and images.

"There are dangers to this you should be aware of, Mynx," Reeves said.

"I know."

"What shall I do if I find them?"

Commonalities to defeat disease, fight aging were one possibility. Anomalies had their benefits provided through quirks of mutations at cellular levels. What had been changed, could change again. If Reeves found an easy way to disable those same genetic quirks, then this project might not lead to the saving of lives, but to ending them.

"Secure it. Flag for my review."

"No deletion?"

"Anything you discover could be found by someone else," Mynx said. "I'd prefer to know, and to prepare, than stay in the dark." Speaking of dark, she'd been in this void too long. There were other things to do, other programs to play with. "I'm backing out."

"I am ready."

Leaving her void felt, for the briefest moment, like a lightspeed plunge through the universe. Everything flashed for a hot second and then Mynx sat back in her chair, centered in the Factory floor. A workstation without a monitor occupied the desk in front of her. Useless to anyone else. Mynx could stick out her hand, follow the black box and its network cable to just about any part of her facility. Now, though, she stood. Stretched.

Dinner approached, and dropping into cyberspace didn't stop her body from demanding calories.

The salad Reeves' drones prepared contained much that began in nature, but nothing that finished natural. Whether the goat cheese texture had been optimized to hit perfect creaminess or the strawberries massaged to a scintillating sweet and juicy blend, refined algorithms and scientific progress optimized every bite Mynx ate. That she devoured the meal while overlooking a world largely left to its natural devices—the ocean—gave her a small smile.

"We haven't conquered all of you," Mynx said to those far off waters. "Yet."

After she finished, and when a drone had replaced the cleared plate with her after-dinner merlot, whose heavyweight flavor helped set Mynx up for sleep, the projection table lit up with an incoming message. A little late to be any Paragon business, but other than Denise calling again begging for access, Mynx wasn't sure who else it would be.

"Answer it."

Celice's face sprang up out of the table, bright in the gasping leftovers of twilight. Unlike Mynx, Celice did not look the least bit calm. Her red eyes hunted for Mynx, she nibbled on her lower lip, a habit Mynx thought she'd kicked by now, and her hair had neglect's scattered look.

"Mynx!" Celice started, and Mynx, boosted by the wine, wanted to be sarcastic but held her tongue. "We're in trouble."

"Is it Thane?" Mynx had lost track of that monster while she'd vanished inside the Factory. A sloppy move, and the frustration must have shown because Celice shook her head quick.

"No, I mean, it is. But I don't need *you* for that. My dad has Thane bottled up in some fortress. I think he's going to try and blow it up. Kill Thane." Mynx wanted to ask how, but Celice kept right on rolling. "Here's the thing, he's pulling most of our drones away, and I need more. Can I place an emergency order?"

"There are channels for that." The blunt answer came as Mynx wondered how Aegis planned to kill Thane, a creature the Champions had all decided was probably invulnerable unless surprised. Aegis already knew dropping bombs wouldn't do the job.

"Mynx, the entire northeast has no eyes and ears right now. Our Paragons are operating blind, the ones that haven't been pulled. Already I'm getting reports of crime picking up. We need help."

"Then I'll send you the reserves and build new ones to replace them," Mynx said, then shrugged away Thane for the person at hand. "Celice, are you all right?"

Celice paused, then fell into a weak smile. "Ever have one of those days when your world gets torn apart?"

"When I was your age, all the time. What happened?"

Rather than answer her question, Celice glanced at something outside the projection window. Squinted at it, and just as Mynx was about to repeat the question, Celice snapped her face back into the frame.

"Mynx, thanks for the drones. I'm getting a high priority from Boston, near where dad's at. I'll talk later."

And with that, Celice winked out. Mynx stared at the space for a minute. Then set her wine down.

Trying to kill Thane? What was Aegis thinking?

"Reeves, prep the jet. I'm going back east."

"Again? And at this hour?"

"I'll catch a nap on the way."

A Champion's life. What a treat.

29

Catch The Killer

Thane's improvised base stood at the road's end, his home and the hill rising up behind it shadowed by a slow going moon. The Paragons cut the power, making the mansion, quite literally, dark. Pixie said an orange glow had appeared for a few minutes—a rogue attempt at starting a fire, most likely—but its subsequent death showed Thane either had little fuel or lacked the will to burn pieces of his own, stolen, home. Regardless, Aegis had a more welcome sight in the moon's silver; drones had been floating in throughout the day and now bobbed in a ring around the mansion. Every so often one would break away, soaring to a nearby charging station set up to deliver rapid energy. The gap would as often be replaced by a new drone as the returning one, and all focused their aim down at Thane.

"You don't think he'd survive all this, do you?" Pixie asked. "I've never seen this much firepower."

"Because Thane's the only one that deserves it." Aegis checked his Tama. It showed, on his left wrist, the drone formation and its climbing numbers. "We can't let him get away."

"There's no chance. We have so many Paragons, so many—"

"It took eight Champions last time. It's only me here now," Aegis said.

Even with all eight Champions, subduing Thane enough for the monster to shrivel down to his more compact, more vulnerable self took coordination Aegis didn't see happening among the Paragons today. Several dozen pulled a night shift with him now. Aegis had only slept a couple of hours after Celice left to head back to New York, but coffee still worked miracles, even on a body as beaten up as his, and Aegis had no idea what most of these Paragons could do.

How could Aegis design a strategy without knowing his own side, much less any tricks that motley crew Thane had holed up in there with him could pull off?

"All eight? I've never heard of that fight." Pixie knew better than to ask the question straight out. "Must have been hidden."

"With good reason."

Aegis didn't expound on it. Didn't want to go back down that path. It'd been fun, defending the planet as a team, but when the existential threats went away, more mundane matters split them apart. Aegis didn't regret it—he'd wound up with the best world, and lost all the drama.

His Tama beeped, set for this particular event to sound like an obnoxious trumpet, almost had Aegis jump. Almost. The eight Champions had their difficulties, but Mynx had always been there for him. And now she'd arrived.

"Took you long enough," Aegis said as Mynx climbed left her custom jet. He never understood why she'd designed the craft to hold only a single person. All the potential joyrides that had been lost because her needle-nosed plane lacked a backseat. "I was about to go ahead without you."

"Fine by me," Mynx said, wrapping Aegis in a hug even though it'd only been a couple of days since they'd last seen each other. Then again, with professions like theirs, it might be good to squeeze the affection out of every moment. He returned it. "Saving the day looks good too."

"As if you've ever cared about looks."

"Hey, I run a whole region too. Wouldn't hurt to remind them why."

If that was her goal, Mynx should have broadcast her outfit across Pacifica. She'd gone full battle suit, but unlike the clunkier versions from her past, this set showed her evolution in both form and function. While black fabric, Aegis wouldn't dare assume it was cotton or some other common thread, formed the base, gold nodes and lines wrapped and ran around her, culminating in small circles in various spots. In short, Mynx looked like a badass microchip.

"So what can I get you?" Aegis said, gesturing towards the encampment. "We've got tactical vests, arms, ammunition?"

"If I wanted to look like you, I would have come that way," Mynx said. "Instead, I figured this would make a good demo for my newest mech."

Aegis had long since stopped treating Mynx with skepticism—getting proved wrong so many times will do that to you—but Aegis couldn't see a single one of Mynx's hulking monstrosities around. That plane certainly couldn't have carried it. By the time he turned his questioning eyes back to Mynx, she held a grin.

"Want to see it?"

Aegis shook his head, sighing, "Just do it already. We have a villain to destroy, remember?"

"We're old, not humorless," Mynx replied. "Don't be a snot."

"A snot? What are you, a five year-old?"

Mynx, confirming Aegis's assertion, stuck out her tongue, then tapped on her left wrist, where what Aegis had assumed was another node turned out to be a disguised Tama. The effect made itself known by Paragons shouting around them, and Aegis followed their looks up at the drones. The four closest to them broke free from the ring and glided down towards Mynx.

"Your new toy?" Aegis asked.

"My friends are everywhere. Easier than packing a suit every time I have to come save you."

The drones settled in above Mynx, rotating their structures—all different configurations, meant for suppression, assault, protection and surveillance—in a slow orbit around their creator. Mynx looked them over for a moment, then stuck out her left arm. The smallest drone, a model Aegis knew as 'Eyes', swooped its meter-long curving arc of a reflective body down. The drone settled against Mynx's arm, covering it, and, though Aegis couldn't see it, he heard the sounds of metal tightening, locking in.

"The nodes," Mynx clarified as Aegis watched. "I've been writing the code into all the models for the last few years. It's quite cool, is it not?"

"Fancy."

Mynx held out her left arm and, apparently following orders, the protection drone—a flat, armored slate coated in small, stunning nubs and twice as large as its spying brother, came down and took its place on Mynx's right arm. The result looked so ridiculous, with Mynx's head tiny between the two machines, that Aegis cracked a laugh.

"Have to say, Mynx, this isn't one of your prettier projects."

"Function over form, Aegis."

"Sure."

With her two arms spread, the pair of drones she'd already connected with triggered a minor burst of their jets, no doubt limited so as not to fry Mynx, and hovered her a meter off the ground. This proved enough space for the latter two, ones bristling with more lethal weaponry, to attach themselves to her legs and up along her torso. By the end, Mynx looked like a cartoon character from Aegis's youth, albeit even more mismatched. A robot warrior made by someone with no sense of symmetry.

"So maybe I have some kinks to iron out," Mynx said, her head barely visible in the mess of metal. "But it's going to work."

"Just don't get yourself, or us, killed." With the strange spectacle of his friend merging with drones done with, Aegis turned back to the waiting Paragons. "Get ready. I'm going to give Thane one last chance."

FOR THE SECOND TIME, Aegis walked alone along the road towards Thane's stolen home. Unlike the first time, he felt whole. If not rested, then not hurt. His body had returned itself to working order, and, with the drones overhead, his mind had the calm that came with overwhelming firepower. What a difference that made. For so long, even after they'd established the Paragons, the Champions, Aegis had fought out-manned, out-gunned, and dependent on his anomaly ability to keep himself alive. Did the odds rest in the hero, or the cause? Aegis had to believe in the latter.

Despite missing lights, Thane's sentries told Aegis to stop with a single shot. A loud crack in the quiet night, and a spark breaking off the ground in front of Aegis had him stop and seek out, with no success, the source. In the dark, and having no knowledge of their weapons, made it difficult to gauge whether Aegis stood in their firing range or not.

Best assume he did.

"Thane!" Aegis could still get a pretty good yell out. The neighboring trees seemed to rustle in response, sending snow rolling to the ground. "You're out of time!"

Threats would be wasted on Thane. He wouldn't cower, or surrender. However, the man, or monster, would talk until fire started being thrown around. Get Thane outside, let him monologue his way into distraction and Aegis would have the opportunity he needed to blast Thane away.

Aegis waited one minute, then two. Negotiated a truce with the hunger pangs in his stomach—Aegis hadn't had a real meal since that lobster roll—and clenched his fists again and again to keep them warm. Kept his gaze straight, staring at that old collection of brick and stone, wood and windows, gone far past its prime, if it ever really had one. Took one more breath, at the third minute, to try another shout.

"Aegis! My friend!" Thane insisted on the ridiculous label for their relationship. The friendship might have been true once, but that was so long ago, felt so many worlds ago, that it was meaningless now. "Have you finally decided to let me go?"

Aegis searched for and failed to find Thane somewhere on the rock ledges. The moon had become less helpful with creeping winter clouds. Not for the first time, Aegis wished he'd remembered to request night-vision gear. The drones would have no problem picking their targets, and the Paragons would shower the place in light once a fight began for shock-and-awe, but that did nothing to help Aegis now. So he kept his face straight and hoped Thane was somewhere in front.

"You know we can't do that." Delivering straight sentences in a shout felt wrong, but there wasn't exactly another option. "Either surrender, you and all of your associates you haven't killed in there, or we're going to take you out."

"Aegis. Come now. Must we start with the threats already? What happened to the negotiations? The barters back and forth?"

"That only works if you have something to trade."

"But I do! Your lives!"

There we go. That was the Thane Aegis knew. The man could only resist a cocky boast for so long. Aegis figured the creeping madness of Thane's angry side had engaged in a steady rot of the man's sanity, and who knew when it would gain complete control.

"Last chance, Thane. Yes or no. The world can't risk you free."

"Ah, the world. What a place you've made!" Thane's voice sounded like it'd moved, as if the man walked across the ramparts. "For all your talk about how dangerous I am, do you ever turn that lens on yourself? How many cities have you cowed with your power? How long would it take Mynx—yes, I see her back there— to topple civilization with her incessant army of drones? Who, I ask you, is the real threat?"

This guy never stopped. Never. But Aegis felt sure Thane had left the house, which made him as vulnerable as the Paragons were going to get. Aegis tapped his Tama. A pre-set message beamed out near-field to all Tamas with a Paragon code set for the operation, one Pixie had chosen: IceMine. Every armband computer would start shivering or beeping, depending on the user's preference, in a second. In the moment after that, well, they'd see whether Thane had the strength he claimed.

"Let's find out!" Aegis broke into a run as he cried the words, pulling two energy rods from holsters on his belt. He preferred his nigh-invulnerable fists, but against someone like Thane, heavier tools were required. Twisting his wrists uncorked the batteries and the half-meter long rods shone red to indicate their lethal electric dose.

"Mynx," Aegis spoke towards his Tama as he ran. "Take him out."

Before Aegis's next step hit the ground, the night died. Overhead, some three dozen drones flared their lights, each one meant to stun a potential criminal long enough for those same drones to knock them out. The lights weren't aimed directly at Aegis, so he saw a clear path, crystal snow leading towards the road-split rock retaining walls.

On those walls, Thane's men, at least twenty—which prompted other questions that Aegis quashed—stumbled around, their long guns flailing. Some managed to get off shots that, in their total lack of accuracy, were as dangerous to themselves as to the Paragons. Thane, though, had vanished.

By Aegis's fourth step, with plenty to go, the drones began the second phase. Darts, energy bolts, and even a few gas grenades, depending on the drone model, rained down on Thane's hapless force. Non-lethal. Aegis hadn't given that order, because, in his opinion, anyone who decided to take up arms with Thane forfeited their life, but Mynx had always been a softy. Sprinkled in among them, with their greens, oranges, purples and rainbow starbursts were Paragons lucky enough to get a projection as their anomaly.

Unlike the drone shots, which hit with predictable power, the Paragon blasts did strange things. One orange ball, lobbed like it had physical weight, burst around a trio of Thane's men and unleashed spiderweb tendrils that caught, snarled, and wrapped up all three. Another, a fairy dust shower that zipped over Aegis's head with enough speed to move his hair, stopped just in front of a Thane soldier and proceeded to dive into the soldier's mouth. Rather than take a shot at a drone, the soldier whirled and began beating on his fellow man, using the rifle like a crude club.

Aegis dove into the mess, whacking with abandon. Thane's force had no cohesion, and Aegis heard no yelled commands. So instead it was carnage. Aegis, a drone armada, and dwindling enemies who started shouting their surrender before Aegis had even taken a hit. Instead, Aegis paused with his right rod over a cowering man—all had similar ragged winter clothes that looked like they'd come from a discount store—and searched for Thane.

"That wasn't so bad," Pixie said, rushing up behind him with most of the other Paragons.

"The real fight hasn't started." Aegis gestured to Thane's men. "Get them out."

A snap-crash-burst of breaking wood, glass, and sundered shingles closed Aegis's order. From the mansion's top, one now bearing a large hole in its center, jumped out the target. Four meters tall and with a body that presumed intense workouts at approximately all hours, Thane grappled with the roof for a second before making a leaping dive towards several drones. To Mynx's credit, her robots analyzed the new threat instantly and began to counter.

To Thane's credit, he was damn fast.

The drones didn't get away and Thane fell in between them, grabbing one apiece in his huge mitts. As Aegis moved towards Thane's landing spot, the monster hit the ground—Aegis felt a tremor—and launched his two drone grenades towards their still-floating brethren. Stored power, ammunition, and who knew what else exploded as the drones bashed through each other, raining sparks and liquid fire down around them. Shouts for help, medical attention, evacuation filled the air as Thane continued grabbing whatever he could and lobbing it at the drones.

The Paragon counterattack came hard and fast, a nova blast of everything they had. Aegis had cleared the kill order for Thane himself with everyone beforehand, and if ever there was motivation to give a target everything, it was the sight of Thane's giant, frothing body. Aegis pulled up short, mouth opening at the unleashed hell blasting its way to Thane. Those orange spider webs were there, and he thought he saw the fairy dust, but both of those paled next to everything from pure blue flame to raw, basic bullets fired from Thane's own, now stolen, rifles.

But out of all that still came thrown bricks, trees, whatever Thane could grab. He yelled now, too; long roars that showed more annoyance than actual pain. That gave Aegis the answer he already knew.

They couldn't kill Thane. Not like this.

"Stop!" Aegis called, his voice amplified by his Tama and beamed to everyone's own arms. "Switch to stun and restrain. Lethal is a no go!"

He dropped the rods; if all that firepower couldn't take out an angry Thane, then his beat sticks weren't going to. Instead Aegis pulled, from a holster around his back, what looked like a long syringe with a trigger on the end. A faint blue liquid sloshed in the weapon's tube, which ended in a diamond-pointed needle. Thane didn't have a monopoly on hard skin, but his existence had been the primary motivator for developing the weapon. Now, Aegis had a chance to use it. The change in tactics took a second to manifest with the heat cooling off as the drones swapped to stunning electricity, to grappling cables that struck and wrapped themselves around the now-visible Thane and tied his arms and legs to his aerial adversaries.

A move that gave Thane new ammunition.

With a wordless roar, Thane threw himself around, flinging his arms, kicking his legs, and sending the drones crashing into each other. Some scattered down to the ground, pushing the Paragons to save themselves and their friends rather than focus on the source. Chaos, disaster.

And a clean shot.

Aegis ducked as a drone's fiery crash swept over him, keeping the syringe ready in his right hand. His boots kept grip on the ice beneath the tossed snow, and in a few long lunges he'd nearly made it to Thane. Had almost managed to stab the monster when, with a howling spin, Thane lurched his gaping maw right at Aegis.

"You get uglier every time," Aegis said, cocking his arm to stab the syringe right into Thane's mouth.

Thane replied in a spit-filled roar, misshapen teeth coming right for Aegis in a bite from jaws wide enough to wrap around the Champion's head.

Until something big, messy, and metal crashed into Thane's side and knocked the monster to the ground. Aegis brushed Thane's saliva off his face and saw Mynx wielding her mismatched collection with what could have been beautiful precision if it wasn't, in fact, awkward engine blasts, stunning bolts, and clunky rocket dodges to avoid Thane's counter-punches.

Mynx took one right hook on the metal plating of her defensive drone, with Thane leaving massive dent, but rather than retreat, she used the strike's momentum to grab hold, with a steel cable launched from the attack drone wrapped around her right leg, of Thane's outstretched arm. She triggered all of her drones' jets, slammed herself towards the ground and rotated, sending Thane over her head in a windmilling move that ended with him crashing head-first into the ground.

A normal adversary, whipped around like that, would be either dead or out of the fight. Aegis figured Thane would be stunned for a few seconds or less, so he used them, dashing towards Mynx.

"Up and up!" Aegis shouted.

Mynx, standing, heard the call and held out her drone-coated right arm towards Aegis. He jumped, and Mynx tilted the arm, letting Aegis use the wide drone body as a ramp. He stepped over her head and kept going, up the drone on Mynx's left arm. As Aegis ran, the drone decoupled itself, boosting further upward so that when Aegis reached the end, when he jumped towards Thane, he flew more than three meters up in the air.

When Thane rose, shuffling snow off his back, to his full height, when Thane turned towards Mynx with every intention of pounding her into oblivion, Thane saw Aegis's flying form streaking towards him, plunging the diamond syringe into one of the few, slightly, vulnerable parts of Thane's massive, angry body: his neck.

Aegis didn't hang on. He drove the syringe in, pulled the trigger, and dropped, and as soon as he hit the ground, Aegis delivered a series of hard kicks to the backs of Thane's knees. The blows sent Thane kneeling, the monster's hands reaching for the syringe, pulling it out. Thane gave one more cry, but already its force had diminished, its rage vanishing into a wordless growl. His body followed, Aegis standing over him as Thane shrank, shriveled as the syringe's drugs operated on the one weakness Thane's enraged self had: his mind.

Apinya had come up with the device, in the Champion's typically obtuse, infuriating way. Thane, Apinya had decided, couldn't be hurt while angered, but he could be persuaded. The anomaly blocked threats to his body, but not a sedative's sly whispers. The good feelings that turned Thane's rage into placid contentment, if delivered through a soft, harmless solution, would get through Thane's defenses when everything from poison to radiation to direct assaults failed. So for two decades now they'd kept Thane interred. For two decades they'd kept him pacified, and as Aegis stared at the old, wasted man in the snow at his feet, shivering in the cold, he could only wonder why they hadn't killed him sooner.

"I'M TAKING HIM," Mynx said.

They stood over Thane, who slept that deep sleep of the chemically-controlled. Pixie and the other Paragons had taken Thane's various mercenaries—some were already talking, saying they'd been hired to be here by anonymous directors—and were shipping them off to processing centers. The drones were leaving too, launching back to their normal patrol sites across New England. Only a couple stayed behind, monitoring the slumbering target.

"You're not hearing me," Aegis replied. "He dies. Now."

But he didn't lift his foot, didn't clench his fist to deliver the blow, because Aegis could read Mynx's face. That set look of hers saying Aegis would find the drones holding him back if he tried.

"It won't work. You'll break the hold, and then he'll come at us again," Mynx said. "We've already tried this."

"He's older now. Weaker. Look at him."

"Did he seem weak a minute ago?"

No. No he had not. But if they didn't try now, then when? Aegis spread his arms, looked at Mynx. Pleaded with his eyes for another option.

"We still have the island," Mynx said. "It's out there."

"Let him free? Are you joking?"

"Hardly. I'll drop him. If they don't kill him, he'll be trapped. Dozens of kilometers away from anywhere. Harmless."

Aegis stared at Thane's body. So frail. So weak. One good stomp would end it, Aegis felt sure. But if he was wrong? If Thane came roaring back? He didn't have a second syringe ready, and there were too many vulnerable people here. Too much risk. The old him might've done it, the one with a taste for gambling, for the bravado of it all.

"Take the monster, then," Aegis turned away, started the trudging walk back towards a transport that'd take him home. "For our sake, Mynx, I hope you're right."

A Good Show

Of all the spaces in Chicago that had changed as the Paragons overhauled the world, McCormick Place, a palace of windows, coiffed landscaping and sloped white roofs had rebuffed the anomaly influence. Like the city's traditional landmarks, McCormick Place stood as a signal to what had existed before. Unlike the city's traditional landmarks, McCormick Place was liable to get coated in bright banners bearing mythical heroes and worlds far stranger, somehow, than Earth.

Kat could see the setup from the train station, and even if she couldn't, the outfits of the passengers getting off around her would be clues enough. At first, the anomalies had seemed the death of the mighty and miraculous film and fiction heroes, but as it became clear few anomalies matched those conjured-up abilities, and even fewer the selfless morals, storytellers dusted off the age-old icons and watched as they soared to greater heights than ever before. Kat had enjoyed them too, as a kid. Then she'd lost her parents, and now any anomaly with great powers put her on an unstable edge. When she bothered with entertainment, she'd take it straight with normals. No PTSD for her, thanks.

Even so, the crowd's enthusiasm—a family to her left rattled off all the members of some hero team Kat didn't recognize, a couple to her right plotted out the timetable to see all their favorite actors, and genuine laughter permeated—pushed a smile on to her face. Not that she was having fun—never—but she had to fit in. Who'd go to a convention like this and be sour?

As Kat neared the massive buildings, she sidestepped her way out of the crowd to scalpers hawking last-minute day passes. A tap of her Tama to another's and she had a badge hung around her neck, declaring Kat a visitor of 'Eternal' rank, which, the scalper assured her, would guarantee her entry into just about any event she could want.

She didn't know where Calvin might be, but Kat could make guesses; the biggest shows, the biggest stars.

Once passed the doors and through the line for a necessary coat check—winter cold outside, blasting heat inside coupled with thousands of people would make for a sweaty day—Kat sifted to a vacant spot against the window and pulled up the conference's app on her Tama. Set a schedule.

"Hey, I know you," said a slippery voice Kat remembered well, mostly because the woman's ability had made her such a pain to catch. "Still making good reps off of me?"

Xia hadn't changed much in the three years since Kat had traced her. She'd been one of Kat's first catches, an anomaly Kat had found cooking in a diner. Xia had been lax with her cover, turning out dishes at such a fast rate that the diner had a reputation for getting food out no matter how tight the time. When you could flash-fry with your hands, turning out chicken fingers and fries by the thousands wasn't all that difficult. When you could do the same to a person, that made you dangerous.

"I'm doing fine," Kat said. Xia sported an emerald dress, fairy wings folded along the back with a dark crown, and a pair of teenage children trailed her, looking from their mom to their Tamas to the costumed wonders passing by. "How are you?"

The trackers had guidelines on interactions with anomalies they'd traced. Examples, given that traced anomalies covered the range between grateful and murderous. Over time, the general consensus settled on keeping calm and keeping your distance. Just because an anomaly had been traced, didn't mean they couldn't get their ability-driven revenge.

"Oh, you know, living every parent's dream," Xia said. "Working for the Paragons. No choice in that. And here I am with my kids, trying to have a fun day and forget, for a moment, the life you locked me into, and sure enough, the person I strangle in my dreams every night shows up!"

Kat nodded behind Xia, to her kids, both of which had picked up on their mother's escalating anger.

"Those yours?"

"Of course they're mine. Not that you'd care." Xia pulled a plastic wand from her belt, pointed it at Kat. "You just take. Use. Then leave."

De-escalate. That's what Kat was supposed to do. But she was tired, there were a lot of people around, and Xia had a stupid wand in her face.

"If you don't want to see me, I'm not stopping you from leaving."

Xia worked through this. Seemed, for a moment, like she would hit Kat with the wand, and Kat moved her arm up enough to block. That action, that reminder of the back-and-forth fight that'd destroyed half the diner and wound up with Kat burned and Xia unconscious and traced, untangled the angry knot forming in Xia's mind. The emerald fairy turned her back on Kat, announced to her kids that they were leaving. Kat watched Xia take two steps away before the anomaly stopped, turned back to her, nearly clipping someone in the crowd, and shouted with that ever-pointing wand, "You want to see a real villain? That's one. Right there! She'll ruin your life!"

Kat couldn't deny it.

THE TRACKER WANDERED. Blended in with the crowds and walked through the enormous convention center. Every so often her Tama would beep at her, announce that a show she'd pegged as being high value was starting and Kat would angle in that direction to scope out the line, but she wouldn't go in. Couldn't handle sitting, because then she'd get too far into her own head.

Mynx, the Champion who started the tracker program, never hid its purpose, or the price that trackers would pay. They were recruiters by force, and their targets—victims?—would be pushed into a sort of paid servitude for an organization they had obviously wanted to avoid. Mynx couched all of this in heroic high-flung language: that trackers were doing necessary, valued work that wouldn't make headlines.

Kat hadn't been ready for the hate.

Xia wasn't the first of Kat's anomalies to come back to her with a life turned less than ideal after Kat's interference. Sometimes the response was a dour acceptance, freedom's loss salved with the hefty reps conferred by the Paragons. They'd give Kat a half-hearted glare and move along. Rarely, she'd get ones like Stanley, who rolled something better after they left behind the paranoia inherent in being a rogue anomaly. Most of the time, Kat earned a confrontation. A word slurry tasting like guilt, like Kat had stolen something from them, when they, in fact, chose to break Paragon law. Physical threats, like what Xia might have done had they met on a quiet street and not in a heavily patrolled convention center, tended to die away once the anomaly remembered that Kat had beaten them once, and she could do so again.

Didn't make those moments fun, though, which was why Kat spent more and more time cloistered in her apartment. No conflicts there. No reckoning with her life choices.

Laughter snapped Kat back to the present and she realized she'd wandered into a huge vendor hall. Booths selling every comic and movie toy imaginable littered the area, and for every physical stand, there were a half dozen virtual ones; simple posters with Tama codes that would allow you to visit discount markets or special storefronts on the Internet.

The laughter had come from a performance going on in the space's center. Kat thought she recognized the man standing on the raised platform, microphone near his lips as he railed off a series of jokes so insider-specific that Kat felt slightly embarrassed she could follow them. Being in her apartment so much meant she caught a lot of shows.

A *lot* of shows.

She joined the crowd, hanging near the back and listened to the set. Kept looking around. No sign of Calvin. Not that her odds were all that great, with a crowd this size. A crowd starting to get to her too, gnawing at her composure. If Calvin didn't come striding into view soon, Kat might just bounce for the day. Come back tomorrow.

The comedian ran his jokes into another series, one Kat didn't know, so she allowed some new arrivals to nudge her away and out of the set's natural pull. Anxiety worked its magic on Kat's stomach, and a confirmation of the hour made clear that it was about time for a meal. And if she needed food, it chanced that Calvin might too. Everyone had to eat, right?

IF THE VENDOR hall had been a cluster of competing offers, the dining area offered competing scents. Apparently mass entertainment transcended cultural boundaries, as Kat picked up everything from curries, to fryers, to the distinct spicy flower smell of plant-based sausage. Operating on a similar appetite schedule, the crowds descended on the space with Kat, cramming into lines and holding out tickets for free samples or meals won at the convention's various contests.

Kat moved deeper, where the crowd thinned as the appealing entry stalls grabbed most people. Here, encircling a giant bar offering themed drinks in green, eco-plastic cups large enough, Kat felt, to hold her entire arm, splayed two and four person tables with light chairs flexible enough to accommodate the patrons and costumes at this particular party.

Alcohol came with familiarity's promise, relief as Kat pressed herself into an empty bar stool. Some screens overhead showed clips either completed or in progress, though a couple had breaking news bits concerning a violent affair in New England. Apparently Aegis himself had been there, along with a fleet of other Paragons.

"Thane again," the bartender offered, following Kat's eyes to the screen. "They can't keep that one put away. Ought to just end it."

"Right."

Kat wasn't in any mood to discuss the higher question of death vs. life for a criminal like Thane, so she accepted the bartender's verdict and ordered a light brew. After she received it, took a sip, she took a slow turn on the stool to look back out over the tables. The crowd.

And saw him.

It should have been obvious. Calvin seemed like a loner, like her. He'd make his way here, to this odd oasis at the center of it all. Kat couldn't see his face, but he wore that same hat, the same ratty jacket. No costume for our hero. Calvin ate something, his back to the bar as he hunched over the table. An easy target.

Found your anomaly, Gordon. At the big convention, dining hall. Come meet me now, with the bounty.

That message ought to get Gordon running. Kat didn't like admitting to herself that beating Gordon to this one gave her the biggest rush she'd had in a while, but that was life, apparently. Maybe one day she'd take the trackers up on their benefits package and see a therapist about that. About a lot of things.

But not today.

Kat slid off the stool. Slow-walked with her beer in her left hand while her right slipped beneath the fold where her jeans collided with her cream, loose sweater. Pressed up against her hip, with a special chip that let it disarm metal detectors—something the trackers received to assist in their non-lethal ventures —was a slight stun gun. Short range, loaded with nerve-numbing darts.

She slipped it out, palmed it till the barrel faced Calvin's back. Went right up to him, pressed the gun against his neck, and whispered, "Hey Calvin, why'd you run away so fast?"

31

Beneath The Streets

Chicago's undercity had survived the years by remaining invisible. While downtown's surface had been remade to fit the pods, the Paragon-forced redefining of capitalism, the grimy streets beneath stayed resilient. Zhan-Yo stepped out a full block away from his destination, wanting to walk for a minute in this place, with its deep golden lights, long shadows, and constant churn from heavy freight and waste vehicles getting rid of the things humanity produced but didn't want to see.

Voices carried down here too, from workers performing tasks no drone or AI could prove profitable. The same complaints; the reps, the cold weather—though down here the harsh winds from the lake were cut—and the constant grind inescapable by the common man. That last thought brought a smile; Zhan-Yo shouldn't think like that, like some philosopher. He wasn't some wine sipper preaching to scribbling university students.

No, he was a revolutionary, and these workers down here were his subjects, even if they didn't know it.

Sylvie requested the meet up near the spot she'd chosen for their world-bending assassination. Zhan-Yo didn't like that word, which draped like a greasy cloth over his noble aspirations, but he had to admit value in calling things by their true names. Aegis had to die so freedom could live. They could not best Aegis and his Paragons in a straight fight, so assassination it would be.

A heavy, welded door marked the entrance. An old-fashioned keyed bolt sat above the handle, with nary a Tama scanner in sight. How long had it been since Zhan-Yo carried a keychain? Heard the jingle as he tried to remember which applied to the specific lock?

"Do you have a key?" Wexley asked, stepping from another pod behind Zhan-Yo. He hadn't chosen to make the walk, and cast looks about like he was afraid goons would attack at any moment. "Or is Sylvie expecting us to wait out here?"

"She'll let us in when she's ready."

Wexley shook his head. The man had bundled himself head to toe in garments Zhan-Yo could only describe as office luxury. Black, thick, and woolly. Zhan-Yo preferred the lived-in comfort of his puffy jacket, the same one he'd worn for years. Then again, Zhan-Yo had reached the ladder's top. Wexley still climbed the rungs. Just as Zhan-Yo refused to judge the undercity workers for doing their brutal jobs at the bottom of the city, nor could he judge the apparel of someone trying hard to escape it.

Luckily for Wexley, Sylvie opened the door not two minutes later, at the precise moment their Tamas vibrated to announce the scheduled meeting's start. One that, on both Zhan-Yo and Wexley's calendars, had been marked as a high importance dinner. Something that would keep out the calls and keep quiet the questions.

"Welcome, gentlemen, to the last place our Champion will ever see." Sylvie stepped aside and beckoned the pair with an elaborate swoop.

If this space would house Aegis's final moments, Zhan-Yo found it suitably awful. Scrambled pipes, steaming vents, grated wires and more ran across the ceiling, breaking every now and then to gift a patch to fizzy fluorescent lights whose blue-white glow drained any hope.

Sylvie's chosen place kept going too, and the 'walls', as she shuffled Zhan-Yo and Wexley along, revealed themselves to be boxed battery packs for solar storage. Black cubes bearing small screens displaying the collective panels on buildings far above to suck in enough energy to keep the city working. A high tech initiative clustered into a low tech environment. One, from the lingering smell, that had been used to store waste for eventual incineration in a past life.

Towards the back, Sylvie indicated a maintenance door. It, too, was locked and bore no less than three red-lined signs declaring civil and criminal penalties should the wrong person dare open it.

"We lead him through the access tunnels to this door," Sylvie said. "He opens it, we finish him in here, then get away through where you came in. Simple."

"It's perfect," Zhan-Yo said.

"You make it sound so easy," Wexley countered. "Aegis won't be alone. And what about the drones? As soon as he realizes it's a trap, he'll call them in. This close to the city's center, they won't be more than a few seconds away."

"Check your Tamas," Sylvie replied. Contrary to her late night rendezvous, Sylvie's outfit tonight glimmered silver-gray, with slits packed with armored plates. Two bulges at her wrists were, Zhan-Yo figured, bolt knives ready to launch at a gesture, and her waist sported a belt with up-close and far-away weaponry. All this gave her suggestion a sinister edge. "You'll find your answer."

Zhan-Yo's Tama didn't hide the problem—towards the top center of its screen, on the back of Zhan-Yo's wrist, a big red X covered the circle that, as it filled with white, showed signal strength. Zhan-Yo couldn't recall the last time he'd seen that red X—he could maintain a connection on flights to anywhere in the world, in most basements, and out in the middle of Lake Michigan. This chamber here, beneath Chicago's streets, wasn't even all that deep. Which meant . . .

"It's the generators," Zhan-Yo said, noticing Wexley still staring at his own Tama as if it'd become some disgusting creature intent on devouring his hand. "That's the difference."

"Not quite," Sylvie replied. "This building is shielded. Lead plates are all around us, encased in these walls, to ground and seal in any overload. Can you imagine what would happen if these generators blew underneath the city?"

"Makes me wonder how you have access to this place?" Wexley said.

"I don't ask you how you do your job," Sylvie said, and Zhan-Yo noticed the two had, once again, positioned themselves like duelists. "I assume you pay your employees, yes?"

"Of course we do."

"Sylvie." Zhan-Yo tried, but she ignored him.

"You pay them in reps, but that's only one currency. Staying alive, as it happens, is another."

Zhan-Yo suppressed a flinch. Another stain on his dream's pure flag. If he was being honest, the flag was more a dirty rag these days, but at least it was still there. Still able, maybe, to fly.

"So this is where we stage the weapon transfer." Zhan-Yo dragged the conversation back to relevance.

The central room had the capacity. Square, with an open floor meant to give space for the necessary equipment to move and service these giant energy buckets. A dozen or more people could wait in here, ready to ambush Aegis when he came through the maintenance tunnel.

"We're going to put cameras in the corners, and at the middle points," Sylvie explained. "We'll catch it from every angle. This won't just be an assassination, it'll be a cinematic event."

Wexley slipped Zhan-Yo a look that asked whether, really, Zhan-Yo thought Sylvie had any sanity left at all. Zhan-Yo had no answer, but it didn't matter, so long as they accomplished the goal. So long as they eliminated the Champion.

Sylvie continued talking through the coming modifications to the place and Zhan-Yo tried to absorb it all. In explaining secondary traps in case the drones made it down anyway, the maintenance access door jiggled. Wexley slid in front of Zhan-Yo in an instant, drawing a small, legal stun gun from his jacket. Sylvie looked at the weapon, met Wexley's face, and laughed.

The door opened and two men dressed like Sylvie—silver-black tactical gear with armor plates—climbed in. Zhan-Yo recognized neither, and the two ignored Ziran's top executives as they reported all-clears and objective updates to Sylvie. When they finished, Sylvie gave a single nod and dismissed them.

"Wait," Zhan-Yo said to them as the two grunts turned to leave through the main exit. "What is your role, here?"

"They're going to take down Aegis," Sylvie said.

The two turned back around to look at him. Zhan-Yo started to think of them the twins, despite the fact that they looked nothing alike. Big and bulky, sure, but otherwise their skins were opposites, one had longer ears and the other a longer torso. Their faces did have one thing in common: a straight stare so often found in goons. However, lurking beneath that surface and visible in their relaxed muscles, their straight eyes and the utter lack of questions on their lips . . . was the total lack of moral fiber necessary to work on a job like this.

"Have you ever fought a Paragon before?" Zhan-Yo asked. "An anomaly?"

"Here and there," the one on the left said, as if Zhan-Yo had questioned whether he watched movies. "Not a Paragon. Not that dumb."

"They're qualified, Zhan-Yo," Sylvie said. "As good as you're going to find. Nobody's out here advertising hunting Paragons. You don't live long doing that."

Zhan-Yo nodded. Glanced at Wexley. "Take my jacket, if you would."

"Z," Wexley said. "I don't think—"

"This is not your decision to make."

Wexley slipped the coat off of Zhan-Yo's shoulders and the older man stretched his arms out. Felt those muscles pop into place. He meant to follow up on Chloe's offer, get some harder practice. As it was, these two would have to do.

"I've fought one," Zhan-Yo said, stretching his arms. "On a bet. Years ago. I lost, badly. Because I underestimated him. I assumed a Paragon was nothing more than his power, like most anomalies. A profound mistake."

Though Zhan-Yo didn't show them, he had a scar on his left

calf, from where the Paragon had split his bone. No power there, just a merciless stomp. So far as Zhan-Yo knew, that Paragon still lived out there somewhere, and Zhan-Yo owed him a debt—he'd learned a lesson most only realize in their live's last, fatal moments.

"So what are you saying?" Sylvie said, her arms folded as she leaned back against the side of the room. "You want to spar with them? Teach them what it's like to fight a Paragon?"

"What I'm saying is that if these two cannot even handle me, Aegis will make short work of them."

"This is ridiculous, Z," Wexley said.

But the twins apparently didn't think so. They gave a look to Sylvie, who shrugged, and then set about splitting around Zhan-Yo, setting the ostensible boss of this whole enterprise on his own in the middle of the room. Wexley finally understood he was not, in fact, going to stop this from happening and backed over near Sylvie, huffing one sigh after another.

Zhan-Yo, though, felt alive. Felt the adrenaline's rush and excitement that comes with physical conflict, with knowing his life would be in play and it would take every ounce of energy he still had at the day's end to . . .

Win.

Zhan-Yo quick-stepped to his left without turning all the way, jabbing with his elbow at the shorter one's throat. A potentially lethal move against the uninitiated, capable of rendering the windpipe into nothing more than folded tissue, but Sylvie's hired hand made a startled deflection, punching up Zhan-Yo's blow so that it struck the man's cheek instead, snapping his head back. Zhan-Yo took the distraction that bought to jack a right-legged kick into the reeling man's stomach, bouncing him into the sidewall. The whoosh of stale air exploding from the man's lungs meant Zhan-Yo had some time to play with the other one.

Who came at Zhan-Yo with his hands raised up in front of his face, a boxing stance. Taller than Zhan-Yo, twin number two doubtless had Zhan-Yo on reach, so he decided to take hands out of the game. Spinning from his kick, Zhan-Yo dropped into a leg sweep, prompting Twin Two to quick-step back.

Playing it safe. That might work here, but every second Aegis stayed alive gave time for Paragons or drones to home in on him and ruin everything.

"You must attack quickly," Zhan-Yo said, straightening. "Every second against the Champion benefits him, not you."

Twin Two understood, and he waded back in, this time lighter on his feet. If Zhan-Yo tried the same sweep, Twin Two might jump it, or race to beat it, delivering a strike to Zhan-Yo's unprotected head. So Zhan-Yo made to close the gap with a sudden burst towards Twin Two. Sylvie's hired man, rather than trying a frantic jab, instead opted for a hug, catching Zhan-Yo as he closed and wrapping him in Twin Two's mammoth arms. He squeezed, and Zhan-Yo felt like he was going to pop.

But Twin Two wore a belt like Sylvie, and that belt held any number of lethal weapons. Zhan-Yo's pinned hands could feel a gun's grip, and he pulled it out, flipped it towards Twin Two's stomach.

"You're dead," Zhan-Yo managed.

"That's not fair," Twin Two said, releasing Zhan-Yo. "We weren't going full armed."

"I didn't give you any rules. Aegis won't either," Zhan-Yo said, trying very, very hard not to collapse as he sucked in air. Wexley came up to him, helped Zhan-Yo get his jacket back on. "Don't mess around. Once he's in this room, you go for the kill, and you do it fast. Sylvie, I approve. Make it happen."

"I'll keep you apprised," Sylvie said, more than a hint of calculation in her voice and, Zhan-Yo thought, surprise at her boss's abilities.

Wexley walked Zhan-Yo out of the building, signaled pods for them. As Zhan-Yo climbed into his, taking big breaths and wondering whether he'd have bruises, Wexley kept the door open and leaned in, "Once this begins, we can't go back. If Aegis gets down there, he has to die, Z. If those two fail . . ."

"Sylvie and I will make sure they don't."

"You?"

"Wexley, if this fails, we're done. Ziran might go on, but I will not. I've waited all my life for this one chance, and I don't have a second one to spend waiting for another."

The answer seemed to satisfy Wexley, who let the pod's door shut and gave Zhan-Yo a slight wave as the pod drove him out of the golden, greasy depths and into Chicago's bright night.

32

Airborne Delivery

Charon. The boatman who brought the newly dead, or the unwise adventurers, to Hades. Mynx had been trying to think of the name for an hour now, a puzzle easily answered by her Tama but one she wanted to solve on her own. Partly because she just wanted to—having machines solve all her problems made her feel useless—but also because flying high over Atlantis and Pacifica was really, really boring.

Not that the nighttime sky, once Mynx made it above the clouds and tinted out some of that harsh moonlight, wasn't beautiful. She'd just seen it so many times now that—

"A personal lift from a Champion herself?" Thane's voice sounded dry, like he'd sucked on a dozen lemons. "Whatever did I do to deserve this honor?"

Her private jet had no passenger seat, but it did have luggage space. Space now occupied by a sedated, restrained Thane. Sapped of his anger, Thane shrank down, shriveled away until he looked barely fit to be alive. There was some danger in keeping Thane this numb, a chance that his muscles could weaken so much that he'd die in the back of the jet. Frankly, Mynx wouldn't care if that happened, but for one thing:

She wasn't a murderer.

Those words didn't hold for every Champion, and Mynx had, either herself or through her drones, killed before. But killing to defend herself in a fight, or to stop a catastrophe was one thing. To end Thane because she could seemed . . . wrong. Aegis didn't seem to think so, but he could have his views. She'd make the choices that kept her nightmares at bay.

"You terrorized a lot of people and could have killed a lot more," Mynx said, her words wrapping around the cockpit and sliding back towards Thane. "Do you even remember?"

"Of course," Thane replied. "I hold on to everything, even if I can't use it at the time. I know you kept Aegis from killing me, and I thank you for it."

Was that actual contrition?

"Why did you do it?" Mynx asked.

"Oh, my explanation is simple. I was bored, and I was offered a chance to not be. They fulfilled their end, and I did mine."

"Who offered you a chance?"

"Now, Mynx, just because you have me tied up in your rather nice plane doesn't mean you get to ask me all the questions you want."

"Actually, that's exactly what it means."

Thane rasped a laugh. "Does your plane have any water in it, or am I cursed to go without?"

The jet had water, had everything from pre-prepped meals to an automatic defibrillator primed to go off if Mynx happened to have a heart attack in transit. But all things targeted towards the cockpit, not the back, and Mynx's charitable drive had been slain by the night's long flight. It'd been her own choice to make the journey, but it would be an exhausting one nevertheless.

"You've survived worse," Mynx said. "Do you know where I'm taking you?"

"Mynx, it has been so very long since I was privy to your secrets. Even in this state, I cannot guess."

Another lie. Thane very much could guess, and like this, with his mind heightened even as his body decayed, he could probably tell how fast they were going, maybe even judge their location from the pull of Earth's magnetic poles or some such ridiculous thing. Anomalies redrew possibility's boundaries all the time.

"I made this place because of you," Mynx said. "Though by the time I prepped it, we already had you so well contained that Aegis figured it would be more dangerous to move you."

"One of many things that brute has mistaken."

"It worked pretty damn well for almost thirty years."

"Yes. You kept the greatest mind this world has ever seen sedated and locked away. What a brilliant plan."

"A dangerous mind, Thane. You chose your side, you knew the costs."

Thane didn't respond to that. Which, good. The autopilot program did its job keeping them on track, and they were nearing the point where Mynx had to start sending out her code sequence. She used a screen plugged into the narrowing nose, one normally tasked with displaying reports on the jet's operating condition but that had now flipped to five static blood-red bars into which Mynx, through careful finger swipes, drew the passcodes.

"Thane, I don't know if you can feel much through those sedatives, but I would start trying."

"They are like weights. If I lift hard enough, perhaps . . . "

Not that Mynx wanted Thane to shrug off those drugs yet, but what happened next would kill him otherwise.

"I'm not going to promise you'll be safe here, but I do guarantee the rest of the world will be safe from you."

"From me? Mynx, even if you've found such a place, it doesn't matter. I won't be the last anomaly to threaten the world you and your friends have built. There will be more, or some normal will find where you've hidden all their old toys and blow you to pieces with them. All empires fall."

There were so many reasons Mynx preferred cold, hard logic to the vague philosophies of people like Thane and Apinya. Problems ought to be solved, not thrown out into the void. Threats ought to be concrete, not abstract and menacing. She wanted Thane out, but his endless cocky replies deserved a little bit of a smacking too.

"You know, Thane, there won't be anomalies like you for much longer. I'm close to solving your problem. We'll be able to control future generations, save the deadly ones from hurting themselves. From becoming like you."

"Because that will certainly make you the heroes in this story."

"Better than people dying through no fault of their own."

"I always thought you were the smart one, Mynx. The one most able to see the end right when it began. That's why you made all of these drones, right? To carry on your quests now that you're too old and broken to do it yourselves?"

Mynx stayed quiet, drew more passcodes. They passed the outer shell, headed towards the interior, and the smallest slip would get the jet, and both of them, annihilated.

"I think you know as well as I do that there's only one end to this. Humanity is taking its time, but the power always increases from one generation to the next. Someone's going to be born, or get their hands on the wrong switch, and then boom. All your work is gone, all the time you wasted trying to make this world work will be gone in a flash. And not a single soul will care, Mynx. Not when the ash is falling from the sky, when the buildings are collapsing and the Paragons are lying dead in the streets. Nobody will thank you, nobody will celebrate you."

The jet's tablet chimed, her defenses had accepted her codes.

"I had a family too," Thane continued. "People that loved me, that I loved. Do you know what happened to them?"

Mynx knew.

"Do you know what I did when I found out who I was? The very next time my friends were joking around. They pushed me down, part of a game, but I was tired. I was a teenager, and do you know what I did?"

Mynx closed her eyes and started counting down.

"I knew I'd get strong, by then, but I didn't know what I would lose if I kept following that energy, grabbing it, swallowing it until nothing was left but the rage. When I finally spent that, following them back home, the only ones left were all of you. Ready to use me. To test me. To contain me."

Almost there.

"But, Mynx, I cannot be contained. I cannot be held." Thane's voice grew stronger, and Mynx heard the telltale creaks of Thane's bonds as they stretched against the growing monster behind her. She gripped the flight stick, flipped the plane off autopilot and adjusted their course to account for Thane's growing mass. "I grow, and grow, and break free."

"Are you done?"

The bonds snapped. The jet shook as Thane turned behind her, his large body brushing against the plane's sides as he shifted, as he brought his head right up behind hers, his sagging, older skin pulled tight against a suddenly-massive skeleton. His warm, fiery breath reeked of madness.

"Yes." Thane whispered.

"Good."

Mynx's count hit zero and she pulled back on the stick while thumb-tapping a bright orange button near the stick's top, placed for emergencies just like this one. The jet's sudden rise threw Thane back from her seat, pressed him against what should have been the jet's floor, what was its cargo doors, which were now very open. The monster that had terrorized New England, that had haunted the Champions for decades, their secret and, at times, their unspoken savior, shot off into the night, down towards the one place on Earth he would never be able to leave.

By the time Mynx corrected for the stall and told the autopilot to take her home, and entered all the passcodes to leave the island, when endless night was the only thing in front of her, she leaned back in her chair. Before, she might have cried, or gasped for breath, or gripped those armrests with everything she had to keep from shaking. Now Thane's words were one more threat among a million others.

Not that they didn't touch her. No, not that she was immune. They wormed their way inside her and festered there. Whispers in the dark, waiting for her, always.

It would be hours before she made it home. Mynx opened a

small side box, slipped out a bottle, and popped one of the pills inside. She would sleep, and the drugs would make it dreamless.

Peaceful.

33

Accepting Reality

Aegis jogged in the same winter running outfits worn by everyone else on the paths, the only difference the metal around his neck. The medal bobbed against his upper chest, where it hung as he ran through the expanded Central Park in light morning fog, blowing up as a warm spell extinguished snow with a vengeance. Awarded to Aegis by the last President of the United States, not all that long before the Paragons removed her from power, the medal signified grand service to a country whose drive had become so corrupted, along with the rest of the world, as the Champions had risen to power.

The politicians had seen the anomalies as tools to be used. Courted and connived. They'd never expected the Paragons to fight back.

Those battles had been much harder than last night's shock tactic blast to take out Thane. Not necessarily the military elements —coordinated anomalies tended to make short work of anything except each other—but public opinion. Laws and regulations. The glue holding society together.

Aegis passed by another jogger and gave her a nod. She returned it, did a double take. Aegis caught the look and held back a laugh, tromping towards a bridge. He'd pass underneath, come out the other side and be at the park's north end. She'd never quite be sure what she saw.

The Paragons, for all their gusto, their revolutionary enthusiasm, had wound up putting most of the lawyers, the senators and representatives around the world right back in their places. Existing contracts, statutes, and all that stayed the same, and elections still happened, or began in those countries that didn't have such things, to fill those same positions. Above it all, though, the Paragons loomed, and the Champions stood above them. A constant arbiter, threat, and peacekeeping force guaranteeing lawful obedience by sheer power. Thus far, Aegis felt, they'd managed to not abuse that power.

Not enough to throw the world into chaos, anyway.

A Tama shake interrupted Aegis's steady steps. His daughter's face showed on the armband, and because answering a daughter's calls is a dad's duty, Aegis tapped to answer.

"You're getting in the way of my peace and calm," Aegis said.

"Not my fault," Celice replied. "Looks like the world can't go a day without you."

"What is it now?"

"Chicago. Apparently the Paragons there are spooked by something."

Aegis had promised he'd check in with them after Boston, hadn't he? Guess it'd be too much luck for the Paragons there to actually solve the problem themselves. Aegis shook his head as he continued to jog, the fogged pine trees his only sympathetic witnesses.

"Did they give you any details?"

"They're hoping for a call back." Celice paused. "But I did get a message from Mynx. She delivered Thane."

"Another toy on her island of misfits."

"Hey, at least we don't have to deal with him anymore."

Aegis couldn't argue with that. Problems so rarely seemed to leave his list. He ought to crack some champagne for this one.

"Fine, I'll circle back. Tell the Paragons I'll call them in an hour."

"You got it, dad."

So much for his third lap.

WEAPONS, because of course. Innis, the Paragon lead for Chicago, stumbled over the explanation, owing both to his lack of information on what was going on in his own city and his red-faced embarrassment as that lack became increasingly clear. Some group, from somewhere, was sending illegal weapons to someone.

"You're really illuminating this for me," Aegis interrupted, waving off Innis' fractured sketch of how these weapons might be arriving. "Look, if you know this little about what's going on, then why are you contacting me?"

"We're hoping you have some ideas about who it might be?"

"In case you haven't noticed, Innis, I'm in New York. You are in Chicago. They are not, in fact, the same place."

The fire-bearded, burly man burned as red as Aegis had ever seen a human being. Innis reached for a bottle of water off screen, which gave Aegis a chance to look past the floating monitor. The noonday, gray winter skyline spread out beneath those windows, and the sight worked its usual wonders. A reminder of his job, his purpose. The world's people couldn't be perfect all the time, but he had to save them anyway.

"All right, Innis. You said you have some suspicions, right?"

Innis gulped his drink. Wiped his face with his hands. The bright blue Paragon uniform looked tighter on him than usual— stress weight, or too much holiday egg nog?

"I, we, think it might be Ziran." Innis winced as he said the word, as if uttering it might summon some technological device demon to devour him. "They're, uh, they're the only company we know of that might try something like this."

"Care to elaborate?"

"It's their leader, Aegis. Guy by the name of Zhan-Yo. He's old guard around here, known for talking a lot about how much better things used to be."

Aegis sat back in his chair, shrugged. "He can have his opinions. You have more than that?"

Innis looked off-screen again, coughed. Maybe another Paragon was in the room for moral support. Strange. Innis had always been a more forceful Paragon. Ready and quick to get behind an operation or condemn a mistake. Now he looked sweaty, afraid.

"I'm sorry Aegis, I'm spooked. We got a tip yesterday, while you were busy with Thane up there. Said straight out that Ziran's plotting the end of it all. A takeover." Innis leaned forward, his face getting so close to the camera that Aegis could count the man's gigantic nose hairs. "You don't think they might be listening to this, do you? Could they?"

"A tip from who?" Aegis wasn't so far removed from the days when the Champions would get calls pitting them against some person's or company's rival. An anonymous letter, message, even a panicked victim showing up with a story and disappearing, all designed to get someone crushed. "Do you think you can trust it?"

"It'll be easy to find out. The tip came with a time, date, and place."

"For the transfer? Or for coffee?"

Innis huffed a weak chuckle. "For the transfer, I think."

"So here's what you do. Celice already requested extra drones from Mynx. You send them to watch the transfer, record it, and stop it if it's actually happening. Anyone gets away, you do the clean-up."

Yes, it was an obvious suggestion. Paragon protocol emphasized using drones when practical—much easier to replace a machine than a loyal anomaly. Though, given that Aegis himself liked to ditch that protocol on occasion, he could understand someone else forgetting it. They were supposed to be heroes, and sitting in an office didn't make you feel like one.

"Don't know that drones are going to work for this one. Tight quarters, underground. If it's Ziran doing this, they've at least thought we might find out about it."

Again, Aegis shrugged. "Innis, you're the leader out there for a reason. Figure it out. The drones are good enough to get through a tunnel, and if they're not, you've got Paragons you can call on to help. I trust you."

"So you're not coming?"

"Not coming. I have to plan a summit and make sure Thane's cleanup goes well. Apparently all these thugs working for him were hired by the Elementals. Which means I need to have a long talk with them."

Innis looked like he was working his way towards a protest, but before the big man could get his mouth open, Aegis told him to call again if trouble occurred and closed the connection. The monitor drifted down and away, Aegis took his sigh and embraced the view. He'd done it. Said no to a Paragon in need. It should have felt terrible, like a betrayal, but instead . . . he felt liberated?

He *was* getting older.

"Dad!" Celice announced a few minutes later, arriving from her lower level where she conducted Atlantis Paragon logistics like a maestro. "You're still here? Innis sounded so concerned, I thought you'd be gone already."

When Aegis filled her in, Celice didn't look disappointed, but wrapped him in a tight hug. Strange. A reward for saying no? What had happened to the world?

"I can't believe you're actually staying," Celice said, stepping back. "We'll go out tonight, to celebrate. How long has it been since we've done that?"

"Since I scared away your last boyfriend?"

Celice laughed. Still the most beautiful sound.

"Probably. Stick around and maybe you'll meet the new one."

"The new one?"

34

Tables Turned

Of all the possibilities Kat had imagined for her life, sticking a stun gun up to a harmless-looking young man's neck was not one. There'd been the usual dream careers thrown out, the realities of anomaly versus normal life hidden during her pre-teen years. Why taint her ideal future with chances an eight year-old could neither control nor fully understand? Kat grew up watching the Paragons consolidate power, her lessons shifting from one year to the next, from framing anomalies as an unusual minority to discussing them as partners and, later, as superiors.

By the time she'd made it to what functioned as college, her family had been destroyed, those childhood dreams shredded by a wholesale shift in society that created two classes, and hers did not hold the power. The choices were stark; she had no reps, no relatives that cared to speak with her after what'd happened, and no connections. What Kat did have, what she'd developed when her old friends had discovered first loves or found passions to pursue, was a realist's eye. Success, survival, those two things were one and the same. For a normal in her position, being a tracker gave her the best chance at both.

"Calvin," Kat said to her frozen hostage. "I'm going to need you to stand up, and then we're going to walk out of here, okay?"

Calvin gulped—Kat could see it in how his throat bobbed—and set both hands on the table, then shifted one to the cup holding his drink. Kat followed the hand, realized the foam-covered beverage was beer. Calvin really was here for a vacation, then. Kat almost felt bad ruining it.

"I don't want to hurt anybody," Calvin said, sounding like he meant it, the sad sentence of someone hunted through no fault of their own. "I promise."

"I'm sure you don't," Kat replied. "But there's people that want to hurt you, which is why we need to leave."

Calvin nodded, rose. His height made keeping the stun gun at Calvin's neck hard, so she pulled it away, kept it hidden in her jacket's loose cover. The dart would have a harder time piercing Calvin's own thick clothes, but maybe Calvin wouldn't know that. And she could always shoot more than once. With her other hand, Kat took Calvin's motion as an opportunity to slip a little extra insurance into the man's jacket, a transponder that might come in handy should this encounter go sideways, as anomaly encounters always could.

"Can I finish my drink?" Calvin said, nodding towards the beer.

"Do it slow," Kat replied. "No tricks."

Calvin nodded, grabbed the cup and raised it towards his lips. "I really was having a good day."

"I'll bet," Kat said. "If you make this easy, you'll be right back in here. No risk."

"Promise?"

"Promise."

Calvin stuck his right hand out towards her. A shake? Kat almost laughed. Such a formal way to seal such a rough deal for Calvin, but if he wanted a drink and a handshake, Kat could give him that. She was taking so much else. With her finger firmly on the stun gun's trigger, she reached out with her left and gripped Calvin's hand. He shook once, a strong shake, then let go. Kat dropped her hand, and stared at it. She couldn't seem to feel her own fingers anymore. Or her feet. The room, too, seemed to be spinning ever so slightly. It was a miracle the stun gun didn't slip from her other hand to the floor. Kat tried to focus her eyes, tried to take a step and couldn't manage it without leaning on Calvin's old table, thankfully anchored enough not to fall away.

"Here, sit down," Calvin said, moving Kat into a chair across from him.

She tried to form a sentence, a coherent thought, but the connections between ideas and words seemed blocked, fuzzed somehow.

"Do you know why I'm not a Paragon? Why I'm not playing your game?" Calvin said, finishing his fries while he spoke. "It's not because I don't like'em, don't think they're not a good thing. Hell, without the Paragons, I bet anomalies like me would get treated like freaks."

Yeah. Like freaks. Like her sister. Kat tried to focus. Calvin blurred. Her lips were numb.

"I don't get the chance to talk to too many people," Calvin continued. "Partly my own fault, I guess. You ever know how hard it is to start a conversation when you're the opposite of what people expect? That's why I put my name in for a fight the other night, you know. Not because I thought I'd win, but because that bartender asked me if I wanted to. She was nice about it."

Another round of fries. Kat reached for her Tama, on her left wrist, but Calvin caught her hand. Guided it gently back to the table.

"I started to value that a lot. Kindness. When your own father thinks you'd make him a pretty penny being loaned to people who want to use your skill, you start out thinking it's fine. You're helping. Then you see, on the Tama or whatever, how a real family works, and it's not so fine anymore." Calvin finished the fries, took another swig. "Kat. You weren't going to be kind to me, were you?"

Kat fought to keep her head off the table. Calvin's words bounce around in her skull. Something in her stomach curdled and her heartbeat felt like an earthquake. Her Tama vibrated a warning, but she couldn't make out the screen.

"That's what I thought. See, I didn't answer what I asked before.

About why I'm not with the Paragons?" Calvin stood from the table, stepped around to Kat's side and helped her cross her arms, give her a spot to lay down her head. "Because they wouldn't be kind to me, Kat. They would use me. Just like my father. Just like you." Calvin sighed. "Sorry, I might have overdone it. You're not looking so good. I think you should get help, otherwise this might kill you."

Drunk. It didn't make sense, but it was the only thing that could tie these sensations together. Kat hadn't had a single drink, and yet she felt more intoxicated than she'd ever been before, and it was getting worse. Plus, the nearest trash bins were not within her rapidly decreasing stumbling distance.

"How?" Kat managed, fear pushing through the haze to mumble out the words, speaking into her shirt sleeve.

"They didn't tell you what I can do?" Calvin said. "That's why they want me, Kat. Because of this. I would say I'm sorry, but I'm not. I don't want you to die, really, but if that's what it takes to get them to leave me alone?"

Calvin stood, put a hand on Kat's shoulder that felt like it was a million kilometers away, and then he left. Kat tried to follow him, but her head felt so, so heavy. So much easier to leave it there on her shoulders. Her Tama beeped, there on her wrist about one centimeter away from her eye. The device flashed a warning about her blood alcohol levels. Above recommended amounts, and rising.

No kidding.

Then again, her stomach's increasing nausea aside, this wasn't the worst way to go. Kat's world faded, spun away into nothing, and she closed her eyes as her Tama began to beep again and again. The things were good little gadgets, always ready to tell you when you were in trouble. As if she didn't know.

As if she didn't deserve it.

The Knife Cuts Deep

Zhan-Yo had gone to countless dinners, been in so many high-stakes meetings that tonight's engagement ought to be a no-sweat affair. But sweat dogged his afternoon, so he'd already showered twice to cleanse it, and now he shivered as he tromped between the pod and the downtown restaurant, a little-known, high quality outfit specializing in curry fusions. They believed—correctly, it turned out—that you could add curry to just about anything and make it better.

As a result, the rich coconut milk blanketed Zhan-Yo's senses as he walked through the single automatic door. A real, live hostess greeted him, though the place didn't rise to true luxury by using an actual pencil and paper to track reservations. The hostess's computer agreed with Zhan-Yo's Tama and the code displayed on its screen. Two seats, six o'clock. Late enough to avoid the unfashionable happy hour and early enough to ensure a decent bed time.

A glance at the full four seats along the small bar confirmed Zhan-Yo's suspicion that he'd beaten her. Then again, of course he would. Sylvie would be more cautious, would ensure her reason for being somewhere existed before actually arriving. He resisted looking out the sole front window to see if Sylvie lurked across the street.

"Will this be fine?" the hostess, whom Zhan-Yo had followed automatically, said, indicating a small, cloth covered table with prime proximity to nothing of consequence.

"You will keep those two other tables empty, as noted in the reservation?" Zhan-Yo said, gesturing at four-tops within potential listening distance.

The hostess looked confused for a moment, as anyone might with such a request, but a look at her Tama confirmed the order, and the cost, Zhan-Yo had negotiated with the restaurant's manager earlier. A flat rep fee equal to their average order, and a small price to pay for privacy. She left Zhan-Yo alone with a glass of water, and he took in the brick walls, the bustling pots from the kitchen, and the buzzing conversations between the restaurant's other guests.

He also realized how nervous he felt. Zhan-Yo almost laughed, before stopping at the realization an older man laughing to himself alone might cause more interest than he cared to generate. He was too old for this sort of thing. Far past the age when people ought to be dating, and far too involved in deadly matters to consider flighty passions and their distractions.

But.

Sylvie had worked for him, or, really, with him for over a decade now. In that time, Zhan-Yo had come to trust her with everything. Secrets that would get him imprisoned, murdered, impoverished, or all three. Sylvie extracted them with her wit, her conversation, her incredible ability to find his weakest point and exploit it. She was a very, very dangerous woman. But, when he led a giant company, with little risk in his daily life, perhaps he needed a dangerous woman.

"Haven't I told you how much I hate this place?" Sylvie said as she appeared over his left shoulder, sliding past him and taking the seat across. "All of this curry ruins my diet."

"And yet, you never say no when I ask."

Zhan-Yo delighted in their little rituals. That neither of them, for example, dressed up or down for the night. That, in scheduling the evening, Sylvie would never reply, leaving Zhan-Yo to guess whether she'd show, except she always did. And now another one, when the servo-robot came by and Sylvie gave her the order for the wine. The same vineyard, the same vintage. He wasn't sure what they'd do when the restaurant ran out.

"We sent the signal, and it's been received," Sylvie said after the robot had wheeled itself away. "We're in motion."

As if there had been any doubt. When Sylvie set to a project, it went according to plan.

"I don't want to talk about business," Zhan-Yo replied, desperately wanting to do just that. Still, Aegis would not be arriving tonight. He could wait. "But congratulations. At last, it's beginning."

Vague terms were a must in public. Speaking about sensitive matters in a time when every robot could be feeding data back to the Paragons was a game, one with dire consequences for its losers.

"So do you think, next time we touch our glasses, it will be in a different world?" Sylvie said. She rested her fingers around her stemmed wine glass, still empty. "With us on top?"

"A dream, though not the only one," Zhan-Yo answered. "But it is . . . strange to think that such a dream could be so close."

"That's a dreamer for you," Sylvie laughed. "You've always been one of those. Up in the air. Living in imagined futures even though you have the resources to make them real."

"Resources like you."

Sylvie cocked her head as the servo-robot came back with the wine. From its central cylinder, spindly arms arose to grip the wine bottle and remove the synthetic cork with a precise pop achieved through calibrated, focus-group tested pressures. Every tiny charm helped one restaurant stand out from another, and the robot added to its routine by slow-pouring Sylvie a taste first, asking in an Italian opera singer's deep voice whether she approved.

Sylvie drank the wine in a single gulp, no swirling or wafting required, and set the glass down. "It's superb."

Now it was Zhan-Yo's turn to laugh, and he did as the robot refilled her glass and poured his. They ordered egg rolls and spicy curries, which the robot took without comment except, at the very end, repeating the selections before motoring away to the next table.

"You called me a resource," Sylvie said, and all the laughter fled from her voice. "I find that offensive."

Zhan-Yo froze for a second before his years of directing a massive company slid self-control back into its place. "I apologize, but it's true. We would be nowhere near as far without you."

"You would be nowhere, in fact."

Zhan-Yo shrugged.

"Say it."

"What?"

"That you would be nowhere without me."

There were options to be evaluated here. Zhan-Yo could see the dinner's course laid out in paths, each one stretching off into a fuzzy future.

"We would be nowhere without you." He chose the safest one he could think of.

"And that, right there, is why," Sylvie said. "You give in too easily. You're so damn smart, Z, but so afraid to risk anything at all."

"So this is what I get when I ask to avoid business?"

"Without business, there's only the personal, right?"

They were firing verbal salvos back and forth, wine sips serving as temporary truces inevitably broken when the next line came to mind.

"You are all knives, Sylvie. There's more to life than cuts and stabs."

"Like curry dinners for two?"

"Yes, in fact," Zhan-Yo had a chance to change the conversation's momentum here and he took it. "I find these dinners to be the best parts of my life."

Sylvie took the words in, looked at Zhan-Yo. They weren't all that far apart in age, in skill, in drive. In another life, perhaps, such a pair might blossom. In this one, Zhan-Yo could tell by that look, she was coming to a decision that would end such a blossom forever.

"Z," Sylvie started. "I don't think—"

"A compliment, Sylvie. Nothing more."

He had tried an advance, and retreated, he hoped, with his force intact. While they both regrouped from the exchange, the curry arrived and invited a pause while they both took bites. Zhan-Yo's carried heat, a cinnamon spice, and a soft orange color lathered over the synth-chicken and peppers. The rice held its composure just long enough for a taste before disintegrating in his mouth. A satisfying way to lick his wounds.

"I don't get that close to anyone," Sylvie said. "It's not a great way to live, but it's the only way I can."

"Because of the danger?" Though, Zhan-Yo thought, he too kept everyone at a distance and spent his days as far away from real danger as anyone. "I can understand that."

"That would be the easy answer." Sylvie looked past Zhan-Yo, into the bulk of the restaurant. "But really, it's because I don't understand other people. Their emotions. What they need. Only how to kill and corrupt them."

Sylvie smiled, in a slanted way that soaked the joke with acid truth.

"That can't be all true," Zhan-Yo replied. "You lead an entire group of soldiers. They follow you."

"They follow the reps." Sylvie finished her glass of wine, poured another. "I'm not looking for pity, Z. I'm not some young girl looking to absorb wisdom from you. I've made my choices, and I'm happy with them. I'm also happy to have these evenings with you. They're refreshing."

So that's what he's worth, then. Refreshing. Sylvie could consider Zhan-Yo whatever she wanted, though, and it would be untoward for him to push against her decision. Compromise. Integrity. Values that had helped him stay at Ziran's top for so long rose to sway his hand to raise his glass, clink it against hers. A clear sound signaling the round's end, and a switch to the night's most necessary topic.

"I've decided I want to be the one," Zhan-Yo said. "When he responds. You will let me know."

"You being there risks everything. We can handle it."

"We will need a leader that can appeal to hearts as well as minds. I must be strong, and the world must see it."

Sylvie watched him. Zhan-Yo looked back. He would show no

cracks. No weakness. He would not say that he wanted to be the one to kill Aegis because he'd never, in all his training and all his years, delivered a death blow before. He would not say that he needed this because the coming road would be paved, he feared, in blood.

He would walk that road, no matter what it took.

AFTER THE PLATES WERE CLEAN, they left the restaurant and Zhan-Yo walked with Sylvie along what were first busy, crowded streets where fresh frozen snow ground beneath tires and boots, then to quieter ones where the fluff had been left undisturbed, frozen now in clumps along the curbs and buildings. Eventually they came to where the snow couldn't reach, and only running melt rivulets gave hints to what lay above.

Zhan-Yo hadn't wanted to talk business at dinner, because the business, such as it was, would take up all night.

36

Insertion

It didn't matter that she'd done it hundreds of times: when Mynx woke up in the afternoon her body felt wronged. As if the organs had shuffled around in her sleep in some mystery dance and only now, upon waking, were hustling to get back to where they belonged.

"Tea." Mynx croaked—dehydration, another late night symptom, lodged in her throat—as she pulled herself out of the bed.

At her words, the bedroom's blackout curtains slid back slow to reveal, in the least painful manner possible, the southern California sun. Despite the chilly season, it seemed brighter than usual today, and Mynx squinted until she managed a look straight down at the floor, at her feet as scuttling drones raced across the wood to collect her slippers and slide them on. Slippers that had micro fibers built into the soles, guaranteeing a level of traction fine for a forty year old, but essential for someone pushing seventy.

"I've re-arranged your schedule to accommodate for your late departure," Reeves said, failing to adjust his voice for Mynx's emerging headache.

"Clear it," Mynx replied. "Today's a waste."

"Unfortunately, I can't do that. It seems someone is attempting to approach the Factory unannounced."

Mynx struggled to push that thought through sleep's remaining sludge, and failed. "Unannounced?"

"Yes, it appears to be Dr. Jones. She is approaching rapidly in a pod."

"Well, Reeves, stop it."

"I have tried. It seems she has overridden the link."

That, finally, pierced the fog. Overriding a pod's systems was not a light undertaking. For one, at the slightest tampering, any pod in Pacifica would send an emergency alert to the drones for support. For another, if tampering continued, the pod itself would engage in a series of cascading system failures designed to render the vehicle nothing more than an expensive chair until those same drones arrived. For Denise to take control of a pod, it meant she had serious skills beyond her biological bent, or serious gear, or both.

"Skip the tea," Mynx said. "Scramble the drones, and get me some coffee."

If this were twenty, thirty years ago, Mynx would have darted from the room. Leaped off the edge of the adjoining deck and caught one of her old suits in mid-air. Thus equipped, she'd have flown back over her house and intercepted the intruder with warnings and lethal threats. As it was, Mynx's muscles were still plenty sore from the drone-suit, already designed to exact the minimum exertion on Mynx's part. So, while Pacifica's Champion didn't exactly hobble from her room, she didn't do much dashing either.

Instead, two vision drones, essentially hovering disks designed to project images on the fly, whirred their way in front of Mynx and showed the rogue pod and its rider. Denise, eyes buried in her Tama, sat in the pod, seeming unconcerned. By now she'd made it through the Factory's outer gate—Reeves ought to have stopped Denise there, but apparently the AI was having issues today. Denise approached the delivery entrance and exit, built large to accept pod trucks for drone shipments, without incident.

"Tell me we're ready for the intercept? It'll be embarrassing if she can get all the way to my door," Mynx said as she went down the short hall towards the kitchen and a much-needed pot of coffee. While Mynx preferred tea, when she needed a quick boost she would turn to the bitter, dark friend.

"Set. Turret drones are enabled, and I have gladiators waiting for her."

Mynx went into her kitchen, a steely ensemble she'd long ago lost any interest or skill in using. Waiting on the counter, doubtless deposited moments ago given the smoke climbing from its soft, teal edges—Mynx loved seafoam, and she used it liberally—was a stiff mug of the black stuff. She carried it out to the deck and sat at that long table, watching the projection as Denise's pod slowed near the door.

Denise emerged wearing a loose dress, with several bags hanging from her shoulders. Also, she had a sheen covering her, as if Denise had read up on the dangers of UV rays and the benefits of being cost-conscious and decided to start drenching herself in cheap sunscreen.

"Reeves, what's she wearing?" Mynx waved off the vision drone and turned to the bigger, better feed on the table.

Denise walked up to the looming gladiator drones, each three meters tall, each with a black-metal hand extended palm out towards her. A clear message to halt, and one backed up by a frankly absurd array of weaponry visible on both drone's backs, sides, and those same outstretched palms. Not only could Denise be stunned, knocked unconscious, or gassed to sleep by these peace-keeping machines, they could also render her into several other states of matter, all of which were incompatible with Denise's continued existence.

Yet, Denise did not stop. She walked up, took a look at the drones, managed a big breath that suggested the confidence in her plan was somewhere short of absolute, and then continued. Right past those hands. Right past the destructive machines Mynx had spent so long perfecting to make intrusions like this an impossibility.

The feed swapped, showed Denise, apparently heartened by her continued life, heading right to the delivery door and, pressing her Tama to the door's lock, opening it. Heading inside.

"Reeves," Mynx said slow. She hadn't even had her tea yet, and her day was falling apart. "What is happening?"

"I'm . . . not certain."

"Probabilities?"

On the table, Denise went into the Factory, looking around. A little lost, then. Which discounted the idea that Denise had somehow hacked inside Mynx's secure systems and corrupted everything. A map, presumably, would have been among the things Denise would have stolen in such a stunt.

"I'm not detecting any system intrusions," Reeves said. "But I am querying the drones now."

It felt a little like a movie, watching Denise wander around Mynx's home and sanctum. Admittedly, this movie made Mynx's stomach churn, lacked a good soundtrack, and any supporting cast. But there was still time for a salvaged ending, one with Denise torched or taken. Or both.

Mynx took a sip. The tea burned her tongue, and rather than cursing or spitting it out, Mynx swallowed it. Just the kind of day it was.

"The drones say they didn't fire because you were the target."

"Repeat that."

"They're saying they didn't register Denise, but you walking up to the Factory."

Mynx waved her hand at the feed on the table. Zoomed in as Denise, who seemed to have finally figured out where she wanted to go, marched deeper into the Factory. That sheen.

"Reeves, you looked into Denise's business ventures, right?"

"I compiled a full dossier, yes."

"Can you tell me how her company makes most of its money?"

"When the university stripped the funding, they turned to bioengineering. Genetic testing for other companies, mainly."

Denise, again tapping with her Tama on a lock that should have been impassable to her, went into the tracker section of the Factory. A move that made clear her end objective. That had Mynx curling her hands—cracking knuckles and all—into fists.

"Would it be a stretch to say she could replicate DNA, and perhaps make it into a film?"

"Cells could be grown into such a thing, yes."

Mynx shut her eyes for a long moment. Then snapped them open. Regrets could come later. She needed to act.

"I need you to seal off the tracker database," Mynx said. "And I need you to bring me a suit."

"The database is now sealed," Reeves replied. "As for the suit, we do not have any ready. Except for the drone protocol?"

"The drones won't fire on her. I need something with manual control."

"Mynx, at your current vital levels, medical recommendations state that you should avoid active combat."

Denise walked past the rooms where Mynx developed tracker gear—better tracers, better suits—without sparing any a glance, going right towards the holy grail at the end. When she reached it, while Mynx tried to figure out what to do, the door that ought to have been sealed, with its locks overridden, swept open for her.

"Reeves! I thought I said seal the chamber?"

"It is sealed," Reeves said. "The only person who could possibly enter would be you."

"She is me, Reeves." Mynx put her forehead in her right hand, leaned on the table.

All the countermeasures, all the security in the world couldn't protect Mynx from herself. A thousand after-action ideas swam through her mind, all useless in the moment. Literally every part of the Factory was designed to respond, to protect, to serve Mynx, and the easiest way to accomplish that had been to tie her genetic signature into everything. Someone might be able to guess or hack a password, but Mynx's own genes? That would take some doing. Even the locks that relied on her ability had a failsafe tied to Mynx's genetic code, because anomaly abilities could be unstable. Genes wouldn't change, shouldn't be duplicable.

Yet, Denise had done it. Because Mynx had given her the tools.

"Perhaps it is a limitation in my programming, Mynx, but I am unable to follow?"

"Nothing to do with your programming, Reeves. Get a suit ready, please." Mynx took another drink as she watched Denise plug something into the workstation, the only one with hard access to the database. "And, if you would be so kind, open an audio channel to Denise."

"You will be live as soon as I am finished speaking."

The table crackled, popped slightly as the audio feed kicked in. Denise, apparently, heard some noise on her end too, as she looked up and around, searching.

"Denise." Mynx worked to tamp down the frustration she felt. "You are trespassing and engaging in an illegal theft."

Denise checked the monitor, which, no doubt, displayed some bar explaining how much anomaly data had been siphoned onto that drive of hers. Mynx wondered if she could order Reeves to cut the power to that part of the Factory, but even if such a move could work, it could risk the integrity of the database, or affect any number of other projects in progress. A chance not worth taking.

"This doesn't belong to you," Denise said, trying to find somewhere to look. "This isn't your DNA. You didn't make it."

"So that excuses breaking into my facility?"

"This should be free for everyone! So many might benefit from access to what you have here." Denise flung a hand towards the workstation, as though showing off a prize on some techno game show. "We might cure diseases, could stop, like you asked me to, aging itself. We could end death!"

"If you knew how many times I've heard those words over the years," Mynx said. "Grand promises left unfulfilled for baser passions. Do you really want all of this to cure the world's ills? Or to end your own?"

Normals proved time and time again that they harbored a corrupting envy for their anomaly cousins. Whether it sprang from a belief in being cosmically wronged when no abilities poured forth at puberty or from a desire to prove themselves the equal of their gifted counterparts, the most dangerous normals nurtured this cancer until it burst out in a desperate move just like this one.

Denise had to know she had no chance of success. Had to know she ruined her career and her life by taking this step, but she stood there, doing it anyway. She didn't bother answering Mynx's question. Instead, at a chime from the workstation, Denise turned and yanked her portable drive free. Jacked it into a slot on her Tama and ran from the room.

"Reeves, she couldn't have copied the whole database," Mynx said, swapping the feeds to watch Denise run through the halls.

"The logs show only thirty percent," Reeves replied.

"Enough to play with, I suppose."

"Do you want me to activate the drones again?"

"And have them wave their hands at her? No. Keep an eye on her instead, watch where she goes," Mynx said. "When she stops, we'll take our data back."

Denise had managed to get her prize. Whether the scientist knew what to do with it, Mynx couldn't say, but she didn't plan on giving Denise time to figure that out.

37

Champion Of The Computer

For his least favorite place in Bastion, Aegis found himself here too often. Technically a part of the visitor tour, the Paragon tower's third floor served as the home to the vast collection of trophies, keys to cities, and some frankly bizarre gifts from nation heads who'd felt the Champions deserved some memorabilia to help them recall their battle against this or that marauding menace.

"Doesn't help, though," Aegis said to a scrawling scroll hanging down a soft cream wall.

Lit from above and designed to look like an accolade from ancient Rome, the scroll called out in old Latin—which Aegis couldn't read, but a plaque beneath helpfully translated—a long day and night where the Champions took down anomalies that had, through mind-warping abilities, convinced the Vatican that they were the Apostles returned.

Aegis couldn't remember any of it. A blur. More and more of his legacy dissolved from his own mind these days, slipping down crevasses he couldn't explore. On the one hand, the change distressed him, as losing any part of who Aegis had been was . . . distressing. On the other, Aegis didn't mind fewer nightmares, didn't mind losing yet another picture of a face bashed in or bloody bodies left behind as the result of an anomaly gone bad.

He worked his way through the tour line, arranged chronologically so that the beginning held individual awards as the Champions built their origins for themselves. Most belonged to Aegis, of course, this being Atlantis and his home. The other Champions had agreed to donate a few things for this museum and frankly, Aegis hadn't pushed for more. His ego alone could fill the halls.

Leaving the ribbons, the group-sized plaques and certificates grew in size and signatories, and the Champion roster grew too, finally reaching the full eight that had served as the world's protectors for a dozen years before becoming the world's rulers. Aegis winced as that word flashed through his mind. Rulers had a foul taste to it, sounded a bit too much like what a villain might say. Champions, guardians—those sounded better.

The tour didn't end so much as transition. From one room to the next, the mood changed from amazing exploits to constant messes made in a world run by normals. Messes cleaned up by the Champions, and the escalating disasters that led to the Champions creating the Paragons and assuming ownership of a humanity strung out to sanity's edge by rogue anomalies, paranoid normals, and a global economy on the brink.

Aegis stopped at this transition. While he didn't need to puff himself up with the trophies, he didn't need to revisit those terrible years either. When the Champions had turned on their former allies and destroyed their power. Ripped nations to the ground and built them back up anew. Those years hadn't been about breaking villains, but breaking civilizations.

He turned and went back through the award rooms, this time taking more attention to the photos. Broad displays showing the first Paragons, the Champions. Always eight of the latter, though not always the same. There had been losses, especially among the early Paragons. In some of the pictures Aegis stood next to people he didn't recognize, not by face. Not till he read the list of names beneath.

His Tama buzzed. A message from the Paragons in Chicago.

They'd identified the when and where for the weapons transfer and were putting together a strike force. They were going to hit the site in advance, and soon. If Aegis had left when Innis first asked he could have been there . . . what had felt, in the moment, a freeing decision had been maturing during the day. He'd said no to helping his own Paragons. Celice and Mynx could say whatever they thought, but at the end of it, that's what Aegis had done. Innis had asked for help and Aegis had refused to give it.

Aegis had come down here to try and find perspective, look at all of these placards for ventures so much more important than an illegal arms sale. These weapons were likely not going to destroy the planet. Likely wouldn't even be noticed. But what Aegis saw, in these rooms, were the Champions helping everyone, always. Some missions ended with accolades like the Roman scroll, yes, but near that trophy was a simple pressed flower from a small Japanese town that had needed help excavating its people from a sudden, dire quake. Another, a letter from school children trapped in a bus that'd been caught in a flash flood.

Minor stuff, but major to those they'd helped. If Aegis could have saved a single life by being in Chicago for this, if he could keep some Paragons from getting hurt, then wasn't it worth it?

His Tama buzzed again. This time an active call. Celice.

"Hey, what are you doing, dad? You're not upstairs?"

"Just living in the past," Aegis replied.

"Well, your future dinner reservation needs some attention too. You're not going to make us late, are you?"

"I suppose that would be rude, wouldn't it?"

Aegis began making his way to the elevators. At this point in the evening, there wouldn't be much competition. A quick ride to the top, a quicker change into something decent for his daughter's no-doubt fancy destination, and he'd be off to a night of charming conversation while his own people fought for their lives.

"You look sad. Is the idea of a night out really that bad?" Celice quirked her face in the Tama's screen.

"Chicago's starting the operation now," Aegis said.

The elevators had been designed to let signals in and out, important when you might have a long ride going from top to bottom. So when Aegis tapped his floor, he could hear Celice start to make a series of impassioned, protesting points about how Aegis had made the right call, these Paragons were adults, and they could all handle themselves. She was right, on all counts.

And yet.

"Let's push the reservation back," Aegis said, punching another, slightly lower number on the elevator's screen as the ascent started. "The Paragons should be working with drones. We can see through them, right?"

Celice sighed loud enough to carry through the Tama's mic. "I'll get us an extra hour. That should be enough."

"Thanks, Celice. I'll buy, tonight."

"You're buying every night for the stress you put me through."

Before Aegis could reply, Celice blinked off from the call. The elevator made its way up to the designated floor, and Aegis exited into what Celice affectionately called the Command Center. Monitors abounded in the open space, where the only walls were Bastion's outer shell. Many of those same monitors, too, moved, shifting around based on Celice's commands and their own programmed logic. Right now, a large screen quartet had made their way to the center, where chairs, tables, and random snacks formed Celice's actual post.

Celice herself wasn't here—likely getting ready for this dinner— but she'd made the call for Aegis, and those four screens held everything he could possibly want to know about the Chicago operation. On those screens Aegis could see the city getting dark—a function of winter's absurdly early sunsets in the north—and six Paragons had assembled in what looked like a side street somewhere downtown. Aegis spoke commands to Polly, Bastion's resident AI, and she flipped two monitors. One, on Aegis's far left, shifted to show an overhead map of the city with the Paragon's precise location. Another, on the far right, swapped to faces and lines; health data taken from Tamas so Aegis could see exactly who was on the team, and whether they were still alive.

Right now, of course, everyone had bright green numbers next to their names.

The middle two monitors held two views; one, a farther out camera feed from a drone, and another the direct visuals from one of the Paragons on the ground. Dima was the name, and Aegis used his own Tama to bring up his stat sheet. Relatively new, but with the powerful ability to alter the magnetic polarity in objects through his eyes. In a metal world, being able to cause things to split apart or pull towards one another could serve all sorts of useful ends.

"Dima," Aegis said, and the camera jerked as the Paragon reacted to his absolute boss and general legend coming through his earpiece. "I'm just checking in. What's the status?"

"Uh, hi, sir," Dima said. "We're, ah, checking in too. Confirming gear and the plan."

"Mind turning up the audio receiver on your Tama so I can hear?"

"Of course not, sir."

Aegis didn't say anything more. Clearly Dima's nerves were on fire, and if they were heading into an armed conflict, Dima didn't need to be worrying about Aegis watching his every move. Once the Paragon adjusted his Tama, the central Chicago sounds began to leak through. There was the same vehicle traffic—all those pods—that Aegis would hear at street level in New York. But here, sandwiched between buildings in a less-traveled section, the ambient noise felt far more distant than it should have.

Which meant Aegis could make out Innis' speech to his team. As those things go, the speech hit the usual booster notes, coupled with pairings and the instructions not to kill if it could be helped, but not to hesitate if it would mean saving a Paragon from injury or death. Dima paired with another, more experienced Paragon named Sabra, who could accelerate time in small, dinner plate-sized pockets.

As for where they'd be going? Innis pointed towards an even tighter alley that descended down towards Chicago's under city. When Dima pivoted, Aegis caught the dimmer lighting, the slight steam coming as generated heat from the machines working beneath encountered the chill air. Depending on the view, the golden glow and silky tendrils could be ominous or beautiful.

With Innis leading, the Paragons began their descent and, almost immediately, the video feed fuzzed.

"Signal loss," Polly answered Aegis's about-to-be-asked question. "The concrete gets in the way."

"Why aren't the drones following?"

Aegis kept his audio link to Dima muted—he didn't want to distract the Paragon. Instead, he listened to their murmured discussions and watched the skipping, blurred images coming his way.

"Innis ordered them to keep their distance," Polly replied. "For the same reason. If a drone loses signal and encounters a novel situation, it's difficult to know what it might do."

Aegis would trust Mynx to get her drones programming right for that kind of scenario, but he wasn't there. Innis was, and the Paragon had every right to call the mission as he saw fit. Speaking of, Innis issued orders for the group of six to set up around a door leading into some power generator building.

"Dima," Innis said, the Scot's voice sounding tinny through the audio transmitter. "Take care of this, would you?"

"On it."

The Paragon walked up to the door and, while Aegis couldn't see Dima's face, he could imagine what the young man did. As Dima's eyes shifted focus, the door began to push against locks and bars that soon began their own attempts to break away. With everything straining against its bonds, it took only a few seconds for the metal to bend and for the door to collapse forward with a groan. Innis stepped in front of Dima, caught the door and shoved it away.

Dead dark stared back at them.

"Seems odd," Sabra spoke, standing behind Dima. "Isn't it easier to meet with the lights on?"

"Maybe we're early," Innis replied, an edge to his words. "Let's go. Slow and easy."

With Innis leading the way, and Dima towards the middle of the pack, the Paragons began to enter the building. As they did, Aegis felt that telltale unease, a sensation born from walking into far too many traps. Sabra had asked the right questions—who would conduct a transfer in the dark, and if they were here early, wouldn't ripping a door off the front be a clue that the meeting place had been compromised?

"Polly, unmute my audio," Aegis said.

"Done."

"Dima, can you hear me?" Aegis tried. The picture coming through was worse than ever, a swimming mass of picture fragments and swaths of black. As if Dima's camera had plunged into the darkest ocean depths. "I want all of you to back out of there. This isn't right."

Dima didn't reply. Nothing changed on the picture either. The audio coming back came in fragments. Curious, at first, and then becoming more and more alarmed.

"Dima?" Aegis tried again.

"It doesn't appear your transmissions are getting through," Polly said.

"Really."

"I've mapped their location. It's indeed a generation station. The electromagnetic interference is breaking our links."

Great. Aegis leaned forward. The picture on the monitor had shifted from black to a spotted gray, as if someone had turned on a light. Clipped shouts burst through the feed, along with bangs, and in less than five seconds after the color shifted, the feed died. Audio too.

"Polly, get it back."

"I'm trying, sir, but it seems like the source has been damaged."

Aegis stood, because sitting seemed too close to doing nothing. Had he lost teams before? Seen friends fail and die, or groups he supervised fall apart in the moment and come back with casualties as a result? Yes. Yes. Of course. That was part of being a leader, the cost exacted on his soul. And every time it burned because if it had been him there, if Aegis had been in that dark room, with his experience and his near invulnerability, he could have changed the outcome.

For most people, saying their mere presence could shift a dramatic event was an exercise in vanity. For Aegis? It was fact.

"Polly, get my plane ready," Aegis said, heading towards the elevators.

"Yes, sir."

Celice wouldn't be happy, but Aegis couldn't see himself going to dinner without knowing what happened to his Paragons. Without helping his team.

It's what Champions did.

38

After Effects

The convention had been prepared for emergencies. Kat learned that much in the smeared intervals through which she rose and fell from consciousness. Drones poured over her, supervised by the ever-more-rare human physicians and paramedics. Gordon told her, later, that they'd given her so much water in so many different ways that he worried they were going to drown her from the inside.

Oh, yeah. Gordon was here, now. In her apartment, where she'd just woken up after a dreamless night punctuated by occasional, surging bursts of nausea. Evidence that those blips weren't entirely imaginary lay in the large bowl by the bed. She'd need to give that one a thorough bleaching before making brownies again. Her guardian snored lightly in her desk chair, his neck bent back over the top of it in a position Kat would have picked as being far too uncomfortable for slumber, but Gordon had a knack for making a bed out of anywhere.

Seeker, though, woke up with Kat and padded his way up the bed to cover her face in licks. She let the dog have his fun. No doubt she needed a shower anyway, and the cost of a little bit of dog slime was a small price for the sheer happiness on Seeker's goofy face.

"Wish I'd taken you," Kat muttered when Seeker gave her a chance to breathe.

Not that the convention had allowed dogs, but even so . . .

"You're awake?" Gordon pulled himself upright, leaned towards her. "Feeling better?"

"As hangovers go, this one isn't too bad." Really, Kat only had the dimmest headache. If medical drones could do this after a night of drinking, well, she'd have to consider making them a regular part of her benders. "Thanks for the help, by the way."

"After your taunting text, it was the least I could do."

Kat rubbed her eyes, sat up. Her stomach lurched a bit. Okay, so a little worse than a headache. "Calvin did it. The anomaly."

"Oh, you mean you didn't drink yourself into oblivion in the early afternoon?"

Gordon was joking, but he put the tiniest, tiniest bit of real concern in there. As if he thought Kat might do just that.

"I'm not the happiest person alive, Gordon, but I'm not that bad," Kat replied. "Did you see Calvin at all?"

"He was gone by the time I got there, and, you know, I had bigger problems to attend to. He's probably left the city by now."

"You can check." Kat waved a hand at her workstation. "Launch my tracker."

"You traced him?"

"Almost as good."

Gordon wheeled the chair back to the living room and Kat followed, rinsing out the bowl and collapsing on the couch as Gordon set to work, launching the tracker program which, thanks to Kat's general disregard for securing her tech, logged right into her profile. Among the usual news and updates on reps earned by her various anomalies, there were other options for Gordon to select. Namely, one for linked pings.

Pings did what their name implied; beamed back coordinates for as long as their tiny, hard-working batteries had life in them. Useful if Kat found an anomaly to trace in an area, like, say, a crowded convention, that didn't lend itself to a full confrontation. While she'd gone up to Calvin with the stun gun ready, she'd also slipped the ping onto the man's jacket as an insurance; supposedly Calvin was deadly, and why take chances?

"All right, I'm impressed," Gordon said, selecting the ping's signature. "Though I keep forgetting, you're pretty good at this."

"No reason why you should remember. None at all."

Kat mentally ran through the years dating, the dual tracker career they'd had, and the many, many times Gordon had forgotten this or that key element of Kat's life. The man had a mind like a sieve. Or, rather, as Kat had learned the hard way, Gordon only held fast to those things he really cared about.

"Whoa, look." Gordon pulled himself away from the screen, spread his hands. "I'm not going to get into a fight, okay? You're an hour away from nearly dying, and we've got this deadly anomaly running around, so—"

"Prioritize. Yeah. Look at the map and tell me where he is."

Gordon gave her a leveled stare that promised this conversation would be revisited, and held it until Kat rolled her eyes and nodded towards the monitors. Seeker, curled beneath her left arm and resting his big fluffy head against her chest, sniffed. The dog understood; now was not the time to get dramatic.

"You want to know where he is?" Gordon swiveled as he spoke. "I bet he's long out of town. Took the first train and . . ."

Gordon's voice trailed off as what began as a city-wide map of Chicago zoomed in deeper and deeper, showing Calvin, or at least the ping Kat had tacked onto him, were both in the city and not all that far away. Calvin didn't seem so flush with reps that he'd be staying in the more expensive neighborhoods. And this, Kat saw as she leaned forward to get a better look, was far from a luxury neighborhood. Near *Carver's*, the ping's location put it squat in the an industrial wasteland.

"I'm waiting," Kat said.

Gordon shook his head. Took another look at the monitor, as if it might have been lying to him the first time. "He might have thrown it off."

"Sure. Waited till he got all the way out there to do it, too."

Not the best argument—Calvin might not have found the ping

until he'd reached wherever he was staying and then cast it off on some random street rather than downtown—but the fact that the ping was moving, at walking pace, suggested otherwise. Kat resisted the temptation to believe Calvin was some super-spy, able to find the ping and savvy enough to stick it on someone else just to mislead them. That way led to madness.

"Are you ready?" Gordon's transition from caretaker to tracker happened in an instant, and he bounded up from the chair as he spoke. "He's not far. We can catch him now."

Kat really did want to say no. She'd escaped death and had no desire to run right back into it again, but Gordon seemed like he'd go for Calvin no matter what Kat chose, and she wasn't about to let him get credit for her tracking skills. Scooting out from under Seeker, pushing her lingering headache to the back of her mind, Kat made her way out of the bed and moved past Gordon to her closet. Going after an anomaly in a long t-shirt and pajama shorts in winter didn't seem like the best idea.

The move also made her reckon with who had brought her back here, who'd changed her from her convention outfit to something more comfortable for what must have been a long night.

"Hey, Gordon?" Kat said, turning back to him as Gordon started pulling on his tracker gear. "Thanks. For yesterday. I mean it."

"No problem," Gordon replied. "You found Calvin, I saved you, think that makes us right about even."

"Because that's what this is about." Kat readied a good glare to blast Gordon, but the tracker had that joking half-smile on his face that put the lie to his words, and Kat swapped to a sigh and a renewed focus on her outfit. "You have all your stuff here? I'm not a hundred percent on what Calvin can do, but he's not playing around."

"Stun gun. Tracer. Incredible athletic ability, yep, think I've got everything."

"When he's beating you, I'm not going to help. I'm just going to watch and laugh."

"Kat, when did you get so mean?"

. . .

GORDON PAID for a pod to take them directly to where the ping pegged Calvin, but at the last minute canceled the ride so it dropped them a block away. On her Tama, Kat looked up the coordinates and found Calvin's locale was home to a working-man's cafe, the kind that offered eggs, bacon, and potatoes with portion sizes large enough to decimate any diet. For all the work done by governments before and after the Paragon's rise to power to push people towards healthier lifestyles, humanity, in Kat's opinion, remained stalwart in defending hollandaise, scones, and heaping pancake piles.

The sidewalk here was wider than usual, accounting for, perhaps, the sprawling density this far west in Chicago. More room for bigger streets, more rumbling pod trucks carting loads from work sites, less people, but more stuff on the sidewalks. As if the stores and block-sized apartments around here used the cement between their doors and the street as extra storage space. This being winter, snow took over the sidewalk, but lumpy, odd-shaped piles hinted at junk hiding below.

"Haven't been to a place like this in a while," Gordon said as they left the pod.

"What, you're only hunting rich anomalies now?"

"Kind of." Gordon had the decency to sound a bit embarrassed. "If you ever went to work for the Paragons proper, you'd get that too. They send me all over for high-profile targets, and most of those are anomalies that have used their powers to, well, get out of spots like this."

"One more reason for me to stay here, then," Kat replied, taking a deep breath. Still winter crisp, but with an undercurrent of cooking oils and plastics. "I prefer this to the lux lands you live in, where everyone's sporting suits and a need to show off."

Kat knew she was stereotyping, just like Gordon; but this was still her city, still Chicago, and the need to defend all its quarters rested deep in her heart. Maybe because she didn't have a family, the city had filled that void. At least, the parts Kat found herself frequenting.

"I get it," Gordon said. "I'll keep my comments to myself." They went past a hardware store, a sign in the window advertising drone repairs, and came closer to the café, Kat guiding Seeker on his leash before Gordon put a hand on her shoulder to stop her. "So what's our strategy here? Go in and take him out?"

"Last time I sneaked up on Calvin, he almost killed me. I say we don't give him a chance."

"Agreed. Let me punch in a clearance."

On his Tama, Gordon tapped in codes, alerting drones and Paragons in the area that a tracker operation was about to take place, with the potential to get violent. Kat had those codes too, though Gordon apparently had higher access, because the approval came back almost immediately. If Kat had asked to get physical in a crowded space, she'd probably have to talk her way through a Paragon's questioning before getting the okay.

One of many reasons why she preferred hunting anomalies outside the city, or in *Carver's* basement, without drones to deal with.

"You want to go first, or me?" Gordon asked once he finished his Tama business.

Kat looked around the street. Mostly deserted, too early in the morning for the lunch crowds, but late enough that anyone seeking a dawn-adjacent coffee had already slaked their thirst. The squishing pod wheels rolling through slush was about all they could hear. As settings for a fight went, this one hit all the marks.

"Me," Kat said. "You stay back. He'll recognize me, but he seemed willing to talk last time. He might hesitate long enough."

Gordon nodded. "And Kat? If this starts to go wrong?" He pulled aside his jacket, revealing the stun gun, yes, but also something else. Something very illegal except for authorized holders. "After what happened to you, the Paragons gave me permission. If Calvin gets violent, we're supposed to take him out."

"I'm not shooting that thing."

"Hopefully we won't need to."

Killing. Something Kat had done before, though always in defense and always with regret. Some anomalies wouldn't accept surrender, tracing. Even after getting stunned, getting enrolled in the

Paragon's cycle of work requests, they'd come back for Kat, looking for revenge. Trackers had unlimited license to defend themselves in those instances, and Kat could deliver blows hard enough to break a neck or compress a chest. Those moments, though, played over and over in her nightmares, and she had no desire to add to them.

With Seeker, she left Gordon one shop away from the cafe, a little place calling itself The Breakfast Nook and advertising, on a foldable sign placed on sidewalk ice, a double sausage special for a rep price so low it made Kat's stomach growl. In their hustle, Kat realized she hadn't had breakfast, coffee, or anything really since the day before. Maybe if they took care of Calvin fast, she could grab a bite right here . . .

A tiny alley served as a starting gap to the cafe, and with Seeker enjoying a leash-pulling set of smells on the walk's left side, Kat looked right as she approached the cafe's glass windows. The big panels had fogged on the edges, with icy crystals making a natural lattice where the cafe's heating failed to win out against the day's cold. It was beautiful enough that it took Kat a second to notice the face framed within that lattice, one that saw her as she set eyes on him. Calvin sat at the window table, a big coffee mug and a finished plate of eggs-n-something in front of him, along with a real, live, ratty book. They held eyes, Calvin's going from surprised to exasperated in that same time frame. Then he reached out and put his left hand on the window, right near Kat's face.

Whether it was intuition, instinct, training or just plain luck, Kat started to dive as Calvin's hand went up, so when the entire window shattered, its glass blowing outwards towards Kat and the sidewalk, she'd already made it low enough to dodge the worst damage. Concussive force rolled over her, shoved Kat back along the sidewalk into the drift at the street's edge. Seeker barked, and Kat curled up, trying to protect herself from the glass, and trying, trying not to fall apart.

That sidewalk had been smaller than this one, with patches of faded green from grass clippings left to molder by her father's haphazard mowing. Too cheap to get a drone, too busy to excel at household maintenance, Kat had landed right in one of those patches when the force had thrown her away from her own front porch.

She'd been running back from the playground near the summer sunset, had made the critical last turn to head down the walk splitting their yard to the two-story, light blue-with-white-shutters house, when the front door opened. Her mother, hair and eyes wild, began to yell in a voice Kat had never heard before. High, sharp, and telling Kat to go back, to run away. The sight, sound was so strange that Kat had stopped, had asked her mother why, when Kat noticed the light. Soft white dominated the color of their home's lamps, but this was a rosy orange and it grew, its fuzzy edges expanding behind her mother and in the windows on her right and left. Her mother turned back, saw that light, took a step towards Kat, waving for her to run.

A flash, a cascade of pops and a curling rush of hot air threw Kat to the ground, where glass flew against her body. Her face burned, skinned on the concrete. Her neck and hands and legs sparked as shards poked through.

"Mom?"

"Mom?" Gordon said, leaning in close. "Stay down, Kat. Help's coming. I'm going after him."

Gordon left—from her angle, Kat only saw his boots turning and stomping away—while the sidewalk glittered as winter light played off the shattered glass.

Breathe.

Other people streamed out of the cafe now, with two, an older man and woman, coming Kat's way. Asking her if she was all right.

Seeker. Where'd he go?

Kat moved to stand, when her two helpers grabbed her arms and pulled her up instead.

"Don't want to be putting your hands in all that, I think," the man said, struggling to put logic back in a world that seemed to have lost it. "Don't know why a window would break like that, but glass'll cut you up for sure."

"Here, let me help you," the woman added, dabbing at Kat's face with a few napkins likely taken from the cafe.

"My dog." Kat said, trying to see around the hands of the woman. "Where is he?"

"Janey's holding him," the woman said. "He'd cut his paws on this glass just like you would."

The words threw Kat back too. The same things her neighbors kept telling her as they pulled her away from her house, from the burning wreck. Of her mom, running towards her, there was no sign except a blasted black patch on the smoldering front steps. Kat had called out to her, her father too as help arrived—more human than drone, back then—but he'd never emerged either. Her sister, gone. It'd be hours yet till someone managed to tell her what had happened, what could happen with an anomaly gone undiscovered.

"I'm fine." Kat shook herself free of the hands, the help. "Thanks."

Her suit, that white tracker-grade gear, had done wonders here, sealing off her body from those glass shards. The connected contacts had their own protective mechanisms, expanding to coat her eyes with a hardened film. Temporary blindness for a fraction of a second, but worth it to keep her eyes safe. Given the size and number of jagged pieces around her, Kat would have been a shredded mess had she come after Calvin in street clothes.

Calvin.

With Kat's evident lack of life-threatening injuries and, therefore, drama, the cafe escapees transitioned to looking at and muttering over the shattered pain of glass. The ensuing freedom gave Kat the chance to reclaim her dog from the young girl holding Seeker back, and try to figure out where the anomaly, and Gordon, had gone. The answer, apparently, was nowhere in sight.

Seeker barked at her. Impatient, all-knowing. She let his leash go and the dog sprinted off, jumping over the glass and skipping around the crowd in an absurd athletic display that had Kat, who followed with crunching steps and apologies to those she pushed aside, feeling way too jealous. Seeker might have been her pet, her best friend, but he was far more than just those. Arguably, Seeker was Kat's greatest weapon. In fact, screw the arguably. Without that dog, Kat's career as a tracker would've been shorter, bloodier, and pathetic.

The husky took a hard right at the next intersection, throwing one tongue-wagging glance back to make sure Kat ran hot on his heels, and then kept going. When Kat rounded the corner, she nearly fell into Gordon, who leaned on a post, hand to his chest. With Seeker bounding on, Kat only had a moment, and Gordon gave it back to her.

"Keep going," Gordon coughed. "He waited for me around the corner, punch knocked the wind out of me. I'll be right behind you."

So Kat went. Calvin was far more than the usual anomaly target. A dangerous power plus savvy and skill. Kat had taken down explosive anomalies who knew nothing beyond their reliance on their ability, who tended to collapse when thrown from their comfort zone by a stun gun or charging canine fangs, but Calvin seemed like he could adapt. His power, too, seemed different. Anomalies only had one mutation—at least, so far as Kat knew—yet Calvin had nearly killed her with alcohol poisoning and now had blown a window apart with a touch. So either he was a new terror, or Kat hadn't yet figured out his core ability. Regardless, Calvin was a unique flavor of dangerous. No wonder the Elementals wanted him.

Seeker had cut across the street, weaving between a few pods, and dashed down another cross-cutting alley with trash bins and smoking vents. Kat made the same maneuver, banking on the pod's hard programming against ramming humans to keep her alive. Emergency sirens filled the air as drones and rescue pods raced towards the damaged cafe. A high-stress backdrop to the slopping sound of her boots scattering slush everywhere she stepped, the acrid vented industry mixing with the cafe's pent-up kitchen pleasures.

Midway down the alley, Calvin turned to confront Seeker's barking charge. Kat came round the entry corner—her hand brushing the cold brick side—and yelled for Seeker to stop. Calvin waited a dozen meters away, the dog between them, Seeker looking back at Kat as if to say, in a very fluffy voice, *I had him!*

"Good call," Calvin said. "Don't have anything against your dog."

He looked like a man who'd been up all night watching the windows. Bags sat under his dark eyes, and his clothes seemed more ramshackle than before. Kat didn't know how many outfits Calvin traveled with, but these had seen scraps and escapes, telling their tales in stains and rips. Yet, even with all that, Calvin stood tall, his arms relaxed at either side. Ready.

"You told me, before you tried to kill me, that you felt hunted." Kat figured she could try diplomacy with this distance between them, figure Calvin out, and give Gordon a chance to pull himself together. "Still feeling that way?"

"What would make you say that?"

"Exploding a bunch of glass in my face, for one."

"That was supposed to kill you. Which is harder than it should be."

"Because your heart isn't in it."

Kat didn't know she was going to say that, but she felt it and spoke the damn words because they were the truth, and that meshed with everything she'd picked up on Calvin. Why she'd approached him with a stun gun instead of shooting him from across the convention floor. Why she'd tried to tease the power out of him in *Carver's* even though it would have been easier to kill Calvin right there. Kat didn't read evil in him. Fear, danger, sure. But evil?

"You don't know anything about my heart."

Kat still had the stun gun in her pocket, had the grappler on her suit ready to fire from her wrist. She could even launch the scanners and use their bright flashes to blind Calvin for a second. Instead, with Seeker looking at both of them, Kat left her hands clear. Wide and open. Calvin, for his part, seemed as frozen with indecision. Turn his back and Kat could take him out from behind, run towards her and she'd have time to draw and fire before he'd get close, not even counting the dog.

"Know what's going to happen if you run?" Kat tried a different tactic. "We'll keep hunting you. So will others. Constantly. You're getting too big a name for yourself, Calvin. There's no more hiding. It's time to come in."

Calvin's reply was cut off by a new voice from above. Two pacification drones, human-sized ovals laced with non-lethal ways to subdue someone, floated into the alley and angled towards Calvin. In a voice intended to sound like someone's soothing mother, they ordered Calvin to lay down, that things would be fine if he would surrender. Calvin broke his focus on Kat, looked up towards the drones, and knelt to the concrete ground. For a second, Kat wondered if Calvin would give up that easily, if either her words or the drones pushed Calvin over the line into surrender.

Until, on his knees and leaning forward with his hands on the ground, Calvin lifted his left hand up towards the descending drones. The gray, slushy concrete beneath Calvin shimmered, like a glass of water disturbed by a small tremor, before the air changed around Calvin's outstretched hand. Like a fog, but dark gray and heavy, Calvin's mist spread out towards the drones, wrapping around them. Their electric jets whined, sputtered, and extinguished as their repeated calls for calm crackled out and died.

"Seeker! Here!" Kat said, and the dog obeyed, getting well away from whatever Calvin was doing.

The fog continued to thicken, until Kat couldn't see anything on its other side. She realized, too, that though the drone's engines had stopped, they hadn't fallen. Instead, they were suspended in that fog, parts totally obscured. Trapped, as if the fog had become solid gel.

"Leave me alone, Kat!" Calvin's voice came quiet, like an echo bouncing. "Tell them all to leave me alone!"

"Don't run, Calvin! We can talk!" Kat tried, but she heard nothing back.

Instead, keeping Seeker close, she approached that wall of gray fog. Though, now that she was close, it didn't really seem like fog at all; clear lines, no fuzziness or movement with the winter breezes that shot down these alleys. Kat raised her hand, put it against the gray. Solid. Hard. Like concrete. Calvin had built a wall right here, in between these two buildings. But . . . how?

"Where is he?" Gordon called, still sounding weak, but standing back at the entrance to the alley. "Did you get him?"

Kat shook her head, combing the new wall, looking for the answer. "He made this and ran. I don't know how."

"Out of the air?"

Kat reached out, touched it again. Definitely concrete. "The air, yeah. Trapped two drones, too."

This time, when Kat withdrew her hand, the wall shivered. As she watched, cracks appeared, pieces began to fall and split into dusty fragments as they scattered around her. Seeker barked and Kat heeded the dog's advice, backpedaling as Calvin's new wall collapsed on itself, the drones smashing to the ground with it. The larger chunks of Calvin's concrete, broken up by the crash, shivered and broke down into gray sand, which blew away with the next gust, forcing Kat to shield her eyes as she went forward.

On the other side of Calvin's wall, where the anomaly had been kneeling, was a deep hole, perfect and smooth, as if scooped from the earth with a spoon.

39

Preparation

Sylvie kept him away, even though Zhan-Yo had all the equipment he would need: Two tachi, short, curved family blades sharpened by history and an excellent specialty shop not far from his home, were strapped to Zhan-Yo's back. The loose robes he wore to his marshal arts classes covered up new additions: armored pads like those Sylvie wore, strong enough to stop bullets and ready to redirect heat and electricity, common anomaly elements.

Rather than using this preparation, which Zhan-Yo described to Sylvie the night before, Zhan-Yo sat in the generation station's back room, amid janitorial gear and toolboxes, watching the Paragons come to stop him on an encrypted feed from his Tama. They were fighting towards the station's entrance, though the picture quality became crap after Sylvie cut the lights. Amid the blurs and blinks as powers flashed, Zhan-Yo tried to find Aegis. He recognized some of the Paragons in the blitz—Innis, that red-bearded blusterer was all over Chicago's airwaves proclaiming this and that Paragon initiative —but Zhan-Yo thought Aegis would be the first one inside.

"We're sealing the doors now," Sylvie's voice came from Zhan-Yo's Tama, patched in through the mission's secure, local line. "Take them. Try not to kill if you don't have to."

Sylvie's order looked hard to follow. The Paragons certainly weren't playing by the same rules. They'd come in hot, blasting into Sylvie's thugs and acting with the confidence you're not supposed to have if all your communications were cut off. Those half-dozen Paragons ought to surrender, and at first Zhan-Yo figured Innis's presence boosted their drive, but now, as they threw themselves into Sylvie's forces in the generator's central room, it became clear they simply thought they couldn't lose.

At first it seemed like the darkness might serve as an edge for Sylvie's forces, springing with their night-vision helmets and smashing into the Paragons, an initial burst that succeeded in pushing the Paragons away from their only exit and past the point where, Sylvie declared, their communications could be completely severed. The Paragons, though, grouped together, carrying the opening assault's only victim, someone Zhan-Yo couldn't see until she'd recovered enough to ruin their plan. Whomever this Paragon was, as Innis and the others fought a desperate, moving battle in the dark, she'd been dragged along until they'd reached the main room. Then, just before Sylvie called to seal the doors, the Paragon had woken up, and gone supernova.

A superlative word to describe a superlative result. At one moment there'd been no light and a squad of Sylvie's soldiers surrounding the Paragons with stun guns and paralyzing shock batons, and then everything had flashed so bright as to send Zhan-Yo's Tama feed to static until it had recovered. And what a sight when it did.

If Zhan-Yo's life had a great contradiction, it was his respect, even wonder for anomaly abilities contrasted with his hatred of what those same abilities had wrought. Here, in the room's center, shone a woman who's skin glowed more brilliantly than the brightest light Zhan-Yo had ever seen. A pure silver, so searing that only her clothes kept it from blinding everyone in the room. A power beautiful, terrible, and one Zhan-Yo had no desire to destroy except that her reversal meant Sylvie's forces were now stumbling around trying to take off their useless goggles. A Paragon took advantage of the flash: repelling those thugs he looked at from the floor and sending them to the ceiling, where they stuck, arms and legs flailing.

Worse, with this new light, Zhan-Yo could see Aegis hadn't come. Not only had they managed to seal themselves in a building with deadly Paragons, they didn't even catch their target.

"Sylvie," Zhan-Yo said, standing up and speaking into his Tama. "We have to save this."

"I'm already on it."

"If you don't mind, I am going to help."

If Sylvie had an opinion on Zhan-Yo's change in plans, borne both of desperation and frustration, she kept those opinions to herself.

Zhan-Yo left his back room, which opened into a smaller, dim hallway connecting the maintenance bays with the primary generator room, and, after a quick equipment check, drew the tachi and advanced towards the connecting door. The heavy, insulated steel portal, meant to keep this back area safe in case of some overload, did a strong job muffling the sound. By the time Zhan-Yo came near the door, he wasn't sure whether a fight was still going on in the room beyond. He could open this and find himself against the Paragons alone.

Then again, if the fight had ended, those same Paragons would search back here and find him eventually. Better to risk helping now than surrender, helpless, later. He sheathed his left tachi, grabbed the handle and yanked down to disengage the lock. Zhan-Yo pulled the door open, keeping its bulk between him and what lay beyond, poking his head around the edge to see what fight he walked into.

Sylvie, alone, held the center. She had a knife up to the glowing Paragon's throat, backing her against the wall opposite Zhan-Yo. The other five Paragons, some with light wounds but otherwise looking unscathed, watched her. Bodies belonging to Sylvie's forces littered the space.

They hadn't heard Zhan-Yo open the door because Sylvie yelled, loudly, for the Paragons to back away from her. To the right, the corridor leading to the building's entrance, locked now but with a passcode Zhan-Yo had stored on his Tama, stood unguarded. He could run, get out and, by the time the Paragons extracted some confession from Sylvie, be ready to deny his involvement. Reset back to square one and start again.

Except . . . Zhan-Yo caught Sylvie's eye for the briefest second before she focused back on her opponents. She didn't want to give Zhan-Yo away, because, now, she depended on him.

He would not disappoint her.

Zhan-Yo did not creep, but instead burst into the room, both tachi angling for the center two Paragons. All thought of taking the heroes alive had vanished—Aegis wasn't here, Zhan-Yo's forces were losing, this was as desperate as it could get—and Zhan-Yo's strikes went for kills. Or, they did until an incredible force yanked both tachi from his hands and sent them rocketing up towards the ceiling, where the blades embedded in the metal shielding plates. One Paragon on the right, a young man, had followed his partner's glowing light-eyes and looked Zhan-Yo's way.

"Behind us!" the Paragon yelled, fully spoiling the surprise.

So Zhan-Yo switched tactics, and as the two central Paragons began to turn around, he delivered snap kicks to the backs of their left and right knees. Hard enough to blow them out and send the Paragons to the ground. The young man and another, older woman were to the right and Innis on the left. Zhan-Yo left the leader, as Innis seemed to be moving slow, perhaps he'd been hurt, and went for the other two. The woman stepped up to meet him, and as she did, she seemed to expand and split. There were three of her, one looking young and fresh, a middle-aged version of the woman in the middle, with the original, older one on the right. All three dropped into a kick-boxing stance, shielding the man behind them. Zhan-Yo didn't wait—with numbers against him, speed was his only advantage.

Zhan-Yo feinted straight, as if he was going to plow right over the original Paragon. The younger, older versions collapsed in from the sides, so when Zhan-Yo planted his left foot and knelt into a floor-circling sweep of a kick, he knocked the ankles out of all three. The first impact, with the original Paragon, had the stiffness of real muscle and bone. The other two, though, felt more like water. Less substantial. That factor proved its worth a moment later, when the young and middle-aged versions sprang back with an alacrity impossible for a full-weight person. Before Zhan-Yo had recovered from his own move, the two were on him, delivering a series of hits to his sides. The pads soaked up the hits, which struck with less strength than a normal blow Zhan-Yo would have expected for a woman like this one.

To get away from the rain, Zhan-Yo broke right, pushing through the kidney shots of the original Paragon and trampling her. Not exactly the smoothest maneuver, but he drew the younger version into an almost-blind charge, which Zhan-Yo countered with a spinning high kick. Right to the neck, a move that would have snapped any normal person but that, here, seemed to slush into the younger form, knocking her to the ground but without the telltale crack of bone. The missing resistance caused Zhan-Yo to stumble back, tripping over the older one that he'd just knocked over. The last form, then, took her chance to pounce, with a skull-rattling kick to Zhan-Yo's head.

It'd been a long time since Zhan-Yo had suffered a true concussion, a strike that sent the world into blurs. This one sent the long shadows in the room swirling, and Zhan-Yo's stomach threatened to release dinner's contents while his inner ears forgot which ways were up, down, or in between. The original Paragon rose up over him, her body seeming to bob and weave as if they were on a rocking boat and not a sturdy concrete floor.

"Give up," the woman said. "You're done."

Done? The fight had barely begun! He only needed a minute, or an hour, to put himself back together. His whole cause couldn't end here, not because of some low level Paragon. He tried to tell her as much, but when he opened his mouth, all the light in the room vanished. In the sudden dark, Zhan-Yo thought he heard Innis and the young man shouting to each other, thought he heard the

Paragon standing on him ask a question. This was the moment. He had to act, and without the light, there was nothing for his damaged head to spin, so Zhan-Yo struck. Straight up, with all the strength he could muster. He caught her soft stomach, and with a coughing grunt, the Paragon fell back off of him. Zhan-Yo tried to stand, wobbled and fell over onto the very Paragon he'd just struck.

She tried to grapple him, getting her arms around his neck as Zhan-Yo's back pressed her against the floor. He squirmed, instincts pushing past mushy senses, and he delivered shot after shot with his elbows even as the other two forms fell on him. One of those shots must have connected, because the Paragon's arms relaxed and both the young and middle-aged forms, their scrabbling hands reaching for his face, vanished as if they'd never been. Zhan-Yo simply breathed for a second. Tried to piece himself together, get his head to stop, to squash the mounting fear of what it might mean to fight an army full of abilities like this.

The world had surrendered to the Champions and their Paragons. Not because the world couldn't fight, but because the fight could only have one winner.

"Lights up!" Sylvie's voice cracked above the sounds of scuffle, and, though Zhan-Yo hadn't realized Sylvie still had more operators in reserve, someone answered her call and flipped the generator station's lights back on.

The blue-white glow gave the reason why Sylvie felt she could give that command. She stood over the prone forms of the woman who'd lit herself up, and the young man who seemed to be the one messing with polarities, as objects—like Zhan-Yo's twin blades— began to fall from the ceiling as their weights made connections with gravity. The two Paragons Zhan-Yo had struck from behind were struggling to rise, until Innis moved between them and put a massive hand on each of their backs.

"Keep yourselves down," Innis said. "Less chance they'll kill ya that way."

"We ought to kill you," Sylvie said to Innis. "My men weren't supposed to be hurt."

"Neither were mine."

Zhan-Yo managed to get to his knees, the general nausea playing in his gut subsiding enough, the world stopping its spinning enough, to permit an attempt at standing. An attempt that quickly swapped to a leaning fall against the nearest wall.

"You weren't supposed to bring anyone else," Sylvie fired back, thus far ignoring Zhan-Yo's plight. One of her knives began its plummet from above, and without taking a glance from Innis, Sylvie plucked it from the air like it'd been a falling leaf instead of a sharp blade. "You and Aegis. Alone. That was the plan."

"The plan changed. Aegis isn't coming." Innis sounded as frustrated as Sylvie, and Zhan-Yo had to wonder if that was because his team had been injured, or because Aegis still lived.

Some of Sylvie's thugs were starting to come 'round now too, rubbing their faces and getting to their feet. Sylvie, with a series of gestures, set them to work binding the Paragons with zip-ties and healthy applications of stun gun darts. If you wanted to be sure a Paragon couldn't use their ability, just keep them unconscious.

"You're a traitor?" One of the Paragons Innis held down sputtered. "What?"

"None of your business," Innis growled, and before he had to defend himself any further, one of the thugs put the Paragon to sleep. "The plan's a bust, Sylvie. Now I've got to take care of this. You should've just let us leave."

"No," Zhan-Yo spoke, his voice weaker than he thought it'd be, but it still carried along the echoing metal walls. "The plan has changed."

Sylvie finally picked up that Zhan-Yo was not all right, and she stepped across the room to give him a shoulder to lean on, "What happened?"

"A little kick to the head. I was slow," Zhan-Yo replied, then looked over at Innis. "Take him too."

Aegis led vast anomaly network, just as Zhan-Yo ran a vast corporation. When situations were dire, Zhan-Yo didn't hesitate to go in person to rectify the problem, to save his business, his employees. These Paragons were in trouble, and Aegis had a habit of getting himself personally involved. He would come for these. He wouldn't resist the call to be the hero.

"Sylvie, we need to send a message. To Aegis. Tell him that we have his team," Zhan-Yo said, leaning on Sylvie and keeping his eyes closed as much as he could. "He'll come, and we'll take him when he does."

40

Actions Come With A Cost

Of the things Mynx didn't want to do so soon after fighting Thane, gearing up for another assault listed pretty high. Still sore, still tired, Mynx nonetheless awoke to Reeve's report that he'd traced Denise Jones back to her lab. All through yesterday, Denise had zipped around the L.A. area, never stopping for more than an hour at a time. A pattern, Mynx felt, that fit right in line with someone gathering what they'd need to make a getaway, or a last stand.

Not that Denise would find it easy to leave the city. Reeves, on Mynx's instruction, had invalidated Denise's IDs and frozen her accounts, using the unilateral power that would have taken a tandem team of courts and police in the pre-Paragon world. Ripe for abuse? Maybe, but that was the whole point; the world had to trust the Champions wouldn't run wild with their power, because the world didn't have a choice. At any rate, should Denise attempt any legitimate escape, she'd be picked up by drones or humans when she tried to scan her Tama.

That Denise hadn't been caught yet suggested she had help. Everyone knew the Champions could clamp down on a criminal, Mynx could be seen on billboards all over Pacifica detailing all the ways to get yourself on the Paragon's naughty list, so Denise probably planned for it. Recruited some hapless saps to help her with the promise of becoming anomalies someday, a deal that sounded destined for low-budget afternoon programming. Yet Mynx, and the other Champions, had seen the mystical fruit of potential powers dangled over so many common criminals by delusional would-be masterminds that the cliched plot points of yesteryear had a depressing home in today's reality.

"You think she's going to stay there?" Mynx said, back at her projection table.

She wasn't wearing her robe, was sipping harsh black coffee, and had already taken pills meant to soothe away her muscle soreness. Today's cloud-scattered sunlight and the ocean's pounded waves, whipped up by an overnight cloudburst, echoed Mynx's violent thoughts. Pacifica's Champion prepared for war, and it would be a swift, total one.

"The pod she's using has been freed to the pool, and while there's frequent traffic to the lab, she hasn't left," Reeves replied. "It is, of course, impossible to predict irrational human behavior, but the indications are that Denise is staying put."

"She's trying to race," Mynx said, flipping the projection on the table to a circling drone's live feed of Denise's lab. "She must think she's so close to cracking the secret that with a few more hours, she'll be able to have her own army of makeshift anomalies."

"The realities of scientific work make that outcome doubtful."

"You're not wrong, but, like you just said, humans are irrational." Mynx finished her coffee and held up a single hand with a finger pointing towards the sky. "I think it's time we show how irrational she is."

"Not your best line, but it will do," Reeves replied, beginning the process to send some of the Factory's designated drones over to Mynx.

"Reeves, remind me to adjust your opinion algorithms. You ought to think everything I say is gold."

"On the contrary, I must occasionally present a humbling argument, as it has been exhaustively shown that humans with high egos get themselves killed at higher rates."

"So you're insulting me to keep me safe?"

"Yes."

There were times, many times, when Mynx wondered if she'd done too good a job with the AIs powering the Champion's homes. Unlike the drones, which had limited ability to flex outside their programmed parameters, Reeves could do anything his connections allowed. This meant being sarcastic, yes, but also allowed him to tap into Pacifica's pods, its electrical grid, monitor every news feed that played to the internet, etc. Thus far, there'd been no AIs going crazy or embarking on a mad war against humanity like in the movies and books, but that didn't mean it couldn't happen.

"Mynx," Reeves said as the first drone attached itself to Mynx's left leg, followed quickly by another on her right. "I must also advise against taking any personal action here. We have enough drones to flatten or take Denise captive without your literal involvement."

"I know that," Mynx said as a third drone, larger than the first two, wrapped itself around her chest. While the set she'd worn against Thane was a haphazard collection made of drones that happened to be there, these hometown creations stayed at the Factory for when Mynx needed her max-level gear, and their perfect fits showed it. "But Denise has to know we'll be coming after her. I'm too old to draw this out, Reeves. I'm going to finish this now so I can actually get some sleep tonight."

By the time the drones attached themselves to her, Reeves had gladiator drones ready to escort Mynx to Denise's lab. Too big, now, to fit in a pod, Mynx powered up the battery propulsion systems in her new legs. They had enough power to get her to the lab, but probably not for a return trip; the individual drone engines couldn't lift the combined weight of Mynx and the suit for all that long. It shouldn't matter—after the attack, Mynx could disengage the armor and take a relaxing pod ride home.

"Reeves, lock down the Factory while I'm gone," Mynx said after she'd glided over her own roof and landed amid the four drones waiting to escort her. "Nobody in, even if they scan as me. I'll pass along a verbal code when I get back."

"And what code will that be?"

Mynx rattled off of precise sequence of ones and zeros—her birthdate in binary. Too long for someone mimicking her voice to guess, and it scratched that little trivia itch she had.

"Also, Reeves, keep running the tests. Even if Denise made this whole idea up, I want to see if there's any truth at all to it."

Would you stop looking for the greatest treasure just because one of the hunters turned out to be a cheat? No. Mynx had been betrayed before, would probably be betrayed again. It'd never stopped her from pressing forward.

"Of course." Reeves said. "You also have an incoming priority call. From Aegis."

Mynx almost swore. If Aegis had already put himself in more trouble, forced her to fly back to the East coast, Mynx might have an aneurysm right here and now. She had her own business to take care of, and couldn't keep being at Aegis's beck and call whenever the Champion caused some ridiculous problem.

"Patch him through."

It took a second, but the tenor in her ear changed, picking up the telltale wash of a jet engine screaming through the air.

"Mynx. You deliver the package?"

Thane.

"I did," Mynx replied. "Sent you the details on that too."

"I know. Just being polite."

Aegis must have really wanted something if he was trying to butter Mynx up with small talk. The man was normally as subtle as a trainwreck. Yet, of all the times for Aegis to get talkative, this wasn't what Mynx wanted to deal with now.

"I have a situation here, Aegis. What do you need?"

"I might have lost a team, Mynx." Aegis let the frustration in. "In Chicago. Celice wanted me to stop being active, so I stayed. Now I'm heading there."

Losing Paragons wasn't a small thing. Anomalies were rare, anomalies that could make effective leaders, enforcement officers, or reps to the community were even rarer. That's why Mynx had made the drones in the first place, so Paragons didn't have to put themselves at risk for the small stuff. Or, as the drones kept getting better, for the big stuff. Aegis's team should have stayed back at the office and directed the assault via video feed, and Mynx said as much.

"They would have, except the target wasn't in an area with good signal. An underground generator."

Mynx set the start sequence on her suit, tied it into the gladiator drones so they'd fly together. If Aegis needed her help, and she had the feeling the ask was coming, then Mynx needed to deal with Denise quick. And get Reeves to brew some more coffee, because apparently the world had lost its mind. The electric engines came on with a soothing thrum, and Mynx floated up a meter off the ground. From here, on the rise leading up to the Factory, she could see a fair way south into L.A. proper, old and new buildings mingling their blocks and swirls together as commerce all around. Drones, yes, but also flying transports, pods, and other craft following flight plans that kept them clear of each other. Reeves submitted hers, and as soon as Mynx flicked it on with a double blink, a broad, translucent green wave appeared in her visor, showing the exact route she'd be taking to get to Denise's lab.

"The drones can operate with a signal loss," Mynx said. "They're less predictable, but better than nothing."

"Know what'd be better?"

"Don't say 'me'. I'm busy, Aegis. At least for a while."

"You chickening out?"

Mynx smiled to herself. Aegis, after all these years, kept bringing it back like they'd never changed. The friendly taunts, the 'we've got to save the universe' vibe, he'd always been the biggest believer in their own heroics, while the rest of the Champions, Mynx included, understood they only had these powers due to random chance. Yet they'd stuck with Aegis for years, at least in part because he made them feel like they were the heroes of childhood stories and triumphant movies. Together, they could save the world, and together, they did.

They had.

"I have a fight of my own today, though I'm not excited about it," Mynx said as her suit and the accompanying drones began to follow the flight plan, launching them up and over the closest homes to the Factory. "After that's taken care of, I might be able to head your way, but you'll have to wait."

"Can't do that. My team might still be alive. Can't put your thing on hold?"

"No." Mynx had no desire to get into the implications of leaving rogue DNA in the hands of someone like Denise—give her enough time and Denise could probably distribute what she stole across the internet, publicizing the private genetic makeup of anomalies to any actors, good and bad, that might have ideas for it. "This one's important."

Aegis sighed loud enough for the mic to pick up, "Remember back when we had more than just you and me?"

"I do." Beneath her, now, stretched remade highway. With pod efficiency, Pacifica reduced much of its roadways and returned them to parks, to homes. Some designers chose to build around the existing foundations, using the concrete pillars that once supported cars and trucks as the cores of vertical farms and apartments. "They're still out there."

"Think they'd come?"

Mynx knew the other Champions would. If necessary. What she really focused on, though, was how Aegis kept talking. The man was not one for long conversations, even while in transit. He could have been studying up on his mission parameters, memorizing blueprints, the ancillary stuff that turned haphazard misfires into razor-sharp executions.

"Aegis, if a threat required all of us, the Champions would come together. They'd forgive it all."

Silence, and for a brief moment, Mynx thought Aegis had ended the call right there. What had been pitched as a separation to run the newly formed Paragon regions across the world was, well, just that; a pitch to convince a war-weary public that their protectors were still united. That they weren't one more argument away from turning on each other.

"Well, at least you did," Aegis said, finally. "Thanks, Mynx. Good luck with yours."

"Take the drones, Aegis. They'll help you."

"Yeah. I will. Later."

Aegis clicked off, leaving Mynx with a weird, empty feeling in her stomach. Aegis sounded so lost. At once musing on the past and getting ready for what sounded like a violent future. More than anything, Aegis sounded like he was done. Not looking forward to this, like Mynx, now starting in a descent towards the lab, didn't look forward to what was about to happen. Forming the Paragons should have ended this.

Instead, the world seemed to be getting worse.

41

On Approach

While Mynx traveled in a lightning-fast ball, Aegis took the coach variant: a private Paragon plane, running on standard hydrogen jets at a slower, more stable velocity than his Champion counterpart. The Paragon jet made up for its relative sloth by providing amenities, like room to stretch his legs, broad windows, and a large monitor where Aegis watched the incoming message that had driven him to end the call early. Separated from the pilots and the sole attendant, with a gesture to close privacy doors, Aegis sat across from the meter-wide screen and hesitated.

His Tama told him the message was from Ziran. The company. Sent to Aegis personally, something that had never happened before. He knew, though, that Ziran had its headquarters in Chicago, and while Aegis wouldn't consider himself the most clever of the Champions, a nervy feeling tied this message to what he'd seen, in parts, earlier. The question was whether this would show his team's remains, or offer a deal to get them back?

"For your sake, I hope it's the latter," Aegis said, tapping his Tama to start the playback.

"This is not how it should be." The voice, grainy, un-edited and un-optimized, said as a Tama camera's blurry picture centered on a grimy space and the half-dozen tied bodies filling it. "You were supposed to be here. Not them."

The camera held its focus. Aegis leaned towards the screen. He thought he could pick out Innis, there, head down. Dima too, though he looked unconscious. Which meant the others were all probably Paragons as well. At least they were bound, which meant that none, for the moment, were likely dead.

"I know you will come, because that is who you are," the voice continued. It sounded male, older. "But you should understand why." A breath. "You would not hear us if we yelled, if we screamed or showed up at your door with demands. So we are getting your attention in the only way that will work, by letting you play the hero. You will try to rescue them, and we will be waiting, and we will have our conversation."

Aegis couldn't place that voice and it bothered him. Most villains took some perverse pleasure in announcing their names, in detailing their motivations, their plans as if the Champions would all be struck down in awe. Instead, this voice continued rambling on about some shift in society. Equality and this and that. Arguments that Aegis himself had made decades ago when he'd led the fight for anomaly rights, for the sanctity of those who happened to develop powers. The old world had decided living weapons must be controlled, so the anomalies took that control for themselves.

The video ended with one more call for Aegis to join them, and listed coordinates with the customary threat that the hostages would be executed if anyone other than Aegis attempted to approach. This left open the option for Aegis to have drones and other Paragons burn the site to the ground, writing off the captives as a loss but keeping his own life. That would be the call Aegis would make if he was the monster the narrator of this video thought he was. Instead, Aegis punched in the address and sent along a note to have drones keep it under constant surveillance without approach. Aegis might get lucky, see who went in and out.

After that, he made the call he'd been dreading.

"You're not coming back for dinner are you?" Celice said when she answered.

He'd told his daughter he was going out quick. He hadn't told her where, or that it'd be on a plane.

"Don't think I'll make it," Aegis said. "I'm sorry I didn't tell you before I left, but—"

"You're on your way to Chicago. Think I don't know when one of our planes takes off? You taught me that. Logistics are everything."

"You got it. Knew I did something right, raising you."

On his Tama screen, Celice looked off camera, blinked and rubbed her nose for a second, then looked back. "Chicago's a mess right now, you know that? Innis is gone, so are a bunch of their other Paragons."

"I'm going there to fix that."

"With what, dad? Your fists?"

"If I have to."

Celice laughed, once, that kind of heartbroken chuckle that killed Aegis when he heard it, and he heard it far too often. In that instant he made the promise to himself, to Celice, that he'd be done after this. Hang up the gauntlets and lead from the armchair, not the front. Get that summit together and arrange for a nice retirement filled with dinners with his daughter, and maybe a trip or two to see Mynx out west. He could even work up the nerve to visit some of the other Champions, repair some of those rifts. It wouldn't be easy, but it would be easier than watching his daughter hold back her own frustration.

"Ziran's behind it, or someone in that company," Aegis said, trying to change the subject, to cancel out the emotions and get back to something more comfortable. "They have the whole team hostage. Innis and everyone. Want to talk to me."

"What do they want?"

"I'm not sure. Either way, I want you to put a plan in place to freeze their accounts. Figure out who'll replace their tech."

"That's . . . not going to be easy."

"Which is why you're the perfect person to handle this. Logistics, Celice."

She shook her head, "You're really piling up the debt, dad. At this rate, you'll have to give me the whole tower."

"It's yours," Aegis replied. "Never liked it anyway."

A lie, though not as far from the truth as it once was. He'd begun to feel a little too high and mighty up in his steel throne, looking down on New York. One more thing he could give up after this. See his Paragons to safety with a last go'round, then stride off into the sunset.

That's how heroes did it, right?

Aegis felt the shift as the plane began its descent into Chicago, confirmed a second later by the pilots through the overhead.

Celice picked it up too. "You're almost there?"

"Almost. Listen. Celice. I've made the decision. I'm done after this."

"That's what you said before."

"Guess I'm saying it again, then."

Celice nodded. "Okay, dad. Whatever you say. Go be the hero."

"One more time."

"Sure. Love you."

"Love you too."

Celice blinked away, and Aegis turned to the gray clouds outside as the plane brought him closer to his goals, and farther away from his dreams.

42

Greed Is Deadly

Kat stared at the ceiling and wished Gordon would go away. Seeker evidently did too—the dog's non-stop barking had started as a bad companion to Gordon's endless tirade about how they had to keep going after Calvin, a listing of growing intensity that had pushed Kat onto her couch, where she'd elected to wait Gordon out. A prospect that grew dimmer by the second.

"Think of the reps, Kat!" Gordon shifted his play from protecting society to earning cash, apparently deciding sheer greed might be more appealing than benevolent options. "An anomaly like Calvin has never been seen before! He can do different things! Who knows what he might be capable of?"

"I know he could kill us if he wanted," Kat deigned to fire back, a mistake she instantly regretted.

"Maybe! But not if we both went at him together. He's not psychic, or he'd have known we were coming," Gordon took turns pacing, sitting at Kat's desk chair, and drinking from a coffee pot he'd made but clearly didn't need. "With the tracker, we could ambush him, stun Calvin before—"

"Were you not there an hour ago when he blew a window in our faces?" Kat said. "It didn't matter that we surprised him. He took us out anyway, along with two drones. I didn't sign up for this to get killed."

"You're not going to die," Gordon tried switching tactics again. "Calvin clearly doesn't want to kill us. He won't."

Kat rolled onto her side. Stared at Gordon, "I don't know if surfing around the country taking on these random contracts has warped your brain, Gordon, but trackers die all the time. Anomalies kill people constantly. It's the whole reason we exist, remember? Because everyone freaked out about anonymous explosions, people getting turned inside out or frozen solid?"

Gordon didn't have a ready reply to that one, so Kat decided to seize the momentum and keep going.

"You think this is all some sort of game: get the tracer in, collect the reps, go on and find some more fun. But me? I'm not doing this for kicks, I'm doing it because I can't do anything else. Because if I can keep some anomaly from hurting someone, I should try. But!" Kat held up a hand to stop the obvious objection. "There's a reason the Paragons exist. That all these drones are flying around. That's because some anomalies are too dangerous for us, or for anyone. Calvin's beyond you and me, Gordon. We're not supposed to stop people like him. So let's pass along the ping to the Paragons and let them sort it out."

Gordon, for what it was worth, had a great dumbfounded face. He'd been neglecting to shave during this current stint in Chicago, so the frizzy beginnings of what promised to be a patchy beard framed his dropped jaw at Kat's words. His expression suggested Kat had made some ludicrous proclamation—that Seeker could, in fact, fly, say—rather than the logical conclusion to a series of encounters that had universally ended with the two trackers on the losing side, clinging to life in the city streets or its crowded convention halls.

"Do you really want to be a tracker?" Gordon said, lobbing the question like a grenade.

"Yeah, but a sane one. A live one." Kat dove on it, smothering the explosion with thick logic.

"A boring one, then." Gordon attempted to condemn her with

the label. "When we started this, I thought you wanted to be the greatest. We worked together to trace them all, and we did it, Kat. We were amazing."

"Yeah, and then you left because Chicago wasn't good enough for you."

"I left because you changed!" Gordon included his hands now, waving them with the words like a maestro conducting an orchestra.

"Nah, Gordon, I didn't change. You did." Kat stood off the couch, which felt too calm, too casual for this conversation. "You wanted the chase to be your life. You wanted bigger, better targets. I don't want that. I don't want to throw myself into danger every single damn day and wonder if I'm going to make it out the other side."

"So you're scared. That's it."

Kat didn't do slaps. She did punches. Kicks. Shot anomalies with stun guns when she had to. But did she ever want to slap Gordon right then, right there. Because he was right, Calvin scared her, and Gordon playing that fear as a bad thing was a jerk move. Fear, reasonable fear, kept people alive in this crazy world. She and Gordon were normals. They had no business going toe-to-toe with anomalies that could play with natural laws like Kat could play with dice. Not with the deadly ones, anyway.

"This is done," she said instead. "We're done. Get away from my desk. I'm sending the signal to the Paragons, and that's it."

Gordon stood, looked for a second like he was going to let Kat do just what she said, then he leaned over, clicked the workstation's screen over to the ping's position. They both stared at it. West of town, an isolated area, even more so than where they were this morning. With the sun setting, a ping that far west meant Calvin would be alone. No civilians, few rules and ambush possibilities.

"I'm going after him," Gordon said. "You coming with?"

"Nope." Kat slid in front of Gordon. "I'm calling the Paragons. Right now."

Gordon went over to the door, pulled on his coat. Started putting on his gear. "It's going to take them a while to respond. In a city this big, one rogue anomaly that's not attacking people isn't going to get much attention."

Kat threw a withering glance his way. Gordon wanted to race the Paragons to Calvin? Sounded just like him. Her hands, meanwhile, clicked and typed their way through the emergency intervention form, popping the request, with the ping, off to Chicago's Paragon office. Kat's own rank would be attached to it, assuring a faster response. Too fast, hopefully, for Gordon to get anywhere near Calvin, boasts or otherwise.

"Guess who's not going to get any credit when I catch this one?" Gordon continued. "All me, Kat."

"Whatever."

"A classic Kat counter. All that skill, all that moxie, and when things get dangerous, she folds."

Gordon swung open her apartment door and swept out, Seeker barking at him the whole way. Kat went over, closed it, and only then turned to quieting the dog.

"It's all right Seeker. That's how he is." Kat ran her hands through the husky's fur, rested her chin on the dogs head for a minute, until a blinking light from the workstation drew her eyes back to it. An even faster reply than Kat expected. She clicked it open. Stared. Read it again. Looked back at Seeker, hoping, somehow, the dog's floppy tongue could change the message, and turned back.

The Paragons are currently dealing with other emergencies and are unable to respond at this time. Please issue a general alert for drone assistance.

Not even the usual listing of numbers to call, guidelines to follow. This message must have been thrown up fast. Kat flicked threw a number of news feeds, saw nothing. Not all that surprising that the Paragons would keep something major under wraps, but still, any planned operation would have had a similarly planned outage message.

Kat leaned back in her chair. If the Paragons weren't going to help, that meant drones. Calvin had dealt with those easily enough, and if the Paragons were dealing with a real emergency, any high quality drones would be supporting them. Which meant Gordon was heading towards a dangerous anomaly all alone. Kat looked at Seeker, who gave the same answer he always did when Kat looked his way—a small huff. What she should do was obvious. Go after him. Give Calvin another chance to kill her.

And all she'd wanted to do, after surviving the glass explosion this morning, was drink some whiskey and forget.

43

Spread The Net

During his life, Zhan-Yo pictured himself in many different hopeful futures, and he realized many of those dreams: he'd given speeches broadcast around the world to thousands, made design choices that had gone on to affect the Tamas everyone now wore, and now led the very civilization-bending effort he'd been hoping for since his father had designated Zhan-Yo for greatness. Company CEOs were not immortalized, but philosophers, leaders were.

None of those leaders, philosophers, had found themselves pacing a white-lit room beneath Chicago's surface, hunting for purpose in the six trapped Paragons and double that number of equally bored mercenaries. This wasn't a revolution, the start of something. This was a plan gone wrong with everything on the line.

"We sent the message, right?" Zhan-Yo asked Sylvie, who, leaning against the wall, appeared to be taking a nap.

The generators and the building's armor from the city streets above prevented outside Tama signals. A local network gave Zhan-Yo and the others the opportunity to communicate around the building itself, but the rest of the world was a foggy mystery. And when he'd become so accustomed to having all knowledge on his wrist, having none felt as if Zhan-Yo had been blind-folded, boxed across the ears and then juiced up with caffeine; in short, he was on edge.

"You've already asked that, and the answer's still the same," Sylvie replied. "Stay calm. Nothing ever goes perfectly."

They'd been sending runners to the surface to reconnect, and one had beamed out the short video Zhan-Yo had recorded. The last bait to catch their all-important target. Yet, down here, trapped in this metal box that smelled of oil and sweat, time and space seemed to lose all meaning. His Tama told him it was late. Zhan-Yo, who'd just consumed a sandwich procured from a nearby, clueless deli, felt apart from himself, as if this entire sequence was a surreal joke.

"Nothing goes perfectly, but things can go better than this," Zhan-Yo said, looking at the Paragons. With the exception of Innis, the burly leader, the other five were kept in permanent, drugged sedation. "I didn't want to kill this many."

Innis looked at Sylvie, "You said they'd live. That was the deal."

Sylvie sighed the same sigh Zhan-Yo's mother would when dealing with him, his siblings, and the trouble they caused. One that spoke of suffering an endless line of indignities at the hands of morons she was, nonetheless, obligated to oblige.

"Deals work both ways, Innis," Sylvie replied. "You said one or two, not five. Unless you can get them all to agree to take our side, I think we'll have to resort to a more permanent solution to this problem."

"What'll it matter?" Innis tried. "You're gonna turn this whole world over, anyway. They won't make a difference."

Zhan-Yo watched the pair. He understood Innis' struggle for his team's lives, of course, even if Zhan-Yo held little sympathy for how Innis had arrived at that plight. Making deals and sticking to them, understanding how much wiggle room you had and whether it even existed at all was part of being a leader. Innis had traded on hope, and luck, and lost.

The thugs in the room were much the same. Zhan-Yo wondered, for a second, why he thought of them that way, meat slabs meant to stand in the Paragons's way in exchange for reps. He ought to consider them loyal Ziran employees and learn their names, their families. Yet, this business put such common courtesies far away. Everyone seemed to operate on the idea that less information was better, so they could all disappear after this one night spent changing history.

Many of Sylvie's men nursed bruises or worse. When Aegis arrived, possibly with more reinforcements depending on whether the Champion cared enough to abide by the threat sent in their message, more grunts would get hurt, some might die. The prospect filled Zhan-Yo with . . . nothing. Was this how Sylvie lived? Apart from the consequences she delivered to her own followers?

"Do you know their names?" Zhan-Yo asked Innis, surprising himself with the question that had risen, like a breath, from some instinctual depth he had no control over.

"These? They're part of my office," Innis tried to look at the Paragons, but, being all strapped together in a giant lump, his head couldn't quite make the rotation. "I've worked with most for years."

Zhan-Yo nodded, slow, "Ziran has too many employees for me to know them all, but the ones around me? I get them their birthday cards, know their children and what they want in their jobs."

"Then you understand," Innis replied. "Why I'm here. We all want more. Need more."

"No, I don't know why you're here," Zhan-Yo crouched so that he could look Innis in the eye—also, his legs were getting tired from the standing. "None of my employees would take a bribe like this."

"Wouldn't they? If it meant getting to be where you are?"

"Leading Ziran is hardly a treat." Zhan-Yo thought about detailing his calendar's day-to-day, then realized that schedule didn't apply to him anymore. After tonight, his career was done. If he survived, a new one would begin. Who would step into his position? Would they fight someone for it? "But I suppose I could see the appeal, from the outside."

Innis set his face, his eyes showcasing a drift back to another time, another place. "How long since you've taken orders? Not the type you can question, either."

"A very long time."

Not since his father died. Almost two decades already.

"For me, it's been all my life. Paragons don't have CEOs. Don't have retirements. You're in till you're dead or useless, and the Champions aren't ever either. So I've been squirming under Aegis's boot forever, and it'll never change."

"It's changing now."

Innis shrugged. "Maybe. Maybe your bunch of blowhards here can win. Maybe you lop off his head and tell the world a new player's in town. Know what happens then? The other Champions will come 'round and kick your ass just the same."

"But you must have a plan for that?"

Zhan-Yo had plans for the likely Champion reprisal too, though those hinged on popular support. On a wave of normals fighting for rights that had been stolen from them.

"Sure. Claim it for myself. Atlantis. Once I'm in, we make a show of holding your fodder accountable, then we go on. You get your voting rights back, I get to finally run this region like it deserves."

"You think this is only about voting rights?" Zhan-Yo said. "It's about so much more than that. It's—"

Innis snorted, cutting Zhan-Yo off. "You can keep your preaching to yourself. I've heard a lot of talk like yours in my time, and you know what? You might care, but everyone else? They're just trying to figure out where they fit in your vision, whether they'll be better or worse off."

Now it was Zhan-Yo's turn to sigh and end the conversation. Innis didn't object and returned to his spaced glower at an indeterminate spot on the floor. Zhan-Yo leaned against the wall near Sylvie, his pair of tachi back in their holsters and making the stance more awkward than he'd intended. An outfit like his wasn't made for casual lounging.

"Get another convert?" Sylvie asked, her eyes closed.

"Not quite," Zhan-Yo said. "I'm beginning to wonder if I ever had any at all."

"If you get what you want, does it matter?"

If he liberated a people that didn't really care if they were liberated? Zhan-Yo wasn't sure how to answer that question. If he freed a caged animal that had never known anything different, would it leave? Would it know what to do once it made it outside of those metal bars?

Then again, what happened after wasn't Zhan-Yo's responsibility. He would give the people a choice. What they did with that choice was up to them.

"No," Zhan-Yo said, and would have gone on had one of the runners not burst into the room at that moment, coming in from the back entrance.

Aegis's jet had landed. The Champion had arrived.

44

Crunching Glass

As twilight's last gasps died away behind her, Mynx, with her suit's lights, along with all the drone's, off, looked at the silver lab that now held, among other things, DNA potentially containing the secrets of how anomalies came to be, and how they might never end.

"I'll go in solo at first," Mynx said. Traffic going into and out of the lab made it obvious people were inside. Mynx might not have any sympathy for Denise, but her employees deserved a shot at life. "See if I can't convince Denise she doesn't need to get all these people killed."

"We could send in a drone instead," Reeves countered. "You could interface and project. No need to risk your physical self."

Then why had she flown out here at all?

"No. People change when they see a Champion, Reeves. They fold. Apologize. Give up." Mynx didn't mention that sometimes, when their enemies knew they were doomed, they decided to go out firing away with everything they had. "I'll make it clear it's me, and what the consequences will be if they resist."

Reeves, being an AI programmed to provide risk assessments and assistance on Mynx's orders, did not protest any further and instead pushed the drones' expected positions to Mynx's helmet screen. She looked over the lab's roof and saw, as green spheres, every drone and, with orange projected cones, their coverage. The lab soaked in the orange, and with the artillery on hand, Denise would lose everything if she said no.

Which was why, when Mynx coasted down and simply bashed through the lab's front door, scraping chunks from the walls as she went in with her over-sized drone suit, the Champion had the confidence that came with certain victory.

The lobby that had seemed small and bland when she'd been there in person now felt cramped with Mynx standing two-and-a-half meters tall and a meter wide, twice that with her drone-augmented arms extended and aiming their dart-gun launchers. Start with non-lethal options and progress as needed.

Her entrance showered the floor with glass, caused the hanging white lights to sway, and precipitated shouts, screams, and a blast from someone poking their head up from behind the desk. Mynx's suit, and the drones in general, were made to withstand the physical punch of a bullet, the heat of a firestorm or the soaking water from rain or hose. But electrical bursts? Those were harder.

The shock lanced through her suit, and Mynx's visor lit up with damaged components, fried circuits, and her biggest weapons—white-hot energy bursts triggered by discharging multiple batteries at once—dying off. She felt the heat, too, as cooling pumps meant to keep her drone bits from burning stopped and triggered automatic restarts.

Worse, the stabilizing program faltered in her right leg, and with Mynx, with no human, really, having the strength to keep that much metal stable, she staggered to the right, her aim flying off target, causing her counter-fire to pepper the wall behind the desk with darts far too high to do anything more than deface Denise's signage. Not exactly the crushing initial blow Mynx hoped for.

"Denise is ready for us," Mynx said, wincing at what would be beautiful new bruises along her right leg where the dead drone had pulled against her skin. "Trig overload, Reeves."

The AI acknowledged with a blip, while Mynx busied herself

sending the dead drone through the reset steps to get whatever circuits still worked back online. Not so much a resurrection as a Frankenstein-esque renewal, a meter appeared on her visor showing a far-too-gradual countdown to when Mynx would be able to move again.

"Give it up!" a man's shout, and by the sound, a scared one. "We got you!"

A head poked up from behind the desk. Then another. Both wearing lab coats and looking like they were trying to put on the most determined face possible, if only to pretend they weren't shaking. If Mynx didn't make such a big target, she bet they would've missed her completely.

As it was, the blasts had fried her vocal amplifier, so Mynx couldn't talk to them even if she'd wanted to. So instead she stared, waited for Reeves to do his thing.

Denise's two henchmen? Lab assistants? Mynx wasn't sure where these fell on the broad spectrum of villainous sidekicks . . . crept around the desk, approaching Mynx's suit as though it might suddenly explode—not an unreasonable thought; every drone had a self-destruct option—and holding their static guns forward with both hands. Unfortunately for them, the danger wasn't going to come from Mynx's still-restarting suit, but from the roof over their heads.

The vast majority of drones in operation dealt with surveillance and suppression, crowd control and visual aids for the Paragons. However, what came through the roof represented the future, and the future weighed hundreds of kilos and collapsed on its target with catastrophic force. The twin gladiators shattered the roof, breaking jagged holes and punctuating their descent with metal shrapnel, prompting shouts and scrambling from Denise's buddies. That scrambling; surprisingly good pulling jumps back over the reception desk, was met with calculated doom by the gladiators.

Designed to look like giant, metal humans with an extra two pairs of arms, the gladiators straightened from their crushing entrance, evaluated both Mynx—defend—and the pair of henchmen—attack—and used their lowest appendages, equipped with gripping claws, to rend the desk to pieces.

"Trig non-lethal," Mynx said, deciding she didn't need to leave a massacre in her wake.

There would have been some value in using the raid as a publicity shot; show the world just what would happen if you opposed the Champions. But the idea of using bodies and a blown up lab a safety campaign struck her as a little too close to the villains the Champions had fought against their entire lives. Mynx wasn't against hanging a Sword of Damocles over the populace, but there were better ways of doing it.

The gladiators, using their upper arms, shot precision stun darts at the two enemies as soon as they were exposed, dropping them to the wrecked floor without another sound. The massive machines straightened and angled themselves towards the rest of the lab, waiting for Mynx's signal to continue.

"Well, that was a good opening exam," Mynx said to Reeves as she stood up, her systems having recovered to a point where movement was again possible. "Gladiators obeyed commands, neutralized the threat, and executed a precision landing in a difficult environment."

"Diagnostics show no damage sustained, either."

Mynx strode past the two gladiators, both of which stood taller than her, their thin block heads—packed with sensors and a single, bright blue headlight—fixed on the double doors leading into the lab proper. In front of the door, Mynx hesitated. If they tore through this place, they might destroy Denise's data, and even if Denise had backed things up, the equipment in here was valuable. Useful, perhaps, to someone without such nefarious designs.

"Switching channels to an open broadcast," Mynx noted, the drone dragging the command from her words and toggling the channel while Mynx took a breath. "Dr. Jones! You're surrounded, and you will not win. You have two options; surrender, and save what you've done for others, or refuse, and lose everything."

A little dramatic for her taste, but better to be clear: if Denise resisted, she would, in fact, lose everything.

Shrapnel continued to fall in the seconds following the ultimatum, shards counting time as they sprinkled to the floor, off the drones. Mynx made a mental inventory of the new bruises in her right leg from where the drone pressed against it. Opened her mouth to tell Reeves to find some time for a massage, when a familiar voice shot through the lab.

Coming out scattered and spitting from a damaged intercom system, Denise struck her defiant stance, "You're giving me options now? Because you didn't give me any before!" Denise didn't emerge from the lab, so Mynx assumed the scientist planned to fight. "I came to you with a promise, a hope, and you shut me down. Why? Because I'm not one of your anomalies?"

"Because trust is earned, Denise. Not freely given. You have ten seconds to surrender. Your associates, if any remain, have those same ten seconds. After that, per my right as Champion of Pacifica, your lives are forfeit."

"If you kill me," Denise countered, even as the lab door opened and several more scientists ran into immediate stunning darts from the gladiator drones, "you'll lose all the progress. You'll never find what you're looking for, and then you'll wither away. All of you will."

The timer ticking in her visor the moment Mynx declared her ten second deadline hit zero, so Mynx passed along the requisite signal. One of the drones launched a spider-net over the five captives and the silver-black strands stretched and surrounded their target. The same drone rotated and, using the hole Mynx had already made in the front door, dragged the prisoners out of harm's way. Harm the second drone began inflicting with its top two arms the moment the civilians were clear.

While the world had gained a fondness for energy weapons, with their flashy colors and limitless ammunition—provided one had a working battery—Mynx understood the value of a good, solid shell. The gladiator drone did too, and punched holes in the wall dividing the reception desk from the lab. Every bullet carried through the building, plunging through equipment, walls, and people, if any were left. When the projectiles hit the building's end, defined through the bullet's integrated computers and the continuing miracle of GPS, the bullets triggered a single reverse charge that packed enough punch to drop them, safe, to the ground.

An ultimate weapon wasn't one that could destroy, but one that could destroy its target alone.

"Last chance, Denise." Mynx tested her movement, lurched by the gladiator drone. "Don't be stupid."

Sharp static burst over the intercoms. Too damaged now, maybe, to give Denise the words she needed to save her life. Mynx told the other gladiator to hold the lobby and made the crunching move inward. The walls, not designed to withstand heavy assault, fell apart like dusty crackers as Mynx's drone arms ground through, their engines serving as the force behind Mynx's tearing motions.

First came the offices, including Denise's own, where Mynx had sat only days earlier, wondering if she'd found the solution to life's inexorable problem: that it had to end. Mynx crushed the computer with her left arm while her right ripped away the makeshift hallway, getting to the actual, refined part of the structure: the lab.

The gladiator's warning shots had pierced the airtight seal here, big punctures in the shiny silver shell evident. Mynx followed their lead, using the holes as openings to rend her own way through. The whole way, Mynx set her voice to repeat a call for Denise, and she kept tabs on the outside dragnet, but so far her target scientist hadn't made a run for it. Which meant Denise had been perforated by the warning shots, or had decided to end her time on this Earth without a sound.

Inside the lab itself, Mynx waded through 3D printers set to string out flesh and bone; useful things if you wanted to test human DNA tweaks, if a bit hard to look at. Mynx kept going, though, because she caught a glimpse of her quarry.

Denise wouldn't be going anywhere. The premiere geneticist had strapped herself to what looked like a black office chair, complete with plastic wheels looking foreign in the lab's metallic world. The chair had been secured to stands, with a frightening number of clear bags hanging on them, IV tubes dangling from those bags and heading right into her body.

Mynx would have loved to say that Denise was the first person she'd seen try to turn themselves into an anomaly. Would have loved to rock back in her massive drone suit, screaming in shock or surprise. Instead, as the dozens of prior genetic manipulators and their failures cascaded through her memory, Mynx sighed long and low, until it turned into a groan and then a growl.

"You're like all the others," Mynx said. "You're going to end up like them too."

Denise shifted her head to stare at Mynx. "I can feel it, you know. The change. It's happening."

"I'll bet you can," Mynx replied, then muted her speaker. "Reeves, have the drones back out and set a shell around the lab. Two hundred meters. Denise is going to be making a mess."

"You think you get to keep it all for yourselves," Denise continued on. "This secret. This power. That's not why I'm doing this, though. I'm close. The aging. We're almost there."

"Ran out of time, right?"

"Because of you."

"Denise, you could have had all the time you needed." Mynx blinked with her right eye, shifting the status reports hovering translucent in her visor until she found one giving the readout on her battery power levels. "You were just greedy."

Her visor said Mynx had enough juice left for a short flight. And, looking at Denise, a short flight would be the thing to do; the geneticist's skin had turned splotchy, with wide and scattered circles of red and black forming along her body. Denise had chosen athletic wear for the occasion, as if her first post-anomaly transformation would be a 5k through the campus. A run she'd never make. Denise had closed her eyes now.

That always happened.

"What did you do with the database?" Mynx asked.

"Integrated it. Probably lost now that you destroyed my lab." Denise pulled herself back long enough to defend her honor as a researcher.

"You didn't back it up?"

"No time. I knew you'd be coming." Denise gave a wet cough,

and her eyes opened again, for the first time showing a bit of alarm. "Something feels off."

"I bet." Mynx looked at the lab's ceiling above. Not reinforced and easy to break through. "Denise, goodbye."

"You're not staying to see?"

"I've already seen the end of this particular show."

"What?" Denise burst into more coughs. "What do you mean?"

But Mynx didn't care to answer. She activated the drone engines, which lofted her from the lab floor up and through the roof. She leaned forward, watching the faint red circle Reeves had painted around the lab and flying until she'd crossed outside of it. Around the circle, like light poles, stood or floated the drones. A vigil for the end.

Anomalies by their nature were living risks. Chances that sometimes came up with miracles, most of the time with minor touches, and rarely with catastrophic failures. Those last ones identified themselves with finality—the child would hit puberty, mention feeling ill, their skin would turn as their blood fought against the transformation happening inside until, inevitably, bang. Others had tried to remove the random chance element with a forced insertion of anomaly genetic material. Like a rogue virus, the body attacked it with furious abandon. Unlike a rogue virus, the strange cells that made anomalies what they were defended themselves, and did so with prejudice.

"Everyone loses," Mynx muttered.

Aegis had said that once, summing up how the anomaly part of themselves chose to fight that battle. So when Denise's broken lab vanished in a sudden, concussive fireball expanding from right where Denise had been sitting, Mynx could only acknowledge that the anomaly DNA had done what it promised. When Denise's blood fought back, the anomaly genes had employed the nuclear option.

"Trig catch protocol."

The heat washed against her, while Mynx's drones leveraged targeted lasers too precise for human hands to fry away shrapnel streaming out from the blast's center. Those parts of the lab that didn't fly outward collapsed with the fading fire, leaving the frame and scattered wall patches too stubborn to fall. Thus ended the life of Dr. Denise Jones.

"A waste," Mynx said. "Reeves, find out who owns this lab and tell them they have a mess."

"Of course," Reeves replied, his ever-stately accent providing the rock for Mynx to hold on to. "I take it Dr. Jones is no longer a problem?"

"No longer a solution, either." Mynx began plotting the fastest route home. "If there's a fresh pot of tea waiting for me when I get back, I'll be much happier."

45

Tunnel Time

The maintenance tunnel looked as though it bore a grudge against its function; slop water clung to the circular exit, positioned near the river and filters straining any foul material before contact with Chicago's hydro ecosystem. The gate, bearing not a Tama lock but an old-fashioned physical keyhole, sported rust more green than orange, moldy bits making their homes. City lights washed out the riverbanks around Aegis, but vanished into the tunnel's black maw.

"But that's why you're here," Aegis said to two hulking gladiator drones, newly flown from the Factory, to Chicago. "Keep me safe and all that."

The drones chimed an affirmative. No words. His great, big, mute bodyguards. A million reps to build each one'of'em and Mynx couldn't even plug in a voice. Then again, as Aegis looked at those narrow, robot heads, maybe it's better they couldn't talk. Least they couldn't annoy him too much.

Aegis did not have the key for this particular gate—it'd been a decade since he'd held a physical key—so he reached out with his hands and gripped the bars. He wore gloves, black with light blue slivers to go with the assault gear coating him like modern medieval armor from head to toe. Seeing as he'd been invited, Aegis figured stealth wouldn't figure much into this mission. His one concession to strategy, on advice from Celice, had been to use the maintenance entrance and dodge any traps waiting at the main door.

The bars refused to budge. Aegis kept himself super fit through a strict regimen he'd developed forty years ago and never altered, but his anomaly abilities did not include the power to rend metal from its foundations. His Tama, in sight on his wrist, flashed a query from one of the gladiator drones, the words appearing in big block text that, to Aegis, emphasized its robotic origin. Whether Mynx intended the font as a joke or not, Aegis took it as a sign the robot-led apocalypse would have a sense of dire humor.

"Go for it," Aegis said, letting go and stepping well away from the grate.

With synchronized flashes from their lowest arms, the gladiator drones lanced searing hot, blue-white energy through the grate's bars. The lasers faded out through the bars, careful not to burrow holes through the sides of the tunnel beyond. Impressive tech, especially compared to the often-wild damage caused by anomalies. When the grate teetered and fell outward, Aegis caught it and lowered the piece to the ground, leaving them with a wide open entry into Chicago's undercity.

"So when you lose signal, you going to be all right?" Aegis asked.

His Tama flashed again, stating that the drones would follow their Protector protocol. Whatever that meant. Of the many, many things Aegis told himself to learn and knew he never would, Mynx's various terms occupied a middling space on the list, right between how to play bridge and when to quit.

"Well, my metal friends, it's time to save some Paragons." Aegis pulled the tactical goggles over his eyes as he stepped up and into the tunnel.

Before he'd gone more than a stride, though, one gladiator drone, bending down to fit within the tunnel's narrow confines, grabbed Aegis with its middle arms, the set that had twin claws on the ends, and pulled Aegis back. The other drone took Aegis's place at the front, marching and pausing a few steps in. The drone behind him gave Aegis a slight push in the back.

"So that's how we're doing this?" Aegis said.

The drones didn't take to arguing, not responding in any fashion to Aegis's question, so the Champion took his place in between the drones as they began their hike into the dark. Not that Aegis couldn't see—his tactical goggles flipped quick to lowlight vision's neon green while the drones blanked their own lights, relying on sensors more precise than Aegis's eyes to keep track of where their metal feet were going.

Inside, the tunnel stank of moldering . . . stuff. Not human waste —Aegis didn't care to reflect on why he knew, so well, the various offal a human body could produce—but rather the washed down leaves, oil stains, trash, and the other random detritus that found its way into hidden holes like this one. The utter lack of a breeze once they made it past the tunnel's first curve served to thicken the mixture, until Aegis wondered if they'd stumbled into some portal to the worst possible dimension.

Like an oasis in a rotten desert, the tunnel widened after too many disgusting minutes to accommodate tubes. The big pipes funneled in from their respective homes to a triangular space illuminated by Aegis's goggles in the faintest greens. Little light down here, little reason for it. Supporting columns traced the lines from the incoming tunnels to the outgoing one Aegis and the drones had just traversed. The reason for the space, and thus the columns, became evident as soon as Aegis set foot into it and felt his boots sink into a mass of soft matter. A collecting pool for biomass; gather enough organic waste here and a suction truck would take the crud and turn it into power.

His Tama flashed. Bright, and Aegis held his left wrist away from his eyes until he could, with his right hand, pull up his goggles and take a look:

Take cover.

Survival, for Champions, often came down to split second chance, something that Aegis had seen in the spotlight, bearing every aspiring villain's target. So the moment he read, comprehended the words on his Tama, Aegis fell back, sacrificing his footing to make himself smaller. A dart, invisible but for a slight whistle, shot through the area where Aegis had been standing.

Aegis could have fought in the dark—he had the gear, the training, but the two drones decided this skirmish would be better conducted with bright flashing lasers, nerve agent cluster bombs, and angry orange flame throwers. The artillery, from one and then both drones, seared away the gloom as Aegis blinked his goggles back to the normal spectrum. Aside from the flame thrower's roar, the burning weapon positioned front and center on the gladiator drone's torso, the lasers were silent and the cluster bursts emitted slight pops, giving the attackers-turned-defenders opportunity to fill the air with their screams.

No, not screams. Orders. Aegis pushed himself up as he parsed the words, trying to get a look at what the gladiator drones were tracking with their precise, unending fire. Shapes moved in the shadows, dropping to the ground when the drones scored a hit. Counters finally emerged in satchel bombs and tactical EMPs; localized electrical grenades set to destabilize circuitry. The gladiator drones, though, proved as adept with their own countermeasures, zapping the thrown bombs out of the air with micro-lasers.

Did Aegis even have to do anything?

The thought came and Aegis killed it. He broke into a sloppy run through the muck to the right, towards where the shapes seemed to be clustering. While that would put Aegis into the drone's fire, he figured they ought to be able to shoot around him. Hoped so, anyway.

Aegis managed a last step from goop and onto more solid, if still soiled, ground in time to watch drone fire spray out and stick. Most of the intersection now seemed to be burning, with the drones increasingly caught in their own firestorm. Not that the heat did anything to slow them down. The twin drones had pinned the shapes in the right tunnel, behind the opening where the enemy hid just well enough to avoid rapid, total annihilation by Mynx's machines.

And set them up for wholly different defeat.

Aegis used the smoke, a thick black curtain being dealt with, ineffectually, by the tunnel's emergency ventilation systems. Fans spun up, sucking the soot upward, so that Aegis appeared like a phantom as he waded through the murk and into the attacker's midst. Up to this point, aside from the obvious likelihood that anyone choosing to attack those two drones would need to have substantial monetary motivation, Aegis hadn't seen his new enemy up close, and therefore had no confirmation that the half-dozen or so people facing him were, in fact, in Ziran's employ.

In the fire's muted glow, Aegis saw the collected gear, the set faces and musclebound bodies that bespoke of careers spent in whispering distance of death, earning scars and stories at the cost of life expectancy. In these men Aegis saw the world's broken armies, the forces dispersed and disintegrated when the Paragons came into power, people who's whole careers had been thrown aside with a set of signed documents, cast out into a peaceful society with little use for their talents.

Most had adapted, in the manner of veterans since the dawn of time, to the switch from war to peace. Not all, though, and not everyone wanted to. Aegis understood, because he too felt his time slipping away, the point and purpose of his day to day getting muddled by progress. Not now, however. Here, staring at the adversary, the goal was clear.

"Surrender," Aegis said, relying on the filter in his tactical mask to keep him from choking on the smoke. "Nobody else needs to die."

A half-dozen guns rose in a half-dozen hands, pointing his way. Gray-metal and shiny, the guns appeared to be the sort that fired real bullets, not darts. Old Aegis would have laughed at this, shrugged off the shots as they struck his fast-healing skin. New Aegis hesitated. The kidnapped Paragons weren't here. Other fights might lay beyond this point, and Aegis couldn't afford to get himself blown to pieces before he made it to the end.

"Think it's your turn to do that," the nearest commando replied, in a tone that suggested he made the calls for the group. "You're who we're waitin' for."

The man had no clear accent, spoke with no venom, despite the likelihood that several of his team were behind Aegis, either dead or injured in the inferno. Aegis could respect that; the mission above all else. Could use it.

"Then show me," Aegis said. "I'll follow."

The commando didn't waste time, "Get in the middle of us, then. Three behind, three in front. We'll walk you in."

"The drones might get annoyed."

"Then we'd better get moving, before they figure out how to fit in here."

This tunnel, not needing to accommodate as much waste as the original one Aegis and the drones had entered, did appear to be smaller, and its bottom held less muck, so walking felt less like wading through a marsh and more like stomping through a leafy, dirty puddle. Aegis took his position between the six commandos, who kept their weapons trained on him. Behind them, the drones were making noises too; extinguishers whooshing in an attempt to clean up the mess they'd made.

At some signal Aegis didn't catch, the commandos moved, the ones behind him putting their hands on his back and pushing Aegis forward. They went twenty paces or so, around a curve in the tunnel, when the leader held up his hand for a halt.

"Blow the charges," the commando said.

"Charges?" Aegis bothered asking.

"We saw the drones, we prepared for them." The commando punctuated his sentence with a nod at one of the others, who pressed something on his Tama.

Short pops echoed behind Aegis, followed by dirt and cement rushing to follow gravity's orders. Filling in the tunnel probably wouldn't stop the drones for all that long—by this point, Aegis assumed Mynx had a countermeasure for every tactic installed on these things—but it would buy time. The bang also bought Aegis a distraction: beyond the sound, the explosion triggered red emergency lights along the tunnel's upper edges in perfect lines. The glow changed the shadows, gave Aegis a chance.

With his left elbow, Aegis jacked the commando on that side

while he twisted, pulling the second commando behind him in between Aegis and the third close commando on the tunnel's right. Aegis gripped the pinned commando's gun hand and pressed the trigger, pushing the man's arm as he pulled and released, triggering loud cracks as each shot sprang out towards the leading trio. At close range, the commandos couldn't do much to dodge, so they tried aiming their own weapons.

Aegis held his hostage close, buying a half-second's hesitation. Enough for the Champion to fire first and only.

Another shot rang out behind Aegis, and the Champion felt the bullet press into and get rejected by his armor. Aegis pushed his captured commando into the one on the right, trying to work out a way to get around his partner. The shove drove them both into the wall and let Aegis turn towards the one he'd elbowed as the commando delivered another shot, this time to Aegis's chest. Again the armor held, though Aegis could feel early bruises aching.

The commando seemed to realize Aegis's armor wouldn't be breached by his small handgun, so he swapped tactics, raising his aim towards Aegis's head. In response, Aegis kicked up the mud from the tunnel floor, splashing dirt, leaves, and crud all over the commando's face. The Champion ducked left as the commando fired anyway, the bullet ricocheting off the ceiling and, from a grunt somewhere behind Aegis, striking the commando's allies. Aegis took the moment to step forward, squat and grab the commando. Aegis's knees popped in the action, but the Champion managed to lift the muck-covered man up and over, banging the commando against the tunnel ceiling before bringing him down on the remaining two.

The whole set collapsed in a scrambling limb heap, curses filling the tube. Aegis drew his stun gun and lay about with the darts, hitting all six commandos with quick shots to the legs, face, neck, wherever he could strike that didn't seem covered by thicker body armor. Aegis stopped, waited to see if any did anything other than breathe shallow breaths.

"Stay down," Aegis whispered, then began checking the bodies.

The commandos he'd shot with actual bullets were hurt, and Aegis took the minutes to search, find, and apply bandages to the wounds. They'd still need more competent medical attention, but Aegis figured would die there. From the video Ziran had sent, it seemed like they hadn't killed the captive Paragons, and, drones aside, keeping death away from this particular battle seemed like a fine play.

At least until Aegis could be sure the Paragons were safe.

As Apinya, the most annoying Champion, had often said during their time together, a body now is a burden later.

"See?" Aegis said to that memory, standing up from the last commando. "I listened to all your crap."

Aegis went back next, to check out the collapsed portion of the tunnel and see whether he could open a path. Despite his preference for living, breathing Paragons, the drones were useful and Aegis would rather have the killer bots with him than go it alone. The tunnel, though, would not be granting that wish: amid the rock and dirt were collapsed piping, concrete blocks, and oozing water from some busted main. Not a glimmer came through from the other side.

With his Tama, Aegis tried to beam through a command, a question. The Tama told him after several seconds of trying that all attempts at reaching the outside world from here would be futile. No sounds from the other side either, which meant the collapse had been deep enough to block the rescue dig's noise, or the drones had given up and, maybe, were trying an alternate route.

"Guess it's just me, then," Aegis said, before tapping another series of commands into the Tama. The device turned on a small, white light at the top, and Aegis raised his wrist, turning it to face the collapsed tunnel. "Hey, Celice. Thought you'd like to see the trouble your dad's got himself into this time. They blew the tunnel. Trapped those drones outside. Sorry I gave you crap about those, by the way. They did good work. I'd probably be dead if not for them, though tell Mynx she's gotta tune down the fire a bit. A little hot for close quarters action."

Aegis found himself talking for longer than he meant to, recounting the fight, the commandos, the pungent air inside the tunnel. None of this mattered, really, but Aegis couldn't stop himself. He'd never been much of a talker, but here he was, going on and on about every facet of the mission to a recording.

"They had guns. Real guns. I know we've been working hard to get rid of those things, but it looks like we'll have to hit it harder," Aegis said, now walking back past the commandos, still lying in stasis. "We have to figure out why people keep falling into these lines of work. Shut'em down. Think you can figure out a way to do that?" He laughed, once. "Of course you can. You're my daughter. You're incredible."

The tunnel continued and Aegis kept walking and talking in the red light, bringing his voice down as he approached where his Tama indicated the Paragons ought to be. As he went, his words slid away from policy proposals and missions and more towards family, future, and the life he'd chosen for themselves.

"Your mother, I don't talk about her as much as I should," Aegis paused, wondering if even here, in this dark and damp place with a fight lingering, he could open that box. "You've probably read all about her. Know more than I do, maybe." He stopped moving. The break in the tunnel where he'd reach his destination wasn't far off, and Aegis wanted to finish this. "What the stories won't say, though, is that we held on to each other, Celice. There were other Champions, other Paragons, but when the missions went to hell, we had each other, and we knew that. I never felt more invincible than when I was with her.

"I'd be the first one in, draw the fire while she set to work. Blind'em all, make it easy for us to see. Amazing. But the best part, the best thing she did? Your mom had this way of teasing out just the right yellows, whites so that every night we had was magic. Our own private, spectacular sunsets. She'd tell me it was all about the photons, but I was always too busy falling in love with her to care."

A beep from his Tama interrupted the reverie, brought Aegis back. Time had gone running again, and Paragons were waiting for him. So Aegis said goodbye, set the message to send the next chance it found signal, and the Champion marched on.

46

One Last Deal

Despite her full suit and her fluffy dog beside her, Kat would have much rather been inside wrapped in blankets than out in the pouring snow and biting wind that had come to take over Chicago's west side. A blizzard arose as the sun set, an ominous warning as Seeker and Kat left her apartment in search of Gordon and, Kat grimaced at nobody, Calvin.

She'd taken her time getting ready. A long shower, a snack, and the slow piece-by-piece dance of adding armor and weapons. More than enough time for Gordon to reach his destination, to confront Calvin and complete the task without her involvement. Was she a little ashamed about it? Yeah, maybe. A little.

But Gordon had made his choice.

She'd made hers.

The call, though, never came. No message flaring across the Tama in triumph, telling Kat disaster had been averted. Instead, silence. Even after Kat tossed out a feeler, asking if Gordon had struck his metaphorical gold. Because Kat *did not* want to face Calvin again. She knew that deep down. A chill fear clung to her bones at the prospect of going up against an anomaly who seemed more than capable of dispatching her without much effort. Kat preferred her life in her own hands, not at another's mercy.

Seeker, though, made the ultimate call. The dog demanded to be walked, a demand that grew louder and louder as snow started to fall, bringing with it the promise of bounding through soft banks, catching falling flakes in his mouth, and dragging Kat until she slipped and fell. That last one may not have crossed Seeker's mind, but it sure buzzed in Kat's as she struggled to keep the husky on the walk.

Not that they were going far; both the situation's strange desperation and the distance required to get to the west side meant Kat had called a pod. It'd take a few minutes to arrive, so Kat let Seeker pull her around the block in a futile attempt to burn off some energy before trapping herself with the dog in what amounted to a small orb.

On the second lap, as Kat came back 'round to her apartment and the spot on the street where the pod would make its precise pickup, she noticed another soul decided to brave the nighttime snows. A soul staring right at her.

"Beth," Kat said, approaching and wishing the pod car would pull up right about now. "You picked a bad night to visit."

The woman, bundled thick with overlaying coats and pants, kept a straight face that said how little she appreciated the remark, and how little she *did* want to be out here. Kat's suit worked to keep her temperature optimized for activity, at least until its batteries ran out. Beth looked like she relied on old-fashioned clothing to do the job, and that reliance hadn't paid off.

"I wouldn't be here, except some doubt you'll make the right decision," Beth said, her words erupting little puffs with every syllable. "You're working with another tracker."

"How do you know that?"

"Don't play dumb. He saved you at the convention. The video played out all over local news clips."

"So you're not watching my apartment?" Kat dragged in the leash, kept Seeker close, though the dog seemed happy to bite at passing snow. "Not following me everywhere?"

Beth stared back at her, then down the street behind Kat. "We aren't the Paragons. We don't have the resources or the desire to monitor everyone's movements. You're going after Calvin now?"

Beth motioned, with a gloved hand, towards Kat's suit, its pearl-white sheen and smooth bulk a clear indicator of its over-qualification for a simple dog walk. Kat hadn't put the mask down—it receded into the suit's hood when not in use—because with her eyes glowing blue and her face a silver slate, her neighbors would probably call the drones on her. From a distance, with her normal features visible, Kat felt she looked like a somewhat normal person doing a normal thing. Quite an achievement for her, honestly.

"You're not going to intimidate me," Kat said. "I don't care what you have to say."

"So you're going to make him a Paragon thrall."

"Better than a terrorist." Kat's Tama beeped.

The pod approached.

Beth tried a sigh, the wind swallowed it. "I would have thought someone like you understood how important it is to have friends across the spectrum. If you want to survive what's coming, you'll reconsider."

"What's coming? You going to try to destroy the city?" Kat raised her right wrist, snapped it once to ready the single stun dart loaded there. "Should I stop you right now and turn you in?"

Beth eyed Kat's wrist, the light shifting shadows across her face as the pod car rolled to a stop next to them, its tall door sliding open. Snow began blowing inside the vehicle, and the cool blue aura coming from its inside gave truth to Kat's discount pod car subscription—ads played during the rides, but the savings made the suffering worth it.

"We aren't trying to destroy society," Beth said. "It's going to destroy itself. We want to be ready when it does. Calvin would go a long way in helping with that. You would too."

"Then I'll call you when the world ends." Kat nudged Seeker towards the pod car. "Good night, Beth."

"Good night, Kat. Stay warm, and good hunting."

The Elemental watched as Kat helped Seeker into the pod, as

Kat slipped into the plastic-style seat standard for basic pods. Lux subscriptions, of course, cost more and didn't allow dogs. Kat gave Beth a wave as the pod pulled away, heading west towards where Calvin's ping. Where Gordon should be.

"What do you think?" Kat asked Seeker, while a vid espousing some new sports drink—anomaly energy in every bottle!—played in front of them. "Is the world going to end?"

The husky looked at Kat when she asked the question, his tongue flopping out of his mouth, before turning back to the spherical window and resuming his non-stop study of the falling snow.

"Guessing that's a no."

Kat looked at her Tama. Pulled up the ping map. Not long, and she'd be back in it, with one big change: this time, she wouldn't pull any punches, play no games. Kat would have preferred to stay in her apartment, sipping hot chocolate and watching a movie.

Calvin had ruined her night. In return, she'd ruin his.

The Target Arrives

Zhan-Yo never expected to feel this uncertain, this *afraid*. Aegis, according to the last words before Sylvie's hired hands dropped into the dark, walked this way. Through the maintenance tunnel, too; a subtle back entrance rather than a showy blast through the front door. Maybe that's what had Zhan-Yo feeling off, gripping the tachi hilts to steady his nerves: Aegis played the showman, yet here he took the sneaky route.

"There aren't any other Paragons coming," Sylvie said. The two stood in the central room, near the captives. "We've distributed enough false alarms to empty out the current shift, and Aegis seems to want this alone."

"Fits his character."

"I'd admire it," Sylvie said, "if it wasn't so stupid."

"He's not risking anyone else," Zhan-Yo replied. "He doesn't know how we took down the first team. He believes he's invincible, so why risk anyone else?"

Sylvie gave him one of her arch, skeptical looks, "You can read his mind, now?"

"It's part of being a leader. With Ziran, it's similar. I don't throw my staff into impossible problems that I alone can solve. Nor would I charge them with a task they are not ready for."

In those words, Zhan-Yo dealt Sylvie a gentle rebuke. It'd been her idea to set the ambush for Aegis once they realized he planned to bring two new, dangerous-looking drones along. Despite her henchmen losing to the lower-tier Paragons now assembled in a sedated, tied cluster behind them, Sylvie had insisted the mercenaries take point. They'd gone, but they wouldn't be coming back.

Sylvie responded by going through her weapons and gear. The ammo in long, thin pistols worn at her hip along with throwing knives along her left arm. Beyond that, she wore gloves tied to a battery pack inside her chest, ready to deliver a nerve numbing shock if Sylvie clenched her fist and swung. Her suit, the same thick, textured black stuff Zhan-Yo wore, culminated in a fitted helmet that Sylvie pulled over her head, those blue eyes now covered in a transparent screen.

"I want him first," Zhan-Yo said. "He needs to understand."

"Why? Aren't we going to kill him?"

"Revolutions begun in blood tend to end that way," Zhan-Yo replied. "We haven't killed a single Paragon yet. If Aegis resolves to see our side and promises a change, we may be able to keep it that way."

"Don't be naive. That's not the plan."

"Plans can change."

"You're letting hope get in the way of logic, Z."

"Maybe I am."

Sylvie started to say something more, but stopped when creaking metal rang through the generator station. Aegis had arrived. Sylvie took the cue and slipped back into the side room where Zhan-Yo had watched the initial Paragon assault. Close enough to help should Zhan-Yo call for it, but far enough, hopefully, to keep things from escalating.

"He's gonna tear ya apart," Innis mumbled from behind Zhan-Yo. "Can't believe I threw myself in with you wrecks."

Zhan-Yo ignored the Paragon. Innis had been a fount of dire ramblings and coarse insults over the last hours, as if he'd come to the realization that betraying the world's most powerful Champion and the world's most powerful organization in one shot may not have been the smartest play. Pity, though, ought not be felt for those who make their own poor choices.

Instead, Zhan-Yo placed himself, feet squared and knees bent ever-so-slightly, a meter away from the captives and in clear view. He could react fast if Aegis decided to come out from the back hallways swinging, and otherwise presented a strong, if not threatening front. All things pointed to a negotiation, not a slaughter.

The nerves that'd tightened and loosened themselves while waiting for Aegis cooled when the Champion walked into view. With the tactical gear on, goggles down and face covered, Aegis looked far from the modeled icon plastered all over signs, videos, and everything else since Zhan-Yo had been a teenager. The Champions suit made clear his fitness, and the tools locked into holsters along his chest and waist made clear his preparation.

But Aegis looked like a man, and nothing more.

"Are you all right?" Aegis asked not Zhan-Yo, but Innis.

"They're fine," Zhan-Yo said.

"Not talking to you." Aegis waved Zhan-Yo off. "Innis. Are you alive? Are the others hurt?"

A minor setback, but Zhan-Yo let it play. Caring about his subordinates fit Aegis's profile, and it wasn't like Zhan-Yo had anything to fear from Innis's answer: the Paragons were alive.

"Pride's wounded, but not much else," Innis said, not raising his head to look at Aegis. "Think the others are takin' a forced nap. Damn ugly in here."

"I took out a half-dozen commandos in the tunnel." Aegis continued to ignore Zhan-Yo. "Does that cover everyone who hit you?"

"It might. Lotta flashing lights, though. Made it hard to keep a count."

"Those were all of our men," Zhan-Yo tried another interjection. "It's only us now."

This time Aegis didn't wave away Zhan-Yo, but squared up to him, with several meters separating the two leaders. Though Zhan-

Yo couldn't see Aegis's eyes through the Champion's goggles, he had that distinct crawling feeling as Aegis analyzed every bit of him.

"Zhan-Yo, right?" Aegis said after several long seconds.

"Right."

Zhan-Yo would have continued, but some force compelled him to stay quiet. Answer Aegis's questions and nothing more. A Champion, Zhan-Yo realized, had that effect.

"Got your message on the way here." Aegis cracked his knuckles. "Not a good way to negotiate, Zhan-Yo. Not with me. If you'd come to New York, pitched me the proposal, I might've paid attention. Might've tried to find some common ground for us to stand on. Now, instead, I'm just going to destroy you and your company."

"My company has nothing to do with my actions," Zhan-Yo said, wondering why he wasn't in control. This wasn't how the meeting should be going. "I used Ziran for my own ends, not the other way around."

"If that's true, then they'll be able to find other jobs." Aegis shrugged. "But that comes later. Now I care about those Paragons you've got right there."

Zhan-Yo felt the conversation had tilted way past the point of recovery, at least without a drastic action. He reached up with his left hand, gripped the sword and drew it, stopping the blade a millimeter short of Innis's throat. The move, at least, made Aegis stop talking.

"You would not listen to me if I came to New York," Zhan-Yo started, feeling the heat bubbling up in his heart as he spoke. "You have not listened to us at all. I brought you here, in this way, because if I did not you would continue to ignore the normals. You would continue to crush us with your decrees and your drones, you would continue to shackle us to a world in which we have no say.

"You're here, Aegis, because you care about these Paragons in the same way I care about the millions in this city. The billions across this Earth who have no place in your hierarchy, but who deserve one. I want promises, Aegis. I want your word and commitment that the Paragons will be open to normals. That we can have our place in our government once again."

Zhan-Yo stopped to take a breath. It felt damn good to say all that out loud to the opposition, though it would have been better had Zhan-Yo been able to see Aegis's face, which ought to be open-mouthed and stunned. Zhan-Yo kept his own lips straight, his eyes steady. This wasn't a plea nor a gloat, but a negotiation.

Aegis tracked the length of Zhan-Yo's small blade. Worked his way from the point up to the hilt, from there back to Zhan-Yo's eyes. Shook his head.

"You ever read your history?" Aegis said, an exasperated teacher talking to a failing student. "Because if you did, you know that normals have been nothing but bastards to each other for all of time. These last thirty years with us in charge? Peace. Stability, relative anyway. Now look at you. Saying you want back in, and the way you're arguing for it is by taking hostages? Putting that little knife up to someone's throat? How's that supposed to convince me you deserve that power?

"You want to keep talking at me? Fine. Put that sword away. We'll put you in a Paragon cell and I'll send someone around to keep you company every now and then. Listen to you ramble and pay real good attention."

Of all the Champions, and Zhan-Yo had done his homework, Aegis had the headstrong instincts. A man who hammered out problems with his fists, who spoke like a rock and offered no compromises. Why Zhan-Yo thought Aegis would be the one to work with, rather than, say, Apinya or even Mynx, both of who had a reputation for considered thought, he didn't know. This whole operation had been a series of mistakes.

"So you will not negotiate?" Zhan-Yo sighed out the question.

"Nope. Put that sword down, or you're a dead man."

To take a life is a burden. Killing a man meant taking responsibility for all the things that man would never do, the lives he'd never change or fulfill. It's why Zhan-Yo preferred the less lethal route with his martial arts—he could change a mind by breaking an arm, rather than a neck—but here, if he put down his sword, Zhan-Yo's dream would die.

He pressed the blade closer to Innis's throat, careful not to start cutting . . . yet. The time had come for ultimatums. Diplomacy's end.

"Surrender and the Paragons live," Zhan-Yo said. "Take a single step and this one dies."

"Let'em kill me," Innis said, the motion pushing his throat against Zhan-Yo's blade and drawing a red line across the Paragon's neck. "It's my fault you're here, Aegis. The whole thing. It wasn't supposed to go sideways."

"Quiet," Zhan-Yo said. "That doesn't matter."

"For once, I agree," Aegis said, the Champion not picking up on Innis' real meaning. "You were outplayed, Innis. This man had you fooled. Why you led these Paragons into this mess, I don't know, but after we get out of here, you'd better have your excuses ready, and they'd better be good."

Then, before Zhan-Yo could make a move, Aegis flicked his right wrist along his belt and whipped something forward. Two metal balls, linked by a line of wire that flared bright white as it flew and hit Zhan-Yo's blade just above the hilt. The balls looped the wire around the blade, and by the time the wrap had been completed, the wire had melted through the metal, dropping the whole ensemble, minus the hilt Zhan-Yo still held, to the floor.

Aegis followed up his throw with a shoulder strike, crossing those few meters faster than Zhan-Yo could have expected. The hit threw Zhan-Yo back against the wall behind him, hard enough to jolt the blade-less hilt from Zhan-Yo's left hand and force him to crouch forward to keep from falling.

"My own daughter made that," Aegis bent down, picked one of the orbs off the ground and squeezed it, sucking the wire back inside and sealing the second ball to its partner. "One-time burst, but hot enough to melt through just about anything. She's smart, Zhan-Yo. Smarter than you."

Zhan-Yo straightened, coughed away the bruise growing in his chest from the hit. Raised his tachi, and prepared to fight a legend.

48

From One To The Next

Mynx didn't spin the story. While she rode in a pod from the burning lab, Mynx told Reeves to release a statement to the local press. One area that had done well after the Paragon takeover—as reps were generally awarded based on community value, journalism finally found a space it could thrive—the media had nonetheless adopted a hostile stance towards the Champions and the society they'd created. Mynx figured reporters and editors disliked the power imbalance that came with covering individuals holding absolute authority. She wouldn't care, except those same reporters and editors twisted public opinion, and Mynx didn't need some story about a prized scientist's unjust murder beamed out to every Tama in Pacifica.

"They'll know Dr. Jones suffered from a failed experiment with catastrophic consequences," Reeves told her as Mynx coasted in towards the Factory. "These things do happen."

Reeves started listing off incidents within the last few decades where seemingly random explosions had decimated companies, individuals, communities. Reeves knew as well as Mynx that most of those came from Paragon interventions in nefarious acts, regardless of whether those interventions caused more harm than good. The Champion's general operating procedure, since passed on to the Paragons, held a threat's total destruction was the preferred outcome, collateral damage or no. Too many anomalies, or normals with dangerous ideas, existed to play soft.

"Reeves, I want you to include what Denise tried to do," Mynx said as she arrived outside the Factory's front entrance. White cement steps led up to the great mountain facility, gladiator drone guards watched he ascend. "If nothing else, we need to discourage the idea that anyone can become an anomaly."

A younger Mynx would have hated the sound of that, but the innocent hope that everyone ought to have a chance at power like hers had sharpened into a much stronger conviction that very few could handle it. Open the anomaly box for everyone and the world would drown itself in souped-up chaos. The Paragons had enough troubles keeping down the natural anomalies.

"I've added it," Reeves said. "Would you like to proof the statement?"

She should, but right now Mynx craved a fresh cup of tea. A chance to sit down, have a snack and contemplate an early bedtime. So she compromised, "Read it to me while I head inside."

Reeves hit all the right notes, and Mynx had the statement approved and out through the Internet to all the various Pacifica media by the time she'd made it through the Factory to the residence. As she'd hoped, Reeves had read her mind, or interpreted a long history of Mynx's habits, and placed warm tea and an accompanying pot on the table outside. A bowl of fresh berries sat alongside another full of veggie ramen.

What caught Mynx's eye more than either thing, though, was a small pill selection waiting in the mix. Three capsules sporting the black and yellow coating reserved for energy burst chemicals.

"Reeves?" Mynx said, taking her seat and a moment to look out at the crashing waves, which caught twilight's last purples in their froth. "Explain?"

"I have another report for you and, according to past responses to similar data, you may need the stimulation," Reeves replied. "I will pull it up for you now."

Mynx sat at the table, speared a few berries with a well-placed fork and took in the video and diagnostic collage splaying across the surface. The top line data made the problem clear: Aegis had gone in with two drones, and now those two drones had lost their charge. More troubling, the drones predicted that as Aegis had not emerged from the collapsed tunnel or attempted further communication, the Champion had likely pressed on alone. The drones were now working their way around to the generator building's alternative entrance, but, due to fire and electrical damage sustained in a tunnel attack, they were not operating at top efficiency.

"In other words, Aegis is really on his own," Mynx said.

"There's more. Aegis also passed along a video message he received prior to making his entrance."

"Play it." Mynx drank some tea, ate some ramen while Ziran's clear threat played in front of her. She wanted to laugh at the hubris there, for a single organization to challenge the Paragons, but that same hubris wound up creating chills instead. "Ziran's not so stupid to pull a move like this unless they have a plan."

"Aegis already started the process of freezing their operations in Atlantis, but due to Ziran's place in our networks, it won't be easy to extricate them."

"Do the same here. Pull a list of Ziran's top people around the world and send it to the local Paragon offices." Mynx declared the several bites enough. "Every one of them should be pulled in and interrogated, find out what they know. If we're lucky, this move is isolated and our infrastructure's safe."

"If not?"

"We've rebuilt the world once. We can do it again. Get the jet ready. I need to head after Aegis."

"As I suspected. The jet is already prepared to fly. However, I do not believe it is possible for you to arrive in time to change the outcome?"

"Aegis doesn't die," Mynx replied. "I'll get there in time."

As she turned to head towards the jet's launch pad, set in the

Factory's upper reaches, Mynx swiped the pills off of the table. As much as she'd love to get a nap in on the way to Chicago, her nerves pulsed and sleep wouldn't be coming. No matter, she could use the time to look at Ziran.

To find the traitors.

49

Champion's Turn

As battlegrounds went, a dirty underground generator room that looked as though it'd played host to rat armies over the years didn't quite crack Aegis's top ten. Neither did the opponent, Ziran's chief executive and a man, though fit, who looked on the wrong side of his life to be pursuing world-changing revolution. Not that it really mattered—Aegis would knock him senseless, free the Paragons, and get back topside for some late, and much needed, dinner.

Zhan-Yo didn't draw his second blade, instead choosing to advance on Aegis with hands ready, held just above the man's waist. Wading into hand-to-hand combat with a Champion ranked among the most suicidal options one could choose, so Aegis gave Zhan-Yo two steps to reconsider that decision.

Then Aegis pulled his stun gun from his belt and fired. The dart hit Zhan-Yo straight in the chest, right where the heart ought to be, and bounced off.

"Guess we're doing this the hard way?" Aegis said, replacing the gun in its holster.

"He's better than ya think," Innis muttered from the side, hallowed eyes watching from his restraints.

The local Paragon leader vexed Aegis. Innis had misplayed the whole raid, brought rookies to a risky encounter and pulled them ahead without drone support. A tactical nightmare. Aegis would be removing Innis from his command, might boot him out of Chicago entirely and to a far away region where the Paragon could learn what it meant to lead without endangering anyone.

Zhan-Yo tried to prove Innis's comment true right away, quick-stepping into low kicks that tested Aegis's left and right sides with gusto. Aegis let them land, felt the mash as Zhan-Yo's boot connected with tactical armor and Aegis's own power to blunt the impact. For someone who'd taken punches from Thane, Zhan-Yo's strikes felt like a light smack with a pillow. A dull pressure.

"Going to take a lot more than that," Aegis said, accentuating his words with a straight jab right at Zhan-Yo's chest.

His target played smart, dancing back out of the punch's range, leaving Aegis striking air. So Aegis pursued, stalking Zhan-Yo as the latter danced back and around the trapped, stunned Paragons. As they circled around to Innis, Aegis feigned another lunge, buying space. With that, Aegis pulled a tactical knife and cut Innis free.

Innis stared at his emancipated wrists as Aegis flipped the knife into a reverse grip in his left hand, ready for Zhan-Yo to try some-thing, anything. Instead, Zhan-Yo stood there, watching, as if Aegis starred in some fascinating documentary.

"What's your move?" Aegis said to Zhan-Yo as Innis stood. "People know where I am, drones too. They'll get here before long, and you won't be able to dodge around all of us."

"I've dodged all of you for a very long time," Zhan-Yo said, and Aegis felt concern glimmer: Zhan-Yo seemed far too calm for someone who appeared to be losing everything. "I'm stopping now because the trap is ready to spring, and you have sprung it."

The trap hit Aegis hard. Innis's fists punched into Aegis's back, just above his hip, where numbness blossomed. Innis's ability blew out the nerves around his strikes, like a biological EMP device. Aegis had seen the Paragon knock an enemy upside the head and had the person forget who they were, what they were doing, and go through a complete personality transformation. Unfortunately for Innis, Aegis's back had neither brains nor critical muscles, so Aegis delivered a left elbow to Innis' chin and knocked the Paragon to the floor.

No, not a Paragon. Not anymore.

"Well that clears things up," Aegis said, rubbing at his back to clear away the numbness. Innis's ability couldn't hold off Aegis's healing for long. "Is that all you have? A washed up Paragon?"

Zhan-Yo hadn't moved. Ziran's leader watched Aegis, then flicked to Innis, frowning. Maybe Zhan-Yo did only have the soon-to-be-exiled Paragon. Either way, Zhan-Yo recovered his courage and spread his hands like a teacher explaining the obvious to an ignorant student, "Think about what it means, Aegis. Your own lieutenants are turning against you. Your movement is failing. Now is the time to stop, before it all collapses. Give in to change that must happen."

"We've beaten so many that sound just like you. You want change? Earn it." Aegis feinted toward Zhan-Yo but instead wheeled around and delivered a triple jab to an unsuspecting, rising Innis.

Innis crumpled, clear evidence that he'd spent far too little time in the field, that he'd become exactly what Aegis had not; someone who'd forgotten how to fight. Innis struggled to deflect a blow, any blow, and failed, earning a riddled face and what felt like a cracked rib for his efforts. The Champion finished the series with a strike from his left knee, and Innis fell to the ground, cradling his legs like a child. Aegis wanted to tell Innis how embarrassed he felt, how much Aegis loathed not just Innis for this failure but himself as well. How could Aegis have let this one stray so far?

"Get up," Aegis said.

"No," Innis tried, sounding even more pathetic for all the times Aegis had heard him proclaim, with plenty of bravado, about the bold strides his Chicago Paragons were making.

"You were a Paragon once. Are you going to die there, on the ground, or can you reclaim any of your honor?"

Innis didn't speak, and Aegis thought he saw tears in the big man's eyes. A total fall. One Aegis might as well end right now. He readied his right foot—

Aegis didn't feel pain often. And when it came, the aches left quick. A function of his being; a Paragon whose body repaired itself faster than anyone else in the planet. But this stab came from behind, deep, icy, and long. Aegis felt the blade slide near the bottom of his spine. A strike not meant to kill fast, meant to maim, weaken. There'd been Paragons over the years who'd perfected similar skills, who'd brought enemies low with crippling blows. Aegis never thought he'd experience one, never thought the day would come when he'd be vulnerable to the same techniques his forces had employed.

His world kept changing, and Aegis had been too cocky to change with it. Zhan-Yo had him, for a moment.

"You've lost," Zhan-Yo said, voice right behind Aegis's right ear, with logic's stoic weight. "If I twist this blade, no matter how strong your healing, you won't survive. Not now."

Aegis performed a simple calculus, retreating from agony's hot spike to the cold space he went to every time an enemy or disaster forced a choice between life and death. In this pure vacuum, Aegis always came out with the same answer: try. Keep fighting. Never give up. A thousand cliches stacked on each other, each urging Aegis to push and push again. Thus far, the advice had not failed him. So as soon as Zhan-Yo finished his threat, Aegis threw himself back, knocked his head into Zhan-Yo's face and, lunging forward, torqued the sword out of Zhan-Yo's grip. The blade still inside, Aegis felt every cutting shred as it moved in his body. Following the pain came the itching pulse as his healing tried to cope, to seal away veins and organs.

With the sword freed of its wielder, standing over Innis, Aegis turned back towards his opponent. So far, this fight had gone like so many others; back-and-forth wound parade ending when Aegis's stamina outlasted Zhan-Yo. Before, Aegis's endurance had been a given. Now, Aegis couldn't depend on it anymore. He'd need to force the issue.

Zhan-Yo set for Aegis's attack like someone who knew what they were doing, but after Zhan-Yo blocked the first, the second swing, his training gave way to the reality of the Champion's assault. Aegis barreled through Zhan-Yo's forearm blocks, driving his opponent across the cement floor to the hard wall. Bouncing back from slamming Zhan-Yo against the sturdy concrete, Aegis clapped his hands on either side of Zhan-Yo's head before picking Zhan-Yo up, armor and all, and launching him across the ground, until Zhan-Yo rolled to a stop near the captured Paragons.

The sword still sticking out of him protested every one of these maneuvers with deep stabs, and after tossing his opponent, Aegis sucked in one breath after another, trying to keep himself awake and steady his furious nerves. He'd dealt with the immediate danger. Next came survival. Aegis reached back with his left hand and felt for the blade's hilt.

"Don't pull it out," Innis said, still on the ground. "You do that, might start bleeding too fast even for you."

"Trying to help me now?" Aegis gasped more than said, feeling what might have been blood or saliva or both bunch up in his mouth and burble out. "You're a little late."

"Never hated you. But you've lost your way. Leaving us behind. Can't you feel it? The world's changing. Your perfect bubble's bursting and you don't have a plan."

"Stick to fighting, Innis." Aegis sighed through the reply, getting his grip ready and setting his teeth. "You're terrible at it, but at least you'll only get yourself killed."

Aegis yanked. Pulled the sword from his back and flung it to the side even as the shock-white burst drove him to his knees. Aegis hadn't felt pain like that in a long time, maybe ever. Spots danced in his eyes, his every nerve tingled with the expectation of imminent death. Imminent, but not here. Not yet. Aegis held himself in his mind, held Celice, Mynx, the other Champions who he'd fought alongside for so long to create this world these monsters wanted to tear apart. He couldn't let them win.

Bit by bit, Aegis pulled his body back from the terrible void it'd so wanted to fall into. First he steadied his hands, palms on the ground. Sturdy, real. Then his lungs, each inhale restoring cadence to his body, balancing his rapid-fire heartbeat. Rising from his knees came slow, with lashes from the sword's aftereffects radiating out from Aegis's back. But he rose, he stood, and Aegis, Champion of Atlantis, focused on his enemy.

"You're not supposed to be able to heal like that," Zhan-Yo said. "Not anymore."

"Champions don't lose," Aegis replied.

But Champions did get angry, and this Champion had no compunction against taking lives from those who no longer deserved to have them. Zhan-Yo had stabbed Aegis in the back, had refused to surrender. Had waged a war against society. There could be only one price for that. Aegis took one step, two steps and stared down at the enemy.

"It's over." Aegis cocked his fist, ready to deliver a single deathblow.

Two shots struck, simultaneous. Both in his chest, heavy rounds. Aegis could feel them cut in, pierce armor made to defend against common dangers. The sound knocked out his hearing, ears ringing as the impact threw Aegis back. Off his unsteady feet to the ground. New agony came hot, fast, and everywhere. The place, his calculus made to cut the panic wouldn't, couldn't come, and the Champion sank into his oblivion.

50

Way Out There

As destinations went, the place the pod dropped Kat fell somewhere between a modern art installation and a dark, sinister dimension she never wanted to visit. Lights were few this far outside of town, giving the white ones ringing the tall fence around the scrapyard a spectral appearance against the relative black everywhere else. The pouring snow added to the effect, sliding down in clusters according to mystical whimsy. Wind whipped out here too, unobstructed by the buildings breaking up gusts in the city. Enough so that even in Kat's suit, with thermal regulators working overtime, she felt cold licks crawl up her hair and brush her ankles.

Seeker, for his part, didn't mind at all. The husky pounced on snow piles, jumped after falling flakes and grinned his toothy, tongue-flopping grin at Kat as though they'd found paradise.

"Of course you'd like this place," Kat muttered. "One man's wasteland, another dog's heaven."

Across from the scrapyard, behind Kat, industrial warehouses kept them company. Old spotlights loomed over their packed lots, protected and worked by machines with no need for those gray stalks overlooking noisy, continual production. An occasional, distorted bark echoed from the machines' human overseers, likely remote and watching the proceedings from some comfortable office or, as Kat wished, with hot chocolate in hand on their couch. No other souls were in sight.

Kat checked her Tama, buckled into its spot on her left forearm, just above the gadgets clipped to that same wrist. No new messages, and the tracking application showed both Calvin's ping and Gordon's last network connection coming from inside the yard. She'd found the right place, however wrong it felt to be here.

Behind the chainlink gates and rising in spots above the three meter fence were tremendous scrap metal piles. Junked vehicles, drones, pods and things both earlier and later than those inventions clustered among each other in no discernible order. Some shone with recent progress evident in their stainless finishing, while others surrendered their carapaces to orange and red rust. Everything seemed to be waiting, but for what?

A placard on the right gate labeled the scrap yard's owners—not a name Kat recognized—and declared any trespassing as grounds for terrible retribution. Seeing as the Tama lock on the gates had been smashed and the gates themselves opened, if only enough for a body to squeeze through, the ability to carry out the promised retribution seemed to be lacking. Going by the footprints, vanishing as the soft snow fell, Kat figured both Calvin and Gordon had come this way.

How nice of them to leave her a path to follow. Kat didn't even have to touch the gate.

Every step inside, following those footprints, brought Kat past some techno-wreck. Here lay a refrigerator. There, long old-style car doors, and further along a small pre-fab home's crumpled remnants. These scrappers, it seemed, were equal opportunity. Seeker failed to match Kat's interest in the relics, instead pushing ahead along the trail, taking time every few seconds to throw Kat a frustrated glance.

She'd never let him off leash here. Not with Calvin around.

But when they hit an intersection between large piles close to where Gordon's Tama dot appeared, Seeker barked and lunged forward with strength Kat didn't expect. The dog brought forth his genetic heritage and sought to pull Kat like a sled, to drag her to the goal as fast as possible. Kat let the leash go to save her shoulder and its socket, breaking into a run herself to follow, using her spare breath for frustrated curses.

Seeker had no time for stealth.

The dog also didn't have trouble with the snow, now deep enough to make Kat's boots crunch through mounds with every step, and thick enough to make those steps an exercise in keeping her balance, making what could have been a fast sprint on dry ground into a shambling dance that had Kat, for once, grateful they were in a lonely scrapyard. She didn't have much beyond her tracker reputation, and a video of her flailing arms and pumping, sliding legs wouldn't do that any favors.

"Could have gone to *Carver's*," Kat huffed, looking around at the scrap and hoping Calvin didn't have some ambush planned. "Had some whiskey. Nice and warm. Instead I'm freezing out here, looking for you, Gordon."

Around another stripped wiring stack that looked, in this light, like silver snakes, Kat saw Gordon lying in an old car canyon. Calvin stood over him. Sedans and trucks, axles in the air, framed the two. Seeker chose one car as a parapet from which to make his barking call, nose pointed Calvin's way.

Calvin knelt, eyes on Seeker, and reached towards Gordon's throat.

"Hey!" Kat yelled. "Step back. Now."

Kat drew her stun gun as she spoke. Aimed right at Calvin. The gun's range-finder played Calvin's distance in blue numbers on the back of the barrel: twenty meters out. Not a sure shot but not impossible either. Especially since Calvin looked like he wore nothing more than the ragged jacket, shirt and jeans he had on before. The man must be freezing, but he looked at Kat without flinching, no shivering that she could see.

"Call off your dog," Calvin said, and he didn't stop reaching towards Gordon, placing two fingers of his left hand along Gordon's throat.

"I said get back!" Kat replied, starting a slow walk towards Calvin. "If you've hurt him—"

"He's alive," Calvin said, standing up. "For now. I said call off your dog."

Kat could give the signal and the husky would charge, go for Calvin's legs, maybe his arm. Seeker would close the distance fast, but Calvin, from here, would be faster. Kat would not see her dog die today. She didn't want Gordon to die either, but it looked like that might have already happened.

"Seeker, stay," Kat said, and the husky obeyed, stopped the barks, though Seeker's focus stayed locked on the anomaly. "What did you do to him?"

"He came after me, I defended myself," Calvin said. "Same thing I did before. I don't want to hurt people, but you keep forcing me."

"No. You're making the choice. You know the laws."

"I didn't have a voice in making them."

"Not my problem."

She'd had this conversation before with Calvin. It only went one way: they'd banter back and forth until Calvin pulled some stupid move and either killed her or ran. So this time Kat went for surprise. Pulled the trigger. The dart fired straight at Calvin's chest and stuck there even as Calvin started to act. Calvin fell forward to the ground, catching his fall with both hands in the snow. He looked up at Kat, then reached towards her as she finished loading a second dart.

Kat fired again. The second dart lanced through the air and stopped as it struck an icy circle spreading out from Calvin's hand, as though the anomaly had gained a solid ice shield. The dart fell, useless, into the fluff. Calvin's shield grew, cutting in front of the anomaly and sealing the space between the cars. Gordon's body, Seeker, and Kat on one side with Calvin on the other. Frustrating, but could she expect anything less with this guy?

Kat holstered the stun gun, and broke right, scrambling up stacked pick-ups to look over the wall and see Calvin running, slow and sedated, deeper into the yard. She would have leapt after him, around the ice wall, but Seeker's whimper called Kat's attention back behind her. Gordon. She went to him and knelt down, held her Tama towards his own and pulled the vitals readings. Calvin had it right: Gordon lived but his signs were shaky. And without a suit on, his body temp had started falling. Gordon needed an evac, fast. Kat tapped her Tama and put in a quick call for emergency drones. They were out there, circling Chicago's skies and waiting for things like this, but a sharp beep from her Tama confirmed there weren't any near the scrap yard. They'd arrive, but not for ten minutes or more.

Calvin would get away by then, and she couldn't take the chance that Calvin would find the ping and disappear forever.

"Sorry Gordon," Kat said. "You brought me out here. Can't let that pod fare go to waste."

By the time she stood up, Calvin's ice shield had dissolved into a thick pile of frost. The anomaly had scared Kat before, had nearly killed her. Time to return the favor.

51

The Revolution Begins

Saved.

Zhan-Yo saw Sylvia standing outside the door to the back room. Both of her guns in her hands, sighted on Aegis. He followed their barrels to the Champion, who lay sprawled on the ground, wet coughs and still limbs indicating Aegis wouldn't be getting up anytime soon. Zhan-Yo wouldn't mind staying down himself. Aegis had delivered punches and kicks with a ferocity Zhan-Yo hadn't experienced in a very, very long time, if ever. His body had forgotten how to take hits like that, and adrenaline couldn't fully compensate for the bruised ribs, the throbbing knee and the bulging bruise already forming beneath Zhan-Yo's right eye.

"Get up," Sylvia said. "He won't stay down forever."

"You don't think you killed him?" Zhan-Yo said.

Sylvia flicked her icy stare his way. "Sometimes I forget you don't actually do this. Killing any anomaly is hard, but he's a Champion, Zhan-Yo. None of them have ever died."

"Right," Zhan-Yo said.

Aegis and his crew had suffered losses before, Zhan-Yo knew, but they'd managed to escape the reaper's scythe since climbing to their positions of power. Whether by luck or by sending in lesser

Paragons to blunt the harsh blows of the fights against the old governments, the Champions had preserved themselves and, thus, created their invulnerability's iron image. They'd never been beaten, never died, never surrendered to normals. From the red pool beneath Aegis's body, this would be a night of many firsts.

Sylvia, keeping one hand aiming a gun at the Champion, used the other to help Zhan-Yo up. They went over to Aegis together, with Zhan-Yo confirming the other Paragons were still in their temporary comas. Innis, meanwhile, seemed shocked, staring at Aegis with his bearded mouth open, saying nothing at all. Up close, Aegis didn't seem to see them, gaze occasionally latching on to Zhan-Yo or Sylvia's face before drifting off. Zhan-Yo had seen this before. Not a killer, no, but Sylvia had sent proof of her other work. Obstacles to Ziran that needed to be removed, Paragon and otherwise.

Zhan-Yo had seen enough last moments.

"Here," Sylvia said, handing out one of her guns. "Do the final shot lower. Leave the face intact."

Sylvia had it right, and Zhan-Yo needed to focus. This had to play well. This would be the start of the revolution. Zhan-Yo couldn't play dumb, couldn't be a coward, couldn't back away from this. The moment had arrived, and it wouldn't wait for him to be ready. Zhan-Yo's hand trembled as he took the gun, he forced it steady as Zhan-Yo stepped around Aegis to point it, from behind, towards the Champion's chest.

"Three rounds," Sylvia said, exchanging her weapon for the Tama on her wrist, its red light indicating the recording had already started. "And if that doesn't do it, we'll cut the tape anyway and I'll finish him after."

A small part of Zhan-Yo hoped his shots would fail to kill Aegis, that Sylvia could add one more mark to her extensive score and his own sheet would stay clean. Even if the world thought Zhan-Yo a killer, he wouldn't be one. Zhan-Yo had been a ruthless leader, wise and strategic. He'd built Ziran from his father's strong company to a world dominating one. None of that made him a villain. None of that made him evil. But this?

"Are we ready?" Zhan-Yo asked.

"Ready," Sylvia smiled, the producer urging her star to the next scene.

"Hurry up, or you'll lose your chance." Innis had found his legs, he stood now and watched. "Aegis won't stay down long."

"Shut it," Sylvia snapped back. "Or I'll have another body to dispose of."

The words knocked another hole in Zhan-Yo's mental wall. Sylvia spoke like one of those seedy thugs, talking of body counts and what to do about them. Murder played a part in the plan, yes, but the point of it all rested in the revolution. He'd talk to Sylvia after this, make sure she understood. Violence and death were unfortunate side effects, not goals to be achieved.

Aegis coughed. Zhan-Yo snapped back. Discussions could be saved for later.

"Let's begin," Zhan-Yo said.

The script rolled off his lips. Memorized, rehearsed and ready. Practiced statements claiming the new future would be a democratic one, would be for normals and anomalies alike. One that could only be built upon the rubble and ruin of the present. The Champions had refused to see the brighter path and so now he, Zhan-Yo, would show them.

"I want you to stand with me, I want you to fight with me to overthrow our oppressors," Zhan-Yo said. "All through human history those who have been trodden have risen up against those who trod upon them. Now we must do it again. Tonight, I send the first signal. Join me, and remake our world into a better one."

He took a breath, aimed. Pulled the trigger.

The bullet bounced off the ground, ricocheting off towards a corner. Aegis had moved. The Champion rolled to the right, grabbed Zhan-Yo's broken sword and its jagged hilt. Zhan-Yo tracked Aegis with the gun as Sylvia drew her own. He had Aegis, but those Paragons sat around him, helpless. If he missed—

Then Aegis moved again, a rolling tackle as Sylvia's own shot flew above the Champion, whose maneuver knocked her to the ground. With his right hand, Aegis jammed the broken sword into

Sylvia's chest, even as she poured another pair of shots into him. Aegis fell off as Zhan-Yo ran up, pulled the Champion away. Sylvia's wound looked bad, her face already turning gray, her eyes finding his. Zhan-Yo placed his hands around the hilt, but hesitated. Aegis had survived the pull, but would she?

"Going to finish him?" Innis said, appearing next to Zhan-Yo and sounding utterly unsurprised at the Champion's sudden attack.

Zhan-Yo glanced at Aegis. The man's eyes had closed, he didn't look to be breathing, and the fresh gunshots across his torso suggested the fatal blow had already fallen.

"He's already gone," Zhan-Yo said. "Help me. We need to get her out of here."

Together, the traitors, the revolutionaries, lifted Sylvia off the ground and carried her towards the surface and the chance of a good signal, leaving a dead Champion in their wake.

52

The Ashes

To say she screamed into Chicago would be underselling it. Mynx had the jet topping its speed limit, burning down its battery at a frightening rate that threatened to overheat its engines. Celice had called, said the drones hadn't been able to get through to Aegis thanks to further collapses in the maintenance tunnel. Other gladiators around Chicago had been called to help, but going to the under-city meant losing signal, and without access to satellite oversight, the drones could fall prey to hacks, bugs, or worse. Celice had been willing to risk a rogue drone in a major population center, but these were Mynx's machines, and she called their shots.

Aegis could survive anything. That had been true forever, and Mynx refused to believe it wasn't true now.

Chicago's city lights appeared as the jet raced in its descent, cutting down through clouds into a blizzard. Bad weather chose the worst time to strike the city.

"Trig rapid eject sequence," Mynx said.

The jet didn't question the choice to bomb out into a snowstorm. Mynx's seat flattened and moved back into the jet's body. Restraints shot across her and pulled tight, pressing Mynx into the cushion. From each restraint, further plastic expanded, met its counterparts, and sealed to keep Mynx protected. She'd have enough air to last ten to fifteen minutes. Plenty long to plummet to the ground. Behind her, the wind's roar filled the jet as the escape hatch opened between the large engine nacelles. With her head facing cold sky, Chicago's lights making a blurred reflection in her mesh, Mynx clenched her fists. Held her breath.

She hated this part.

The locks holding the seat in place disengaged, sending Mynx flying out the back and into the night. Mynx yelled, an unquenchable combo of exhilaration and panic as her stomach jumped. Above her, Mynx saw the jet keep streaking away. The autopilot would take it to an airport. Mynx, meanwhile, hurtled towards Chicago's downtown.

The moment of truth. If her algorithms worked right, if the drones did their job, Mynx wouldn't splatter herself across the steel surfaces of the buildings below. The snowstorm didn't make the descent any less harrowing—the drones should account for the wind, for how thick snow might affect their weight, but every new variable made Mynx more nervous.

Until a bouncing bang jolted Mynx against her restraints and the clouded sky above her vanished as a drone enveloped her. The roaring thrusters slowed Mynx's fall, and she felt the drone turn to dodge around those buildings. Together, they sank towards the street, finally touching down with all the harsh impact of a child settling into bed. Though this bed turned out to be a concrete road with a half-dozen drones landing alongside her.

As with Thane, as with Denise, drones alerted to Mynx's arrival swarmed her as soon as she'd stepped away from the jet's abandoned seat, bolted to her arms and legs and gave her the tools she hoped she wouldn't need. Information splashed across the new visor, what had once been a glass covering for a drone's suppression cannon. Over her right eye, a steady stream of filling bars gave graphical progress to the pinches, tugs, and jolts Mynx felt as her armor assembled. On her left, Chicago's current Paragon alerts played out, with Aegis's predicament nowhere on the list.

Of course Aegis would choose to keep his rescue mission to

himself. Probably under some ridiculous reasoning like keeping other Paragons from getting caught in the same trap. Poor logic for a leader whose charges had all accepted the risks when joining the Paragon's peacekeeping forces. Mynx didn't hold her drones out of danger for fear they might get damaged. Aegis ought to have gone in with all the support he could muster.

In the seconds stuck waiting for her armor's green light, Mynx read through a few of the other headlines. Standard minor fare, but enough of it in a city this large to keep the Paragons busy. One high priority med evac call for a tracker that'd nonetheless take time due to its remote location. Unsurprising that the tracker had been somewhere sparse, surprising that the person putting in the call was also a tracker. Chicago's number one, in fact.

"Reeves, keep tabs on this one," Mynx said, the visor tracking her eyes and highlighting the med evac in question. "I'm curious to hear the story behind it."

"Of course."

The suit pinged its readiness and Mynx didn't waste any more time, loping over the stopped pod cars and heading towards the entrance to Chicago's under-city. As she went, Mynx put out the Champion-priority alert to the local Paragons, ensuring plenty of reinforcements would be following her in. Anyone who thought they'd get Aegis alone would find themselves very much outnumbered.

Her right view overlaid with a familiar face. Celice, calling yet again. Mynx could have blinked to block the call, but she had a few seconds to traverse yet, and she understood the panic that came when a loved one might be in danger.

"You're on the ground?" Celice asked.

"Heading towards his location," Mynx replied. "Two minutes out."

"I still can't get ahold of him."

Of course not. Aegis hadn't emerged from the underground. Mynx nearly called Celice on the remark, but saw the red-rimmed eyes in time.

"I'll get there soon." Mynx tried being reassuring—machines

didn't need pep talks, so she was out of practice. "Your dad's a Champion, Celice. He'll be fine."

Words Mynx knew she shouldn't say. Promises like that only put heroes in bad spots when they inevitably proved false, but Mynx couldn't help it. Aegis wasn't a normal, wasn't a Paragon soldier. Aegis had survived the worst things Earth had conjured up and kept on swinging. Regardless, Mynx didn't get to hear Celice's response; she rocketed down a sloping street into the undercity, the call fuzzing and fading as Mynx approached the generator building's signal disruption.

Given the late hour, the silent emptiness down here didn't seem strange. The quiet did, though. With the signals cut, Mynx's visor killed its overlay. Comments from Reeves or beeps notifying Mynx that her drones were in position disappeared, leaving the Champion with the background thrum of a living city. Mushy snow blew in from above, melting in patches as grates and vents everywhere expelled heat. Golden lights dripped their honeyed glow as Mynx clanked her way towards the generator building.

From a distance, Mynx could tell the building's front door no longer sat on its hinges. Something, someone had torn it off, and the barrier leaned against the building wall, presenting an unobstructed, dim way inside. On either side, shut down in pre-coded stasis, were the gladiator drones that ought to have saved Aegis. Looking at them, Mynx leveraged the scanners in her drone armor to learn both gladiators had suffered minimal damage, and had been shut down through standard Paragon code words. The commands only Paragons would know to speak. Up top, the gladiators would double-check anyone telling them to stop with the Paragon's current database to make sure the order came from a real Paragon, but with the signal loss, Mynx had them coded to take the words on faith. Otherwise, innocents might die.

Now, Mynx wondered whether that security had cost a Champion his life.

The building and its entrance had, thankfully, been designed to move large equipment, so Mynx managed to make it inside with her armor intact. When her scanners picked up no dangerous noises—

heated chatter, the distinct clicks of rounds being loaded—she rushed the rest of the way through, gouging out pieces of the walls in the process.

No attacks came, no force yelled threats or assaulted Mynx from the shadows when she made the central room. Five Paragons sat bound in the middle of the room, one awake enough to turn his head towards Mynx. Beside them, on the ground, laid Aegis.

"I think he's dead," the Paragon said. Without her visor's connection to the vast web of information, Mynx had to rely on old skills of deduction to discern the Paragon was both young and distraught. Not likely an enemy. "I don't, I don't know how it happened. I woke up and he was like this. But he wasn't with us when we attacked."

"How long were you out?" Mynx clomped over towards Aegis, looked at the Champion and let the scans run.

He'd been shot numerous times. The visor overlaid the wounds on his body, highlighting them in red blotches. No breathing. No registered heartbeat. Mynx swallowed the instant emotion, forced herself to stay here, in the moment. She had to get Aegis out of here. Then she could figure out what happened. What to do.

"A long time. I don't even know what time it is?" the Paragon's voice jolted Mynx from the shock, and with her left hand, she reached her drone arm towards the bound Paragons and fired a precision burn that cut through the alert one's hand bindings.

"It's late. Take care of yourselves," Mynx said, picking up Aegis. "Get out of here. Write up what you know."

"It wasn't supposed to be like this," the Paragon said as Mynx turned back to the exit and began her run to the surface, towards the only thing that might yet save Aegis. "We were supposed to win."

53

No Giving In

The scene had a final battle's look: Kat came running around broken washing machines to find Calvin standing tall, centered beneath an old plane's white fuselage which straddled its own towering scrap piles to drop a shadow over Calvin's head. The plane's wings were bent and broken, forming skeletal overhangs, their twisting branches and the metal sheets strung between them providing a bulwark against the falling snow.

Kat made the connection when she noticed the scattered, molded furniture on the ground around Calvin. As though formed from clay, a chair, firepit, and what looked like a makeshift twin bed built from car parts made a circle around their owner. Safes sat locked off to one side, providing ballast to a leaning locker.

If nothing else, the Paragons would get Calvin a better home.

Seeker seemed to agree; the husky stood heavy on his four paws next to her, teeth bared and the lowest growls bubbling from his throat. Too quiet for Calvin to hear. Snow continued to gather in his fur, making the dog glisten in the spotlights, as though she'd covered him with jewels for a winter ball.

Like Seeker would stand for that.

Music began to play in her mind, a deep rhythmic pounding

that called forth conflict on an epic scale. A war that might be waged between gods. Yet here stood only one. An anomaly, ready to deliver a smiting to the uppity normal. The fight deserved a good guitar riff. The wind's howling would have to work.

"Not running anymore?" Kat called to Calvin. "Would've thought you'd keep going. Seems to be what you do best."

"I'm tired," Calvin said, the wind snatching the occasional word and making off with it. "I'm so tired. I've been chased my whole life from one place to another and I just can't do it anymore."

"I didn't ask you to run," Kat replied. "Didn't ask you to fight, either."

"But you're making me. Aren't you?"

Of all the anomalies Kat had traced, the ones she'd hunted down through back alleys and surprised in resplendent office buildings, Calvin made her feel the worst. Most who fought were defiant, had escaped the system for so long that they thought they could never be beaten. Or they panicked. Begged to be left alone. Claimed that they weren't hurting anyone and that it would all be fine if Kat would just turn and walk away.

As if Kat had a choice.

Anomalies were dangerous. Ones who didn't register, doubly so. When they asked Kat to give up, she fought, and won. When they begged her to leave, she refused, and returned the anomalies to the only place that could keep them under control: their own brethren.

"I am making you choose," Kat replied. "You either give up and let me trace you now: no bruises, no broken bones. Might even have time for a beer before bar close. Or we mix it up. See what happens. Maybe you get away, but you won't make it far. It'll be me, or Gordon, or another tracker and you'll be right back here, wondering how you can be left alone and knowing the answer is standing right in front of you."

Calvin, his face half in shadow from the spotlights above, shrugged. "Guess I can't see it."

Of course not. Why would he get easy now?

Kat snapped her fingers and Seeker jumped forward, paws scrabbling on the snow as the husky bounded towards Calvin, coming in from the right while Kat ran at him from the left. Prompted with a dog and a charging tracker, Calvin kicked out to the side, his foot rattling against the over-hanging metal and causing it to shake, several chunks of ice to drop. With his left hand, as Kat closed, Calvin caught the falling ice and stuck out his right palm towards her. Between the two of them, the air fogged, Calvin's hand spraying out the fine dust. Sparkles appeared and grew as Kat realized it wasn't just smoke, but ice. It didn't take much calculation to understand what a sheet of sharp ice flying towards her could do. So she dove, face forward sliding along the snowy ground.

Seeker, barking all the way, charged through the forming ice, striking from the side and scattering Calvin's attack. Brittle flakes flew everywhere, a miniature snowstorm with a husky in the middle jumping and tearing. The sight would have been funny without death's dire possibility. Kat pushed herself back up, reached for her stun gun. She'd already hit Calvin once, and her fervent prayers hoped the dart would slow the anomaly soon. Unless Calvin's ability kept him safe from the sedatives, which would be just her luck.

With his ice cloud obliterated, Calvin backed away as Seeker turned towards him. The husky, barking, planted his paws and rushed forward.

"Come on, doggie," Calvin said, dropping the icicle. "Come right here."

The anomaly reached out, touched the hanging metal fuselage with his right hand and pointed his left towards the dog. Seeker leapt, going for Calvin's throat and slammed into a sudden gray metallic wall, spreading out as though Calvin had unfurled a steel umbrella in the air. Seeker collapsed to the ground, and the metal fell next to the dog a moment later, too heavy to stay in the air. The morphed disc came to a point, as if Calvin had conjured a giant top out of nowhere.

The tracker and her target again stood across from each other. Kat had her weapon aimed. The anomaly breathed hard, glaring back at her.

"If you hurt my dog," Kat said, "I'm going to forget that I'm supposed to take you alive."

"If you want to make it through this, you should forget that anyway," Calvin replied. "And I didn't bring your dog to this fight."

"You still attacked him. Stop trying to act like you're the good guy."

Enough words. Kat fired. The dart lanced out, covered the full distance between Kat and Calvin in a micro second, only to slam into another, smaller metal shield and bounce to the floor. Kat sighed, slipped the stun gun back into its holster. Snapped her left wrist to switch from the flash orbs to something a little more useful in a close fight. Took a step forward. Raised her arms as if the two were in a boxing ring.

"You didn't really fight at *Carver's*," Kat said. "Now's your chance. Straight up. You versus me."

Not that Kat had any fair fighting intentions. She had to keep Calvin close, get him invested in a brawl instead of running away.

Calvin laughed. Hoarse and tired. "Can't do that. No time."

If Calvin didn't want to play the game, then Kat would have to force him. She feinted straight, and Calvin, still keeping his hand on that metal—Kat made the connection—launched out a pointed steel lance that Kat sidestepped. She dashed towards Calvin's left side, towards that fuselage Calvin had his hand on. Calvin tracked her with his left hand, launching ever smaller silver missiles her way; sharp, shimmering, narrow needles. After they formed, Calvin pushed them towards her, but the needles didn't have much momentum on their own, and Kat slipped past them.

Despite the show of fists, as Kat ducked under another needle, she swept Calvin's legs out from under him with a low kick. The anomaly, reacting slow to the move—the first stun dart doing its work?—fell with the swipe. He hit the snow with a grunt, and rolled. Kat followed, again drawing the stun gun. The anomaly didn't have a hand on the metal anymore, so no steel shields. Kat aimed, when Calvin reversed the roll, snapping himself back towards her and raising his right fist, his left buried in the snow. An ice blast shot out, blinding her mask and coating the stun gun, jamming its trigger.

Useless. Kat threw the gun aside, wiped the white off of her mask and stared as Calvin began to scramble away.

"You can't run Calvin," Kat said. "Stop."

Calvin actually did. Turned back towards her.

"Thank you," Kat said. "Hands up and away, please."

"You know, you're right," Calvin said, raising his hands ever so slightly away from his waist. "I'm cold. I'm tired. Sick of running. All this goes away if I let you trace me?"

"All of it." Kat took a step forward, watching. The idea that Calvin would give up, right now, seemed ludicrous. "You'll have a home. Hot food. A dog of your own if you like. Pretty good deal."

"I'd be a Paragon."

"If they want you for that, yeah." Close to him now. Kat reached for the small tracer on the back of her belt. One injection into Calvin's forearm and it'd all be done. "Good reps either way."

"Problem is, I don't care about reps." Calvin jerked his knee up, tried to hit Kat in the stomach.

Except he'd telegraphed the whole thing. His eyes watching her, catching his breath right before the move, his muscles twitching and his left foot's ever-so-slight shift in the snow to ensure balance. All that gave Kat the signals she needed to block the blow with her left arm and deliver her own gut punch with her right. Calvin dropped to his knees, planted his hands into the snow to catch himself.

"Not my problem." Kat lined up the tracer with Calvin's left arm.

"Nah. You've got other ones."

A vice closed on her feet. Locked her boots and then her ankles, covered by the snow, into place. Kat looked down. No way Calvin had planted a trap of some kind here. The odds that she'd walk into it were too low. So then . . . Calvin rose up as Kat leaned down, brushed away some of the snow and saw what held her. Solid ice. Thick and wrapping all around her feet and up to her calves. She couldn't move.

"Bye, tracker," Calvin said, pulling the tracer from Kat's hand and tossing it. "Hope your dog's all right, and that I never see you again."

The anomaly turned and shambled away, feet sliding through the snow. As if he'd won the fight.

Hunting anomalies rarely went according to any plan. Too many variables. Too many physical laws broken. So you had to be quick on your feet, quick with your mind. Kat may not have expected to get the Popsicle treatment in the junkyard, but that didn't make her helpless. Just meant she had to shift tactics. She raised her left wrist, looked right at Calvin's retreating back, and fired.

The cable launched out, aimed slightly to Calvin's left. The steel end, linking to her mask and its visual targeting, timed its turning jet to shunt itself to the right as the cable passed Calvin, wrapping itself around the anomaly over and over. The cable trapped Calvin's hands to his sides, sealing them tight as it rocketed around. When the cable ran out of thread, Kat snapped her left wrist back towards herself and the cable responded, reeling Calvin in like a big fish, the anomaly struggling against the binding in the snow.

"You're not the only one who can make people stick around," Kat said as Calvin brushed up against her front leg.

"If you don't let me go, I'll find some way," Calvin said.

"Be quiet." Kat took one of the spare stun darts from her belt and jammed it into Calvin's shoulder.

Apparently two darts did the trick. Sent Calvin to a quick and not particularly pleasant sleep. Mission accomplished. Anomaly caught. Kat gave herself a breath, maybe three, there in the slow-falling snow beneath the plane's wreck. Let her heartbeat slow down from its frenetic pace. She'd survived another one.

Now Kat had to figure out how to get out of here. She didn't exactly have flamethrowers in her suit, and the ice Calvin had put around her feet looked thick.

A huff came behind her and Kat felt a subtle nudge from Seeker's nose. Kat twisted, a tough move with both legs trapped, and reached down to give the husky the pets Seeker so clearly deserved. The dog's eyes looked a little confused, his legs a little wobbly, but otherwise he seemed all right. Good enough, anyway, to find a solution to Kat's problem: lick the Popsicle trap to death.

54

The Details Of Ending The World

Zhan Yo didn't think his new revolution's first moments would be spent dealing with a loved one's death. Because that's what Sylvie was, even if he had a hard time admitting it to himself. She'd been his only true confidant, the only one close enough to know his insecurities and his doubts and push him forward anyway. Yet he dealt with her just like she must have countless others.

Contacted Wexley, who said he'd handle it.

Zhan-Yo dragged Sylvie's body to the substation's broken entrance and waited until a pair in masks showed up in a heavy transport pod to take her and the other casualties away. Now Zhan-Yo stood back in his office, at the tippy top of the building belonging to a company that would very soon find itself in all out war with the world. Or at least those controlling it. They left the Paragons behind, witnesses to be found, who might propel the story with their defeat.

Showered, changed. All evidence washed away as dawn lit up Lake Michigan like it had every morning for millennia.

"Tea, or do you want something stronger?" Wexley said as he entered the room. Somehow, even now, the man dressed in a full suit. Did Wexley ever take them off? "I could get champagne if you'd rather?"

"Champagne?" Zhan-Yo said. "Maybe once the Paragons are gone. Any earlier celebration would be premature."

Wexley set the tray, an immaculate blue disk, on top of Zhan-Yo's glass and white metal desk. Twin silver cups, a pot filled with stiff black tea. Wexley filled the cups while Zhan-Yo studied the purple clouds, and together they stood overlooking the quiet city. An unknowing one, as of yet.

"We're already cleaning up the site. Removing the evidence," Wexley said. "The Paragons won't know we did it until—"

"Anna has someone we can trust editing the video. It will be ready soon, and we can choose the time to release it." Zhan-Yo smelled the tea. He ought to need caffeine as he hadn't slept, but didn't feel tired. Or awake. More like a dream state in which nothing quite seemed real. He could have simply smelled the tea, watched the sky for hours. But time remained a luxury neither his reps nor his position could buy. "What did you do with her?"

"We're holding the body," Wexley said. "I thought you might want her to go somewhere else. I know you had something of a relationship."

"She was very good at what she did," Zhan-Yo said.

Sylvie deserved more than that, but not here, not in front of Wexley.

"Thank you," Zhan-Yo continued. "I'll think of something appropriate. I don't know if she has family. We never discussed it."

"I can have that looked into?"

"No. Sylvie maintained her secrecy for her reasons. We won't disturb it. Let them wonder."

The idea of Sylvie vanishing seemed pleasant, so like her. Wexley let the idea float through the office air until it dissipated, then gave his small sigh signaling the change in topic. A re-orient from the sentimental to the strategic. Crass, but essential.

"We'll need to move quick now. The Paragons will be in disarray, but not forever," Wexley said. "We should let the others know before the video becomes public."

An essential switch, but not one Zhan-Yo accepted. Not yet. When legends die, they deserve more than a few minutes remembrance.

"I didn't want to kill him. I tried not to."

"What do you mean? He had to die. That was the whole point of the plan."

"He wasn't evil," Zhan-Yo replied. "If he'd agreed, we could have adjusted things. Brought the Paragons down and pulled us up. It would've worked."

"For a little while, maybe." Wexley gestured to the city below. "You think they would accept us? The rest of the Paragons? They have all the power and no reason to give it up. We have to make them, Zhan-Yo. That's the point."

A deep breath. Wexley, always so focused so driven and so dire. The man always saw the clearest path to the end, but never counted how many bodies would be trampled on the way.

"He was a dictator, Zhan-Yo," Wexley continued, adopting a prophet's tone, desperate to keep his friend on his side. "All the Paragons in Atlantis worked under him. He would never give that up either. A deal means both sides have to come to the table. Why would Aegis negotiate? Now the Paragons will be confused, and we can take advantage."

"To make them weaker."

"We have to break them, Zhan-Yo. There's still champions left. Mynx, right next door. You don't think she'll consolidate? Bring Atlantis and Pacifica together and then we'll be back to where we were."

"Ziran is not an army, Wexley. The way you speak, it's as if you think we'll have to kill all of the Champions to have a chance. I wanted a conversation, not a slaughter."

"I'm with you. But we're not going to get that now. Not with Aegis dead. We've made them angry, and they will come after us with everything. This is a fight, and we cannot lose."

"I'm not afraid to fight, only sad that such a fight is necessary." Zhan-Yo said. "Sylvie wanted a shadow war. She thought that cutting the head would kill the body, but I think you're right. Our cause won't win so easily."

They continued from there to more specific matters, and breaking down the future from the theoretical to the concrete, to times and tasks, cut away Zhan-Yo's lingering sadness with clarity. Yes, killing Aegis would bring problems, would result in massive change from the moment the video made its way to the public. But the world needed that change, and if Zhan-Yo would have preferred it to come without such violence, backing away from a dream because it grew thorns was not an option. When Atlantis learned they no longer had a Champion, Ziran would make its claim to destroy the Paragon's throne.

"Sylvie sent me one last thing," Zhan-Yo replied after draining the tea. "She'd drawn up plans for every one of the other Champions. Begin to implement them."

"So you're committed to seeing this through?"

"Like you said, what we've begun cannot be stopped. If the Paragons decide they have had enough, we will talk. Until then, it will be either them, or us."

55

Saving The Savior

When the handler had tried to introduce her to the smug young man sitting at the table's other end in the restaurant's private room, the young man held up his hand and the handler stopped. That had been Mynx's first lesson in the proper way for a Champion to command a normal, according to Aegis. Swept away from her Los Angeles home to New York after badge-bearing officers showed up demanding compliance, rewards, and a meeting with a hero, Mynx had clung on to the whirlwind and resolved to get everything she could from it. That's what her parents had taught her, after all— opportunities were meant to be seized.

"You're the one they're bringing to me?" Aegis said, looking at her.

Not in the way her dates or people passing on the street might look at Mynx, not with that sort of interest. No, Aegis had those clear eyes that found purpose and stuck to it while forgetting everything else. He locked his crystal blue pupils with hers, threw a limp smile out there, and waited to see what this woman would say about herself.

"They didn't bring me anywhere," Mynx said. She'd learned, in high school and especially in her first years in the engineering program, that a woman has to stick up for herself in a meeting like this. "I chose to come with them. I should be back at school."

"From what they tell me, you're supposed to be right here," Aegis said. He leaned forward, elbows on the table, hands crossing over one another. Still keeping his eyes on her. "They tell you why I asked them to find more?"

"More?"

"Like you. Like us. You know there's a lot, right?"

Mynx had suspected. Secrets weren't well-kept back then, especially this one. The one that would wind up changing everything. People still thought random violence, new technology going wrong could illuminate the increasing waves of random, unexplainable occurrences. Teenagers finding that instead of dreaming about their first school dance, they'd melted a hole through their floors in their sleep. Discover an extra arm that only appeared when they sang, find that every five days their hair would change colors and weirder things still. Reality's physical laws were proving themselves malleable, and everyone noticed.

That's when Mynx switched her major. Because she wanted an explanation, an answer for what happened to her. What happened to everyone else.

"Why me, if there's so many?" Mynx asked, because she didn't know what else to say.

Aegis looked so much younger in person than he did in all the magazine articles, all the pictures that showed him strong and towering over any problem. The Paragon. Invincible. Aegis could walk into a terrorist den and stop them in a single go. Come out without a scratch. This wasn't like meeting a celebrity, not that Mynx had much experience with that either, but growing up in LA, you had your encounters. No, this was more like meeting your God and having God tell you that you were just like him.

"What's your gift, Mynx?" Aegis asked. "That'll give you the answer."

"I can see how things work. I mean, get inside them. Mechanical things. Computers, programs and machines. Those things."

"But that's not all."

"No."

The handler hadn't given her anything to go on, neither had the agents who'd picked her up. Said only that Aegis wanted to see her about an important job. When she'd asked, the suits had acted like movie caricatures, all closed lips or changing the subject. Aegis, though, didn't give her any hints. Mynx looked over at the handler, who wore a blank expression. Either he didn't care, or knew how to look like it.

"Come on," Aegis said. "You're fine. We already know, but I want you to say it. You have to be comfortable with what you can do, or they'll use it against you."

Use it against her? Another glance at the handler. No change. Well. She'd come all the way out here, and Aegis seemed like he was on her side.

"I can change them too."

"Change what?"

"Anything. Machines. Computers. Programs." Mynx took out her phone, set it on the table. "I could go inside this right now and make it do whatever I wanted."

"Even if you didn't know the passwords?"

"Even if I don't know the passwords."

"Good. That's why you're here." Aegis sat back, interlocking fingers clasped behind his head. "I may be able to take a bullet, but what I need is someone who can show me where they are. I can't punch a program with my fist or force open a database. I've persuaded them to start with you, and if that works we'll add more."

Mynx didn't have to ask who *they* were. FBI, CIA, something else. It didn't matter.

"You mean like a movie? A comic book?"

The long, rich history of super teams had come up again and again as these sorts of incidents became more common. People wondering whether now might be the age of super beings and so on. 'Anomalies' would only stick when people realized the powers weren't always good.

"Yeah. Like a movie," Aegis said. "So, you're in?"

. . .

"I KNOW we never planned to use it." Mynx pressed the command that shut the opaque steel chamber and sealed Aegis inside. "But it tested out positive. The chamber works."

"But resuscitation doesn't," Reeves said. "You're depriving the world of a burial that it may very well need."

"Since when did I give you a psychological module?" Minx tapped on the chamber's touchpad to confirm the temp, set the timescale to maximum. Aegis wouldn't leave here without a manual release. "I don't need you to tell me that people will be upset."

"Are you sure? Because the way you're acting now isn't rational."

"The world doesn't know that he's dead," Mynx replied. "The longer we can keep that secret, the more time we have to make a plan."

The words helped. She'd spent the flight back from Chicago controlling her tears. Her anger and her frustration. Now the flurry of things gave her focus. Let her do what she did best: come up with solutions.

"Atlantis will be the first problem," Reeves said, apparently abandoning his doubts about the cryo-chamber.

Minx started the process and stepped back as the chamber hissed and rattled. As gas and liquid flooded her friend's body. One that might still have a functioning brain, organs that could be saved. A soul, maybe, if you believed in such things. Not that they had the capability now to restore them to life, but someday, maybe.

"Really? All your processing power and that's what you give me?" Mynx watched the temp drop, her friend's new home described by a series of negative digits. "I need you to get a list of potential Paragons there. One that might be able to take the mantle to be the next champion. I'm guessing Aegis didn't file a plan?"

"Aegis sent out a general call for a summit, but no succession plan. You don't have one either."

"Set aside some time on my calendar and I'll do it," Mynx turned away from the chamber and started out of the Factory.

The walk out, past the automated assemblies churning along as if nothing had changed, assemblies that didn't care about the hour or working all night, made Mynx feel every year in her bones. The excitement that'd carried her to and from Chicago, blitzing at airspeeds reserved for emergencies and that, no doubt, spooked some sparse towns along the route, had died off to leave lingering nausea and a growing headache. Sleep, though, would be impossible. She'd fall into memories. Thrash herself over what she could've done. Now she needed some coffee. She needed some food. And maybe a grief counselor.

"Celice would seem the prime option for Atlantis," Reeves said. "She has the respect, the knowledge, and the position."

"Celice isn't an anomaly," Mynx said. "We make her a Champion, and what's the excuse for any other normal who feels like they want a shot? Next month we'll have somebody who socked away a ton of reps come in with their own horde of weapons and demand their own title. I won't do it."

They argued. Reeves had endless reasons why Celice ought to be the one to take over for her father and Mynx only had one counter, but hers was the critical factor and eventually she ordered Reeves, using a hard command, to kill the argument. Doing things this way kept the AI from learning, but Mynx didn't have the energy for this fight. Not now.

"All right," Reeves said after the command. "I'll put together the list. Anything else?"

Aegis hadn't died of old age. He'd been murdered. Cut down at a specific spot chosen to keep help from arriving in time. Baited in by people who wanted him dead. That would earn them nothing unless they planned to keep moving with it. They would either kill more Paragons or Champions or both. And the success they'd already had would bring hope to others with the same ideas. Which meant Mynx had to come up with a plan not just to stop this group, but to prevent any others.

"Aegis and I knew we had to have an idea for succession. For what comes next," Mynx said, sitting down at the overlook table and watching the waves while one of the drones trundled out with her coffee. She closed her eyes for a second, embraced the breeze slipping through her activewear outfit designed to accommodate the drone armor. Breathable, comfortable, and a reminder of what she'd tried and failed to do.

"So you want what?"

"You said Aegis sent out a signal for a summit. I think we hold it. I'll reach out to the Champions. One by one. We bring everyone together and hash this out. We all get behind a plan. Once we've done that, anyone thinking they can kill one of us and change the world will know that won't work."

"The Champions haven't been all together in years. You split up because of your differences. How do you think that's going to work now?"

"We don't have a choice," Mynx said. "I wish we did. The world's not that nice."

"As ordered. I'll find times for each of them."

The waves curled over and crashed into each other. Inexorable. Constant. Governments across the world rose and fell, and had since the dawn of humanity. The Paragons had lasted only a few decades. Was this it? Would this be the end?

"Reeves, boost drone production. All of them, but especially gladiators. The armed variant."

Civilizations didn't die without a fight. The Champions wouldn't either.

56

The Old Or The New

Seeker licked her free in what Kat figured would be the record time in dog-ice-licking circles. She'd always considered his slurping, slobbery tongue a weapon of mass destruction, and her freed feet served as Exhibit A.

Kat stepped out of the remnants of Calvin's trap, brushing the rapidly freezing dog saliva from her boots, more grateful than ever for her suit's temp-regulating abilities. In the scrapyard, with breezes howling, her suit told her the outside world at this early hour approached zero degrees. Calvin, still knocked out from the stun gun dart, didn't seem too affected by the cold; eyes closed, every breath puffing a gray cloud towards her. Peaceful in its way.

She had the tracer in her left hand. Wouldn't take much to move Calvin's coat out of the way, deliver the injection and forever subject Calvin to the rights and wrongs of Paragon rule. That would be fulfilling her job, her contract, and avenging Gordon all in one shot. So why did she stare at the device like an alien creature that'd taken up residence in her palm?

Beth. The Elementals. Kat didn't get an offer like that every day. She'd been living in Chicago for a long time now, chasing anomalies through the streets and beyond. What did she have to show for it? Some reps, a modest apartment not suited to serve the dog she owned. No social life, unless you counted the fights at *Carver's*. The every-so-often bar binge when Kat just couldn't take the solitary screens anymore. The Elementals might offer something new.

Of course, they might take Calvin and kill her. Or abandon her, leaving Kat to face the wrath of whichever Paragon wanted Calvin most. She could lose everything. The question really became, how much was her everything worth? And if she lost it, would it really matter?

"What do you think?" She asked the dog. Seeker, busy sniffing all the metal bits and pieces, wandered over and plopped his body at her feet. "I know, as long as you get to run, get to eat, you really don't care, do you?"

Her Tama beeped. A message from Paragon forces in Chicago. They'd finally worked their way down to her spot on the help list and now medical and capture drones were heading over, complete with staff. Real-life humans, who could make real-life judgments about what Kat was doing standing over a wanted anomaly instead of binding him, tracing him. Her choice now had a short deadline.

Well, she could do something right now. Things that fit both sides. Kat removed some cabling from a pouch on her waist belt, the rudimentary capture material you had to have around if you expected captives. She knelt down, pushed Calvin over, wincing a bit as his face smashed into the snow. She tied Calvin's arms behind his back, and clasped his hands together. While Kat wouldn't say she had total confidence in what Calvin's anomaly ability could do, she had a pretty good idea that it came from those hands. That putting one hand against something and the other in the air would allow Calvin to change reality. Transmute, or whatever the word was. That would explain how Kat found herself so drunk so fast, if Calvin had taken the alcohol out of the beer and sent it straight into her. Explain how he shattered the cafe window by sucking the air and shooting it into the glass.

The thing with anomalies, they were all mysteries until you figured them out.

Kat sighed. Now there was killer thought. She ought to write it down. Mysteries until you figure them out. Brilliant.

She cleared away some snow so Calvin's hands wouldn't freeze when she turned him back over, and after she had him looking skyward again, Kat brushed the flakes off of his face. She'd be delivering a product to one side or another, and it needed to be in good condition.

"I must be tired," Kat said. "I'm laughing at my own thoughts. Talking to myself." She looked back east, past the scrap piles for the oncoming drone's lights. "You have an opinion Calvin? Which side?"

"Uhh," Calvin moaned, jerking Kat's attention to the anomaly. His mouth didn't speak so much as hung open, and his eyes had that dazed glaze that the recently awakened tended to have.

"You shouldn't be up yet. Not for another hour or more." Kat crouched over Calvin, tried to assess the risk. She didn't have any more stun darts. But she did have her feet, and sometimes a blunt method serve just as well. "Are you going to fight back?"

"Don't know," Calvin replied.

They sat there, Calvin gradually mush-mouthing his way back to sentience while Kat watched for trickery. Seemed like bound hands and now, after Kat took additional assurances, bound feet, killed Calvin's desire for combat. Or maybe Seeker, who'd begun licking the anomaly's face with reckless abandon, goofed away any anger. Kat only stopped the husky when she became concerned Calvin might actually drown under all the slobber.

"It's what you get," Kat said as Calvin gasped for air.

"Fair," Calvin said, his voice tired and weak. "I suppose I did try to hurt the dog."

"Hurt? You could've killed Seeker."

Calvin tried to shake his head. "No. Not hard enough. Would never kill a dog."

Kat wasn't sure she believed him on that score, but the drones would be getting close and choices needed making.

"So I have a question," Kat said. Calvin rolled his eyes towards her. "If you had a choice, would you go to the Elementals or the Paragons?"

"Neither."

"Not an option. Pick one."

"Elementals then. Screw your Paragons."

The Tama beeped again. The drones had picked up Gordon and were heading her way. Too late to run away with Calvin, or hide him. So she might as well get some satisfaction.

"Sorry, wrong answer," Kat replied.

She reached, pulled open Calvin's jacket. The stained, ratty t-shirt beneath gave more evidence to the kind of crap life Calvin had led before this moment. The Paragons, at least, would improve his wardrobe. With his arms tied behind his back, finding the bicep wasn't as easy as it could have been, but Chicago's best tracker had the talent to maneuver Calvin's body around to get the proper angle. Kat set the tracer against Calvin's arm and waited for the anomaly to say something, to protest or anything, but Calvin kept quiet.

Kat pulled the trigger.

Three seconds later, her Tama beeped again. A different, brighter and happier tone. As if Kat ought to be thrilled about the new Paragon she'd just added to her cluster. Kat tucked away the tracer and looked at her newest addition. "It's in, working. You'll start getting Paragon stuff within a few days. You'll report to the Chicago office and they'll get your rep accounts going. Start setting you up with contracts. It'll be a lot better than what you had."

"What do you care? You've probably got dozens of us working for you without a choice."

"You don't work for me." Kat pointed back through the scrap-yard, where the drone's lights appeared even as the horizon grew brighter.

"So that's it? They take me and I never see you again? I'm a Paragon now?"

"You're whatever you want to be, but choose carefully. If you break away from this, the next time one of us catches you, it'll be to kill." Kat didn't say she avoided those hunts. There were trackers who preferred the one-time rep bonus from a lethal engagement to dealing with taking captives. She preferred to dodge the scars that came from taking lives. "My advice? You find a way to love the life you get. It might not be so bad."

The drones were two-man vessels—still called drones as none of the crew flew the things. They came down from ten meters up and lowered flat platforms to the ground. Four normals, wearing Paragon blues with the designating red badge on the shoulders that said they had no powers, that said they were restricted to certain duties, clambered off. Kat answered their questions, quick and clear as they loaded Calvin into the captive drone. The anomaly didn't struggle, didn't say anything as he vanished into the mechanized beast. The captive drone didn't wait for its friend, but rotated around and headed back towards downtown.

"You guys were busy tonight," Kat said to the leader, who looked about as tired as her.

"A lot of problems. A lot of Paragons down." His eyes slid away from Kat's, hiding something. "I don't think any of us are going to have an easy day for a long time."

"That sounds ominous."

The man shrugged, offered her a lift, which Kat declined. They'd be going to the city center, way past her apartment. Besides, the last thing Kat wanted now was more forced conversation. Just one more question, and she'd let the crew go.

"Gordon? Is he all right?"

"We got him up there. He'll need some rest. Light medical, but he'll live."

Kat started walking with Seeker as the medical crew rejoined their drone, and she managed a half wave as the craft flew overhead, back towards the city and the rising winter sun.

57

Final Goodbyes

A good shower could do many things, but it couldn't wash away grief. Zhan-Yo took his time, a luxury afforded by a schedule cleared under the guise of illness, a deception that would disappear in spectacular fashion once Aegis's death and Zhan-Yo's part in it broke loose. He thought Sylvie would appreciate the slow morning, how he left Wexley to the clean-up at the office and took charge of what he, himself, needed. Sylvie had done that best, never giving concern to modern life's thousand pestering problems. Always focusing on the most important.

Zhan-Yo couldn't, however, stay beneath the warm water forever, and went for the opposite shock by heading out to his balcony. The purple dawn grew to a gray morning as the clouds multiplied, and a few spare flakes dared to drift down. The gods, apparently, were not willing to weep for either Sylvie or the Champion. As omens went, Zhan-Yo chose to read the weather as acceptance; a normal winter day would give all the attention to his announcement.

The mechanical gods, though, were busy. Drones clogged the sky, floating slow over the city in such numbers that made clear something had gone wrong. Zhan-Yo glanced at his Tama and saw no alerts. The Paragons weren't willing to break the news them-selves, and hadn't come up with another story. With Innis paid off and thoroughly subdued, Zhan-Yo expected no less. Chicago belonged to Ziran, now, and he wanted to shout that news down to the people beneath, who kept looking up, wondering.

They would know soon enough.

His Tama rang, and Zhan-Yo swiped, glanced at his wrist and saw Wexley's face fill the screen. Still in the same suit from hours before. The man never switched off. No wonder he had no family, no relations to speak of. If Zhan-Yo didn't know better, hadn't seen emotion take over Wexley, he'd assume the Paragons had planted him as a spy. Something their Champion artificer Mynx would have cooked up, a drone meant to behave like a man.

"I heard you're going home the rest of the day," Wexley said. "Do you want me to postpone? I have the video ready now."

"I want to put Sylvie to rest," Zhan-Yo replied. He'd already spoken with the body-clearing crew. They had her waiting, and he knew where he would bring her. "Let me take care of that before we open the box. Be ready to make the moves when I call. We need to beat the Paragons to the announcement. Chaos is our strength."

"Your recording will do that," Wexley said, his voice honey. "I think it'll do much more. Can you imagine what they'll feel, all those anomalies, when their hero dies? When their perfect utopia cracks and crumbles?"

"Don't get poetic. There's too much work left to do." Unusual for Wexley to show passion at all, much less in an outburst like that. Zhan-Yo made Wexley wait while he pulled out a cigarette, lit it, and took a nice long pull and let the ash curl on the end. "What do you think their response will be?"

"The Paragons will strike hard and fast once they figure out who and where you are." Wexley's brief foray into the realm of lofty proclamations died without a second thought. "After you finish with Sylvie, you'll need to go under. Don't expect to come back to your apartment."

Of course he wouldn't. There were plans for this. Zhan-Yo

looked through the door back at his home. Small, sparse and made for a man who spent more time at the office. He wouldn't miss it.

"You'll know when I'm secure," Zhan-Yo said, then gave his friend—Wexley had earned that moniker, at least—a curt nod. "This is the beginning."

"No, it's already begun." Wexley replied. "Don't take too long. We need you free and alive. No more sacrifices."

"Sylvie made her own choice. Not one I desire," Zhan-Yo said. "Follow the plan, Wexley."

"Of course. Take care, Z."

The master of his company, the spark of a new revolution, stubbed out his cigarette in the ashtray on the table before turning to head inside, saving one last look at all the marks on the wall counting the days to freedom. He wouldn't need to add another.

58

An Old Fire Still Burns

What had looked like a great lunch died when Reeves told her about the video. When Mynx played it above the table. Every agonizing minute of Aegis alone in those dark tunnels, outnumbered and still not afraid. He believed in his invincibility to the end, or pretended to. But then, Aegis personified the belief in heroes. His will made the world recognize them as the future. The first Paragon, the one who blazed the path for all the rest. Chosen by genetic chance, but it's what he did with that die roll that mattered. Now what Mynx would do with hers, what the other Champions would make of the world Aegis had left them, that she couldn't know. Only that they all would have no choice but to come to the summit now. After this, there could be no doubt the Paragons were under attack.

"How many calls?" Mynx said after the video stopped.

"About a dozen already. I'm blocking them, because I assumed that's what you would want." Reeves, as imperfect as he was, could be a blessing. "Do you want me to start letting them through?"

Mynx rubbed her forehead, shut her eyes. She hadn't done much more than sent an initial message, a quick contact out to the Champions to say it's time to come together. Nothing to the public, and silence wouldn't be enough to keep the government in order.

The normals demanded security and a predictable day, and the Paragons had to provide it. All the same, Mynx couldn't come up with a palatable statement right now. The Paragons had public relations folks that could, but they would be as ill-informed as everyone else. Aegis had been the media savant, conjuring inspirational nonsense out of nothing. If Mynx stood in front of the cameras now, she'd probably undermine any remaining confidence in the Paragons.

"No," Mynx said. "We're not ready. Tell any who calls that a Paragon statement will be coming, but not yet. Not yet."

She went to the balcony's edge, looked down over those rocks, the sand to the Pacific ocean. She reached down, opened the gate that swung out beyond the glass edge of the patio and revealed the narrow stair carved into the rock. She could have built over the rough stones, made a flashier, safer walk but that would spoil the view. So instead Mynx made her way slowly, with drones hovering behind her, ready to assist if she fell. Every step sure, and before too long Mynx made it down to that sand and, ditching her sandals, felt the cool, soft grains between her toes.

"I've been running the models that Dr. Jones developed," Reeves said.

"The fraud?"

"For a fraud, she had some innovative ideas."

The AI's voice came from the speaker in one of the drones, and it followed her as Mynx walked into the ocean and felt cold water's liquid kiss on her shins. In the middle of the day, there were only a few people within sight, none near her. Near the Factory. Whether that was because they all had seen the video and assumed Paragons weren't safe right now, or just random chance, Mynx couldn't say.

"She only wanted to be like us," Mynx said. "That's all they ever want."

"Perhaps. But there are some possibilities here. Would you mind if I began setting up some trials?"

Would Mynx mind if her AI struck out on his own to try and stop the world from growing old? What other projects could Reeves get into if he started being independent? But then, what did it matter really? Humankind was destined to struggle against itself, to persecute the powerful no matter how much they did for the weak, and who cared if Reeves found his own pathways to that same power? Someone would tear Reeves down eventually too. A depressing circle.

Mynx caught a salty wave in the face, and she sputtered out the bit that made it into her mouth. The ocean telling her such thoughts were pathetic, a waste of time. True enough—Mynx may not be able to stop a collapse of the world she'd designed with her friends, but she could fight the change. Could make it cost. Utopias deserved to be defended, after all.

"Do it. Find a miracle, Reeves, because we sure could use one," Mynx said. An aggressive defense of the Paragons, the Champions would require fighters, and Mynx could think of no better one than Aegis's daughter. A normal, but one who would not rest until she'd found her father's killers. "Have you contacted Celice yet?"

"I've tried. There's been no response. She's gone dark."

Mynx would find her. She'd collect the Champions and build a defense, root out the rot. Maybe, if Reeves found a solution, she'd bring Aegis back from his deep freeze too. All miracles, all worth believing in. She was a Champion. She would fight, and she would win.

"Reeves? I want to know who made that video, who had that sword. We will find them, and we will destroy them."

Not For Nothing

Your father's gone.

Celice had expected the words for a long time. Ever since she'd turned twelve, when she began to understand the full extent of what her father did, that both her parents risked their lives endlessly to better a world that wouldn't stop hurting them. Aegis said he'd wanted to tell her the truth even earlier, that he'd been so afraid he might disappear one day without getting a chance to say goodbye.

So he'd said it. All the time until the farewells became a joke to her. Aegis wouldn't fail, wouldn't fall, and as Celice had learned more about the Paragons, she'd become determined to help her family. Do what she could to help keep her father's words from ever coming true.

Pizza sat on the shelf behind her, along with microbrews cooling in the fridge. Waiting all night and now into the morning for Aegis to come back, stick to that dinner he promised her. Shouldn't be such a big deal, a father and a daughter sitting down, having a meal, talking about the normal things. She'd called off the boyfriend, but he wasn't really that because, let's be honest, you don't date someone like Celice. Not once they found out who her father was. Was. She'd have to say that now. Was. The word banged around her mind like a sledgehammer.

Deep breath. Watch the city. Hold on to the chair.

Aegis loved that about her. Rational. Logical. Able to see what really needed to be done and what was most important. Aegis wanted to punch everything to death. He'd accepted a leader's mantle because it'd been thrown on him. Celice, so her father said, would deserve it. Though Aegis would never say exactly where Celice would be doing this leading—as a normal, Paragon law forbade her from becoming a Champion. Without Aegis declaring otherwise, Celice wouldn't be a Paragon either.

Celice turned away from the cityscape, stood up from her father's chair. If Aegis had really died, there were procedures she needed to follow. Paragons to alert and processes to kick into motion. Outlined in a special digital locker Aegis had shown her a long time ago, one available to only the two of them. Nobody else could know about the plan, to prevent panic or scheming. If some disaster were to claim them both, Celice guessed, the Paragons would have to figure things out for themselves.

She punched up the locker on her Tama and started walking towards the lift. It wouldn't be long before word started getting out and people asked questions. Atlantis and her Paragons would need a ready response. Opening the locker, its contents spilling virtual icons all over the screen, sent a thrill. Everything in it had been updated, and recently. The day or night after Aegis had been shot. As if he'd known he might die soon.

"Then why," Celice said to herself as she summoned the elevator. "Why did you go?"

Polly, the tower's AI, had enough sense not to answer.

The plan, in the event of Aegis's demise, called for a whole slew of Paragon movements. Various promotions would kick into effect, others transferred across the seaboard, all in the name of keeping the center of Atlantis power in Manhattan and a clear chain of command to the other regional centers. All logistics, all stuff Celice had found fascinating in a vacuum. The text looked like nonsense to her now. She read it anyway. Looking, failing to find her name. No mention of her, what she did or what she should do now. The executor of Aegis's plan had no part in it.

Aegis, her father, had kept her out of his succession. A hundred potential reasons simmered, then boiled away as the elevator descended through the tower. Celice slapped her right palm against the steel cage. Of course he'd do this without telling her. Of course he'd strip away the one thing she had left out of some excuse for her safety.

She hit tower's office floors, stopping at the operations level. A giant command center ringed with screens and display tables so Paragon officers could monitor and direct in real time. Celice had spent hours here just watching as her father's heroes saved the city, Atlantis, the world from all sorts of threats. Now, though, it seemed like some signal had sent the Paragons home early. Only a couple old stalwarts manned the screens, neither bothering to look towards Celice as the elevator doors opened.

These were supposed to be the new guardians of her father's legacy. People who's biggest responsibility had been directing Paragon traffic. Not her, not Celice, who'd done everything while her dad used his fists to save the world. Anger mixed with grief mixed with frustration and Celice knew she should take time. Spend the day upstairs, looking over the city and doing nothing but marinating in the past. Tomorrow, she could deal with the future. Grapple with Aegis's plans.

Instead, Celice punched a new destination into the elevator. A very low floor, beneath the ground.

Her father had always counted on her to do the right thing. And Celice would. As the elevator descended, Celice cleaned out the digital locker. Deleted every document, keeping only the couple of videos Aegis had left for her alone. She'd play those later. They'd keep her up, energized, motivated. Atlantis would need to change. The Paragons, too. They'd been peacekeepers for a long time, but someone had declared war. Celice would find out who, and when she did, her Paragons would be ready to fight back.

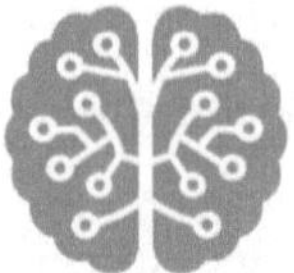

The Rotten

Thane struck the water off the island's shore at a speed that should have turned him to chum, and the impact would have done its lethal work if Thane hadn't fallen for several minutes before, if Thane hadn't worked himself up to a maddened rage strapped in Mynx's plane before she kicked him out of it. Instead of disintegrating, Thane's huge, nearly invulnerable body splashed with a sound not unlike a lightning bolt's crack. He dipped out of consciousness, giving his life to waves that washed him onto the island's rocky shore.

Since then he'd feasted on moss and mushrooms, caught a few fish with his hands when he could work up enough rage to charge his old limbs. Thane, though, had spent the time contemplating the drones floating silently out near the horizon. A fence to keep the problem in. They didn't bother Thane in the cavern overlook he'd found above his washed-up entrance, and the drones didn't change their patterns when Thane noticed the island had other visitors. Many, many others. Mynx hadn't made a private prison just for Thane, she'd stuck him in with the other inmates.

Soon, Thane would leave the cave, journey towards the closest set of fire-smoke drifting up, carrying cooked meat's smell on the breeze. He'd spent his time, nearly emaciated himself, coming up with a plan that would get him off this island. Thane would find the hole in Mynx's fence, and he would escape.

And she would pay.

READ *on for an excerpt from* CHAMPION'S CALL, *the Hero's Code Book Two— available* FREE *by signing up for my new release newsletter through the* QR *Code below:*

An Excerpt from
CHAMPION'S CALL
THE HERO'S CODE BOOK TWO

She ran the tests without opening her eyes. Flexed her legs, her arms, turned her neck back and forth, and felt nothing. For the first time in the week since she'd fought Calvin in the scrapyard, Kat wasn't sore, wasn't bruised, and wasn't sick from the thick cold she'd caught while duking it out in a frigid night. Couple a healthy body with a bed she'd spent far too much reps on, and Kat felt like she could lie there all day. She'd feel a little lazy, because Kat had done pretty much nothing all week long, but why not? Hadn't she earned it?

Nearly dying deserved some time off.

A thick, slobbering tongue smacked Kat's face, left a dripping line along her cheek. Hot breathe lathered her, and paws pressed her shoulders into the mattress as Seeker, Kat's husky, attacked. She'd made a mistake, given a sign that she was awake. A critical error.

"Seeker, stop it," Kat said with no enthusiasm and less force. "I'm trying to sleep."

She earned another lick for her troubles. Kat squirmed, tried to put forth a minimum effort to get Seeker off without fully opening her eyes and giving in to the day, but the dog didn't move.

"Tap, tell Seeker to leave me alone," Kat said.

"Seeker, bad dog. Not cool." Tap, her apartment's A.I. said. "Let her sleep. Not chill to wake someone up on the weekend, dog."

The surfer bro theme. Kat swapped Tap to it every winter, because the laconic attitude reminded her of golden beaches and sweltering sun, everything Chicago did not have on a February weekend. Seeker, though, obeyed to Tap as much as he did Kat, and continued slobbering away. At a certain point the dog crossed the licking threshold and, sensing her time in bed had reached its end, Kat rolled herself away from Seeker, sitting up and pushing her chestnut hair out of her eyes.

Another gray day in the midwestern winter, going by the window to her left. What a shocker.

"Tap, the usual," Kat said, holding a finger up towards Seeker, now down on the floor but looking like he might resume his assault at any moment. "If you jump up here, Seeker, I'm not getting you anything."

The 'usual', a spread from a nearby third-shift diner, came with fried eggs, rye toast, and random fruits the place had available. A delivery drone dropped it in the package slot outside Kat's window not long after Tap had placed the order. Just enough time for Kat to pull on some clothes, splash some water on her face, and start the coffee brewing. With a kitchen not much larger than her closet and a stove-top that preferred shorting out to heating up, Kat had taken the easy way out and boarded the take-out train.

It helped that the diner always threw in spare bacon for Seeker, who munched on the charred pork with gleeful, teeth-snapping happiness. Kat envied the dog's endless joy, as she picked at her own food over the coffee table from her couch. A leathery thing long since banished to doggy doom, the couch cushions remained comforting, and gave prime viewing to the massive monitor serving for Kat's work and entertainment. Right now, as the creeping clock went past mid-morning, she had Tap scrolling through her messages, reading the interesting ones and deleting the rest.

Not that there were many these days. The Paragons were still a giant mess. Ever since that video came out, the one that seemed to show Aegis dying—a horror that Kat refused to really believe—the Paragons in Chicago had seemed leaderless. Nobody had posted new anomaly contracts in the region, and the Paragons themselves answered her calls with pre-programmed messages stating that things were being dealt with, not to worry. While Kat could afford to wait, given all the anomalies she'd traced already who kept churning out reps for her, other Trackers weren't so fortunate and had responded by littering message boards with increasingly panicked calls for work. It'd only been a week, but apparently a lot of people in her profession didn't keep much saved away.

Then again, given the likelihood you'd die in this business, maybe it made more sense to spend for the moment than save for the future.

"Hey Kat," Tap said after concluding another boring message extolling the Tracker to update her beneficiaries in case of an untimely demise. Like she had any. "Just gonna say, you might wanna pay attention to this next one. It's from someone you might care about."

Tap's sun-drenched tone hid the under-the-hood calculations pretty well—Kat had no doubt the 'someone you might care about' line came from knowing everyone Kat bothered to contact through her computer—but she perked up from her breakfast's dwindling remnants and watched the screen as Tap pulled up the words.

"Hey Kat," Tap read, his surf voice ill-suited to Gordon Holyoak's midwestern lingo. "I know you might not care, but I'm getting out of the hospital today. Guess they think I won't die anymore, which is nice. But, uh, I don't know anyone else in town that would bother to show up and help get me to where I'm staying till I'm ready to get back to it. Do you think you could? I'll even buy you dinner. Not that it'd be enough to cover what I owe you, but, if you're around at four, think you could? And thanks, Kat. Thanks for everything."

Gordon. Able to pack so much sincerity into a paragraph, and so much callous ignorance into every other part of his life. Kat stared at the words, then told Tap to send a reply.

"Hey Gordon. Glad to hear you're not a corpse. Yeah, I'll get there at four. If you're up for dinner, you better believe we're going to the most expensive place that'll take a man in a hospital gown. See you soon, Kat."

Tap zapped the message away.

Too harsh? Nah. Kat finished her breakfast, drumming up excuses for her curt reply and why it was so very justified. Gordon had shown up in Chicago a little more than a week ago, roping in a bunch of Trackers into chasing after a dangerous anomaly without telling them anything about Calvin. That the anomaly could take anything he touched and transmute it through his body into something else. A concrete wall could be shifted into flying stone spears. Air could be shoved into glass, blowing it into shards. Alcohol could be sucked—Kat's stomach churned at the memory—from a beer and sent right into someone's blood, instantly toxic.

Nobody had died, but Gordon had found himself perforated by ice inside his own body, damage Kat didn't even notice—the medic that'd picked Gordon up told her after she'd reached out, trying to find out if Gordon was still alive. As for Calvin, he'd been traced, picked up by a Paragon drone and taken to wherever the dangerous anomalies go before they're released as loyal servants or, failing that, imprisoned somewhere. Those were details Kat didn't want to know about.

Why blunt enthusiasm for a career that already suffered from more problems than solutions?

Anyway, now Kat had a plan for the day. Review her rep accounts. Take Seeker for a long walk. Find something for lunch after. Get ready and get downtown by four. Either Gordon would be up for dinner, or she'd drop him off at whatever place he'd be using to recover, and from there... who knew. Odds looked good for a night in, with something warm to drink and something happy on the screen while Kat waited for another anomaly that needed capturing to pop up on the board.

Given the chaos enveloping Atlantis in the wake of Aegis's death, Kat felt a little strange to have a schedule so devoid of action. As if she ought to be out in the streets fighting for... something. But, aside from the drones swarming the skies in huge numbers, the city around her hadn't changed. In the last week, the streets had the same crowds, the restaurants served the same food, and if she picked up a few nervous whispers, noticed the regulars at Carver's drinking more than before, that wasn't too scary.

The Paragons were built by the strongest, smartest anomalies on the planet. They'd figure out how to keep on going, and Kat wanted no part of that process.

"How about that walk?" Kat said to Seeker, dropping the breakfast trash down her chute to the building's waste-to-energy incinerator. In a way, by eating disposable containers, Kat powered the building. How noble. "I need to stretch my legs, and you need to burn off your crazy."

Seeker agreed, grabbing his leash from the hanger near the door. Kat slipped on her boots, clipped the leash to the dog, and was in the middle of her did-I-forget-anything look around when someone pounded on the door. The heavy, fist-banging sound had Kat lunging for her desk and the secondary stun gun she kept holstered to the desk's bottom side in a concession to paranoia.

"Tom? Who's there?" Kat asked, keeping the gun leveled at the door.

"Haven't seen this dude before," Tom replied. "I can scan your records and find a match? Have to say though, he looks like he's having a rough time."

"Any weapons?"

"Nope."

"Seeker, stay," Kat said, then opened the door.

Standing there, blood dripping from a big, oval stain around his stomach, was the very same anomaly that'd put Gordon in the hospital a week ago, that'd nearly killed Kat at the same time. Sweat shone on his midnight skin, and while Calvin had upgraded his clothes from his old rags, the new ones already bore rips, stains and scars. If the past seven days had been a whole lotta nothin' for Kat, Calvin had been catching much worse.

"Please," Calvin said. "They're going to kill me."

Kat took a step back. Seeker growled.
"Who?"
"The Elementals."
Oh. Shit.

Continue the adventure with Champion's Call, available for free with newsletter sign-up or at your favorite retailer:

Acknowledgments and Author's Note

Paragon's Fall begins a new series exploring something I've always found interesting, namely, what happens when folks who used to be, physically, unstoppable find themselves very much stoppable. When your self-identity is wrapped up in something that falls victim to time.

Could you change? Would you?

As ever, this story is brought about through Nicole's endless support in letting me play in fantastical universes. My brothers, parents, and in-laws all bring a joy and wonder to my life that encourages exploring the vast reaches of science fiction and fantasy. Their support is everything.

Readers, too, fire the creative furnace. Whether through five star (or less!) reviews, messages passed through the infinite web of social media, or simply a ping on the sales chart that says someone's taking a chance on my stories, that powers the drive to keep on keeping' on. So thank you, and I hope you enjoyed this novel and the rest of the series.

About the Author

A.R. Knight spins stories in a frosty house in Madison, WI, primarily owned by a pair of cats. After getting sucked into the working grind in the economic crash of the 2008, he found himself spending boring meetings soaring through space and going on grand adventures.

Eventually, spending time with podcasting, screenplays, short stories and other novels, he found a story he could fall into and a cast of characters both entertaining and full of heart.

A.R. Knight plans on jumping through to other worlds and finding new stories to tell in the limitless borders of our imagination.

Thanks, as always, for reading!

For more information:
www.adamrknight.com

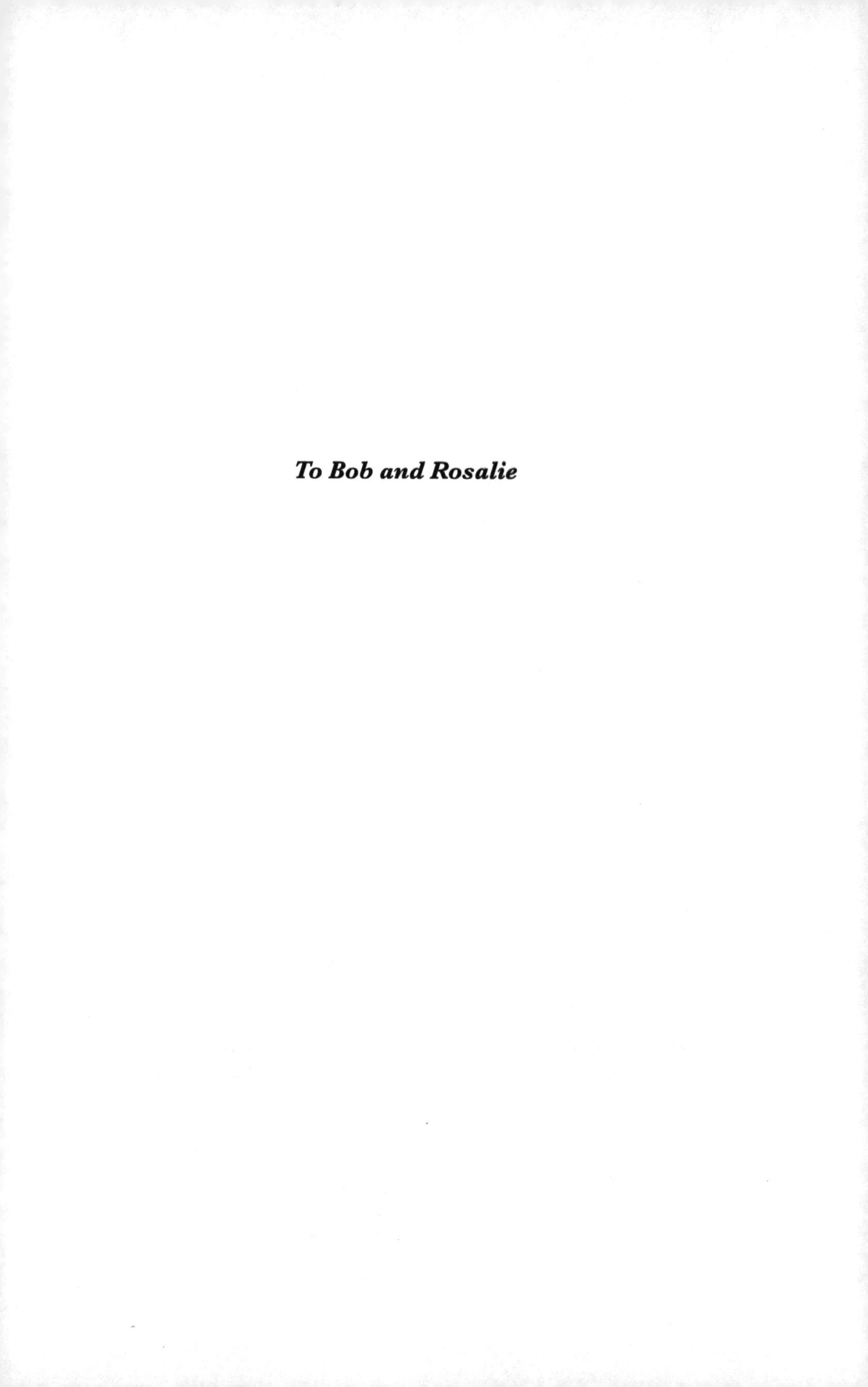

To Bob and Rosalie